0 316 903 337 57

MOST LOVING MERE FOLLY

When the artist husband of Suspiria Freeland dies of poison and Suspiria admits her love for a garage mechanic fourteen years her junior, public opinion assumes her to be guilty. She is acquitted and the couple marry, only to realise that their real difficulties are just beginning. She is a cultured woman, an artist; he is sensitive but uneducated and there is always the public, waiting and hoping for the ruin of what is considered a marriage that cannot last. This novel is a study of passionate and fated love and its struggle to come to terms with the kind of love as it has to be lived out in everyday life.

by the same author

writing as Edith Pargeter:

The Heaven Tree Trilogy

THE HEAVEN TREE
THE GREEN BRANCH
THE SCARLET SEED

THE MARRIAGE OF MEGOTTA

writing as Ellis Peters:

Inspector Felse mysteries

A NICE DERANGEMENT OF EPITAPHS
BLACK IS THE COLOUR
OF MY TRUE LOVE'S HEART
THE KNOCKER ON DEATH'S DOOR
RAINBOW'S END
FALLEN INTO THE PIT
DEATH AND THE JOYFUL WOMAN
THE GRASS WIDOW'S TALE

The Brother Cadfael Chronicles

A MORBID TASTE FOR BONES
ONE CORPSE TOO MANY
MONK'S-HOOD
ST PETER'S FAIR
THE LEPER OF SAINT GILES
THE SANCTUARY SPARROW
THE VIRGIN IN THE ICE
THE DEVIL'S NOVICE
DEAD MAN'S RANSOM
THE PILGRIM OF HATE
AN EXCELLENT MYSTERY
THE RAVEN IN THE FOREGATE
THE ROSE RENT
THE HERMIT OF EYTON FOREST
THE CONFESSION OF BROTHER HALUIN
THE HERETIC'S APPRENTICE
THE POTTER'S FIELD
THE SUMMER OF THE DANES

MOST LOVING MERE FOLLY

Edith Pargeter

LITTLE, BROWN AND COMPANY

A *Little, Brown* Book

First published in Great Britain by Heinemann in 1953
This edition published by Little, Brown and Company in 1992

A CIP catalogue record for this book is available from the British Library.

ISBN 0 316 90333 7

Photoset in North Wales by
Derek Doyle & Associates, Mold, Clwyd
Printed in England by Clays Ltd, St Ives plc

Little, Brown and Company (UK) Limited
165 Great Dover Street
London SE1 4YA

'If indeed we must assume that nobody can be aware of the nature of his own desires nor plumb the depths of his own most secret inclinations, at least each may survey what he has done and face the consequences of the decisions he has ventured.

'Passion means suffering, something undergone, fate's mastery over a free and responsible person. – Passionate love, the longing for what sears us and annihilates us in its triumph – there is the secret which Europe has never allowed to be given away; a secret it has always repressed – and preserved! Hardly anything could be more tragic.

'But married love is the end of anguish, the acceptance of a limited being whom I love because he or she is a summons to creation, and that in order to witness to our alliance this being turns with me towards day.'

DENIS DE ROUGEMONT:
Passion and Society

CONTENTS

CHAPTER ONE:

Collision Between Two Worlds

1

GREAT LEDDINGTON is still twenty-five miles from the factory fringe of London, and produces no electric clocks, biscuits, nor bentwood furniture to this day. Thirty years ago it was a small market town, surrounded by comfortably prosperous farms and rich nursery-gardens, and linked with the capital by a good and rapidly developing road. At the end of the twenties the first restless wave of Bohemia, reaching out after something more remote and archaic as a setting for always potential but never-realised pearls, washed over it and gave it, for a few years, a hectic self-conscious vogue. All its derelict mills became studios, all its more crumbling cottages were taken over by earnest sandalled women and their frail parasitic young men, and aestheticism broke out like a rash between the hay-fields and the shire stud and the good stone cross. Some people still regard this as the heyday of the town, and its subsequent history rather as a decline and fall.

Suburbia, in its more ambitious form, followed Bohemia hop-skip-and-jump along the high road in a ribbon of villas, keyhole estates, petrol stations and road-houses in by-pass Tudor. The infection reached Great Leddington, found a fashionably preoccupied territory there still not overcrowded, and spread into a growth of new housing estates hanging on the edge of the town. The district now led a treble life, with some disinterested fraternisation, but little understanding.

The outbreak of war in 1939 suddenly erased much that was false from the picture, for Great Leddington was no longer remote enough for those abortive aesthetes who had the money to move elsewhere. They uprooted themselves and took wing for Ireland, or the Outer Hebrides, or the lesser-known villages of Cornwall, leaving behind them an astonishing, if small, residue of genuine artists, who had somehow become entangled in the original invasion in their search for space and cheapness, or who now found well-appointed studios going for a song because they were too near to the bombing.

Once Bohemia had abandoned it, Great Leddington was a practical paradise for artists, far less expensive than London, far more peaceful in ways which had nothing to do with the incidence of bombing, yet conveniently close to town, and from long experience adept at that cold metropolitan tolerance which refrains from mocking eccentricity less out of sympathy than indifference. It was possible to work there without exciting curiosity or inviting interference. To the beauty and serenity of a country town it added the urbane attitude of a city. After the war costs went up there, but so they did everywhere. The ribbon development along the road scarcely affected the farming side of the town, and served to keep out new invasions without disturbing overmuch the survivors of the old. So they remained, and Great Leddington was used to them, and made no complaint. They were not the kind of people who could not be ignored; most of them were quiet, hard working, not very well off, indistinguishable in the street from the tradesmen and housewives of the town. A few, according to art critics whose writings Great Leddington vaguely heard about but never read, had a certain distinction, and so were counted amoung the assets of the place.

The fact remained, of course, that they were an alien race. Local people had friends among them, rather as they might have cultivated friendships, equally without comment, among the French or the Dutch, and even learned to speak, for friendship's sake, a few words of those outlandish languages. But the foreigners remained foreigners. Great Leddington, rapidly accomplished in the adaptation of country prejudices to new sophistication, looked upon them always with cool, incurious, civilised eyes, and stood ready to claim their accomplishments and reject their distresses, to acknowledge them as sights, and hold them at bay as human beings.

But the artists did not care. They were there precisely because they cared essentially for only one thing, and to that they devoted themselves. They had kept their eyes fixed on it all through the war, not because they were unable to see right and wrong, or danger and safety, but because these seemed to them minor matters, to be endured, evaded and transcended by any means whatsoever in the pursuit of that one sacred thing, so durable above their transcience. When other people lost sight of it in the smoke, it was all the more essential that they, who could still see it, should abandon everything else, and serve it.

Theo Freeland had painted all through the war, kicking aside casually, almost unnoticed, two or three tentative offers of commissions as an official war artist. He was not capable of being an official artist of any kind, or of going where he was sent, or doing what he was told. As for his wife, she had gone on steadily making pottery the whole time, and she was at it yet. Could there be anything more unimportant, during a world war? True, she had turned out occasionally at night and driven an ambulance, with a fierce efficiency and ruthless fury which arose, probably, from her feeling that this chaos of the world's imbecility had got between her and her wheel, and must be cleared out of her way before she could proceed. She was not popular with the W.V.S. She never said the right things; she had a derisive smile, cool, personal and reserved, when others said them. She was one of the aliens; she always would be.

On the surface, however, the two streams of Great Leddington's life appeared to flow very equably together. It needed a natural catastrophe of hurricane proportions to shake them apart into their divided beds; and in the mild latitudes of near-suburbia storms of that magnitude are few and far between.

2

Suspiria leaned on her forearms, and watched the bowl grow between her hands. It had opened like a lily, coiling the prints of her fingers higher and higher round its rising rim, until it hid the jagged shape of the asbestos bat on which it was rooted, and now it was of the exact spread of the wheel itself, and still growing.

Sometimes, though rarely, she fell into a kind of trance when she was throwing, through her eyes which were dazed with the whirling concentration of the wheel, through her ears which were drowsy with its heavy, purring note, and the faint, slippery hiss of the wet clay through her entranced hands, which fell into a voluptuous rhythm, loving the creaming smoothness and ardour of the clay as they caressed it, and feeling themselves as passionately caressed; and then she lost the impulse to control this tension of creation, and let it run away with her, and made monstrosities, prolonged beyond her wish, grown out of her conception.

Tonight her will was too acutely alive in her to let her wander into that closed tower of self-indulgence. There was another and more intense pleasure in directing exactly the shape of her creation, in feeling form flow down from the centre of her personality, and out through the braced intelligence of her palms and along the strong, soiled fingers to the alert and responsive clay, where it sprang into visible being.

The rim of the bowl opened, flowering. She smoothed it in the soft hollow between her thumb and forefinger, until the edge of the silvery-blue clay glistened like glass. In the background of her consciousness she heard the car, but without relating it in any way to herself or any part of her life. Stepping back from the wheel, she watched the shape of her bowl flow round as perfect in its poise as a spinning top.

She groped into the slurry of water and clay which surrounded the wheel, and fished up impatiently two or three improvised tools before she found the piece of hoop-iron she wanted, bent at right-angles, with an obliquely finished edge. She set the wheel moving faster, and bending, pressed the shaving-tool inward along its surface to cut round the base of her bowl. The wheel shrieked and jarred, and a long, pleated tongue of clay flew outward from the knife and fell into the mess of water. She pressed inward firmly against the outward force of the wheel's motion until she was satisfied, and then dropped the knife into the slurry with as little regard as for the discarded thong of clay, and smoothed the new surface with her finger-tips. Instantly taller upon its narrow base, the bowl revolved, immaculate.

She heard the house-door crash open, heard Theo's voice roaring for her. A quiver of annoyance made the shape of her pleasure tremble for a moment, but was smoothed away again as quickly. She reached for a ragged little Turkish sponge, which leaned on the end of its stick out of a cracked jam-jar, and mopped out the excess moisture from the bowl. She forgot Theo, though she knew he was there, falling about in the living-room, and yelling to her to come and entertain some odd creature he'd picked up on his way home. Let him yell! He was seldom so far gone that he couldn't avoid smashing things, and he was almost never sick. It might be as well if he fell down quickly and went to sleep, of course, but the odds were that he wouldn't do much damage, even if he stayed lively. She let his shouts flow past her ears with an impervious calm, full of the lovely thing she had just made.

A bowl, one would think, is a sufficient description of a certain fixed and understandable shape; and yet the infinite range of its variations has never been half explored, and the whole of time remaining will hardly be enough to exhaust its possibilities. She had been fully six minutes in making this one, which was unconscionably slow, but the shape stood, and the glistening surface, on which the marks of her fingers spiralled faintly, had not suffered for her slowness. Her hand was in, she had the mood on her for manipulating beauty.

Intermittently she heard her name being called. Poor

Theo! In a little while she would rescue him. She took the asbestos bat by its corners, and twisted it free from its anchoring clay. It slid to the pressure of her hands, and she eased it clear and stood it aside to dry. Then she moistened her four wedges of clay once again, and pressed another bat down on them, twisting it tightly into place. She had a pitcher to make for some woman Theo had brought in from London once. She couldn't remember her name. Not a bad sort of person! She knew about pots, enough to select at sight the one piece Suspiria was never going to sell. Nor would she offer to try to make a second like it!; it was a jar she might live her life out and never recapture. But she had been moved to promise something of her best, because of that unerring election of what she herself loved.

She unrolled another lump of clay from the damp cloth in which it was wrapped, wet her hands in the surface of the slip which lay lake-like round the wheel after two hours of throwing, and slapped the clay into the middle of the revolving bat. She centred it strongly, and began to draw it up into a cylinder.

The crash which resounded from the living-room was no louder than those which had preceded it; it was merely the final pecking blow at the damaged shell of her serenity, letting the world in upon her in a flood of exasperation and rage. She felt the cylinder of clay slur out of the true, and watched it revolve under her eyes with an ugly, lopsided motion. She rummaged along the near edge of the bench with one hand for a palette-knife, sliced the distorted lump of clay from its place, and kneading it together roughly, rolled it again into its cloth. It was over. Her divided mind had loosed its hold on the mood for making things. She might as well go. If she got Theo to bed, and his crony out of the house, she might be able to go back to her work with a whole heart. There was all night yet.

But she was bitterly angry. She swept off the lights with a furious lunge of her elbow, because her hands were thickly coated with wet clay, and it was second nature to her to manipulate every piece of domestic apparatus in the house, on occasion, without benefit of hands. In the sink in the work-shop she had only cold water, and on cold days preferred to clean herself in the scullery. She hooked the door to behind her with her toes, and it shut with a slam which rattled the sieves along the wall.

In the stone farmhouse corridor, broad and reverberant as a cave, her steps echoed loudly. She heard Theo's voice in triumph: 'Here's my wife!' and someone falling over himself – probably drunk, too. A hand fumbled at the door; he wanted to make his escape, perhaps. She swung her arm, and swept back the curtain.

Theo was sprawling in a chair, trying to haul himself up by the bookshelves, from the lowest of which he had spilled a pile of books as she came in, but she stepped out of his reach, holding her glistening silver-grey hands cupped before her, and looking with imperious surprise at the young man who stood nervously gazing back at her from the doorway.

Not the usual kind of lame duck Theo picked up – not at all! True, his tastes were not at all narrow, he was as likely to attach to himself an inoffensive suburban type as one of his own rackety equals. The only person one need not expect him to bring home like a beloved brother was the person he was never likely to meet. And how did he come to meet this one? So young, and gawky, and allergic to eccentricities, with that shut face of outraged respectability on him, and those large, inimical and apprehensive eyes. There was no need whatever, she thought critically, for so determined a reserve, he could have very little of anything to hide. As limited as a small bottle, and as obvious as a fair-ground ornament. Not, however, as ugly! Not quite pretty enough as a child to stop maiden ladies in the street, perhaps, not quite handsome enough as a young man to set up notable and flattering jealousies among the girls in his circle, but always liable, with those fresh and unwary good looks, to the occasional shock of being too clearly approved. He stood rather self-consciously against the door, looking at her defensively and wondering what to say; and it was clear to her, even in the way he held himself, that he did not like feeling in the slightest degree ridiculous. What was Theo doing with an innocent little shop-walker like that? No, she corrected herself at once, not a shop-walker. His hands, however conscientiously washed, were slightly seamed with oil in their deeper lines. Then she remembered where she had seen him before. Of course, George Grover's young man from the garage! There was no longer any mystery about him, except how he came to let himself be inveigled into this. Most young men working for private employers have had to find ways to defend their precarious leisure. Was this one too soft-hearted? Or too poor-spirited? Or both?

Theo waved a hand benignly towards his unlikely companion. 'Spiri, this is a friend of mine – name of Dennis Forbes. Be nice to him! Very fine fellow, my friend Forbes, drove me home from George's. Got a queer idea I'm drunk, both of 'em! But kind, excessively kind!' He looked upon her with pride, while she stood immobile in the curtained doorway, holding her clay-covered hands away from her overall, and regarding the stranger with the shadow, but not the substance, of a severe and faintly derisive smile. 'I've been calling you a long time,' said Theo, willing to sound injured, but incapable of holding for a whole sentence a mood so directly opposed to his present feelings. 'Didn't you hear me?'

'I heard you,' she assured him, her eyes flickering downward over him in one quick glance. 'I was working.' She looked over him at the boy Dennis, who had made no sound yet, beyond an embarrassed murmur in acknowledgement of the introduction. 'I'm afraid you're hardly used to hearing men in my husband's state quite so voluble, Mr Forbes. If you wouldn't mind amusing yourself by listening to him for a few minutes, I'll wash off this clay. There's whisky in that cabinet there, and glasses. Will you help youself? And better give him one, too. There'll be trouble if you don't, and it won't have any appreciable effect. This is about as far as he goes.'

Her voice was cool, limpid and low, but he heard the acid note of irritation in it, and was painfully daunted. But for that, he might have stammered some quick excuse, and got safely away. Why didn't he? If he didn't understand that that was the only thing she wanted, to be rid of them both, he must be worse than stupid. Her look had said it, and her movements, and her intonations; yet he stood there, dumbly accepting the mere resigned words which covered her rejection of them both, that furious, silent rejection. He couldn't think of anything to say. When she turned to go back to the scullery, hunching her shoulder to fling back the torn curtain, his nervous resentment goaded him across the room to lift it aside out of her way. She was taken by surprise, but she understood; it was a bid for the initiative, an attempt to assert his balance and ease, in a situation to which he was anything but equal.

He was clumsy; in the circumstances how could he be anything better? He brushed against her closely, reaching over her shoulder, and clutching so hastily at the curtain that the third ring, which was already hanging by a thread, tore loose, and let his hand fall against her breast.

He recoiled at once as if the touch had burned him, muttering an incoherent apology, his cheeks flaming with mortification. For an amazed instant their faces were close together. She saw the affronted grey stare of his eyes, wide with chagrin; he had no control over his eyes, however he might shut down that impenetrable reserve upon the rest of his features. He was too young to be able to hide himself completely behind smooth brown skin and good, bold cheek-bones; however severely he compressed even that soft and vulnerable mouth of his, his eyes would betray the lost, bewildered and angry boy within. Whatever he had expected, she did not square with it. She could see him frantically trying to make sense of her, and helplessly failing.

'I should get that drink, if I were you,' said Suspiria, with an unkind curl of her lips. 'You need it!' And she turned her back on him, and went to wash the clay from her hands.

3

Now he was fairly in it, and flight was no longer even a possibility. He couldn't turn and sneak out while her back was turned; she knew his name, she'd remembered where he belonged, he'd seen it in her eyes. So it was too late to hope for anonymity. Here he was stuck with her husband, who was imperiously reminding him of the whereabouts of the whisky. Better shut him up, at any rate! As she'd said, it could hardly make much difference.

He was furious at the chatter of the glass against the bottle. Good God, why should *his* hand shake? It was she who ought to be feeling humiliated. He pushed the glass into Theo's hand, and turned his back upon him angrily. The full, fluent voice went on lauding the vanished woman, and expounding the excellences of her work, which filled the shelves behind him. Not nice, bright china, but plain pots and vases and jugs, a bit heavy and undecorated to his taste. Was that what she made? He didn't see that it was so wonderful. There wasn't a nice, stencilled pattern or a flower among the lot! Some of the colours were nice, but they weren't finished properly; even the shapes weren't all symmetrical. And fancy raving about a wife like that, as if she were something to be proud of! Why, she was just a slut! What else could you call her? Her house was dirty, and cluttered up with muck. You'd think she'd at least keep this room decent, in case anyone came, but she didn't seem to care a rap. Why, if anyone had caught his mother with her parlour looking like this, she'd have died of shame. This one just kicked the filthy paint-rag from under her feet when it got in her way, and took no more notice of it!

And look at the woman herself, with her hands clotted up with clay, and her overall stiff with it, and smears of clay and colour even in the hair at her temples! Fancy living in the middle of a chaos like this, and for ever as dirty as a farm-hand, he thought, with a mechanic's partial vision. If that was what being an artist entailed he was thankful there wasn't one in his family; his mother would go mad. He liked the arduous and pathetic cleanliness to which he had been bred, the virtue which had always been held up to him as next to godliness; for he was by nature and training a young man very obedient to the demands of virtue.

'My dear chap, you haven't got a drink! Fill up! I want to show you what I'm working on. Better bring the bottle! No, wait for Spiri, though – can't have a proper party without her.'

She came in with a resigned and angry quietness, unwound the scarf from his neck without a word, and began to extricate him from his coat, a long and complicated business because of all the hand-changing it entailed. Theo's solicitude for his glass, almost empty as it was, was the one thing which drove her for a moment into laughter. When she had the coat over her arm, she tilted Theo back into his chair with a perfectly assured and indifferent hand, and brushed her fingers across his ruffled hair with a gesture which assorted oddly with her disregard of all the worse disorder round her. She was not ungentle, but she was not gentle, either; she did what presented itself to be done, waiting to get through the inevitable delay in her plans. That was all it meant to her.

She let her husband go on talking, while his flow of words slid from her senses without a mark. She hung up the coat, and came across to where Dennis was hovering miserably and eyeing the door. She had taken off the overall, but the result was hardly more flattering, for she was still in old grey slacks and a dark red jersey blouse, and the slacks were dappled with occasional smears of clay as high as the knee. He admitted to himself that she wore them better than most women, being as slender as a boy; and maybe she might have been justified in presenting herself in them if they'd been reasonably clean and possessed of the ghost of a crease. But not many women would want to be seen like this. He hadn't realised how slight she was. What on earth did she do with her husband when he came home in this state, and she was left to deal with him alone? She couldn't possibly get him up the stairs. Anyhow, it wasn't a proper job for a woman, putting a drunk to bed; not even her own husband.

'I'm quite aware that I have clay in my hair,' said Suspiria, in a tone equable but cold, 'and I fully agree that I must be a fairly electrifying sight. You'll probably feel much happier about it if you drink this. It makes most things look considerably better. That's why Theo takes so much of it so often – all a part of the search for ideal beauty, no doubt.'

Dennis came out of his trance to find her holding out a glass to him, and became uneasily aware that he had been staring at her long and intently. There was no bitterness against her husband in the sour joke. She took this kind of thing quite for granted. If she was hitting at anyone, it was at him – at Dennis Forbes, who had done nothing whatever to her, who had gone out of his way to bring her old man home safely, and was now being made to squirm for it. And if once he got out of here, he'd take good care never to come within reach of either of them again.

'I'm sorry!' he said furiously, accepting the glass with too eager a hand because it gave him something else on which to concentrate. 'I didn't mean to come in and disturb you, but he would have it. And he wasn't steady enough on his feet to stick up by himself. I'll go, as soon as he forgets about me.'

'That will probably be some time,' she said with a wry smile. 'At this moment he loves you far too well to let you go easily. You'll have to view the thing he's working on, if you don't have to vet all the other stuff too. I'm afraid you've had rather a trying time with him. Where did you find him?'

'He came to the garage for petrol. Mr Grover thought—'

'—thought I ought not to be driving,' said Theo from the rim of his empty glass. 'And how right he was! Grover likes to take good care of his customers, provided he doesn't have to lift a finger himself. Good old George, found me a nursemaid without putting himself out an inch – not an inch!'

She looked at him over her shoulder with no personal anger, rather indulgently, in fact, but still with that dedicated rage against the situation burning in her face. 'I wish he'd been a couple of hours longer finding a sucker to be responsible for you, that's all!'

'If I hadn't brought him home,' said Dennis, outraged, 'he'd probably have ended up by being run in. The sergeant's on the main cross-roads tonight – he'd never come looking for gratitude, the Lord knew, but she couldn't even be civil. For all she cared, her husband could have been in a ditch somewhere; nothing mattered but whatever it was she'd left there at the back of the house – that precious work of hers that had given her dirty finger-nails and a navvy's hands.

'It would have done him good,' she said, with a lift of her slight shoulders, 'and I should have had some peace.' She saw the scandalised rage in the boy's face, saw him tongue-tied between the desire to give vent to his feelings, and the inability to be rude to a lady. Even such a lady as I am, she thought, equally touched and irritated by his helplessness. He'd been very well brought up, this child. If she had even known how to make concessions to his prejudices she would have done it; but she knew she could never hope to keep it up long enough to be convincing. 'You've been very kind, I'mn sorry if I shock you. But don't expect me to pretend my programme hasn't been smashed. I don't feel in the least obliged to assure you that it doesn't matter a bit! It matters like hell!'

Theo, leaning dangerously across to set down his glass upon the table, said brightly: 'You married me, my love! For better or worse, for richer or poorer – remember?'

She steadied him with a tolerant hand, and he put his arm round her waist, and held her swaying with his weight; and all the while her cool and critical eyes never left Dennis's face. She answered in the same tart but impersonal tone: 'Maybe I didn't know how much worse and how much poorer it was going to be. There ought to be reasonable limits, don't you think, my heart?'

'Til death do us part, my angel, is limit enough!'

She smiled, and her long, large hand spread its spatulate fingers upon her husband's shoulder. Dennis felt a fool, and resented it bitterly. How could you find your way among the things these two said to each other? One minute you were trying to guess how light a breath it would take to blow their marriage apart, and the next they were making oblique jokes at your expense, and leaving you high and dry out of their world, a funny little creature who thought he could improve on a mutual understanding far too subtle for his comprehension. 'I'm sorry!' he muttered, hardly knowing why he should be apologising.

'My dear man, for what? It isn't your fault, it's hardly even Theo's. Let me get you another drink!' She was a little sorry they had teased him, he looked so rattled and so apprehensive, feeling his way cautiously along the barriers of their unfamiliar conversation to find a way through. At the suggestion of a way of escape he jumped in eagerly. 'No, thanks, I really ought to be going, I haven't been home yet.'

Suspiria would have been willing to let him go, but Theo was not. He came out of the big chair exuberantly, and lunged across the room to fold a penitent and loving arm about Dennis's shoulders.

'No, can't hear of it! Should feel criminals if we let you run off like this! Take no notice of my wife, she was badly brought up – can't tell lies to save her life. 'Tisn't because she thinks 'em so wicked, it's because they're beneath her dignity. She won't go that far out of her way for anybody – not you, nor me, nor the Lord Chief Justice. Say to her: "I'm afraid I've come at an awkward time," and what d'you get? From anyone else: "Oh, no, not at all! Do come in!" Not Spiri! Oh, no! She says straight out: "Yes, you have!" She likes you, she's even glad to see you, but, damn and blast you, you *have* come at an awkward time. Come on, let's get out of her way till she forgives us.' But he hadn't plotted a wavering course to the curtained door before he was reaching back for her with the other arm, sweeping her along with him into the stone corridor. 'Let's all go! Let's go and look at Spiri's portrait. Best thing I've done for three years. Shark of a dealer wants it, but I'm not selling – it's too good to sell until we're flat broke.'

Suspiria braced herself resignedly under the weight of his arm, and wound her own about him with the expert gentleness of old custom. She looked across at Dennis, and felt with a dual sympathy and impatience his unhappiness at being handled. He was like so many of the humble and respectable, she thought irritably, insensitive enough to any mental contact which passed beyond the obvious, but physically one skin short of normal. One would have to be for ever either explaining something to him, or protecting him from the suspicion that there was something to be explained. As for Theo's imperious embrace, the young man flinched and fidgeted under it with a fourteen-year-old's embarrassment; from before that age, his kind shunned being touched by any but their contemporaries and fellows, with whom they went closely wreathed for a few years in a brief banditry before girls broke into their lives. And Theo should no doubt have realised, even when drunk, that he was neither a contemporary nor a fellow. The trouble was that Theo held himself to be all men's contemporary and all men's fellow. It had never been fully borne in upon him that humanity had sub-divisions.

'You haven't been monkeying about in the studio, have you? I left everything the way I wanted it. She doesn't tidy,' he confided to Dennis blithely, 'she untidies. If she's short of a hand-rag, she takes my paint-rags – when she doesn't tear up my shirts.' Proud and fond, thought Suspiria, even before Dennis could be felt thinking it, as of a clever toddler's pranks.

She slipped her hand within the open door on the right of the passage, and put on the light, and received eagerly the shock of delight which rang like a clear note of sound from Theo's easel, the clangour and gaiety, the shout of the dark-hot blue and the magenta, and the quivering mauve. Nothing but two dahlias and an aster that she had dropped this morning from her basket, and he had picked up for their scream of exultation. By tomorrow he would be tired of them, but she would never forget them. They had set in front of her eyes the colours of a glaze which she had never yet captured.

'It screeches!' said Theo. 'Or am I too tight to be able to stand it tonight? This afternoon I liked it. It had a texture, thick and waxy and cool like a dahlia, you could almost smell that peppery vegetable smell. Is it still there?'

'It's still there.' But she knew he would never like it quite so much again, because it had succeeded in saying everything it had to say while it was still technically only half-finished, and therefore it was most truly finished for him, and to touch it again would be supreme waste of time. He was never interested in things which were finished.

Dennis advanced gingerly, looking round the methodical chaos of the large room with uneasy eyes, and flinching most of all from the canvases propped against the wall, and the two or three Watman boards lying on the long bench among the tubes of colour and the mottled rags, and the litter of rough sketches. How if he should be expected to produce opinions? He was willing to say he admired the fellow's paintings, even if they were totally incomprehensible to him, but if more should be required of him he would be miles out of his depth. He didn't know the proper terms, and all modern pictures seemed to him equally mad, and a good many ancient ones not much better. And yet there must be something in it, if so many superior people said so. Anyhow, he wasn't going to lay himself wide open in front of these people; he'd have to stick tight to safe generalities. With wary eyes he examined the flowers and their portrait, still in high bloom while the originals lay limp and shrunken on the bench. He was a little encouraged, because they were recognisably dahlias and an aster. But why should they be made to look as crude as that? And anyhow, the thing was nowhere near finished.

In the event it was easier than he had expected. Theo asked him nothing. It was a monologue of self-examination, to Dennis's mind immodest in the extreme, though of course you had to make allowances for a man who was exalted drunk. The satisfaction of being among his own pictures steadied his feet, or else the worst was wearing off, for he led his nurse-maids round the room with hardly a lurch, weaving his way among the canvases with a wild dexterity, setting up first one and then another in the best light on the bench to be viewed and criticised. The woman strolled silently at his elbow, propping him occasionally with a resigned hand, and watching Dennis out of the corners of her large, oval eyes with a satirical, gleaming look. He took such pains to look critically intelligent as each canvas was displayed, and had his soft young mouth ready curved into words of wary appreciation, but his eyes, scared and hostile, fended off every assault as if it had been made against his virtue. He knows, she thought, that I know how completely he's at sea, poor child! But her enjoyment of his predicament was something she believed she was successfully keeping to herself. It was a wonder she went to the trouble of trying!

The portrait stood propped against the wall on the bench, its back turned coldly on the room. Theo hoisted it tenderly in his arms, and turned it for them to see, setting it well back where the light fell most gently. The canvas was almost square, and she was a coil of braced curves within the square, curled into a large, plain chair, with her arm crooked over the back dangling a book. The book was there only to provide a point of blue-black, fixed and steady within the coiled tensions of her body and limbs, and the only other stillness in it was her face, lifted aslant as if she had paused to consider something she had just read, and been brought up erect and taut by the whip of her own thoughts. A wild, potential but still look, about which like the swirl of her vivid possibilities the patterns of profound colour span, red-hot red, deep, silvery green and iris-grey, and filling the corner of the canvas, the deep, thick olive-green of her best celadon jar, smoking into the lighter green of the chair. The greys were so lucid and airy that you could put your hands into them, and bathe to the wrist.

That was what Theo saw when he turned his treasure to the light. For Dennis there was only the blunt, expected bewilderment, threaded by the little shock of gratitude that the subject was at any rate recognisable. At least there was a face, a perceptible face. He clung to that as to his salvation.

Theo said: 'By God, it's even better than I remembered it! All my life I wanted to get a grey like that. Look at the space, look at the air! You could throw your arms round her where she sits, bless her! About the jar I never felt so sure – that counter-roundness coming so far forward – but then, that's Spiri, too. I wanted it to balance that other spinning plane, of course, but sometimes I wonder if it isn't pulling the whole thing over.'

Suspiria, moved to malicious mischief, and quite unable to resist the stab, said gently: 'Well, Mr. Forbes is your guinea-pig, why don't you ask him what he feels about it?'

Dennis hated her with a burning bitterness which astonished him. He muttered hurriedly that he liked the colour. It seemed the safest thing to say. Retreating defensively, he added: 'I don't know much about it, but it seems very effective to me.' That was a good word, effective! Simple enough to come naturally from a layman like him, and yet it didn't sound silly. He heard her small, derisive murmur of agreement, and sweated with dislike of her.

Theo sat down in the one rickety chair the studio contained, and settled himself to contemplate his darling. Dennis had no choice but to stare at it, too; it seemed impolite to become bored with it before its creator tired of displaying it. It was pleasanter looking at the copy than the original, because the woman in the picture was gazing beyond him, and he did not have to meet those dark eyes of hers which stung him into such discomfort.

It was very like her, this painting, he saw that more clearly every moment; and it told him things about her which he had not noticed for himself, the natural rhythmic elegance of her movements, the erect, almost arrogant poise of her head, the unassertive distinction of her features, which grew gradually in his mind out of details he did not realise he had recorded. The eyes were of a dark greenish-brown, like the darkest possible hazel; the nose straight, narrow and fastidious, between fine high cheek-bones placed rather widely for the width of her face; the mouth both full and long, with a resolute but thoughtful set to it. Her hair was black, straight and short, cut closely to the shape of her head, not for fashion's sake, though the result looked fashionable, but to keep it from getting in her way, and to ensure that it demanded the absolute minimum of her time and consideration to keep it in order. Looking at the woman herself, he was not aware that he had noticed any of these things, but his conviction on seeing them in the portrait was that he recognised, not discovered them.

'Pretty, isn't it?' said Suspiria, with faintly acid sweetness.

He knew she was making fun of him, but didn't know with what more subtle word to cancel out her contribution, so he said nothing. He looked to Theo for help, amazed to realise that while he had been staring the flow of words had ceased. Theo's chin was on his chest, his head nodding heavily; even when the awareness of being watched stirred him awake again, and he raised his head, his eyelids were seen to be dropping.

'At last!' said Suspiria, and shook him gently by the

shoulder. 'Come on, time you went to bed! You're dropping off to sleep where you sit.'

'Nothing of the kind!' said Theo, quite distinctly; but he rose at her hand's prompting, and allowed himself to be turned towards the door. 'What do they put in the beer these days? Or did you dope the whisky?'

'Of course!' she said serenely, slipping her shoulder closely under his. Beneath the drowsy bulk she looked smaller than ever. Dennis, whose heart had leaped with joy to think he would be able to slink away, turned back from the very threshold of escape to realise that this was no job for her. Much as he wanted to get out of this alien world and stay out of it for good, it surely wouldn't hurt him to stay for ten more minutes, and relieve her of the job of getting her husband to bed. He felt impelled to make the offer. She looked up at him for an instant with an astonishment so blazingly sincere that she seemed a different woman, and then without a word surrendered the weight to his arm, and went before them through the doorway.

By the time they had climbed the stairs, and entered a large, low-ceilinged bedroom, she was having some difficulty in hiding completely her amusement at the heavy weather the boy made of it, with all his good intentions. She could have handled it herself without difficulty, but she left it to him, and him to it, with impersonal forbearance, and waited for him below. He was not a fool, he would see through her if she stayed upon the scene; and perhaps it was worth smoothing things over a little, for his sake, since she was hardly likely ever to see him again upon the same terms. Let him enjoy his chivalry if he could, and feel a man of the world, gracious, competent and sophisticated. When he came down the stairs he looked more like a ruffled and perspiring boy just gratefully rid of a job which had taxed him to the limit.

He said in a constrained voice: 'He's asleep! He dropped off as soon as he was flat. I shouldn't think he'll stir for about twelve hours.'

He could see his own relief and eagerness reflected in her eyes, which smiled full into his with a bright elation which was certainly not meant for him. She was thinking of only one thing, that her old man was safe out of the way for the night, and in five more minutes she would be rid of the other nuisance, too. She was promising herself a speedy return to her precious pots – what was so special about them, anyhow? In the Midlands they turned them out by the thousand, much more elaborate specimens than these, and with no such fuss and bother about it.

'You've been very kind! Won't you have another drink before you go? You must need it, after that!'

'No, thanks, really! I ought to get home.'

He needn't worry any more about escaping, *she* wasn't going to put any obstacles in his way, she could hardly wait to push him out of the house. Oh, she did it with an air, all right! She got him to the door in a few seconds, and almost before he knew it they were out on the quarried yard before the house, looking down the track to the road.

'The moon's up, you'll be able to see your way.'

'I shall be all right, I haven't got very far to go.'

'Good-night, Mr. Forbes! Thank you for taking care of Theo!'

'I was glad to help,' he said untruthfully, but in the best traditions of his training. 'Good-night, Mrs. Freeland!'

The door closed with almost insulting alacrity as soon as he had gone a few steps. She would be flying back through the stone passage, back to her workshop, plunging her hands into the clay again, sinking herself deep into her mystery. Probably she would be laughing, he thought, half for joy at being free, half in contemptuous amusement at the recollection of his awkwardness and simplicity.

It didn't matter now, he reminded himself gladly, lengthening his pace along the cart-track. That was the last of the pair of them, as far as he was concerned. He'd never have to see either of them so close again, and he'd take jolly good care no second situation like tonight's should ever involve Dennis Forbes. Once was enough! Now forget them!

He hustled them to the back of his mind, and set out as fast as he could on the walk home.

CHAPTER TWO:

Venture into Unknown Territory

1

MRS. FORBES was a woman with a strong competitive spirit and a natural instinct for domestic perfection, who had all her life had to make do with inadequate material. Before her marriage in 1920 she had been the middle one in a large family in the industrial Midlands, in an overcrowded house without amenities, where there was never enough food to make cooking anything better than a problem in distribution, never any new clothes except for the eldest, never any leisure or any privacy. Even her husband was small and insignificant, and accepted by her in the same spirit of making do with what she could get, since she could not have what she wanted. In the same way she managed to be truly fond of him, for she had learned to perfection the art of shortening her sights to the range of her weapons.

If she had ever had any hopes that her opportunities might be enlarged by the marriage, the Depression effectively killed them. Her husband spent three demoralising years on short time, and eighteen months without employment of any kind, and dwindled away from shame and discouragement to half his former size, and a grey shrivelled silence from which he never really recovered. He suffered the conviction that he was a failure in everything he had ever touched, and that there was no good reason for his existence at all; a common occupational disease among the unemployed, but one for which neither medicine nor psychiatry had stirred themselves to find a palliative, much less a cure.

It was a fundamental need of Mrs. Forbes' nature that she should have something to be proud of; and if she could not have the accumulation of possessions which would have given her status in her own and other eyes, it was all the more necessary that she should be proud of what she had. Cleanliness, order and neatness can be had without spending, and she made do with them through all the bad years. She turned out her husband, on his trips to the Labour Exchange, well-brushed and regularly shaven, never without a collar and tie, a witness to her dogged assertion of respectability. The standard was never allowed to sag, because only by this fanatical adherence to every rite could she buttress her self-respect upright against the crushing weight of the world.

In 1931 Mr. Forbes went south on a wildgoose chase after rumours of jobs going in light industry, and though nothing materialised in that line, he managed to get a temporary job in a furniture warehouse. A death made the temporary job permanent, and the following year he found a small insanitary cottage in a back lane on the country side of Great Leddington, and his family came down to join him. The old defiant assertion of respectability began again in new surroundings, but with fresh optimism, since a job is a job.

But it was the war that really changed things for the Forbes family. It was not only that there was suddenly more than enough work for everyone, but rather that the pressure of necessity produced, for the wrong reasons but irrevocably, the social revolution which acknowledged them as human beings, with rights and needs. The younger children began to bloom and grow, because for the first time they were ensured a reasonably fair share of the foods they needed, and even the older ones benefited to a lesser extent from this belated measure of justice. Suddenly their health was a matter of public concern, and their rations protected. Albert, when he was called up in 1940, was bringing home weekly wages of which his father had never dreamed in all his life. Marjorie left school and went straight into a factory, and was soon earning what seemed to her mother a fabulous sum for a girl of fifteen. Harold, who was bright and plausible, got himself an office-boy's job soon after leaving school in 1939, and was a junior clerk, and well thought of, before he, too, had to go into the army. So they were almost rich, even if they could not spend their money on precisely the things they had always wanted.

Now Albert was married, and so was Marjorie, and the council house into which the family had moved in 1947, on the edge of the newest estate in the town, was wonderfully spacious for the parents and their three remaining children. Albert was felt to have married rather above him, into a greengrocery business with three shops in the town and its environs. The shades of social significance involved were infinite in number and infinitesimal in degree. His wife's family had got hold of him pretty tightly, and his calls at Lancelot Road were becoming few and far between. Marjorie, on the other hand, had married somewhat beneath her, a milk-roundsman who came from a large and turbulent family out at Copping Common; and she was for ever back at home pouring out her complaints against Stan, and his mother, and all the lot of them, though she always stood up for him if anyone else joined in the condemnation. Harold was too clever to have got caught so far, and as for the other two, they were too young to be thinking about marriage as yet.

It was the five years between Harold and Dennis which had induced Mrs. Forbes to think of her youngest son as still hardly more than a schoolboy. After all, the other two had actually been in the war, while even Dennis's military service had been spent safely in England, and involved nothing more dangerous than barrack-room larking and extreme boredom. More like a sort of game, she thought indulgently. The first three had been brought up in the hard years, Dennis and Winnie in the stimulation of prosperity. They seemed to her still children, though even Winnie was eighteen, and working behind the lingerie counter at Haddow's for the last three years.

The older children had always considered that Dennis and Winnie were being spoiled, and had done their best to reverse the trend; an attempt which had had little effect upon the young people concerned, but had served to accentuate the five-year interval which cut them off from their critics, and had made them seem younger than ever to Mrs. Forbes. So she was not disposed to take very seriously any of Winnie's many and ephemeral boy-friends, nor to lose any sleep over the insinuating appearance of Iris Moffatt in Dennis's life. Almost before she realised what was in the wind, they were walking out steady.

It had been Iris who made the going. Dennis had never taken much interest in girls, or rather his interest had been so diffuse that none of them had managed to establish a claim on him. He danced in the winter evenings, if he couldn't find anything better to do, and occasionally he had been known to go off somewhere on his motor-bike with a girl on the pillion instead of a boy; but it was so seldom the same girl twice running that no one had ever expected anything to come of these jaunts. There had never been many ways that a girl could hope to get hold of him, until his interest in her awakened naturally; but Iris had found one of them.

Iris had a brother who belonged to the same darts club, and she took to meeting him on club nights, always with some reasonable excuse. Brothers, however dumbfounded by such sudden attentions from their sisters, are not notably quick on the uptake; and even if they do see through the manoeuvre, family loyalty may bar them from giving the game away. At any rate, no one had warned Dennis what was in the wind. Even so, Iris had to work hard to take the affair past the accidental stage. It was six weeks before she managed to get herself invited out on the pillion, and several months more before she got him trained to a proper routine, which included appointments with her at least twice a week. Then she felt fairly safe, for he was a good-natured boy, and not likely to make any violent struggles for his liberty. He liked her, and enjoyed her company, and they got on together very well, on the whole, and he hadn't yet realised that there was more to be had than that.

Mrs. Forbes wanted the best for her youngest son, and had not thought of having to let him go for some years yet. But there it was, and Iris was a nice, steady girl enough, and would make him a good wife, if it should come to that. After all, she had to be prepared for it to happen sooner or later, and it could easily have been worse. So she sat back quietly among her new possessions, and watched Iris gradually tightening her hold about Dennis's innocent neck. If she had hunted him down, it was because she wanted him. Who wouldn't? Such an attractive boy, a good worker, steady in his ways but plenty of fun – the girl might well think it worth going to some trouble to make sure of him. Nor did it seem to Mrs. Forbes such a bad foundation for a marriage, if one partner knew exactly what she wanted, and the other merely had no objection. That was how her own marriage had started out, so she knew it could turn out well.

And then, just because of one night when Dennis should have met Iris and didn't turn up – just because of one disappointment after months of steady, reliable companionship – it all began to go wrong.

2

Dennis loitered to straighten his tie at the mirror over the parlour mantelpiece, and his eye was caught, not for the first time recently, by his mother's two big pottery vases, biscuit-coloured things made in a square shape, with the edges sheered off and painted red, a big bunch of flowers stencilled on the side, and a jazz sort of handle. Lately he'd caught himself looking at these things with a seriously studious eye, because they were so different from anything that Freeland woman had in her house.

All those simple shapes, all that roundness on her shelves, roundness that made you cup your hands instinctively when you looked at it, as if to feel how much tactile satisfaction such a shape could give you. He touched one of these vases, suddenly. It felt dry and brittle, and the angles stuck into his tentative hand in an uncomfortable way. Still he could not help being impressed by the floral decoration, full of so many colours. Surely it must be affectation to prefer those plain things, those patterns, where there were any, made of three brush-strokes, perhaps one thin little branch in leaf coiled round a jug, or three reeds and a bird hinted at, as if materials were rationed – surely it was a kind of pose, to choose that in place of such lavish colour and shape as this? It might be clever to put over the idea that those skimpy designs were more artistic, because they were easier to produce. Perhaps she couldn't do anything as elaborate as this! He wanted to be pleased with the idea, if he had to think of the beastly woman at all, after the lapse of almost a month since he had seen her. But the minute he had put the thought into perceptible form, he knew it was not true. He could think of a lot of things to say against them both, but they had no affectations, they were almost terrifyingly without them. So that couldn't be the answer; whatever they were, they weren't phoneys.

He was aware of his mother on her knees somewhere behind him, industriously polishing the linoleum round his feet. He asked impulsively: 'Mum, do you like these vases?'

She looked up momentarily to be sure on which ornaments she was being asked to pronounce, and said warmly: 'Yes, of course I like them. What a question! What do you think I keep them there for, if I don't think they're pretty?'

'Well, but do you think they'd be reckoned *good*? I mean, in an artistic way?'

'Oh, my goodness, I don't even know what you mean by that! I should think they would. Your Aunt Win gave twelve-and-six each for them in one of the biggest shops in London. And that was before things went up the prices they are now, too!'

He hesitated, his lips apart, not knowing what he wanted to ask, nor who was to answer it. She reached up and gave him a smart pat behind to move him out of her way. 'Move over a bit, there's a good boy! I want to do where you're standing.'

Dennis stepped aside obediently, and watched her

continue instantly her polishing of the already bright. 'What's the idea? You've done there once this morning, by the look of it.'

'What a story! I haven't touched it since Thursday. Winnie's bringing that Ferriday girl in with her for a cup of tea before they go to the pictures tonight. I want it to be nice – you know what that family are! I'm not having that mother of hers carrying any second-hand tales round about our house.'

For some reason he was deeply offended by the thought of his mother scrabbling about on her knees, frantic to remove the last grain of dust which might be used as ammunition against her. As if even her house-pride had to be in reality a kind of house-shame, and her impregnable fortress of cleanliness really existed only to provide a shell for her fear. 'I wouldn't make any fuss for them,' he said, sharply frowning. 'Surely we're good enough as we are.'

Indignantly, as she scrambled to her feet and faced him, she retorted: 'We want the place to be presentable when visitors come, don't we?'

'It always is presentable. I wouldn't put myself out to fuss like that just because you're expecting someone – trying to make it look as if no real people lived here at all! I wouldn't do it for royalty!' he said, almost violently.

'Oh, wouldn't you, indeed? What big talk we're getting from you, young man, these days! I'll have things as I want them in my own house, thank you very much, and if you don't like it you'd better get on out. You're going to be late again, anyhow, if you don't get along soon.'

He saw that he had annoyed her, but because of his own inexplicable sense of outrage he could not be sorry. He knew he was behaving badly, and had better get his half-baked ideas straightened out in his own mind before he began throwing them at her. He didn't know what was the matter with him, going off without warning like this. He was as taken aback as she was, and a good deal more upset.

'But you're not having them as you want them,' he said perversely. 'You're breaking your neck getting them up like you think Mrs. Ferriday'd like them – or anyhow, so that you can shut her mouth with them. It doesn't seem to have much to do with what *you* want.' He turned his shoulder on her, because he knew he was putting himself more spitefully in the wrong with every word, and he thought he had better go, before he did worse.

'What a bad-tempered little brat you're turning out to be lately,' she said warmly. 'Nothing around here seems to satisfy you, these days. None of us does anything right for you. I think you'd better go and set up on your own, the sooner the better, and see if Iris can please you, since we can't.'

He took his coat, and flung out of the house as if he considered himself the offended party. Perhaps he was, from the moment that she laid her finger upon the sore spot by sheer accident, and accused him roundly of what was his disease. 'Nothing around here seems to satisfy you, these days.' Did she suppose he liked going unsatisfied? Especially when he hadn't the least idea what was missing from his diet! How could it be true that it had anything to do with those Freeland people? It was only thinking about the vases that had brought them back into his mind. And yet he had sometimes found himself going over and over the words and actions of that disruptive evening, as we do dissect the occasions which have left us feeling inadequate, to see if we cannot arrive at some rearrangement of the facts more flattering to ourselves. Sometimes, with frequent repetition of the doctored version, it is possible to adopt it as the truth, and relinquish the recollection of those bits which fail to fit in. But he hadn't managed it where the Freelands were concerned. The man had been a capricious drunk, and the woman an uncivil slattern, who didn't even subscribe to the elementary rules of human conduct, such as being polite to visitors. He wasn't in any doubt about what they were. Then why should they still, even in recollection, be able to make him feel a miserable, inexperienced bumpkin?

It was the slight to himself he still felt most keenly. Never before had he found himself marooned in a situation like that, where even his attempts to follow the language looked gauche and obvious, while those two daunting people, not particularly impressive, not very well-off, probably not even very gifted, yet strode through the complexities of their whole difficult world with so much assurance and conviction. Why, the damned woman had even made it seem right and inevitable that she should apologise for nothing and be ashamed of nothing, so superbly justified had she felt herself to be in her preoccupation with more important things than either her husband or Dennis Forbes.

He dug his hands deeply into his pockets, and walked quickly, along the neat, white-kerbed roads of the housing estate, trying to leave his dissatisfaction behind him. What on earth had got into his vision, that he could compare his own clean, decent home, and wholesome, respectable family with those intellectual tramps, and make his own world come out of it on the debit side? It didn't make sense. And his mother was right, as usual, he was late for his appointment with Iris. Serve him right if she hadn't waited, he thought, with a leap of his heart which felt incredibly like a convulsion of hope; but he knew she would wait.

She was standing on the corner, close to Haddow's window, when he reached the town centre. He saw the bright red of her new winter coat as soon as he turned into the street, and knew the prim way she stood, toes just lined to the edge of the kerb, bag tightly under her arm, looking self-consciously before her with that bright, painfully unconcerned look, trying to make herself believe that no one knew she was waiting for a young man, and the young man was late. Why should it be more humiliating to wait for him than to make him wait for her? But Iris hedged her life about with hundreds of little pretences, fending off the constant small disappointments and discomfitures which beset the path of the commonplace, by asserting that they simply did not happen, or if that could not be maintained any longer, that they did not affect her, that she was above them. She was one of the great majority who have to protect themselves by such psychological evasions, being without any special natural armour of her own.

Another kind of girl would have waited there, he thought, with head reared, frankly looking along the street for him, perhaps would have frowned her annoyance at him when he appeared, and charged him outright with his unpunctuality. Iris didn't risk that. She came a few steps to meet him, with a relieved but injured smile, tightly magnanimous, and slipped her small, gloved hand in his arm. They fell into step together as they said: 'Hullo!' and he added rather glumly: 'Sorry I'm late!'

It was more than she could rely on getting out of him these days, and she was grateful for it. 'Oh, well!' she said, surprised into too rash a concession. 'I know there must be a good reason.' So much of her conversation these days began with: 'Oh, well!' that it amounted to a confession of her perpetual need to make the best of a state of affairs by no means satisfactory.

'What shall we do?' he asked, halting on the corner, where one road led away to the preposterous little park, and one into the main shopping street. 'Do you want to go to the pictures this afternoon? May not be many more Saturdays as nice as this.'

'Well, I've got a few bits of shopping to do, if you don't mind. I wouldn't be long. Then I thought we could have a little walk, and get tea early, and go to the pictures after. If that's all right with you?'

He made no objection, though he hated shopping; it was one of those things he'd got to get used to, sooner or later. She abandoned him outside two or three shops in their progress through the crowded streets, and her last call was at a draper's in the square, close beside the garden which bordered the plain brick museum and art gallery. While he waited for her he strolled along to look at the late asters and the last of the fuchsias, and then to read, no more than the surface of his mind following his eyes, the notices on the board outside the door. There was always some little art show on there, and sometimes an evening lecture on some item of the town collection, or a piano recital on Sunday afternoon. This week, it seemed, there was an exhibition—

Now why did *she* have to crop up again, just when he was forgetting he'd ever seen her and her pottery? There it was: 'Modern English Pottery by Suspiria Freeland', and the hours of opening; and somewhere inside there, he thought, was the real secret, if he knew how to look at it, the thing she lived by and for. He suddenly felt strongly how much more satisfied he might be if he understood about the pots, and how fine it must be to know about any amount of things – not in the sense of having a lot of facts by heart, but to know to your own content, to have authority in your own mind. Saturday, 10 a.m. to 10 p.m.! This was the last day of the exhibition, and he was presented with the opportunity too late. He stood staring at the notice with an intent frown, wondering if he might not be passing by for good the only road there would ever be to one extension of his personality.

Close to his shoulder, following his fixed stare, Iris exclaimed: 'Why, that's that woman you know – Mrs. Freeland!'

He looked too late and too long at the fuchsias, and then said too quickly, as his eyes returned to the notice: 'Oh, yes – so it is! I don't *know* her, though. I only saw her that once, really, and that was enough.'

He knew that the tone was not quite what he had intended, even before Iris's insinuating hand had crept into the crook of his arm. She was looking from the poster to his face, with long, slow, sidelong looks; and in a moment she said, at once too brightly and too warily: 'If you want to see it, we could go in there, instead of going for a walk. We've got plenty of time before tea.'

The very thought turned his inside to ice. Never in her life would Iris have thought honestly of paying to go into an art gallery. No, what she wanted was to see what it was that was eating into him. She was quick to feel any new tension in him; she had to be, after all the work she'd put in on him. If there was anything funny going on in his mind about that woman and her work, Iris felt she had better find out at once what it was, and study how to deal with it. What he couldn't understand was why it should seem to him so horrifying a prospect, having to lead a suspicious and watchful Iris round a few stands of pottery which neither of them would know how to criticise or approve. But he swung her away from the gallery with an almost violent gesture of repudiation.

'What, me? Waste a fine afternoon on those things? At a bob a time? Not much! Come on, let's get out of town for an hour or so, while we can.'

She went with him docilely enough, but the hand continued with insistent, reminding pressures in his arm, and as they crossed the street by the Post Office corner she looked up into his face with an uneasy smile, and asked almost soundlessly in his ear: 'Love me?' It was a trick she had when she wanted to point out to him how deeply he was committed to the situation. The more blithely she asked it, the more gingerly was she feeling the crackling of the ice under her feet. Every: 'Yes, don't be silly!' every: 'Of course I do!' erected another acutely pointed thorn in the way of his retreat. And yet what else can a fellow say, attacked like that in the middle of the street?

'You shouldn't ask questions like that in the middle of a zebra crossing. You'll have us under a bus!'

Once on the opposite pavement she said, pouting: 'I don't believe you do!'

'I shan't much longer, anyhow, if you get me cut off in my prime. Have you finished now?' He meant the shopping, but it sounded to her ominously like an ultimatum in the matter of her artful complaint against him; so she let the subject slide for the moment, though she did not forget it. After all, nothing was lost yet. Even the easiest of men turns obstinate now and again; the thing to do is to pretend not to notice it, give him no occasion to dig in his heels and turn the playful contention into a real one. So she skipped along beside him towards the open fields and the long green walk of Church Lane, and began to be brisk and talkative about the whist drive at the Social Club last night, and – with elaborate artlessness – about the arrangements for her cousin's wedding, which was to take place at Christmas. A week or two ago he might have missed the implication; he did not miss it now.

They came back into the edge of the town for tea, over which she presided with a conscious grace and dexterity, still nudging him, with every show of old familiarity with his likes and dislikes, into a due acceptance of his position. Then they went to the pictures, and sat in the back row, which again was a kind of unofficial acknowledgment of the regularity of their attachment. Iris marched in there firmly, leading Dennis by the hand, for he was always blinder in the sudden dark than she; and soon her shoulder was fitted closely into the hollow of his, and her head was feeling for its comfortable rest against his cheek. He put his arm round her, because it was the only way to establish his own comfort in that position, but it did not seem to her to fold round her shoulders as satisfactorily as usual.

Moving her lips against his cheek, she asked in the merest breath of a voice: 'Love me?'

'Oh, for God's sake!' exploded Dennis, in a voiceless scream of exasperation, suddenly throwing every instinct of placatory caution headlong in the dark.

He heard her gasp and hold her breath, felt her rigid against him for a moment with shock and fright. Then, silently, she began to cry, and went on and on until he thought she would still be sniffling into her handkerchief when the lights went up. He was almost grateful that it was a sloppy film in any case, and the few rows in front of them were moist with more vicarious tears. He supposed, without cynicism, that it would hardly be possible for the casual eye to distinguish between tears caused by that sickening little girl on the screen and those caused by Dennis Forbes. So he let her alone, rightly judging that any attempts at comfort or intimidation would only involve him in a scene difficult enough anywhere, but almost impossible here in the dark, surrounded by strangers at uncomfortably close quarters. If he apologised and said he did love her, the relief would keep her in tears for ages, and the noise might get out of hand. If he told her to shut up and stop making a fool of herself, despair would produce the same effect. Left in suspense, she was at least stealthily quiet about it, for fear of driving him to extremes. She wanted him to know she was crying, but to be reassuringly aware that as yet no one else knew it. And after all, what had he done? It was due to happen sooner or later, when she kept popping that infuriating question into his ear; he couldn't have kept it in much longer.

And she shouldn't have mentioned love. Suddenly he saw how fatal that had been. If she'd kept it carefully out of all their conversations he might never have noticed how singularly absent it was. Of course he didn't love her! She didn't love him. No doubt she thought she did, because she had no idea what the word really entailed, and she had certainly decided that he was a creditable partner, and elected to have him, which was as far as her definition went. But this, whatever it was, had nothing to do with love, suddenly he was quite sure of that. He didn't know yet what it really was, any more than she did, but he knew it had to be something infinitely larger and more convincing than this. Or else they could keep it!

Suddenly, with a little calculating twin flare of hope and shame, he wondered if Iris would think it wise to make a strategic withdrawal, and ask him to take her home as soon as they came out of the cinema, and whether, if she showed no sign of suggesting such a move, he could tenderly suggest it for her. If he could persuade her that she ought to have an early night, he might have time to get back to the gallery before it closed. If he wanted to! He was still not sure that he did. But *if* he did!

When the lights went up, Iris was in a state of limp and hostile calm, but her eyes were dry, and her handkerchief out of sight. He looked at her with an expressionless face, carefully avoiding any intimation of penitence, and asked constrainedly: 'Shall we go?'

Outside it was cold but still, and the streets were a murmur of strolling people and a glimmer of lights and shadows, busy, alert and populous. Among the broken fragments of other people's conversations and the dappling confusion of lights, it was easy to move islanded and anonymous, more alone than in solitude. They recovered themselves a little, and began to wonder if anything had really happened at all.

'Would you like some coffee?' asked Dennis, still avoiding apology. 'We could call in at Wards', if you like?'

He knew he had made a mistake by the way she jumped at the offer, and remembered too late that Wards' Café had deep alcoves in which a quarrel could take place, even to more tears, without attracting attention. Once she got him in there, who was to say when he would get out again? It was almost a quarter to nine by the church clock. However, there was nothing to be done but follow her in, and hide with her, unwillingly, in a dim corner, where they sat glumly over coffee and biscuits until the waitress was out of earshot.

'I don't believe you're a bit sorry,' said Iris then, opening the attack directly, her blue eyes, slightly reddened with weeping, reproaching him miserably over the steam of the coffee-cups.

'I'm sorry you felt so badly about it as all that,' said Dennis, hedging a little for the sake of peace. 'Sorry I said it, for that matter, but I couldn't help feeling it. Of all the times to start that stuff—'

'You didn't dare answer me honestly,' she said.

'Nobody can keep repeating it every five minutes, and not get sick of it, anyhow. Look, it's no use talking about it now, when you're upset already. Drink your coffee, and let me take you home.'

'So's you can go and enjoy yourself somewhere else, without me! I'm just in your way now, you'd rather get rid of me,' she accused, between anger and fresh tears. 'You don't love me at all!'

'I don't think either of us has got much right to talk a lot about love,' he said abruptly. 'It's a big word. We'd do well to use it pretty sparingly until we know what we have got. You're a nice girl, I like you a lot – if I didn't, I shouldn't be here. Can't you wait for the rest?'

'It sounds very nice,' she said bitterly, 'but I know there is more to it than that. You're not like you used to be. You've changed a lot. I believe it's got something to do with those Freelands,' she said, firing shots at random. 'I'm sure there's something you never told me about that business.'

'There never was anything to tell. He was drunk, and I drove him home, and I couldn't get away for over an hour. I hated it, and I'd be only too glad to forget about it, if you'd let me.'

'Then why is it you haven't been the same since?'

'I didn't know I hadn't. What on earth do you suppose I want with people like that, anyhow? They're not my kind.'

'I know they're not – better keep reminding yourself of that. They're not your kind, and they won't bring you any good!'

'Who's talking about them? What have they got to do with it? Look, we'd better call it off for tonight. I tell you, you're barking up the wrong tree. There's nothing different about me – I don't know what you're fighting about. You're all excited over absolutely nothing – nothing at all.'

'I don't call it nothing, when you suddenly say you don't love me!' The tears began to ooze, and it was all he could do not to shout at her in a way which would have finished the affair once for all. Instead, he went on talking gently, persuasively, reasonably, because it was after nine o'clock, and there was less than an hour left, and unless he reassured her she would devour it to the last minute.

'That's not fair! I never said any such thing, and you know it. Come on, now, this all started out of nothing. Let's go home and sleep on it, and tomorrow you'll hardly remember it – only to wonder what on earth it was all about.'

She was already sorry that she had pushed the dispute into the open, for she knew in her heart that he had slipped from under her thumb so far, and hardened so inexplicably, that if she pressed too hard now he would spin far out of her reach, and it was doubtful if she would ever get him back again. Recovering from the recklessness of despair, she drew back to more secure ground.

'I am tired! Oh, Dennis, I hate quarrelling with you!'

He paid the bill, and took her home. She made the most of the quarter of an hour's walk, and kept him for a few minutes saying good-night when they arrived at her gate. They heard the church clock just striking the half-hour as they halted there; it was nearly five minutes fast.

'I'm sorry we spoiled the day between us,' she said, arduously accepting half of a guilt which she felt to be entirely his. 'It was all rather silly, I suppose.' She turned to face him, and her hands slid up to take him by the shoulders. 'Dennis – you do like me, don't you?'

'Of course I like you! Don't be silly! Now don't fret any more. Just go and sleep it off, like a good kid!'

'Come to tea tomorrow – please!'

'I can't tomorrow, I've got to go to my sister's to fetch something for Mum. But I'll see you Monday evening.'

'Promise? The usual time?'

'Yes, I promise.' He smiled down at her, and she wondered at the way the faint light from the cream-curtained window lit up the sudden bones of his face, making him look excited, and even younger than his twenty-two years. He reared his head, looking beyond her, back towards the town; she felt how his body was arched like a spring to be off from her, and longed to keep hold of him, but she knew her only hope was to let him go.

'Kiss me good-night!' she asked him, raising her lips.

He kissed her, and held her a moment, and the cold young cheek was smooth against hers, and had a fresh, frosty smell all its own. 'Good-night, Iris! Be a good girl!'

'Oh, Dennis, darling!' For a moment she did truly love him. The pain it involved astonished her, but it did not matter, for she never felt it again. 'Good-night, then – see you on Monday!'

She went quickly through the gate, and down the garden path into the shadow of the house; and there she halted, flattening herself against the wall, and waited, listening to his brisk steps as he walked back towards the town. When he thought she must be already safely inside the house, he began to run. There was something terrifying to her in the suddenness of it, and the ardour. He ran like a boy let out of school, wildly, at full speed; a man running for his life could not have sounded more in earnest.

Then she knew that she had lost him, that it was all over.

3

Suspiria was standing in a corner of the room, listening to the dissertations of a critic who bored her horribly, and to whom she could be polite only with considerable difficulty.

She had avoided him for more than two hours, but now, since it was within half an hour of closing time, she felt that she could bear him. He was being complimentary, but to all the least satisfactory exhibits in the show, and she found his half-informed stupidity infinitely more depressing and irritating than the frank incomprehension of some of the improbable people who had paid a shilling to come in. A few late-comers were still appearing; there were awkward gaps in some of the bus services on Saturday nights, it was growing cold outside, and this was as cheap a way of being warm and sheltered for half an hour as any other. There were perhaps a dozen people, mostly in this category, moving desultorily from stand to stand, as she yawned gently into the bronze chrysanthemums in her green celadon jar. A few had the strained look of would-be aesthetes, most were impervious. One or two looked at things as if they really knew what to look for, and lingered where she herself would have lingered. She was curiously following the progress of one of these rare specimens when she heard the door swing again, and looked round to see who had entered in such a hurry, and so late.

She knew him at once, and yet she stared as if she had never seen him before. What was he doing here, the incongruous creature from Grover's garage? He was not being led by some intellectually ambitious acquaintance, for he came in alone. He did not make any pretence of being at home here among her children, for he looked round him, as the door swung from his hand, with those same wild and apprehensive eyes he had worn when he brought Theo home. And he had been running! He was out of breath, his lips parted, his brown hair blown into a tangle, and a high, bright colour glowing under the tan of his cheeks. And now that she came to look more intently at him, touched by his haste to reach her creations in time, she saw that the apprehension in his eyes was more than half eagerness and excitement.

As though, she thought, watching him intently over the critic's oblivious shoulder, he was standing on a frontier ' – like stout Cortez, when with eagle eyes he stared at the

Pacific, and all his men— ' Only it was Balboa, of course. If it matters! This boy was neither of them, to be truthful; more like one of the mercenaries who looked at each other with a wild surmise, silent upon a peak in Darien. But they needed all their courage, too; more, perhaps, not having the authentic demon to drive them. It is very dangerous to open a door upon a new world, all unprepared and without maps. The door is liable to slam behind you upon all the familiar, and leave you loose among the marvellous.

And for what? she thought, speculating wildly. What inducement could he possibly have to cross all his spiritual and cultural frontiers by coming in here? Her origins were far too mixed to leave her any neat notions about the fitting of artistic appreciation into the social compartments. A boy from a garage could as naturally warm to the beauty of form and colour as the most expensively educated ornament of the universities. But not this boy. He knew himself that he was jumping over a river in the dark. His eyes were frightened of the unknown width of it, and the danger of drowning, and awed and excited about what he might find on the other side. And what did he know about the other side? Only that she and Theo would be there.

'Excuse me a moment!' she said. 'There's somebody I know. I must go and speak to him.'

The critic looked round for a celebrity, and could not see one; and when he thought to discover one in a deceptive form by following Suspiria's purposeful advance, all he could see was a young man in a grey gaberdine raincoat, far too young to be a lion, and without the seedy sophistication proper to even the most junior members of the Press. He was standing in front of a double pedestal on which stood an olive-green bowl, below, and a great, full-bodied jug of unglazed red stoneware above. The young man gazed at them doubtfully, even with some distrust, but without hostility. There seemed no reason for Suspiria to approach so ordinary a specimen, nor could thought suggest where or how she could have met him.

She was aware, when she came to his elbow so quietly, that he did not know she was there; and therefore she could study the changes and responses of his face with deep curiosity, and know that she was seeing, for a moment at least, the truth of what he was and what he felt. She had to make the most of the moment, for as soon as he turned and saw her watching him he would retreat behind all his defences, and begin to try and assess the effect he ought to be making on her, in defence of his deeply-resented ignorance. Now he was crystal. He was used to the lavish and exuberant ceramics of the fair-ground, or, worse, the modified, arty form of the same thing, which had the raucousness of the fair-ground without its unself-conscious gaiety. In this full, fruit-like roundness, entirely without decoration, the handle a short, sturdy bow to fit and fill the hand, he could find nothing but dullness and lack of imagination. It was so *plain*!

People for whom life has been enforcedly plain to poverty for generations do not choose plainness when they can choose for almost the first time. They find their way back to it through cycles of excitement and indulgence and satiety, to discover in the best of it many other qualities besides its simplicity. There was no reason in the world why he should yet doubt his own rejection of plainness, except that the self-consciousness of the age possessed him as it possessed them all, and the fact that others could praise and choose what he instinctively rejected made him hesitate, and hedge, and look back again and again to try and adjust his vision. He suspected, fatally, that there was something here he ought to admire, and that he could not find it.

There were some playful little pieces grouped together on the next table, some painted tiles, some feather-combed slip-ware dishes in bright candy colours, and several figurines of children. Perhaps the shapes were still austere for his taste, but they were lively in decoration and colour. She saw the ready gaiety of relief in his eyes, saw them dwell longest upon the delicate marbling of the dishes, and she knew he was thinking of iced cakes in several colours, teased into the same wavy pattern. They did look almost edible; she was not fond of them, but technically they were good, and they had a right to be there to balance the more monumental pieces.

'We call it feather-combing,' she said. 'It's done with a sharpened quill, drawing one slip out into another.'

He had not expected her to be there, she could see that clearly. His astonishment and withdrawal were equally instantaneous, and he stood looking at her for a moment with lips parted, still rather breathless from running. He didn't want to move back into himself and shut the door; he was only afraid not to. She had him at a disadvantage here, because she was within her depth, and he was out of his, and he could not afford to give away any more points. And yet he continued to look out at her, from the safety of his defences, with a wary eagerness and hope.

'Oh, good evening! I was just looking – I wondered how it was done, it's so delicate.'

'They never run into one another and make a mess,' she said, 'just lengthen out in those fine lines after the quill. On a flat surface it isn't difficult. I didn't know you were interested in pottery. But perhaps you often come here?' He was not sure that she was not laughing at him a little, but if so, it was a surprisingly gentle laugh.

'Well – not very often.' He had never been there before, though he had lived in Great Leddington since he was two years old. He wondered if she could tell that by looking at him, and was afraid that she could, and he moved back a step into the salving darkness of his shell. She saw that he was folding and refolding the little catalogue so tightly in his hands that he would probably never get it straightened out again. Better save him the chagrin of noticing his own nervousness, then, by telling him about everything herself, if he showed any signs of wanting to know.

She took him by the arm quite naturally, with easy authority. 'I shouldn't waste too much time on these little things, if I were you. Shall we go round quickly?'

She held him for only a moment, and then they were moving onward together round the long, light room; but he could still feel the hard, direct touch of her fingers, so different from Iris's insinuating approaches. Her movements beside him filled him with a sense of excited pleasure, so exact and assured was she in every gesture. This evening she had on a dark green corduroy coat and skirt, and there were no traces of clay. She looked rather more than a hundred per cent alive, and almost handsome, with the ends of her short black hair just reaching her cheeks and lying there like the tips of feathers folded close, and her long mouth brightly painted the fierce luminous red of holly berries. Her feet were small, narrow and elegant in court shoes. Plenty of girls of his acquaintance dressed much more expensively, even more smartly, he thought, but side by side with her they would never be noticed. It was something to do with the personality, nothing that could be bought and put on. Even if you disliked her, you could never ignore her.

She said very little, supposing that unless he had questions to ask, her work could very well speak for itself. He was too acutely on the defensive still, in spite of a sort of confused warmth of happiness he found in her company, to ask many questions unless he could be sure of phrasing them in a way which would do him credit. She might guess at his total insulated ignorance, but he was not going to let her get a positive glimpse of it if he could help it. Yet his eyes were full of bewilderment and wonder. He did want to know, he wanted intensely to understand everything, but without admitting for a moment that he did not know, and did not understand. Sometimes she thought, as if she stood at a distance to look at them both: 'Why am I bothering with him? What on earth is there in this hobbledehoy to waste my time on?' But she remembered the leap in the dark. Somebody owed it to him to shed a little light on this strange and mapless world for him, and who was there to do it but herself?

'That sgraffito pattern could be better. The drawing isn't strong enough for the shape, do you see that? The design is scratched through the slip to show the colour of the body underneath. It's a pity about that one, the shape is very nearly perfect.'

He did not know what slip was, and was not sure in what sense she used the word body, but he asked no questions. These sounded the sort of thing everyone here was supposed to know already.

About one of her vases she said positively that it was a bad shape, just as positively as she had called the previous one perfect. He could not see why the one should satisfy her, and the other displease her. It was deeply frustrating to be so completely shut out from what she seemed to consider the fundamental laws of form. He continued to listen avidly for every clue, and to ask nothing more dangerous than: 'How do you get that blue?'

'Almost all the blues are cobalt. That one has some manganese oxide in it, too. The greens are copper, mostly. That big jar – you saw it in Theo's picture, too, remember? – that glaze is a celadon. There are a whole family of them. They get their greyish and bluish greens from iron oxides.'

'You have to be a chemist, as well,' he said, lifting a sudden shy glance to her face.

'More like a cook really. You begin by measuring and weighing everything very strictly, and end by throwing in a pinch of this and half a pound of that by touch.'

She halted him before the most beautiful thing she had ever made, or perhaps ever would, and watched in a half-angry pessimism to see its perfection slide by him without effect. Then she forgot him, because the jar was so complete and filled her with so profound a peace. It was well-placed, fairly high and alone against a brownish-grey curtain. It was large – when she was happiest and most sure of herself she had always to make enormous things, to the limit of her reach and strength. This one stood about eighteen inches high, and its outlines flowed upward firmly and urgently from the narrow base, with all the impetus of growth, expanded into a noble and virginal round breast, and then sprang arching together into a narrower neck and thick, smooth lip like a folded petal. The glaze was a full, purplish rose in colour, so deep, lustrous and luminous that it seemed to warm the air round it; and the jar had been dipped to a depth a few inches short of the base, and left to find its own edge, so that it had flowed down lower on one side than the other, like a calm, smooth wave just gathering and thickening at the lip, a wave which had never broken but was always about to break. Beneath it the stoneware of the body had burned in the kiln to a rich brick-red, a smooth rock shore waiting passively for the breaking foam of that purple sea. On the lip and the curve of the shoulder the glaze thinned very slightly to a rosier colour, in the neck and down the flanks its lustre deepened to purple, the lowest fold of the breaking wave darkest of all.

She had forgotten him, but subconsciously she was waiting for him to think of something safe to say. She heard a small, almost stealthy sigh, and then he asked with curious, child-like meekness: 'Can I touch it?'

She looked at him sharply, wondering if it was calculated, but at the abrupt turn of her head he had flushed deeply, and looked confused and almost panicky, as if he were casting about him to see if he had said the wrong thing. She smiled at him, and said quickly: 'Yes, do!'

Encouraged but still abashed, he went forward, while she watched him curiously, to see if his hands had any real hunger, any awareness. They opened, and cupped themselves about the purple roundness just below the breast, and stretched out there against the cool glaze, deliciously braced to touch with every nerve. She felt her heart turn in her with the reversion of his delight. He knew as little about it as a virginal boy knows about the terror and ecstasy of arching his hands for the first time about a woman's breasts, and he experienced it as shatteringly. How vulnerable the young and inexperienced are, she thought, holding her breath. How wonderful and how awful it must be to be at the beginning of all this, and to feel the lightning go through you, without knowing what it is, or what directs it, or where it is going!

He stroked the purple silken surface, his arching fingers leaving it reluctantly. She felt their pain in her own. He looked at her suddenly, and his grey eyes were wide with greed, and his mouth, always the true, tender, irresolute barometer of his youth, was quivering. 'I don't know anything!' he said despairingly.

She thought: 'He's over the edge now, he'll never get back. There isn't any going back into innocence.' And she asked herself for a moment if she really had any responsibility for him; but only for a moment, because it took no longer that that to discover that it was not a sense of duty which was drawing her towards him.

'You could learn,' she said, 'if you want to.'

'What is it? That glaze, I mean? It feels like silk – only alive.'

'It is alive,' she said, 'it's organic, it grew. It's what we call a flambé glaze. You could call them derivative – they came from China. That's copper, too, only used in a reducing kiln. Do you know what that is? Not an oxidising fire – a smoky-burning one.'

'I know! And you can get those colours like that?'

'Once or twice in a lifetime, as perfectly as that. But in a smaller way, yes, pretty consistently, if you know your kiln. Do you like it?'

'It's the *colours*!'

For her it had been the form, before ever the jar had its imperial colouring. But he was approaching gingerly by his own way, and he had plenty of time. She thought now that the moment of emotion, true and poignant though it had been, had caused her to see him for a while as more promising than in fact he was. Most people can be ravished by colour. He had certainly been moved by the form, whether he knew it or not, or he would not have ached to set his hands round it. Experiencing with his body, he believed he was moving only through the eyes, because he knew nothing about his body yet. It was no duty of hers to teach him.

'It's nearly ten,' she said, 'they'll be closing soon.'

They moved on quickly, for already the few other people remaining in the room were drifting towards the doors. She showed him graved and trailed ornament, bowls and beakers and bottles, crackle glazes, and brushwork as spare and fluent as a beautiful quiet voice.

'Does a show like this bring you many sales?' he asked, reverting into shyness now that it was nearly over, and therefore making a particular effort to appear at his ease.

'Oh, most of these things are not for sale. I have to borrow back the ones that belong to other people, when I want to stage an exhibition. Don't take this as a casual selection of my recent work – there are years of my life in this room. Some of the things I liked best I could never bear to sell. Others are where I know I can get them if I need them.'

'The purple one,' said Dennis, 'you kept that one!'

'Yes, I kept that one.'

He glowed because he had been right to like it, even if he did not know why. Away across the town the church clock was just striking ten; by the clear quality of the chime the air was frosty.

'Theo will be coming to fetch me,' she said. 'I think I heard the car a minute ago. Can we give you a lift home?'

She was not greatly surprised when he backed rather hurriedly away from this offer, in a revulsion of shyness. He wanted to go away by himself, to walk home alone in the cold, sorting out the confusion of his thoughts, and reassembling his pleasant, disturbed features into the unremarkable face his family knew. Hearing Theo's steps on the stairs, she gathered up her bag and gloves from the corner where she had left them, and turned again to look at the boy. Should she let it end there, or should she take the one short step which alone was needed to incorporate him permanently into her world? It could not be a very urgent or dangerous decision, and yet she hesitated to take the responsibility for it.

Well, there was Theo. Let him be the instrument of divination, if she didn't wish to be committed. If he remembered, if he claimed the boy, flashing out with recognition and invitation, so be it. It was as good an oracle as any.

Theo came in whistling, and brought a great gust of frosty air in with him, buffeted before the hurrying folds of his tweed coat. He stood aside from the doorway to let two preoccupied lovers pass him on their way out to the last country bus, smiled after their incongruous young backs, as oblivious of art as of the cold, and came across the room in long, jaunty strides to collect his wife. Sober, the lines of his face had a taut and vehement intelligence, which seemed to derive its tension partly from the bones within, partly from the brilliance of the blue eyes. He was forty-five, greying, and habitually lived at a rate which should have aged him beyond his years; but in his good moments he still seemed to Suspiria the youngest of the young.

'Well, Spiri, how did it go?' He looked beyond her at Dennis, who was withdrawing unobtrusively towards the shadows and the door. His face flamed into irresistible laughter. 'Well, hullo! My friend Forbes! What a surprise to see you here! I see Spiri made a conquest that night.' He had possession of Dennis's hand in a moment, and there was no more possibility of sliding away unnoticed. 'I still owe you thanks and apologies for that drive home, by the way. Come home with us now for some supper! Dead safe, I assure you, I'm sober as a judge. It's too early to go to bed yet.'

Suspiria said gently, watching the boy's face: 'Not for me, it isn't. I'm tired. We must get home, and let Mr. Forbes do the same.'

'Oh, really? Well, some other evening, then! Come tomorrow! We'll have some music, and Spiri shall show you her workshop – teach you to throw, if you've a taste for it. What do you say?'

Dennis looked at Suspiria, a sudden, intent look.

'Yes, do come!' she said. 'I should like it very much.'

She saw the answering eagerness leap into his eyes, and was aware of a sense of decision and movement; as if someone who had been standing irresolute for some time under an illegible signpost had suddenly taken his luck and the night in his hands, and set off firmly along one of the unknown roads, with all the conviction of a clairvoyant. Or, perhaps, of a gambler!

CHAPTER THREE:

The Ride to the Abyss

1

THE FAMILY, fallen suddenly silent round the bright kitchen, listened to the diminishing hum of the motor-cycle until it died away in the distance. Even Mr. Forbes looked up over the evening paper, sensing the chill of doubt and disapproval in the room.

'Of course,' said Marjorie then, tying her scarf into a vicious knot, 'you know where he goes!'

'I can't say he's told us anything about it,' said Mrs. Forbes, wriggling a hand into the recesses of one of Harold's socks, 'and since he broke off with Iris I haven't asked him many questions, either. He's grown up, it's his own responsibility. I must say, I never saw any signs that he can't very well manage his own affairs.'

'We shall find that out in the long run, and so will he. Oh, no, I don't suppose he's going to bring his confidences here very much, for the future. We're not good enough for him, now!' Her sense of grievance about her marriage had caused her to adopt that tone about everything, so the family knew how to discount it; but the words were never very far from her lips, and no doubt some people took them literally. 'I haven't asked anybody anything myself,' she said, 'you don't have to. It's common knowledge that motor-bike of his is along the back road to Little Worth all hours of the day and night, except when he's working. Fred brought the tale home from work and I've even had it said to me in the street.

I always let on I know all about it, of course. "Oh, yes," I say, "he's very friendly with those Freeland people." Then they say they didn't know our Den was artistic, and I have to say, oh, yes, always has been, from a kid. Artistic! That little twerp! He knows about as much about art as a rice pudding does! What does he want with people like that? I bet they only want him to get a laugh out of him.'

'The lad can have what friends he likes, can't he?' said Mr. Forbes in mild protest. 'I don't see what harm he's doing, passing his time visiting them, if they like to ask him there. *I* don't know nothing about folks like that, but *he's* a smart lad enough, I don't know as there's anything funny about cleverer people than us finding him nice company.'

'People like the Freelands just *don't* take up with people like us, that's all.'

'Maybe Dennis isn't like us,' said Mrs. Forbes, doggedly darning.

'He's no better, anyhow – he only thinks he is.'

'Well, are they any better?' asked Winnie, who was applying lipstick before the mirror, and turned from the delicate task momentarily with her pretty lips distorted into a Japanese mask, to avoid smudging the effect before it was complete.

'Better? A lot of lazy, shiftless no-goods, if you ask me, like most so-called artists!'

'According to you, then, our little twerp ought to be quite at home with them,' said Winnie cheerfully, and began to run the tip of her little finger over her lips industriously, until the bright, deep rose bow satisfied her. 'So what are you worrying about?' she said then, emerging.

'All the same,' said Harold, flat on his back in the biggest chair by the fire, nursing a cold, 'it's a funny set-up, look at it how you like. Bohemians haven't got any position to keep up, that's all tripe. The only position they've got is what they like to make for themselves, and for all I can see they haven't got any money to set them apart, either. If they were even the same age it would be ordinary enough. But Freeland's in the forties, and she can't be a day under thirty-five. What on earth does he see in it, spending his time up there with them? And anyhow, I should have thought a kid his age would pretty soon have bored them stiff.' The five years between himself and his younger brother seemed a very long time to Harold, as well as to his mother.

'You spend enough of your time running round old Seaton and his wife,' said Winnie, climbing into her coat, 'and they're over sixty, if they're a day. I suppose that's different.'

'Well, of course it's different! Show a bit of savvy! He's my boss! *I*'m not wasting my time. A fellow's got to look after his prospects, hasn't he?'

'We're not all on the make,' said Winnie disdainfully, sweeping towards the door and her latest date in a gust of heady perfume.

'I think you ought to speak to him,' said Marjorie, when the door had closed behind her sister's airy departure.

'I'll do no such thing, and you leave him alone, too! He hasn't done anything wrong, what right has anybody got to interfere with the way he likes to spend his time? He does his work properly, he brings money home, and he's a good boy.'

'You said yourself he was getting difficult to live with. And if there's nothing queer about it, why doesn't he talk about it to us?'

'Because he's twenty-two, and it's his business, and he doesn't think it's any of ours. Difficult he may be, but that's a stage they all go through, sooner or later. He left it late, that's all. He's never given me any cause to worry, and I'm not going to start acting as if he has.'

'Well, of course,' said Marjorie, picking up her handbag, 'if you *like* him being as thick as thieves with that kind of people—'

No, she did not like the strange association, simply because there was no reasonable way of accounting for it, and up to now Dennis had been an eminently reasonable creature. On the other hand, no one knew of anything definably wrong with it. If those were the companions he chose, what business was it of anyone else's? He was of age, and he had done nothing which could be called even irresponsible. If he stayed out sometimes rather late at night, so did many another young man, without being called to order for it. If he had broken off the affair with his first regular girl-friend, so did most young men at least once before they settled down, and not always as decently as Dennis had done it. Mrs. Forbes was even rather respectfully surprised herself when she thought of the circumstances. Iris had made the going from the beginning, and they'd never actually got as far as talking about marriage; he owed her nothing. He could hardly have been blamed if he'd just backed out, stayed away from their appointments, or avoided new ones; that was what many a boy in his position would have done. But not Dennis! He met her when he had said he would meet her; and when he was sure how he felt about it, he told her straight that it was no use going on, said he liked her, and wished her well, but he was sorry he wasn't in love with her, and it would be a mistake for both of them if they continued meeting. No, he hadn't done Iris any wrong. Marjorie, of course, was always down on the younger ones, because they'd been born at a better time, and had a sunnier childhood. She took it out in nagging tales like these. As often as not she was finding fault with Winnie for being pretty, and gay, and admired, now it was Dennis for having engaged the liking of two people of distinction. And after all, the whole family knew how he had first met them, there was no mystery about that.

And yet— And yet Mrs. Forbes knew that he was moving away from them all, gradually, steadily, helplessly. He didn't want to, it was just happening to him, as it was happening to them, and there was no one in the world who could stop the process. When he was at home, which was seldom enough these days, he isolated himself in long silences, thinking his own thoughts, and sharing them with nobody. She did not think that they were invariably happy reveries in which he lived. He seemed to be in a state of perpetual unease, quietly but desperately excited; but if she had tried to prise any confidences out of him, no matter how lovingly, he would have taken fright and run for his life, indignantly denying any knowledge of change and unrest.

And he'd always been such a nice, open, placid child! A

pity, thought Mrs. Forbes jealously, a terrible pity you couldn't keep them like that!

2

When he was on his motor-bike, scudding along the unfrequented roads on his way to Little Worth, under the early frosty stars, and the cold winds of December that stung his lips and cheeks into numbness, he never had the slightest doubt that he was rushing towards an unalloyed happiness. It was only when his hand was at the very door that he remembered with a stab of uncertainty the many disappointments already past, the rapid, sickening descents from exalted eagerness into disillusionment. But always, even when he went home at last enraged and ill with his own inferiority, yet angry with what he took to be the signs that others also recognised it, he was sure that the next time would pay for everything, and waited for it with impatience and passionate hope.

It wasn't as if they did anything to make him feel inferior. They were always nice to him, always pleased to see him. They never talked about art as if it were a mystery from which he was excluded, but always as if it were an integral part of living, with which he must have contacts, since he lived. They didn't expect the contacts to be of the same kind as their own, because every human creature was to them unique, whether they troubled to explore him or not. No, there was nothing in their attitude to him which should remind him of his differentness and ignorance; rather he reminded himself, constantly, whenever Suspiria said something he did not understand, or Theo played music which had nothing to say to him. Most of all, of course, when there were other people there, people of their own kind, people who caught every inflection, and came back with instant, apposite argument, and did all the right things, all the things he didn't know how to do. Those were the worst times of all.

The first time he had found friends of theirs at the house,

he had tried to back out unobtrusively and go away, but Suspiria had been really angry, and taken him by the arm and dragged him inside with such decision that he had no chance to escape. She had presented him very firmly, and thrown him in among them to make his own way, and he had alternated between strident self-assertion and sullen silence all the evening, sweating in horrible unhappiness and hating her for not hiding and cradling him. She had not even given him as much help as she might have done; it had been Theo who had cherished him through the endless hours. And afterwards, when Suspiria had walked to the gate with him, and he had made that ill-judged attempt to make her feel ashamed at having ill-used him, it was he who had got the worst of it, a scolding that sent him away vowing not to go near Little Worth again.

'You are a spoiled child,' she had said vigorously, 'you want to be nursed, and you want to stand on your own feet, too. Nobody can have it both ways. You have a place here, it's yours, and no one else can fill it – no one, do you hear? Either take it, or leave it alone, but don't cry about its being first too big and then too small.'

And like a fool, as he thought in his worst moments, he had gone back again and again for more, always confident that the next time would be different, because he wanted it to be so terribly. What had he ever really got out of it? He had learned to throw a simple cylinder on her wheel, and to do a few little jobs with pigments and glazes, occasionally to her pleasure and surprise. He had sat with people who gravely daunted him round the brick hearth, drinking beer out of home-thrown beakers of warm brown earthenware, or cocktails out of a motley collection of glasses salved from the wreckage of several sets, and had watched the conversation soar out of his reach. He had listened to Theo playing Chopin and Schumann on the piano, and when there were others present the musical comment had usually gone beyond him, too, even though their circle was as motley a mixture as the cocktail glasses. He could always find a slight, somewhere in the course of the evening, perhaps becuase he was looking for one so assiduously. He knew himself that he went looking for them, but he was unable to stop the ill-advised search, because of the endless nag of reason at the back of his mind: 'After all, I'm not really their kind. They let me in, but I'm a bit of a curiosity, not an equal. I don't know the things they know, I don't talk like they do, I haven't got their backgound. I'm just an eccentricity of Theo's and Suspiria's, that's all – a funny little chap she picked up somewhere from among the lower orders.'

Sometimes, when his jealous self-love had found a more than usually bitter taste about the evening, he could almost imagine the women saying to one another, as they drove back into town: 'What on earth can Spiri want with that little tough of hers?' And the answer: 'Well, after all, I suppose he's not bad-looking. A change from Theo, at any rate.' Maybe he wasn't very well up in the ways of Bohemia, but there were some things everybody knew. Artists had their own rules. Probably the prime proof of his lower-class simplicity was that he hadn't tumbled to it long ago what was expected of him!

For there were other evenings, when no one was there but Theo, and Suspiria, and himself, and still others when even Theo was missing. Things were different then; then she had a use for him, she let him work her clay for her, and showed him how to load the big electric kiln built of light cream-coloured insulating bricks, and set him to work on the wheel when she was not using it, sometimes coming to correct his slips, to trim the edges off when he made them too thin and stuck his thumb through them, to set her hands over his and pull hard on them as she taught him to centre the clay properly. She was a hard tutor, she scolded a great deal, but she did not laugh at his efforts, she was always as serious about them as he was, and equally intent. And when he was adroit and quick, when she had stung him to a reckless force and decision which were not natural in him, but which seemed to be essential to this trade, then she could praise, too. She would throw her arms round his shoulders, and hug him to her in fierce, momentary approval, her breast against his arm for an instant as warm and vital as sunlight. When she had something good to show him, whether it happened to be a new and successful glaze or an idea for an improved tool, she would seize him by the hand as soon as he appeared, and tow him away through the house into the workshop to gloat over it with her. She handled him as she handled the clay itself, with absolute confidence and candour.

Sometimes, after these evenings, he could not sleep. It was hateful that he had to share a room with Harold, so that not even the nights could give him privacy in that house. If he turned on his pillow, half-awake, and uttered so much as a name, Harold would stir in his light sleep, and hear it, and the family would have it next day, he could be sure of that. They were already altogether too curious about how he spent his time. He had to lie still, while his mind in the heat of imagination ran away from him into feverish fantasies, and his body ached with a desperate excitement which he could neither control nor understand. Was it even true that Suspiria had singled him out? It was Theo who had first invited him there, but she had seconded the invitation at once, and Suspiria didn't do things like that out of politeness, or out of kindness, either. She had wanted him to come. Was she secretly thinking him an unsophisticated fool for his trouble? He lay curled upon himself in the rumpled bed many a night, rubbing his hot cheeks into the pillow, and breathing deeply to exorcise her name, which came so easily now to his lips that he might utter it aloud, and never know. He was full of a hungry and burning pain which was somehow pleasurable, too. When her hands closed over his, in that impatient gesture to set him right, he felt his heart molten and hollow with desire.

Sometimes he came to himself, in the hard grey half-light of morning, with the shivering revulsion of someone who has just jumped back from the edge of a precipice in the dark, and began in a fury of waking common sense, inexpressibly dreary and depressing, to demand of himself where he was going, and what he hoped to gain by continuing on the same road. But with the first burning recollection of Suspiria everything else would be forgotten, and the end, even if it amounted to no more than access to her presence, seemed to him more than he could ever hope to gain by another route. And by the time his hand was next at the latch of Little Worth he was sure that there was more for him, he could almost feel it already in his grasp.

There was no light in the living-room, this night in December. He left the motor-cycle in the shed, and let himself in without knocking, because whoever was at home must be working, and would never hear him if he did knock. If you were a friend, you could walk in, and go and look for them; the door was never locked. He lifted the latch and went in. A low fire burned on the brick hearth, and cast gleams of light over a few glossy surfaces, leaving the rest of the room in darkness. The matt red arm of a chair, a curved gloss of bowl above a flat glimmering of polished wood, a pale comb of piano keys; these were all he could see. There was no one there.

Because he always thought of Suspiria, it was always on Theo he called, standing in the dark doorway, and shouting towards the studio: 'Hullo, there! It's me, Dennis!'

Suspiria answered him from the workshop, her voice sounding very small and far away, even in a shout. 'Hullo, come on through!'

He shed his gloves and coat and helmet, dropping them in the nearest chair, and went to find her. He knew his way to the workshop now without a light, as if he had really belonged to the house; down the vast, cave-like corridor, and out by the back door, and there were the never-cleaned grey windows on his left, seven or eight yards of them, the whole of one side of the long, narrow shed. There was a strong smell of paraffin as he opened the door, for she had lit her oil-stove to warm the air enough for handling brushes, but even so it was cold in there. He trod through the usual deadening layer of clay-dust, silently along the narrow gangway between benches and racks, past the big wooden block on which she kneaded her clay, and the shelves of bins and tins, most of them discarded from the household, in which she kept her materials. The amount of her paraphernalia still daunted him, just as its nondescript nature still affronted him. She was a brilliant artist, she ought to behave like one, surround herself with order, precision and elegance, instead of operating in this hybrid of a back-kitchen and a junk-yard, where half of her tools were concocted on the spur of the moment out of bits of accidental rubbish thrown away by somebody of ordinary stature.

The hanging screens rattled in the subsiding draught. Through the racks of her drying work he saw her bending over the bench beside the kiln, where she painted, and mixed pigments and slips. She raised her head, looking for him, and he delayed for the pleasure of seeing the quick, waiting gleam of anticipation in her face. She was glad to see him, she wanted him. She never conjured up that expression for anyone unless she meant it. A curved feather of her hair lay across her forehead, her lips were parted, waiting to smile at him. She loved him! She must love him! Why else do you reach out your hand and draw someone to you? Why else do you select so carefully someone who has nothing to offer you, unless he has this? In her world it was nothing out of the way. She was an artist. They looked at these things differently. When you are invited into someone else's kind of world, you live by its rules, surely – it's a part of the invitation.

He came round the racks of drying pots very quietly, rather slowly, looking at her from under his level brows with an uneasy gleam of shining grey eyes. He was flushed and pinched with the cold, his lips looked stiff from the frosty wind, and his light brown hair was untidy because of the way he had dragged off his helmet. A very attractive child, she thought, the veritable smile breaking; especially now that he had given up looking so guarded and afraid. In some ways, of course, a demure little prig, but that was the result of his upbringing, and the veneer was already beginning to crack. And even of demure little prigs one can become curiously fond, once having taken a degree of responsibility for them.

'Hullo!' she said, turning to look at him more attentively. 'What are you looking so mischievous about?'

'I didn't know I was. Am I in the way tonight? You seem to be doing some serious work, and Theo isn't in the studio.'

'He's in London – won't be back until tomorrow, maybe not then if he meets too many of the old crowd. He took some small stuff down for me, too, so I can't complain if he makes it an occasion for going on the tiles. But no, of course you're not in the way. Wait until I finish here, and we'll go inside, where it's warmer.'

He came close to her, looking down with an almost strained attention at the array of green and biscuited pots she had spread before her on the bench, and the saucers and small bowls of pigments, which she kept with a care she gave to little else, except her brushes. 'It's not so cold in here. I don't want to stop you working.' But he was shivering. 'What are you doing?'

'You've never tried your hand at brushwork yet. Do you want to? Or there's some slip you can play with.' She turned her shoulder on him, and went back to what she was doing, reaching for a brush and loading it fully with a dull blue pigment from one of her saucers. She expected him to sit down carefully and quietly beside her on the stool, or stand like a docile pupil at her elbow, and watch while she performed. She expected it, but he could no longer be sure of what she wanted.

'I'm only good for play, of course,' he said in a level voice, not yet even ill-humoured, and watching the wet brush flicker in long, swooping flights across the curve of the beaker. The line thickened and thinned again with the inclination of her hand. She held the pot well away from her, and the brush almost disinterestedly far from the point, and painted from the elbow rather than the wrist, with a beautiful, devoted ferocity. Drifts of dull blue foliage, branches blown in the wind, floating leaves followed her touch round the curve of the beaker.

'You can turn the bases of those two bowls, if you like,' she said, not even bothering to raise her head and look at him. 'You know how to do it – I won't interfere.'

'I might spoil them for you.'

'I know you might. I said you can try.'

But that was not what he wanted; not even to be trusted with what he knew to be special orders. He didn't know what he wanted. Certainly to remain near her, watching her, not to be sent away into the corner of the workshop, to bend obediently over her hand-wheel.

'Sit down, then, and be quiet! Not too quiet! Talk to me! If you want to sulk about something, do it out loud.'

'I don't,' he protested warmly. 'Not unless it's about not being able to run before I can walk.' He sat down on the corner of the bench, as close to her as he could without impeding her movements as she changed from brush to brush, and moved beaker after beaker with its autumnal branches across to the group at her left hand.

'What colour will it be when it's glazed and fired?' He was already used to the idea that the raw colours could give little visible indication of their final glory.

'Greener than this – a deep, greenish blue. It ought to be pretty effective on this light salmon-coloured body. They're a set I've had ordered for some time, and never managed to finish.'

'What kind of glaze will you use over them?'

'A clear, straw-coloured one. There, that's the last of those. I shan't get round to glazing them tonight, I'm only decorating.' She had still two flat dishes to treat, and a round-bellied vase, not yet fired, and four little hand-moulded ashtrays shaped like leaves. She pushed the trays towards him, with a preoccupied but placatory gesture, and a handful of graving tools after them. 'You see what they have to be. Give them ribs, and then paint them. Here's green, brown – the blue, if you like. You can do whatever you fancy with them.'

She went back to her vase, and carrying it briskly away from the bench, set it up with anchoring wads of clay upon the hand-wheel she used for turning and banding, and without looking at him again, she began to score its plump shoulder with a little roller of biscuited clay, spinning the wheel occasionally with her left hand. And that was all she did with him, stroke him now and again left-handed into the motion she required of him, her eyes all the time upon her real objective.

He flung away from the bench after her, and took her roughly by both wrists and pulled her round to face him; but so carefully still that the vase span undamaged with the slowing wheel, only the slightly deeper score of her astonished start marking its full and placid beauty. Her long eyes flared at him, greenish in the dimming shadow. 'What's the matter?' she asked, with a sharp and wary quietness.

'What's the matter! Nothing, nothing at all! Only that you don't even know I'm here. You don't even bother to look at me. Go and play with those, and don't worry me, I've got something important to do! Why do you let me come here, if that's all? Why *do* you! Why did you ask me here in the first place?' He shook her by the wrists, miserably conscious even now that he had not the courage to compel any answer. She looked up at him calmly under the soft, stirring plumes of her hair, and was not even angry. Her voice had a certain severity, but that was all.

'Dennis, let go!' It was a perfectly placid, if testy, order; he obeyed it slowly and sullenly. 'I'm sorry, I told you we'd go into the house when I'd finished here. So we will. If you want attention, you'll have to wait till then, or go and look for it somewhere else. I've got work to do.'

'Then why didn't you tell me to go? I asked you if I was in the way.'

He sounded, even to himself, like a querulous child, and yet she stood looking at him with that glimmering quietness and gravity, not at all as if she thought of him in that way. 'You're not in my way. At least, you haven't been, up to now. You know we like to have you here, as often as you care to come. But my work doesn't go into fixed hours, I can't always leave it behind at six.'

'You don't really want me here,' he said bitterly. 'I suppose I must have been quite amusing for a time, but you're getting a bit bored with the joke now, aren't you?'

'I could be feeling a good many things,' she said, looking at him with a quickening annoyance, 'but boredom isn't one of them. What's the matter with you? What are you accusing us of?'

'As if you didn't know! You took me up for a bit of fun – a novelty. Now my welcome's wearing pretty thin, I see. These proletarian types are only entertaining for just so long – only they never know when to stop, do they? I must have been quite a problem to you sometimes – I'm sorry!'

'You have,' said Suspiria, darkly flushing, 'a quite remarkable gift for vulgarity when you try, I can see that. But don't be so modest about it, that's no gift of your class, that's all your own. Why, you little idiot, what do you suppose this silly talk of proletarian types means to me? Are you trying to fit me in somewhere to suit yourself? You'll have hard work! My father was a pawnbroker in Hackney, and my mother was a farm-labourer's daughter, and I'm a human being. Where does that get you? If you're coming here trying to make yourself important to me because you feel inferior, or because you feel superior, or because for either reason you want a little more fuss made of you, I can tell you, you're wasting your time. As far as I'm concerned, you're a human being, too. You haven't got any privileges or any handicaps but those you've given yourself.'

She was flinging away from him, back to her work in anger and disgust, when she turned as abruptly to look at him again. The taut misery of his face seemed to her altogether too tragic for so small, mistaken and unworthy a squabble. It was not so easy for him, after all; he was dangerously young, he had no idea yet of what he was, or of how he could ever discover it. It was not for her to lock a door against him, even if his fumbling attempts to open it irritated her beyond endurance.

'Dennis! I'm sorry, too! I don't like it when you make yourself smaller than you are.' She let her hand rest for an instant against his cheek, the roller on its twisted wire handle swung free from her wrist, touched him once, heavily, and was gone. 'Give me just ten minutes more, to clean up, and I'll come.'

It was the unexpected caress that set light to all the lingering resentment in his heart, all the tormented self-doubt and self-love which had become molten into the deepest texture of his longing for her. She might have patted a puppy like that, as gently and as carelessly, and expected it to wag its tail and be playfully grateful for the favour. Her touch went into his cheek like acid, with a sharp and bitter pain, because he knew that if she had looked for a more adult understanding from him she had looked in vain, and now with ready kindness had given up the expectation, and accepted him as he was, a poor little pathetic hanger-on, wrapped up in his conventions and inhibitions, incapable of disentangling himself in time to meet her on any ground which would ever be common to two creatures so dissimilar. If he acquiesced now in her resigned acceptance of his inescapable limitations, her almost audible sigh of: 'Ah, well, never mind!' he would have to keep that rôle for ever. And it was not what she had wanted! 'I don't like it,' she said, 'when you make yourself smaller than you are.' But after tonight, if he was silent now, it would be too late to grow.

She had left the vase standing on the wheel, and gone back to her bench, and was beginning to clear away the little pots of colour, to cover them from the dust, and stand them on the shelves of the locker where she kept them. When he came after her closely and quietly, she did not hear him until his left arm encircled her shoulders and pulled her round to him, imprisoning both her arms tightly, and sending the bowl of blue pigment out of her hand, to shatter against the wall and spill its colour in a great stain down to the bench, spattering them both coldly. Wrenched hard against his body, she gave no cry, but her head went back violently against his shoulder, and her hands groped ineffectively for a purchase against his chest, to prise herself away from him. One of the little ashtrays was swept from the bench, and ground to powder under their straining feet. Then he got his other arm under her thighs, and lifted her, and carried her easily towards the door.

She was so light and thin and small in his grasp that his heart felt bursting with frantic tenderness; and she did not struggle, but lay against his breast quite still and quiet now, and he felt her breath upon his cheek. Since he had shut his arm round her he was not aware of having seen her face at all, but he was sure that it held no anger, and no fear.

He carried her along the corridor into the living-room, and in the warm darkness laid her softly upon the long settee, and with his own weight held her there. His mouth felt its way, half-kissing, half-stroking, along her cheek and chin, and whispered through the ruffled silk of her hair, brokenly, breathlessly: 'Oh, darling! – Oh, darling—' over and over. His hands were shaking so that he was afraid to relax them, for fear she would dissolve through them and be lost, though she lay so still now that he was sure of her in every way but this, that he might awake in his unprofitable bed at home, sick with loss, and her accomplishment be only a piece of a broken dream. 'Oh, darling! – Oh, darling—' His hand crept downward, clumsy with longing and triumph and haste, down the slight, sweet, quiet warmth of her body.

Suspiria flashed upward with one hand, set the heel of it under his chin, and springing suddenly into whalebone under him, hoisted a knee into his stomach, and threw him off from her sprawling upon the rug. Before he could recover she was over the back of the settee, the width of the room and a dozen minor hazards between them, and he could hear her laughing, a harsh, angry sound out of the darkness. Grovelling on the rug, winded, shamed, horribly ridiculous, spattered with the bubble of his triumph, he heard her laughing, heard her fingers feeling for the switch of the lamp; and then inexplicably she was still.

If she turned up the light on his unspeakable humiliation he thought he would die of shame; but she did not. She stood there in the darkness, quite still, her hand on the lamp, her eyes upon him, but she did not turn on the light. All she could see of him was the broken look of his body as he gathered himself up slowly by the failing gleams of the firelight, and dragging himself to the settee where her small, helpless feet had rested, put his arms down there, and his head in them, and crouched shuddering, wishing to melt into the merciful impersonal dimness of the air.

What use was it now if they were alone in the house, what use if he knew himself the stronger? That was not at all what he had wanted. She need only bend a finger against him, and she could make him do whatever she pleased. She had only to laugh like that, and he was at her mercy. She had only to despise him, for him to be utterly despicable.

'My poor child! My dear child! You forget the effect years of this life can have on the muscles. Really, did you think you could just gather me up when you pleased? Ought I to be afraid of you? Or was I supposed to be waiting for this?

Did you imagine I had you cast for this part? My poor child, you've been reading too many novelettes! And what should I do now? Run out of the house and stop some car on the road, for help? I would, but it's really a little too cold to carry on with the game. And then, you were not very convincing yourself – so naïve and harmless, much too tame for a wolf. Do get up! I'm quite worried about you.'

But she did not put on the light. Her voice had gathered into its tone a scarifying mockery; if she had not actually been frightened, not for a moment, she had certainly been startled and outraged, or why should she want to flay him like this for a mere clumsy stupidity? He had never been dangerous in his life, to her or to anyone. His poor little gesture had been all a mistake. Why should she want to make him writhe for it?

Dennis lifted his head, and looked wide-eyed into the darkness where she was. She had moved a little nearer, and he could feel the weight of her gaze crushingly upon him. There was nothing he could say that would mean anything. He couldn't come here again, he had thrown everything away. The ache inside his body was pounding through him with the heavy beat of a gigantic heart, because she cared nothing for him, and he had made an image of her which was a childish distortion, and abandoned the reality for it.

'I'm sorry!' he said almost inaudibly. 'I thought— I'll go!' He got to his feet, slowly and painfully.

'You thought I was waiting to be taken, and wondering what took you so long. I'm sorry, I didn't realise how very simple your view of life could be, my poor Dennis. You should have given me some hint beforehand, I might have put up a better show.'

'Don't!' he said, almost crying. 'I made a ghastly mistake. It wasn't your fault, I know. Please forget about it – I'm going, you won't have to see me again.'

He was standing, now, and probably as near to being presentable as he would ever be again. She could see the crushed carriage of his shoulders, the shrinking turn of his head away from her. It was then that she put on the light. He shied at it still as at a blow, but she had to know what she was doing. His voice was not as it should have been, nor had he made the defence she had expected from him. She knew of no reason on earth why she should pity him, still less why she should feel in some way guilty towards him. Everything she had ever offered him had been offered openly; if he had been too clever, or too big a fool, to know what it was, or to take her inviolable word for it, was that her fault? But perhaps the guilt was not for the past, but for the present and the future, for what she was doing to him now, and what would follow from it all through his life.

She had realised, from time to time, that she had assumed a responsibility for him. She could hardly be comfortably rid of it now, just because he made a foolish mistake about the nature of her alliance with him. That wasn't her fault; no, but this could be. If he crept away like this, repulsed with the most cruel ease and lightness, utterly despised, how could he ever again believe that he could be acceptable to anyone? A poor little half-man, creeping jealously through a poor little half-life, afraid to present his slighted masculinity to any woman, and turning his fear into a perpetual grudge against them for being unable to take what they had never been offered! She saw this horrifying vision of frustration rolling outward before Dennis's stumbling feet, waiting to receive him. It was more than she could bear.

'Don't go!' she said, suddenly and urgently.

Out of sheer astonishment he turned, with his hand already on the latch, and looked full at her. It was a poor, silly, bewildered face, maybe, it was not a bad or a fundamentally stupid one. She stood staring back at him, suddenly intent and grave, studying passionately the young, wounded, wary features, the lips still set rather hard for fear of trembling, the hot, bitter flush on the cheeks, the humiliated but direct grey eyes, so wide and light with surprise, and so unguardedly full of desperate love. No, it had not been quite such a simple, quite such a greedy piece of conceit. Perhaps she had known it when her tongue, looking for spears to throw, could find only, again and again, the piteous: 'My poor child – my poor child—'

'Don't go – not yet!'

She went towards him, putting back her head with a deliberate and decisive authority. There was nothing of hers she could not give away if she chose, without asking the permission of any man living. Her respectability was a small thing to give to anyone, she valued it so little, and her integrity was involved now rather with giving than with keeping. It did not seem to her a particularly desperate step to throw her chastity into his arms, if it were done of her own will, and if it could make a whole man of him instead of a maimed one. No amount of free giving could make her less than whole.

He stood looking at her mutely, until she put up her hand, and wiped a splash of blue from his cheek with her handkerchief. The faintest and most preoccupied of smiles touched her lips.

'You can't go home like that! And think,' she said reproachfully, 'of all that good blue you've wasted! Bend your head a little, you've got a lock of blue hair.'

Now he did not know where he was, nor what to expect from her next moment. Probably it was only a new way of making angry fun of him, and in a moment more he would be turned out of the house, having first been tidied contemptuously, comforted briefly, put into his coat like a bad child being efficiently but severely packed off home from school. He could not help himself now; whatever she did to him, all he could do was accept it, make no complaint, and go.

She had imagined him as taking heart again rather quickly, and readily becoming voluble in his own defence, and here he stood waiting, silently and patiently, for her to hit him again. It startled her to realise how fastidiously, in her own flesh, she could feel his acute expectation of pain, and how deeply it astonished her that he was doing nothing to ward it off. He was far too healthily fond of himself to make it secretly welcome, or had been until she and Theo between them had upset once for all the innocent and limited equilibrium of his life. 'Maybe we both owe him this,' she thought, contemplating with resolute serenity what she was about to do.

'I'm sorry if I hurt your pride,' she said, very gently, 'but you hurt mine. I'm not good at having things snatched from me.' Her eyes were large with his nearness, and wonderfully green. He wondered for a terrible, mistaken moment if she could still be making game of him, but instantly caught himself back from a gross folly of distrust. If there was one thing she had more magnificently than any other creature he had ever known, it was her terrifying honesty. His coldness began to be filled with a living and devouring heat. He lifted his hands a little towards her, cupping them achingly to the littleness of her body; but he was afraid to touch her because everything was so inexplicably changed.

'And then,' she said, 'people are apt to resent it when you try to snatch at things they would prefer to give.'

She raised her arms to him, seeing him lean to her, and the sudden tremulous wonder and joy of his face vanished into the darkness of her closed eyelids. She felt his hands enfold her body for a moment with the inseparable delight and pain he had felt when he touched the purple jar, then she was caught up in his arms tightly, his cheek was cold against her cheek, his mouth kissing and sighing and whispering brokenly against her throat, and she felt her own unimagined passion and delight breaking in little, wordless, fierce cries into his ear. It was not a gift, after all, it was a natural cataclysm, a flash of lightning splitting both their hearts, irrecoverably mingling body into body and blood into blood. No, it was not a gift, unless the smaller word will do for a sacramental vastness and violence hitherto unknown, and therefore without a name.

Afterwards the light was out again, and there was nothing in the silence but the soft, silting fall of a few embers in the fire, and her own astonished voice, heavy with tenderness, whispering in a deep, drowned lassitude of delight: 'Oh, my heart – my sweet child – my beloved little heart—'

3

She was thirty-six years old, and she had lived a full and satisfying and rewarding life, uncomplicated by any adherence to conventions, undistorted by any reaction against them; she had had successes, not only in the world's eyes, but even in her own, she had made things she was still proud and glad to remember as hers, and knew that she could make as many more, and the best of the new would always be a little more complete and intact than the best of the old; she had the reputation of a fulfilled and justified artist, and what was better still, the conviction of her own justification; she had liked a man enough to marry him, and live with him in a loose but assured harmony for ten years, and they had had every kind of fun together, and no regrets at all. And yet she had never known love, and never missed it, until now.

Christmas was like a carnival of stars, and the fugitive glimmerings of the aurora which lit in the New Year, faint, fabulous pulses of gold, and rose, and icy blue, were like the monstrous late blossoming of her life, too large for any other garden. She had felt ample enough before to hold every gesture her spirit ever required her to make, there had seemed plenty of room for every impulse and every speculation; but now she was enlarged so exultantly that she felt the warmth of her own joy reflected back upon her from the confines of the night, and the whole house and the arching wood and the open fields were filled with her happiness. Who could have guessed that there remained anything like this still undiscovered, when the world had always already produced so many satisfactions? In the middle of her forever experimental and exploratory content, the limitations of experience suddenly burst, suddenly vanished.

She never questioned what had happened; it was so obviously authentic, so profoundly and intensely right that it would have seemed to her a kind of abortion to examine it critically, much less try to place any restrictions upon it. It was not as if she had gone looking for it. All she had meant to do was to make a single generous gesture towards Dennis's threatened self-esteem, and set him up firmly in his own manhood, against the time when his fancy would incline towards some girl, some contemporary, and leave her behind, scarcely ruffled, certainly no way wronged or guilty of wrong. She had never gone out of her way to appease the conventions, nor even to flout them; usually she was oblivious of them, they seemed to her so irrelevant to all her ideas of responsible human behaviour. Only the little moment of deliberate, cocksure kindness had exploded, and set the world on fire.

And now it was too late to turn back, even if she would have considered retreat for a moment. A reality is a reality. When the constellations turn within its arm, and every hour of the day and night is timed by the incidence of its visitations, it may well be accepted as the only reality. She loved him, and was loved by him. There was no speculation about it, and no room for argument; it flamed through everything she did and thought, it flowered in every clay shape that burst into life under her fingers, and coloured every glaze that came out of her glost kiln elate and radiant in beauty. Nor had it happened only to him, and to her. Every particle of matter in the world about them glowed in the reflections of its splendour, so that every night was a renewal in secret, and every morning a revelation.

Colours had never been so bright and subtle as they were for her that winter, forms so supremely confident in their own beauty, snow so white, people so recognisably significant and immortal, nor herself so ready to meet them and acknowledge them. It did not even matter that love itself was confined to a few rare and brief meetings; the illumination of love continued undimmed between the moments of union, and sustained them in a certainty of its durability and permanence which left no room at all for doubt. So there was no haste, and no greed, even for delight of which there could never be enough.

Day after day through December and January she watched Dennis grow. It was as if all the tautness and suspicion and reserve in him began to melt from the time that he possessed her, as if the warmth of her body and the conviction of her arms accepting him had thawed his defensive coldness, and softened him to stretch out his young length beside her with a relaxed and grateful sigh. Sometimes he seemed to her already taller, as if the release of a spiritual constriction had also set his body at liberty. The lines of his face seemed to lose their sharpness without losing their form. His eyes had a deep, wondering quietness, and when he was not directly troubled by the effort of reconciling backgrounds which must have seemed to him still quite incompatible, he spoke to her in an instinctive way which would have been impossible to the boy whom she had known in the autumn. The voice which had first lost its difficult tensions in the husky, breathless dark, moaning blind, tender endearments into her cheek, and silencing itself against her mouth, could not regain its old habit even in the daylight and the street. He asked her things he could not have asked a few weeks ago, admitted with an open and unpretending humility failures and lacks which he would have fought jealously to cover from sight. She would almost have believed it a recoil into innocence, if she could have credited such a thing; but she did not believe that anyone's life could turn back on itself, nor that recovered ease, supposing it were possible, would ever again fit easily. He had gone forward, because nobody can go back.

She wondered that no one saw how they had expanded, how they shone, how the overflow of their joy in each other was spilled resplendently into all their relations with other people, gilding everything they touched with the reflection of their own unimaginable happiness.

4

They were painting tiles, and had brought them into the living-room and spread themselves and all their paraphernalia upon newspapers on the rug, because the night was glittering with frost, and the workshop was too cold to give their fingers properly fluent play. Dennis had a smooth white tile in one hand, a loaded brush of blue-black in the other, and Suspiria's spare and rapid design before him, a swallow in flight. He was frowning at it with intense concentration, and out of the heart of his need for knowledge he asked without any preliminaries, as he asked her everything now:

'What *is* a work of art?'

It was something which could not have happened a few

weeks before; he would have assumed that this was something everyone about her claimed to know, and that he must on no account emphasise his singularity by admitting his ignorance. Now he asked it without any concealment, looking up at her suddenly across the littered hearth, where only a few minutes before they had leaned suddenly to each other with a mutual impulse of longing, and kissed, and clung.

Suspiria held her cold hands to the fire, and turned to look at him with an alert and startled smile. 'I don't know how to define it. I never tried. I don't suppose anyone ever has, properly.'

'Well, try now! It must be *something*!'

She shut her eyes for a moment, to see in another plane of consciousness. 'I think – a work of art is an image of truth, which somebody has been able to discover and reduce to a form in which it can be –' she hesitated upon the word 'intelligible', but it seemed to her to smell too academically of formulae and the mind '– apprehensible to everybody.'

'And what is truth, then?' he asked, after pondering this definition for a minute or two in silence. 'Because you mean a lot more by it than just the ordinary literal truth, don't you? If you don't know what it is, you can't recognise it in its images, can you?'

This time she did not close her eyes, but continued looking at him steadily with a shining, meditative look. 'I think it's the full realisation of one's own identity, first. And after that, the right relation of oneself to everything else there is to be realised.' She frowned a little, because it did not satisfy her, but: 'That's the best I can do offhand,' she said.

'It doesn't help to give you a quick test for what's really a work of art and what isn't, though, does it? How can you tell, if there isn't any means of measuring it up?'

'With your blood, and your body, and your imagination. Don't trust anyone who tries to tell you there are fixed rules, like certain proportions that you can check up on with callipers. If he tells you that, he doesn't know anything, he hasn't any blood – nor any imagination. I've seen works of art that broke all the rules, and broke them with such authority that you knew at once they were right. The real test is in the full contact with your own personality, and if it rings right, it *is* right. You know it in things as you know it in people's lives – they can be works of art, too, only not enough of them are. People absolutely authentic, absolutely themselves, without any cant, or pretensions, or sidelong approaches. Part of the way of recognising them is in the way *you* approach *them*. It must be dead straight – no preconceptions and no timidity.' She sat with her hands coiled in her lap upon the tile she had forgotten she held. 'You make me talk too much. I can only express myself with my hands.'

'No, you didn't waste it all, really! Only it sounds as if you've got to be a bit of a genuine work of art yourself, to know another one when you meet it.' He grinned at her rather ruefully, but with none of the constraint he would once have felt in attempting such an observation of his own.

'Yes, I suppose you have! That's the beginning and the end of it – that honesty, that integrity – the rock you stand on, the backbone that keeps you upright on such a very little base, the tension that pulls you up to six feet and upsets the law of gravity from upsetting *you*. And now we're getting down to man, who is also a work of art, and an image of truth, and a statement of personal identity at his beast, that is! Some people have so little identity, they're hardly visible.'

He asked, this time with a faint flush and a more resolute smile: 'Could you see me, the first time I came here?'

'You were always perceptible,' she said sombrely, and picked up her brush, and watched it cross the white surface of the tile with a single, skimming stroke.

'But since then,' he pursued, with an unaccustomed and restless flare of mischief, 'I've started out on my career of being a little work of art in earnest, haven't I? You've at least got me centred – just like you centre the clay!' She looked up in surprise and disapproval to catch the last jealous gleam of his outraged self-love, but it was only like a startling glance backward at an old photograph.

'I haven't done anything to you. Things have happened to

both of us. I didn't go prising them into action, any more than you did. And I'm not directing them now.'

'No one's directing them,' he said, with sudden desperate urgency. 'How long do you suppose they can go on like that?'

She put down the tile and the brush, and scrambled across the rug on her knees to take him by the shoulders. 'What's worrying you? What is it you're afraid of?'

The crumpled newspapers rustled as he turned ardently to her, winding his arms about her waist and drawing her close. She felt his heart thudding against her breast, in its sudden tumult shaking them both.

'I don't know,' he owned, his lips stirring along her cheek. 'It's as if we haven't stopped to think, or be afraid, or any of the things we might well have done. I love you so much! Oh, Suspiria, if anything should take you away from me!'

It was seven weeks they had been lovers now, and neither of them had ever uttered a word of doubt, or seemed to feel the need of a glance over shoulder. The world had existed only to reflect their own fulfilled and assuaged faces. And yet this little cry of fear came out of him now as if it had been fully formed in his heart from the first moment of their happiness. She felt a sudden coldness take her senses, as if the shell of delight which had contained them had cracked suddenly, and the frosty wind blown witheringly in. She held him hard against her, passionately protesting:

'What should take me away from you? Nothing will, nothing can! What's the matter with you? You never talked like this before.'

'No,' he owned, 'we've never talked about him. But he's been there all the time. He's there now, painting away in the studio. Some day we've got to begin seeing him again.'

He turned his head, as though he were seeing him at that moment, clean through the wall.

'It isn't that I'm afraid. Well, yes, I am, but not of paying my score. I'm afraid of not doing things right. Talking about approaching things dead straight, and words like truth, and integrity— Oh, can't you imagine how I feel about this? About having to be furtive about it, and hide it, when I want to shout it at everybody, and make a regular song about it?'

Suspiria said in a stupefied whisper: *'Furtive?'* and then, holding him off from her so that she could look into his face, which indeed had a look almost of embarrassment at meeting her eyes: 'Have you had this at the back of your mind all along, then?' It was incredible; she had lived like a happy sleepwalker, while he had been trying to make daytime sense of the whole thing, as if it were not too absolute to be questioned.

'Yes, all the time. At first I thought – Well, after all, *I'm* not so much! – I thought it couldn't last. And if I'd got to get out of it some day, and get over it, better not leave *him* anything to get over. I couldn't see there was very much wrong with that, when he made it so easy. It would have been the opposite of what I'd call really straight, to chuck it in his face and put him to all that hell, if I was soon going to be over and done with, anyhow. You're angry,' he said quickly, 'but I can't help it. That was how I felt. But now, if it's like this with you, too—'

'If!' she said, on a sharply indrawn breath. 'My God, can you be in any doubt about it? What did you think? That I was having a little fun with you, and presently you'd be told: "That's all!" and expect to back out like a good little boy? And would you have *done* that?'

'I don't know! I should probably have crawled after you on my hands and knees, begging you to let me stay. How can I tell? But that was what I'd *rather* have done, if it had ever come to that. Oh, I've known now for some time that it wasn't like that with you at all. But once we'd started hiding it, I didn't know how to get out of the tailspin, and so it's gone on. And now I've said it, I'm no nearer knowing what we ought to do about it.'

'But how could you make such a mistake?' she whispered, raging. 'How could you imagine anything but that I loved you? After that first time, wasn't it plain enough? What does one have to offer, to make things clear to you? Did you think I lived like the novelettes, or something? Picking up lovers and dropping them every few weeks? Dennis, is that all you knew about me?' She knew that it was unjust, and felt that he was hurt by it, but he did not retreat, for to go back now would not solve the problem, nor avoid in the end the necessity of approaching it again, and more desperately. But who would have thought that the idyllic evening would flower into this fury of words and sensitivities?

'I didn't know anything about you? What's the good of pretending,' he said passionately, 'that we've got a perfect understanding, when the only thing we know about each other is *this*. The *only* thing! I love you, and you love me! All right, we know it now, and it's enough, if it's all we know. But how could I be certain of even that, then? And what was the sense of making him go through hell, if I wasn't really any threat to him? But I never liked having to hide it, and now it can't be hidden much longer, if it's what we claim it is.'

'You won't believe me,' she said, with an intense and resigned calm, 'if I tell you that it never seemed to me we were hiding it. I didn't talk about it, because there was nothing to be said about it to anyone but you. It was no more furtive to me than the ark of the covenant was furtive! It was as *private* as the middle of the heart, but it wasn't the same as *hiding* it. I love you!' she said, and for all her quietness it was a shout of exultation. 'I've never loved anyone else, I never shall. If I'd known there could be anything like this, do you suppose Theo would ever have been my husband? And do you think I'm going to pretend this is less than it is, now that I have it?'

'But he won't disappear for us. And he must mean something to you, I know he does. I've seen enough of the two of you together to understand that. So what about Theo?'

'There's nothing Theo can do to separate us. I told you, I love you. No one on earth can interfere with that – not Theo, nor anyone else,' she said, rearing her head formidably, and opening upon him the full blazing challenge of her eyes. 'He means a lot to me. But not this!'

'But you married him. He's your husband, he's got rights.'

'No one has rights to any part of my identity,' she said fiercely. 'I know Theo. He thinks as I think. Theo won't make any claims, he knows where people's rights in one another ought to begin and end. I didn't go looking for this, but I have it, and I'll keep it. There's no way he can alter it, or turn me back from it. But he won't try. He won't want to.'

'I can't believe it! He must love you – doesn't he love you? And if he does, he'll hang on to you tooth and claw. That's what I'd do in his place. I couldn't bear not to, it wouldn't be human. And Theo's human enough!'

'Love me?' She checked at the question, marvelling. 'Does he love me? I don't know! I know so little about it, I've only just discovered it. How can I tell whether he's known about it all along? And yet he seemed satisfied! But then, I was satisfied, too. It was a *better* marriage than most! Suppose somebody had asked him, does she love you, Theo? He'd say yes, and be sure it was the truth. Yes,' she said slowly, 'yes, I see how right you were to remind me about him.' She put up her arms in a sudden passion of longing, and locked them about the boy's neck, drawing his head down to her, rocking him against her cheek. 'Don't be afraid of anything! I'll tell him! Everything shall be as we ought to have it – as honest as you want it. I promise you, my darling! Don't be afraid of anything separating us – nothing can, nothing, nobody!'

He believed her. There was no mistaking this transfiguring ecstasy, it met every test she had tried to propound for him. He encountered it directly, with no preconceptions, because his dreams had never reached half so far, and no timidity, because it was the first time he had ever so much as seen it, and it had leaned to his hand. It rang right, and it was right. An image of truth, absolutely authentic, absolutely itself, and he knew it by his blood, and his body, and his imagination, past the possibility of error. He felt the surging sweetness of honesty restored already in it, and ached again with the added burden of rapture, his mind assuaged, his body in bliss. Mouth to mouth, shuddering and sighing, they clung together in the pool of light the lamp shed over them, as lost to the room as if it had burst away from them, and left them islanded in the milky light of the moon.

Impossible for the heart to bear or the body contain such an anguish of delight, and yet body and heart alike survived exquisitely to the promised and poignant peace. It rang right, and it was right; how could he doubt it, when he lay beside her in this ecstatic calm, loving the whole world for her sake, his heart heavy and holy with desire to give to everyone some part of his happiness? 'Oh darling! Oh, darling—' Nothing left to say but that, and it had the long profundity of all wisdom in it.

Suspiria's head sprang up suddenly from the crook of his arm, her eyes flaring emerald, her cheekbones whitening as the light spilled over them. 'What was that?'

The latch of the door relaxed with a faint and withdrawn click. A moment, and then something which was hardly a sound at all, the softest slur and creak, receding along the stone cavern behind the curtain which stirred along the hem, no more than a shiver in a subsiding draught.

They sprang apart, scrambling to their feet. She put his arm aside with wild gentleness, and ran, and tore open the door. Along the dark, cold corridor they heard, she saw, another door close, and a key turn in the lock, with a soft and unobtrusive but unmistakable finality. They were left staring wide-eyed at each other, scarcely able to make out each other's features now for the clarity of the figure that stood invisibly between them.

'It's all right,' said Suspiria then, with a gentle tenderness, as to a startled child. She came back to him, holding him by the arms, shaking him softly until the brittle whiteness left his face. 'Go home, my darling! Leave me to talk to him. There is nothing to be afraid of – nothing. Only you must leave him to me, it's better for us all. Especially better for him!'

He said sensibly: 'Yes!' still trembling a little with the shock of the echo, which still reproached him. 'Yes, I know! I'll go. Can I come tomorrow? We ought to get everything straight between us, once for all.'

She wondered for the first time, trying to shake the intruder out of her eyes, if it was going to be as simple as she had believed to exorcise the ghost of Theo. It might have been easier, she thought, if the substance, like the shadow, had come into the room and stood between them, instead of releasing the latch and recoiling into its chosen and impenetrable loneliness.

CHAPTER FOUR:

The Futility of Action

1

SUSPIRIA WENT and knocked on the studio door, and when only the slight and measured sounds of normal movement within answered her knock, called out to him firmly to let her in.

'I must talk to you,' she said, almost peremptorily, and waited with confident patience for an answer.

Within the room, suddenly still, Theo's voice said: 'No need for that. You've got nothing to tell me, I've got nothing to ask. I'm working. You go to bed, and don't wait for me.' To all further questions and demands he returned no other answer, and after a few tiring repetitions not even that. His voice was remarkably level and calm, more carefully modulated than usual. At first it was stonily sober, and had a kind of pure echo, as if he spoke in a great emptiness; but after a while it blurred, and she knew that he had the bottle in there with him, and was gradually and purposefully drinking himself into stupor. Because he was more likely to carry this deliverance to its end if she remained there, she went away as he had told her to do, her steps echoing back to him steadily. She went to bed and lay waiting for him to come, but she knew already in her heart that he would not come.

There was nothing new for her in sleeping alone. They had never submitted with any complacency to the tyranny of day and night. When he was working well, and felt like continuing, he would go on all night long if the nature of the work permitted it; if midnight found her in the middle of loading her kiln she would stay and finish the job. Everything passed on this night with a ragged semblance of normality, within this loose definition of what was normal. There was nothing to make her lie awake in the dark, staring at the ceiling, and listening to every sound from below.

He did not come to bed. After a time she dozed uneasily, but awoke readily at the infinitely small and distant and clear clash of the lock on the studio door. Wide-eyed, as if she listened with her eyes, she traced the thread of his footsteps into the living-room, and heard the door shut. His walk was almost painfully steady and distinct. He must have stopped drinking as soon as she left him, and the effects had all been dissipated, probably in a fury of work. As if, she thought, your yesterday or mine can be recovered through a canvas, or through clay, or by any other means of expelling one's own incomparably isolated being into tangible form! It will only turn out to be tomorrow, instead.

She waited a little while after everything was quiet. The shut door did not open again. What now? He was sitting over the fire, or drifting into sleep in one of the chairs. In spite of the few embers left alight, it would be very cold there. She slipped out of bed and drew on her dressing-gown, and with great delicacy, for fear he should hear her too soon, opened the door of the bedroom, easing the heavy latch with her fingers. The air in the house was bitter and clear, as if the frost had entered by every door and filled the rooms with its lucid and sterile breath. Suspiria stood barefoot at the top of the staircase, and looked down into the large, shapeless darkness of the room below, dappled with forms of lighter or darker shadow. A very faint gleam survived on the hearth, but gave no light, only a landmark by which to move. She went soundlessly down the stairs, her hand just touching the freezing coldness of the iron rail.

Theo was lying in a chair drawn up close to the feeble glow of the day's embers, his long legs sprawled out across the hearth, his arms splayed over the arms of the chair, his head lolling sideways so that the face was almost turned into the cushion under him. She stood silent at the foot of the stairs until her eyes were accustomed to the dark, and the loose, thrown-down shape of him gathered to her sight out of the first blindness. At first he looked to her like a dead man, then only like a man sleeping, then she knew that his eyes were open, and his mind braced furiously against the destroying weight of his tiredness, though he was not yet aware of her.

When she moved nearer he heard the sound of her naked feet, soft as it was, and lifted his head, all his bulk drawing together in instant wariness. She felt her breast and lips bruise against the suddenly erected wall of his hostility.

'Theo!' Her voice was low, and carefully without emotion. It was only as if she had touched him, to make sure that he was really there.

'You should be in bed and asleep,' he said in a dead voice. 'You'd better go back.'

'No, I must talk to you. I need to talk to you, and I need that you should listen to me.'

'There's no need to say anything. Perhaps I ought to make it clear,' said the same voice laboriously, 'that I didn't come spying on you. I came for some cigarettes. It was sheer bad luck that you didn't hear me come. I made no attempt to be particularly quiet. But I couldn't help recognising the implications as soon as the door was ajar. I had no intention of intruding.'

'I never thought anything else. All the same, I'm sorry it happened. I'd rather have had this talk with you first.'

'I'm no more likely to have misapprehensions about your motives than you are about mine. So there needn't be any talk. Your feet are bare,' he said, with a strange, distant pity. 'Go back to bed.'

'I want to tell you about Dennis and myself.'

'Why? Do you take it to be an occasion for apologies?'

'No!' she said with violence. 'I'm apologising for nothing! But it is an occasion for honesty, in justice to everybody. Dennis pointed that out to me, tonight, before you came. I want to tell you what I can no more help than he can, or you.

There never has been a time to be ashamed of it, or to apologise for it. There may have been a time when we could have evaded it. But I think that would have been a kind of abortion, too. I wasn't prepared for this, I didn't go looking for it, but no words I know of could tell you how glad I am that it's happened. I love him, he loves me. As far as I'm concerned it's the first and only time, and I see no possibility of any end to it. If you hadn't found it out for yourself tonight, you would have heard it directly from us.'

She drew a little nearer, until the tiny gleam of light was a pale gloss upon her ice-cold feet. She stood looking down at him, and felt the intent stare of his eyes devouring her. He did not move, and she did not touch him.

'I'm very fond of you, Theo. I always shall be. If this hadn't happened, I should have gone on living quite happily in the conviction that I loved you. But the difference is unmistakable now that it has happened. I hadn't looked for it – but you won't expect me to look it squarely in the face and deny that it exists. I might as well swear the earth is flat.'

'With your convictions,' he said expressionlessly, 'you could hardly do that.'

'Nor to deny its right to exist, nor mine to have it, nor his!' Against that heavy stillness of his her voice beat helplessly, forcing the words upon his consciousness with a hardening insistence, because he made no move to receive or reject them.

'You've made everything very clear,' he said. 'There's really nothing more to be said. What do you want from me?'

'I should be glad to hear you say that you understand. And don't blame us too much.'

'What right have I got to blame you?' he said, suddenly harsh with pain. 'I don't own you. Did I ever claim any rights to bend you out of shape? Have I accused you of anything? It's you who make so many words about it. I've made no claims, I'm not trying to confine you. All I want is for you to go back to bed, and let me alone.'

'You could have come a step to meet me,' she said, perceptibly drawing back from him, shadowy into the shadows of the room. 'It would have made things easier.'

But she said it with a regretful coldness, as if she had abandoned the possibility of contact, as if she sighed after it: 'What a pity!'

'Easier! Isn't it enough that I make them no harder?' he said hoarsely, suddenly shrinking together in the depths of the chair in a contortion of unmistakable pain. 'Have I put any obstacles in your way? Or tried to deny you your rights? Don't expect me to be your justification, as well. You're a person, you do what you have to, and you must carry your own burdens. I can't be responsible for your soul!'

'No,' she agreed, chilled beyond expression. 'No, I suppose one can't have it both ways.' She drew another step back, fading into the dark, from which her voice came low and heavily. 'I thought I knew you better,' she said, marvelling. 'I didn't realise we could find ourselves suddenly in different compartments, like this. I told him there was no way you could get between us – that you wouldn't want to—'

'My God!' he said, clutching his head between his long hands. 'Are you reproaching me? Did I make this situation? How am I getting between you?'

'By suffering!' she said, in a soft, protesting cry, and the lamenting sound issued from a darkness in which she was now quite lost but for the floating oval of pallor which was her face.

'I can no more help that,' he said, groaning, 'than you can help loving. You must allow me the same freedom to feel as I allow you.' He drew in his breath hard, wrenching himself round in the chair that he might not even see the half-luminous shape she had left in the empty air where she had stood. 'Go away!' he said, his voice shattering like trodden glass. 'Go away now – stop this! I understand you, if that's enough. Now please go!'

It was not enough, coming as it did out of an arctic estrangement which had no place at all between two such people as they had seemed to be. But she had no right to ask more from him than he could bring himself to offer. Moreover, she began, in her deepest heart, to understand the wall of ice he had erected against her, and had no wish to thaw it too suddenly, for fear of a flood which might destroy him, even if she survived it. The world was not going to end tonight. She said with recovered calm, and almost the practicality of everyday: 'I wish you'd come to bed. It's far too cold to be sitting about here.'

But he did not reply, and the exhausted head lay back now against the cushion with the look of death about it. So she went quietly to the fire, and fed its last sparks with crumpled paper and sticks until it revived a little, and then carefully built a little hollow house of coal over it. It began to draw readily, it was never difficult. Then she brought a rug from the cupboard under the stairs, and spreading it at arms' length, for fear he should recoil from her touch, let it fall over his knees.

'Good-night!' she said, and left him there motionless, looking after the faint sound of her feet as she climbed the stairs.

2

In the morning, when the broad bleak light of a frosty day made it impossible for them to hide from each other, she tried again. It seemed to her that they could not find any means of remaining strangers in the obvious atmosphere of the breakfast-table. But as soon as she reverted to the exchanges of the night the illusion of reality crumbled, and he evaded her with a frigidly veiled look, and went back into his tower of brass. She almost heard the door clang to between them. His lips made the careful, distinct phrases due to his principles, testifying yet again to the essential singleness of human liberty. But when she persisted, he slipped from under her fingers, and went out, and put his head into the house again only to say that he was driving down to town, and would not be back until tomorrow.

She felt him gather up after him, and carefully, jealously carry away, the last trailing thread of his generosity towards her. She knew then that this would not end, however many days she waited for the shock and the revulsion to pass. There would never be a time when he would meet her fully again, and sit down with her in a tried and reliable companionship to discuss the crisis which had overtaken them, and see what could be made out of the breakages. Not because he had frankly found his principles, when it came to the point, a little too heavy to be borne, not because his nature, under the shock of her defection, had rediscovered its own human weakness, and found itself outraged and angry. That she could have understood. Many a man has sincerely held views which, when it came to the point of sacrificing himself for them, he could not sustain. But this was something quite different. He clung to his declared views still, reasserted them as his only contribution to a solution; but they were no contribution at all, since he had withdrawn all his powers into paralysis for fear they should somehow be induced to take action in support of his declaration.

'I don't condemn you—!' No, and I don't absolve you, either! I don't claim any rights in you, but I don't release any of the impalpable rights I've acquired in you over the years. I'm not holding you – and by God, I'm not letting you go! Drag yourself clear if you can, but you won't do it without the reproach of knowing that you've destroyed me, torn me apart in pulling your roots clear, sent me to hell climbing into your new little heaven. I may not be able to keep you from getting there, but I'll poison the air for you, there or wherever you go!

Then she thought, driving herself frantically round the house upon unnecessary and ill-done jobs all the day long: 'No, that isn't altogether fair. It's worse than that for me! He's doing all that, with just that intention, but he doesn't know it. Subconsciously he's finding a way of keeping what he wants. He wants me. If I weaken and send Dennis away for good—' But she could not conceive such an event; it had to become the more distant and undisturbing: '—if I weakened, if I sent Dennis away—'

What then? Theo would relax gradually, assuaged by his power, forgiving for that preference of himself and responsiveness to his suffering every former betrayal. For that, after all, must be how he saw her acceptance of the late and unheralded angel. He would live out the rest of his life upon the bread of this triumph, perhaps not even reproaching her once in the whole sequence of the years, for the sweet taste of his magnanimity in his own mouth.

And if she did not weaken, and did not send Dennis away, but reorientated her life to the new pole in every particular, in spite of Theo's visible and calculating pain, he would rot and die, so that she might know that the loss of his talent to the world, as well as his own suffering, lay at her door. And then let her enjoy the boy if she could, with that burden of regret for ever poisoning her mind.

Love, unless she was greatly mistaken, caused people to will things like that, too. It could destroy, as well as create. That was something she had to know about it, and could hardly learn until the reality of love arrived to instruct her. It seemed to her a terrible blasphemy, this negative power of love, until she considered that every energy in the world is dual, adaptable for good or evil, according to the desire of the mind which employs it. How could the most tremendous energy of all be the exception to the rule?

She was calmer by the time the day had dwindled away to evening again. She had been into town, and shopped, and sat through a half-hour of dreary tea-time music in a café, and the accents of normality had reassured her that time is neutral, and inaction a weapon apt for both attack and defence. When Dennis came she was ready for him, prepared even for the first sight of him, so pale and resolute and vulnerably young, keyed up for a difficult encounter which would never take place.

'It's all right, my dear,' she said with a wry smile, 'he isn't here.'

'Not here?' echoed Dennis, frowning blankly upon behaviour so far out of his scope. 'But didn't you tell him?'

'Yes, I told him.' She watched the boy's face relax from its sharp white tension, between relief and disappointment, and she smiled again, but secretly within herself, in the pure dark centre of her instinctive being, where no other creature had ever penetrated, but this one, it seemed to her, was almost perfectly at home.

'Well, what did he say? What's he going to do about it?'

She wondered if she had only been indulging this same naîve view of man when she, too, had supposed that Theo must intend to do *something* about it.

'He said that he isn't stopping us. He said that he claims no rights in me that would interfere with my rights as an individual. As for what he's going to do— Nothing! Nothing at all, except elude any outright discussion with either of us, and make it certain that whatever happens, he has no part in it – except as the victim!'

To a simple mind like Dennis's, it made no sense at all. He had expected, perhaps, an open and angry contest for her, or a scene of sophisticated renunciation; he was not prepared for the devious shifts to which the mind can go to keep both face and possessions. She explained to him as clearly as one can explain to a beloved creature of experience more limited than one's own.

'If he won't meet us,' said Dennis, setting his jaw, 'we've got to do something about it without him, that's all. It's got to be resolved somehow. If he won't come to any agreement or take any action, we must.'

It sounded beautifully easy, and so it might have been if they could have thought of Theo as an enemy. The boy, after all, had known him only a few months, and seen him, during most of that time, only as a sort of fifth limb of Suspiria's body. But ten years of close companionship cannot be written off like that; and Theo was taking frantic, feverish care not to be an outright enemy.

'Action!' she said, sighing. 'Listen, my darling – if there's anything certain in this world, it's your position with me. What more do you want? You wanted him to know the truth. Well, he knows it. There's no deception about it, there never was. With almost everything in your hands, do you have to be in such a hurry to push Theo into place? Let him alone a little while. Maybe he'll get used to the idea, and come to terms with us. Maybe he'll even help us a little. Give him time!'

'You said yourself,' said Dennis, studying her face with eyes of the most intense and urgent gravity, 'that he means to keep us in the wrong – to be a victim.'

'I did, I know, but in a little while – after all, how can a man get over a thing like that all in a moment? We've been together so long, and he relies on me – he loves me.'

'It's a sign of love, is it, to make these high-flown claims about leaving you your freedom, and then to set out to make you feel a criminal as soon as you want to take it? I don't call that love!'

'It is love, all the same,' she said.

'To want to hurt you? To make you wretched?'

'He knows nothing else to do. He doesn't want to hurt me, he just wants to keep me.'

'Dead or alive! And that's loving you? I don't believe it!' said Dennis fiercely.

'You will, one day.' For a moment she thought of his future without a place for her anywhere in it, and could see only the blank, featureless ovals of young faces about him, drawing his eyes and inhabiting his heart. Then she turned back from the nightmare with a start of revulsion, and taking him by the shoulders held him facing her, closely and gently, until the warm flooding excitement, so soft and passionate, mantled in his cheeks, and his eyes darkened and deepened, opening clean down into the guarded centre of his being. He did not know when his look unfolded upon her thus like a flower to the sun; but when it happened she knew that it was for her, and that no one else would ever enjoy it.

'Trust me! You know you can. I shall never love anyone but you. We can afford to be gentle with other people. Listen – go away now, and don't come for a week. Leave Theo to me, and let's see if we can't do what must be done with as little damage as possible. It will be better for us to remember, afterwards, if no one is badly hurt. And I'm very fond of him! And you liked him, too!'

Dennis did as she wished, without complaint, though the week she had asked for seemed like a year cut out of his life. He kissed her with a solemn, dedicated gentleness, and went away home.

Theo came back from London next day; she had almost expected him to stay away longer, but he came, sober, remote, and looking rather ill. She had made up a bed for herself in the attic room by that time, to avoid the wincing reminders he would suffer from either her presence, or the immediate pain of witnessing her removal. She had taken away all her own things, and made it pointless for him to refuse to accept the change. Moreover, she had met him with careful calm, as if nothing had happened which was not already perfectly understood and acknowledged between them. Within the confines of the house, he lived as fastidiously drawn back from her as he could, answered her impersonally when she spoke to him about indifferent things, withheld himself hard from every smallest service she tried to offer him, and shut himself away from her in the studio or fled from the house whenever she attempted to speak of Dennis and the future. She would not have believed it possible to live with a man for ten years, to know him as well as she had thought she knew Theo, and suddenly to be unable to get near him. It was like trying to hold a handful of quicksilver.

She could not work, with her mind for ever poised alert for some opportunity which never came. Nor, she thought, did Theo accomplish much, though he shut himself into the studio so often, and for such long periods, that he might have been engaged upon a masterpiece. Towards the end of the week for which she had bargained, he began to drink again, and with an intense and purposeful concentration which suggested that all other means of eluding her had failed him. And all the while, as she watched him steadily and waited for him to turn and face her, the accumulation of their days together was fighting for Theo.

During those last three days he hardly left the studio, except to forage now and again for food, and long after she had gone to bed, to creep to his, and sleep like a log until the following noon. He had made sure of his refuge this time; he was not once sober enough to understand what she tried to say to him, and his tower was impenetrable at last. It was useless to persist; she let him alone, and sat empty-handed in the living-room when he hid himself. There would be nothing to report to Dennis, now or ever.

Drifting aimlessly through the house, she tried the door of

the studio and found it open. She did not even know why she had tried it, for there was no reaching him now, and all that long kindness had turned sour for both of them; all the same, she opened the door, and looked in.

He had heard her come, and he swung away from his easel, brush in hand, to stare across the bright room at her with a face at once outraged and impervious. He could not quarrel with her now even for this intrusion, he was too far gone; but still the dazzling blue eyes in the sodden face scintillated with that redoubled awareness they kept always through his body's drunkenness. The core of his mind did not know how to get drunk, it renewed its nervous energy in the disintegration of his physical powers, as sometimes the activities of his hands seemed to quicken their intensity at the cost of his body's torpor. He would go on painting until he dropped and slept where he lay, and this was what would come out of his driven agony, this limpid little still-life, astonishingly coherent and compact from the hand and heart of a man who was falling apart in front of her eyes.

She had never seen it so clearly before. For a moment he was nothing but a pair of great eyes, blind as sapphires, into which she fell drowning as into a vortex of pain. From the height of her own defiant happiness she was plunged into the unimaginable depths of sorrow and loss, and those without reproach or appeal. When the waves went over her fully she drew back, shivering, her eyes closed, and shut the door.

How easy it is to see only one profile of some other poor living creature who happens to be a problem to us! How simple to attribute to all his actions, and even his inaction, the meaning which comes nearest to justifying our own! Perhaps subconsciously he was indeed willing her to feel his suffering, so that she could not abandon him to it, but no one, no one as utterly on the side of life as Theo, could ever have willed to endure the anguish she had seen in his eyes. To want to share a suffering like that is no more than the leaning back in extremity upon any comfort, even the slight and fallible one of hurting someone else with a part of it. They do it to remain alive, the positive duty of man; to remain alive, to go on doing and feeling. What is unbearable must be rubbed off against any creature unlucky enough to come by. There is nothing selfish in it, it is one of the laws of life to survive if you can. And she was blaming him for it, she who in her own extremity had made the situation, and let fall the demon upon him.

The years of their life together were dragging at her memory. She went into the workshop, and damped the green pots which were cracking with their long wait for firing. She swung the wheel, and watched it spin slowly down again into stillness; uncovered the kiln, and looked from the empty blond brick within to her spoiling work, but could not bring herself to care. Almost automatically she began to fill the kiln, lifting each piece with slow, careful hands.

What was to be done now? Whether designedly or not, she had taken Dennis clean out of his old background, and stamped into him the impress of her own mind. She did not think she had set out to do it, but it was done; no, worse, it was still doing, and if he found himself wrested as savagely away from her also in this lost condition, half-made, what hope would he have of growth into any complete kind of creature? He needed her certainty as she needed his promise. And there was the immaculate and erect fact of their love, implacable, demanding its due. And in the studio Theo, who had been deserted by his own beliefs and left to burn, silent and drunken and rotting in his jealousy and pain.

If you cannot, for all your individuality, escape the conviction that you are your brother's keeper, who are you to choose between your brothers?

Something was breaking; she felt it in her own heart, even before Dennis came through the house looking for her.

He was very quiet, and in the passion of her concentration she did not hear him until he came behind her, and put his hands very softly over her breasts, and his lips against the nape of her neck, under the short curved feathers of black hair. He touched her with a wonderfully eloquent delicacy, an adult delight newly accomplished. For her it was like being able to watch a tree grow, the constant miraculous reward for every moment of patience. With every growth in him, she was enlarged. It could not be other than good. It was goodness itself. And yet the eloquence of his fingers could not silence the eloquence of those blue eyes in their extremity of grief and loneliness.

She turned within his hands, and shut her arms about his neck, and held him against her breast silently for a long time. Conviction had changed hands, certainty had gone over to a new home. He was the one who stood gently sustaining her, holding her together between his palms against the disintegrating violence of her divided heart. And he understood more than she could tell him. He said in a whisper, his mouth against her forehead:

'This can't go on, you'll be broken in pieces if it does.' And after a long, quiet minute, while she stretched herself fiercely against the young and erect solidity of his body: 'He's in the studio now, isn't he? I saw the light. Let me go to him! You've done enough.'

'What would be the use?' she said. 'He's drunk. He's been drunk, more or less, for three days. He won't understand a word you say. And what could you say to him that would mean anything?'

'I could tell him the truth – that there'll have to be a clean break. You love me, and you can't go against it. He'll have to give you a divorce, and let you have a new chance of happiness.'

She gave a small, dry laugh, repeating after him: 'Divorce!' and: 'Happiness!' as if they were words she had never heard before, bits of another language fallen from nowhere into his mouth. The ideas they conveyed seemed to her so irrelevant. As if divorce could either set her free from Theo or offer her happiness! It was like suggesting that her brother's keeper could shoulder off the responsibility by resigning as soon as it became heavy to carry.

'There's nothing else for it,' he insisted gently. 'You can see he isn't going to let any sort of friendship survive it. It's better you should come away with me, and get clear of him. Better for him, too! What is there for him here, now?'

'It won't be any use,' she said again. 'If you saw him you'd understand that. But go, if you want to. I don't see how it can make things any worse, for any of us.'

Dennis took her by the shoulders, and turned her softly towards the kiln again. He had what he had always wanted, a moment of ascendancy over her; partly she had given it to him in her weariness, and partly he had taken it from her, but he had it, and she felt how jealously he held it, with what exultant archings of his wings he covered her, for an instant, from the shadow of responsibility for herself.

'You go on loading here, forget about us!'

She heard the door close after him, and the steady receding sound of his footsteps as he walked into the house. She loved him so much that she wanted to believe him effective, and for an instant she even achieved it. It was like wine to her heart; but it did not last.

3

After a while she could not bear it any longer, and crept back into the house, her ears strained for any revealing sounds from within the studio as she passed. When she was just closing the door of the living-room behind her, she heard the shattering fall of glass; even then she tried to go on, and leave them uninterrupted, but after five minutes of straining her ears involuntarily in the dark and empty room, and as many of stopping them with her fingers, she could no longer keep away. She pushed the door wide, and went back along the passage.

The voices hardly indicated anything. Words were indistinguishable, there was only a thick, harsh muttering and shouting, and through it occasionally, with exhausting care and distinctness, Dennis's voice arguing and pleading, over and over again the same short phrases. She did not try to disentangle them; the tone was enough. It had an undertone of shock, as if he had just come through some cruelly optimistic electric treatment, beneficial, no doubt, if the mind survives it. She thought: 'My God, what are we all doing to one another?'

She went in. Theo was standing before his easel, facing

the door, his feet splayed wide to keep him upright. The dead, satiated face and the living, famished eyes confronted her with a contrast of such violence that she saw nothing else for a moment. Then the rest of the scene appeared item by item, fading in from the edges of the circle of which the eyes were the centre: the fragments of the broken glass lying in a pool of spirit, a trampled tube of flake-white snaking out its contents upon the bare boards of the floor, and already trodden furiously about a small area before the easel, where Theo had threshed round in his frenzy of industry without relief; a litter of brushes, rags, tubes, ground colours and oils lying about the bench, and a canvas or two knocked down among the wreckage; the portrait of herself propped against the wall in the far corner, as if he had stood it there for safety before he began to get drunk in earnest. The cool of its greys was like a drink of water in a desert. Nothing else in the room seemed poised and at rest, except the little group of trifles, delicate, graceful and unimportant, out of which he was making one more still-life, with what reserve of vision and dexterity she could not guess.

The room smelled strongly of whisky. Dennis, with a face as white as chalk, was standing beside the bench, pouring a fresh drink with unsteady hands; she heard the siphon stuttering against earthenware, a flat sound like the chattering of teeth. He had tipped the small brushes out of the biscuit beaker in which Theo usually stood them, because there was no other clean vessel in the room, and Theo's insistent demands were hammering in his ears so stupefyingly that he could think of nothing else until he had satisfied them. Both hands, one still holding a loaded brush, came lurching out after the beaker, and fastened upon it unsteadily. She saw how fastidiously Dennis's fingers avoided the touch, how gratefully they relinquished the cup and drew back.

The whisky went down much too fast. Dennis was not saying anything now. No doubt he had tried to give voice to part, at least, of what he had thought was needed between them, bringing it down gradually from its original self-conscious belligerence into words of one syllable, patiently uttered and re-uttered. All without result! Now he knew it was all wasted. He looked more than a little sick with indigestible experience. It took him a full minute to realise that she was there within the doorway, and then he looked at her only briefly, with a white, wordless apology, and lifted his shoulders a little in a gesture of helplessness.

Over the rim of the beaker, staring at her with those blue, blind eyes crazy with pain, Theo said thickly and low: 'Go away, I don't need you! Go away, and take your little dog with you. I'm working—'

It was coherent so far, and then deep complaint thickened into a wordless and indistinguishable mumbling. As much use talking to the wind. She looked at Dennis, and said very quietly: 'We'd better go. You see it's hopeless.'

'Yes,' said Dennis, not moving. The brush was back at the canvas now, all the life left in the hand gathered readily to direct its touch. He swung his shoulder on them, but he knew they were still there, and watching him; she doubted if he knew anything more than this, he was so intensely dedicated to holding himself firmly closed against them.

'How long will he go on like this?' asked Dennis in a rapid undertone.

'Until he drops unconscious, I expect.'

'Couldn't we take the bottle away with us?'

'What's the use? I think he's got another one hidden somewhere. If we leave him this one, he may give up when he finishes it.'

His dulled ears could not have deciphered the whispers, mere breaths as they were, but he knew in his blood that they were involved in some conspiracy against him. Suddenly he turned and shrieked at them: 'Get out – get out! Leave me alone!' It was such a howl of agony that they drew back from him in superstitious horror. He put down the beaker with a crash on the bench, and clawing round by one hand, made a swaying rush at them for a few steps, and then had to recover himself frantically to withstand the pull of his own weight. He lost his bearings slightly, and bearing round in blind anger, came face to face with his portrait of Suspiria across the cold grey yards of air. The lifted face, wildly alert in thought, looked through him and beyond him, and all the whirling planes of colour, charmed into stillness, burned suddenly brighter and clearer, the luminous greys receding magically to give his arms passage round her body.

The two who were withdrawing from him stopped, shaken and afraid, in the doorway, hearing his voice say quietly, with a curiously still and distant grief: 'Spiri, don't leave me!'

Suspiria wrenched herself out of Dennis's arm, and went forward a few steps like a sleepwalker, her hands raised protestingly towards the swaying figure. She felt Dennis's terror dragging her arms down, trying to pull her back to him; but he managed not to speak. It was left to her. Everything, in the end, was left to her. They tore her in pieces between them, dragging her heart in two, but the final onus of choice was always on her.

'Spiri!' Theo was looking at her now as he had looked at the image of her a moment ago, his eyes frantically intelligent and alive in the muddy shape of his estranged face. It was as if he were trying to climb out of crumbling earth towards her, out of a kind of grave. 'Spiri, don't leave me!'

There was not a sound nor a movement from Dennis. He was standing flattened against the door, with his teeth locked hard on his lower lip, and his frightened eyes following her movements in fascination and despair. For a moment he held his breath, for a moment believed her lost; and then he knew that it was over. She had seen the instantaneous flame of calculation and triumph, tiny but clear in the blue eyes, the little flare of vengeful pleasure in her recapture.

She turned, groping frenziedly towards the door, blind with revulsion, like an animal starting back from the rim of a trap discovered only just in time; and Dennis sprang to take her extended hands, to shut a protective arm round her, and half-lift, half-lead her from the room. She clutched at him eagerly, not because she had abdicated her responsibilities, but because for the moment he was the quickest way of escape from the snare, and his will to snatch her away was equal and ardent with her will to go. By the time he had drawn her into the corridor and shut the door hard behind them, he had already lost her. She was out of the circle of his arm, and away into the darkness upon her own firm feet, and all he could do was follow her tamely where he had wanted to shepherd her with passionate tenderness. She did not know how to be weak and in need for more than a few minutes at a time.

A lamentable cry followed them along the dark passage. They heard the easel rock and jar, and then: 'Spiri! – Spiri! – Spiri!—' with diminishing violence until all was quiet, and the living-room door shut, and the curtain drawn between them and him. At the last moment Dennis looked back, bewildered and dismayed by the silence.

'Ought we to leave him alone? He isn't responsible. He doesn't know what he's doing.'

'Oh, yes,' she said, turning in the middle of the room, and staring at him with wild green eyes, as if she would run from him, too, if he came near her, 'he knows what he's doing, all right. Leave him alone!' It was rather as if she had said: 'Leave me alone!' She stood back against the drawn window-curtains, stirring from foot to foot, and plying her fingers in the folds. 'At least,' she said, her eyes steadying upon his face, 'you didn't try to pull me back. You didn't say anything. I won't forget that. What happened? What did you say to him?'

'Not much! It was just no use. I tried to explain – he didn't understand what I said, just looked at me as if I wasn't there at first, and went on drinking.'

'He didn't want to understand. It's his way of protecting himself.'

'Then he began raving, and dropped his glass. You'd have thought nothing existed but whisky, the way he screamed for another. I suppose I just wanted to keep him quiet at any price, but if I hadn't given it to him he'd have got it himself. He's still capable of that, anyhow. I wanted you not to hear – but of course, you did. Look,' he said, bitterly in earnest, 'I can't let you stay here alone with him tonight.'

'Don't be a fool!' she said roughly, shaking her head until the black hair settled in curved plumes across her forehead. 'Are you beginning to tell me what I can do, and what I can't? Of course I shall stay here. This is where I live! That's my husband! Have you forgotten?' The brief indignation of her eyes dulled as quickly. 'I'm safe enough,' she said, more gently. 'I couldn't be safer. There was only one thing Theo could do to me – only one thing he'd have wanted to do. And now that's over. And you're safe, too,' she said, 'at least from losing me – if that's what you think of as safety!' Her eyes dwelt with faintly bitter understanding upon his hands, which lifted so jubilantly towards her at the note of encouragement. 'Without that!' she said.

He recoiled at once, snatching back his hands as if her look had scalded them. An involuntary pity stirred in her at sight of his distress. 'I'm sorry!' she said sharply. 'I can't help it! Leave me alone tonight! You can afford to wait a little while. Go home now, please. I don't want to be touched tonight. Oh, no, no – it isn't your fault. There was nothing you could have done.'

'But I shan't see you till tomorrow night,' he said, drawing back from her reluctantly. 'I must know that you're all right!'

'For God's sake, what can happen to me? Of course I shall be all right. I'll put a note under the stone by the gate for you, in the morning, if you're so worried. But there's nothing to worry about, I tell you.'

But at the last moment she could not let him go without some gesture of exasperated kindness. In the doorway she overtook him, and drew him round to face her for a moment, pulling him down into her arms.

'Don't be angry with me! I can't stand any more tonight!' She kissed him, and her disgust and weariness melted in the instant passion of his responsive mouth, and a terrible tenderness filled her heart. 'Oh, darling, darling,' she said, in a torn and husky whisper, 'what have I dragged you into? What have I done to you?'

CHAPTER FIVE:

A Death

1

SUSPIRIA AWOKE with a jangling start, and lay staring up at the darkness and the faint, bluish frost-light above her face, with wide eyes and vibrating senses. She had not meant to sleep at all. She had intended only to lie down in her bed, and listen for the sounds of Theo dragging himself finally upstairs to the room beneath her attic; but a kind of drugged exhaustion had shut her eyes before she knew she was in danger, and she had gone headlong down into pits, pyramid-shafts, infinities, of sleep, far below the levels of refreshment or comfort. The ascent out of that blackness, sudden though it was, seemed to her a long, laborious swim upward from the deepest and heaviest of ocean-depths, and yet she was flung out into reality at last quite unprepared. She lay groping a dazed way back to the truth of her situation, and remembered why her mind had willed so vehemently to make its temporary escape.

The boy had gone home like a docile child, without protest if not without misgivings. He was so used to the idea that she knew better than he did that he gave no trouble. When he had been through such a complex of shocks as last night's, he no longer complicated everything even with the tender male stirrings of his self-love, which prompted him at other times with nagging suggestions that he ought to be taking the initiative. For both of them, of course. He was the man, it was his part to be stronger. Knowing or fearing that he was not caused him indignation and pain and shame, but not now in such acute form that they could not be completely wiped out when some larger emotion possessed him. In the moments of passionate satisfaction he was eased of all his misgivings, because he knew himself more than adequate. Gentle, adult, triumphantly fulfilled, he shared her certainty and peace, sometimes she felt that he gave them back to her when they were slipping out of her hands. How many people, she wondered, lived long, contented married lives, year upon worthy year, without ever suspecting that such a plane of achievement existed, somewhere far out of their scope? And she and the boy had found their way to it without effort, in a miraculous and tender dexterity of spirit and flesh, lifting each other over the threshold with a lovely simplicity. In that dazzling conviction of accomplishment Dennis was safe from any doubts. And when the extreme of difficulty and distress was exchanged for the extreme happiness, he forgot his own vanity as simply, shaken out of caring whether he cut a figure or not, provided they got through the jungle with their lives. Then he would go softly in front of her, abashed, willing to be guided.

She embraced the thought of him, kissed and dismissed and going away meekly as she ordered him, heavy and full of anxiety for her, while she recoiled into the darkest solitudes of her own nature, and shut herself in there alone with her weariness and disgust. Now, waking, she wanted him for a moment with a piercing insistence, and lay holding the memory of him molten into her body with straining arms. Then the revulsion of her sleeping uneasiness swept over her drowningly, and she sat up in the rumpled bed, and braced herself to listen, all her nerves at stretch.

The house beneath her was utterly still. Outside the window the moonlit, motionless stillness of the night hung as ominously, reflected pallidly on the oblique faces of the ceiling, and the inward-crowding walls. Cold and dry, but only on the unwhitened edge of frost, the folded fields lay pale between their ebony hedges. Within and without, the world was silent.

Suspiria got out of bed, and groped for her slippers. She felt suddenly too far away from the heart of the house, up here under her roof. Sounds from below did not carry to her, or at best only from the bedroom below; and she had not meant to fall asleep. She stood quite still beside her bed, and held her breath to listen more intently, but there was no sound at all. She was lost even to time, but only in the small hours of the morning could there be such a silence, for the distant hum of traffic on the main road did not usually cease until after two, and as frequently began again between four and five. The heart of the night, it seemed, between the sodium lights and the daylight, was like this, hushed and hollow and rounded, like a cave closed by a fall of rock, or the inside of a vault after the withdrawal of a funeral.

She caught up her dressing-gown suddenly, and drew it round her against the startlingly abrupt sensation of cold, though the chill seemed to spring through her flesh rather from within than from without. Very softly she opened the door, and crept out on to the narrow attic stairs. The house did not stir beneath her. Houses, particularly old houses, breathe and turn in their sleep even at night, but now there was nothing to suggest the existence or even the remembrance of life. She went down the stairs. There was only one room below, the big bedroom where she and Theo slept together so many years; only that, and the narrow landing, and the iron-railed stairway down into the living-room. She spread her fingers quietly against the door of the bedroom, and it gave lightly to the touch, with an unmoved ease which assured her that the room was empty. She pushed it wide, and the air within was cold, without the suggestion of a human presence.

In the living-room the fire had gone out on the hearth, and there was no one in the chairs. Something of humanity was left there, a very faint warmth, and a sort of dying vibration in the air, the last tremor of Dennis's voice. She stopped at the foot of the stairs, searching through the faint moonlit spaces of the room, the polished gleams and the matt dimnesses, for the shape of him, reluctant in the doorway, looking back at her mutely as he went out.

Somewhere over there in the town he was lying asleep now, caught back from her into that other and unknown world from which he had emerged to humble her. She knew nothing about it, and had never felt any curiosity, but detachedly she thought of it as a confined place of framed photographs, and sentimental pictures, and neat, guarded relationships, where the kind of woman she was would have a docket of its own, and where they would pretend, if they knew of her, that she did not really exist, but was merely a kind of mental illusion of which Dennis was the unlucky victim. She knew there was a brother, with whom he shared a bedroom. She could imagine, she had seen in his eyes sometimes, his sense of outrage that even the passionate privacy of his nightly memories of her should be invaded. Perhaps he was not asleep at this moment, but lying tightly clenched over the thought of her as over a secret pain, still anxious, already in anticipation burrowing his hand under the stone by the broken gate, to find her morning reassurance which was to help him through the day.

The warmth of remembering him receded slowly; the chill of the night air, trembling on the edge of frost, made her shiver as she stood, and the echoeless emptiness shook itself free of the last lingering tenderness of his youth. She felt suddenly and inconceivably alone. Turning in the inner doorway, she wrenched the curtain aside with a cold hand, and entered the dark tunnel of the corridor. On the left, the kitchen, and the improvised complex of the bathroom and scullery; on the right, the studio. He must be there, there was nowhere else left where he could be. Why was there still this feeling in her that the whole house had been vacated long ago?

She waited for a moment, holding her breath again, but there was nothing to hear. But there was something else to hold her still, a faint breath of strangeness in her nostrils, hardly enough to be called an odour at all, and yet perceptible.

She reached out her hand, feeling the effort by which she

advanced it, and turned the handle of the door, and pushed it open. A knife-edge of light sprang out at her, widening, and with it a gush of wind from an open ventilator in the top of one window, cold and unexpected, laden with a sour and nauseous smell. The door swung wide, and she stood just within the room, looking at the chaos of Theo's night's work; and at Theo himself lying in the middle of it, contorted between the feet of his easel.

His back was towards her, his knees drawn up; he, too, was coiled together over his secrets. She went forward until she stood close to him, looking down at the upturned face, in which the eyes stared blindly. His skin was lividly blue under the bright light, fallen and scooped into gaunt hollows the colour of lead. The bitter smell rose and caught her by the throat as the draught set it in motion. He had been sick, but not violently enough, and far too late. His chin was stained, his jaw half-open and rigidly locked. Nothing remained to call her husband to mind, except the terrible brightness and blueness of those open eyes. Dead, he did not look like Theo any more.

2

She stood looking down at him for what seemed to her a long time, her eyes alert and fixed in a face which had not greatly changed its expression. Something was suddenly broken in her, but it was not any thread of her heart; rather she felt herself tearing loose, of necessity, every affection, every consideration which in this extremity was less than essential. There remained, when she had surveyed the field, only one true essential, and that was Dennis.

Her senses sprang into an exaggerated and sharply painful activity. Theo was dead, Dennis was alive. She had never felt any timidity about selecting her own priorities.

The pattern of Theo's whitened footprints about the floor was like the labyrinths painted on the ground for the ritual fantasies of primitive peoples, the carefully indirect path from world to world. The little beaker of biscuit ware had slipped from between his fingers, and was lying on its side in a puddle of moisture. The broken glass still lay just under the edge of the bench, close to where Dennis had been standing when she interrupted them. The palette was on the floor, too, where it had dropped from his hand, and he was lying partly over it, two or three brushes scattered along the boards beside him.

Her eyes went from the fallen beaker to the almost empty whisky bottle and the siphon. She looked all round the room, and could not recollect that within her knowledge of last night's events Dennis had touched anything else here. The prints of several people's fingers would be on the bottle and the siphon, and who was to say when they had been made? There must be at least fifty people in Great Leddington by this time who followed local scandals with sufficient assiduity to be well aware that Dennis Forbes was a constant visitor at Little Worth, and the incongruity of the association would lead them to make partially correct guesses at its nature. Whatever she did, the truth about Dennis would come out, and the absence of his fingerprints about the house, rather than their presence, might be thought a suspicious circumstance. It must not appear, however, that he was the last, or almost the last, to touch the bottle and the siphon; other prints, more intimate to the house, must lie over his. For whatever other details might be allowed to appear, Dennis Forbes had not been in that room the previous night, had not handed Theo a drink. Many other curious implications she was prepared to risk; but this was something she could not and would not leave to chance.

The siphon looked clear and innocent, the last two inches of spirit in the bottle reflected the light radiantly in amber and gold. Only in the biscuit beaker, precarious on its curved side by Theo's hand, a thin whiteness, a silt, showed under the small cupped lake of liquid.

She picked it up, and watched the heavy insoluble white particles shift round the curve of the base as she turned it in her hand. There was no smell from it but the smell of the whisky; and a drunken man who was not looking for suspicious deposits would not be likely to notice anything amiss. If he could have looked through the ware as through that broken glass, now, he might well have baulked at tossing it down, drunk as he was; but given an opaque cup, its contents just swung into momentary suspension by the discharge of the soda, a man in a devilish hurry to drink himself into unconsciousness was not likely to hesitate. There remained only this small white mud, from which a competent analyst might build a fabulous house of facts.

She asked herself, with an almost detached coolness, what would be the reactions of a trained stranger entering here. First he might well think: he did it himself. Then, what is it? Where did he get it? It won't be found here, whatever it is, but in the workshop – ah, that's another matter! It won't take a competent man long to find it there. Did he go to the workshop to help himself, then, when he'd drunk himself to the edge of suicide? Not unless he took off his shoes to go, and put them on again when he came back! The flake white he dropped and trampled all over the floor isn't dry on his shoes yet, and it doesn't even reach the door. He made us a map of his movements, complete to the last staggering step. He did not go looking for the means of a death among his wife's glazing materials. Not last night. Maybe he had it by him already, maybe he'd lifted it some time ago. Or maybe somebody else brought it to him!

Nothing existed but necessity. A matt surface like that of this unglazed cup ought not to take a good impression of fingerprints. Even from highly finished surfaces washing can erase them, according to the books. But this is not a book; and the prints belong to the fingers of Dennis; and there is always the last, the outside chance, the risk one might, perhaps, take even for oneself, but not for him. She carried the beaker away into the scullery, and washed it very carefully, leaving the tap running for some minutes after it, to ensure that every grain was washed away down the sink. Then she put the cup in its place on the bench in the studio, and replaced the clean brushes in it. With the edge of her slipper she scraped the pieces of the broken glass across the floor, and arranged them beside Theo's hand. The splashes of moisture it had shed in breaking were already almost dry, and in any case would excite no suspicion, being almost underneath the place where the bottle stood. She set her own fingers about the bottle twice, as if to lift and pour from it, and then deliberately smeared the chromium of the siphon, and set her prints there, too. A moment she hesitated before approaching Theo with it, but in the end she knelt beside him, and lifted an already stiffening hand in hers.

It was unbelievable how his fingers resisted her, and how little she felt but the sheer physical struggle with them. Some day she would live all this again without the haste and the urgency which sustained her now, and suffer all the nausea and terror which belonged by rights to this moment. Now she did what she had to do. She laid the hand down again, and the arm rocked a little with the shifting balance. Then she put the siphon back in its place, and looked round a studio which bore, she thought, no positive evidence of Dennis's last visit.

She was covering the retreat of three people; there was nothing else to be done. But which of the three she kept first in the line she knew very well.

At the last moment she looked again at the beaker, and her monstrous uneasiness made its shape quiver and distort as she gazed. Could mere washing wipe out from that porous body every trace of a liquid and an imperfectly soluble solid, which had lain in the crook of it for several hours? Forensic chemists do marvellous things. There might still be traces they could conjure out of the permeable clay, enough even for analysis. How could she be sure? And if they found out so much, they would never rest until they had more. Once they knew that this little cup had held the oxide which had killed Theo, and that someone on the spot had known enough to wash and hide it, they would take it apart grain by grain to find the last faint mark of a finger; and how could she be sure there would be nothing whatever to find?

No, the thing must go. Not into the dustbin, not into shards which could be fitted together again. It must vanish. The risk of leaving it in existence was one she dared not take.

She tipped out the brushes again, and took the beaker away with her, pressing the prints of her hands upon the handles of the studio door, both within and without. The ticking of her watch was the first thing which stung her senses as she entered the workshop; she had taken it off when she began to prepare her kiln, and left it lying beside the wheel. For the first time she began to calculate and hurry, because time had come back with the watch, and she had to work within limits, and with much to do. It was past five o'clock, and she had a forest to make, in which she might hide her leaf.

She kept quantities of her basic glazes constantly ready for use, in covered tubs, so that they needed only the addition of whatever oxide she chose, and some adjustment of the amount of frit or silica to balance the addition. She chose the soft-fired lead glaze, because it need not go beyond a thousand degrees centigrade in the firing, and for all she knew someone's professional curiosity might well interfere before the temperatures necessary to harder glazes could be reached. Risks she had to take, whatever she did, but at least she could reduce them to a minimum.

There were enough biscuited pots to fill a glost kiln. She unloaded the green pots she had put into the kiln in that distracted attempt at normality, last night, and assembled quickly all that she had ready for glazing. The pigments would have little time to dry, but she switched on one element, and stood them on the rim of the kiln over it as she completed them. There were beautiful things there. Her hands dwelt lovingly upon them as she handled the brushes, touching them with a wild kindness because there was no time to linger over them. Heavy blue-black banding and a few blown olive leaves on the beaker, and the rest, the spare, flashing strokes the old Koreans used to create a willow, a palm, a bird; with no time to spare for either hesitancy or elaboration she knew that she did her best work. She felt articulate beauty following her fingers, leaping arched across the broad curves of bowl and jug, vigorous and restive under the discipline of time. Three or four colours she used, to free them from the uniformity which might suggest just such a single bout of work as this; and as they dried, she took them from the warmth again.

When it came to the glazing, a few of the pieces were too large for double-dipping, and she had to give precious extra minutes to ladling the glaze over them; but all the processes were so easy and quick to her hands that there was little time lost. Nearly six o'clock; ten minutes only for the first slow drying, and then she dared wait no longer. She lifted the beaker, now so changed, and lowered it into the centre of the kiln.

Then suddenly she was still not satisfied. The chemical reactions of the kiln can never be calculated absolutely. Suppose there should be some influence left from the spirit and the oxide even yet? Suppose it should combine with the flame to produce an unexpected shade of colour, a stain, a tinge of yellow which might be material enough for the expert? It was unlikely; but she could not be sure that it was impossible, even now. She knew of only one more thing she could do to suppress it for ever. Potters spend a great many of the hours of firing wondering what damage there may be to discover when the kiln is cooled and opened. It went against the grain to plan a deliberate burst, and the desired results might even evade her against all the odds, but she could do what was indicated to encourage it. She took a large jug, one of the green pieces she had lifted from the kiln only an hour ago, and dipped it, draining off the surplus glaze, and set it next to the beaker. Now she knew why the skill of her own painting had ached in her fingers, since it was all to be thrown away. Most of that urgent beauty would be stillborn, spattered with fragments of the burst jug, flattened into a shapeless lump with it, a mass of molten glaze and distorted body. She felt, for the first time, a criminal, almost a murderer, turning back thus against her own nature; but she went on quickly with her loading, drawing out the deep, reproachful pain until the bottom of the kiln was full, and the bat shelves lowered into place like a gravestone over the crime.

By twenty minutes past six she had the brick cover closed over the last of her sacrificial offering, and had switched on the remaining elements. For the sake of speed she must make the necessary heat as soon as possible, and the soft-fired glazes needed no such slow first firing as the harder stonewares. Moreover, it was the rapid ascent of temperature which would burst the raw jug, and make undetectable for ever the form of the beaker. It had stood for over a year in Theo's studio, a few people might remember it and miss it; but no one would ever identify it after today.

Clearing away her materials in haste, she went back into the house. The chilly first hint of daylight was beginning; the moon swam low along the horizon, and while she had been deaf to everything outside the walls of the workshop, the sounds of earliest traffic had begun, faint and constant along the high road. The lane which passed the gate of Little Worth had scarcely a foot on it yet, but there was always the possibility of a passing bicycle heading for one of the farms. She knew exactly what she had to do now, and in what order. First, there was the note she had promised Dennis; while there was still the half of darkness to cover her, she must go down to the gate, and leave it under the stone there. Then the credible morning activities of making coffee and beginning to prepare breakfast. Then, a natural enough action, she would take a cup of coffee to her husband who had worked all night in the studio; and she would find him dead, and give the alarm.

There was so little time left that the note could say only what was essential. It had no endearments, and little information, and above all, no names; then if it fell into the wrong hands it could be less certainly assumed that it had anything to do with Dennis. She had to think of all these things now. She ordered; it was necessary, because only she knew what had to be done and said.

'Don't come in. Go on quickly, read this later. Soon you will be questioned about what happened here last night. You came, but *you were never in the studio, you did not see him. There never was a biscuit beaker*. Otherwise, tell the truth. Come as usual, behave as usual. I rely on you.'

That was all. She did not say that there had been a death

in the night. If he knew it already, why waste words? And if he did not, so much the more convincing would he be when he was questioned.

She ran up the stairs and dressed in haste, and then let herself out by the yard door and ran all down the drive, which was so dry and hard that it would take no prints from her shoes, nor leave any damp upon them. Nothing appeared in the lane as she thrust the note under the stone.

Half-past six, and she was back in the house, and the door shut behind her. She laid the cloth in the kitchen while the coffee was coming to the boil. Her heart was thudding and her ears rang with running, but she could not rest yet. Now she had either to call the police so quickly and urgently that they might be already busy in the studio by the time Dennis passed at a quarter to eight, or else delay until he was safely gone by; and of these two courses the first seemed to her the more convincing, since she was habitually an early riser, and it might reasonably be supposed that she would waste no time in hunting out a tired husband who had worked all night. There remained, however, the frightful risk that Dennis might stop his motor-cycle at the gate just as the police came along the lane, or while they were still at the front of the house, within sight of the gate. Weighing the dangers which every way confronted them, she thought this, on reflection, perhaps the least of them. The sense of caution about their affairs had been his from the beginning, never hers; he would be as defensively careful about retrieving his note unobserved, as if her reputation had really depended upon his secrecy.

When the coffee was made, she poured two cups, and leaving her own upon the kitchen table, crossed the corridor with the second, and let herself into the studio.

The sickness of shock which had failed to reach her at the first confrontation struck at her this time viciously, in the sudden wave of nauseous air, and the extraordinarily pitiful insignificance of the fallen body. She did not have to simulate the sudden violent shaking of her hand as she set down the cup upon the bench, spilling coffee into the saucer as it chattered to rest. The encroaching daylight had faded the yellowish light from the electric bulb, and changed the values of the colours on Theo's canvas. The conflicting rays fought over the body, pulling it this way and that in a shoddy huddle of clothes. He looked curiously small and shrunken by comparison with his living look. She had never thought how irrelevant, how like a discarded and disreputable old jacket, the body of a gifted and beloved person can look when the large motions of mind and spirit have withdrawn from it.

The nearest telephone was a call-box at the cross-roads, ten minutes' walk from the gate; but by crossing the field to the distant corner, and there climbing over the fence, and running the rest of the way, she reached the box in just over five minutes. When the police station answered her call, she hardly recognised her own voice, blown with running as it was. If the effect had been calculated, it could not have been better done.

'Police? Please come out to Little Worth at once! It's very urgent! This is Mrs. Freeland speaking – I've just found my husband dead in his studio!'

3

'You understand, Mrs. Freeland,' said the doctor, 'that I can't give a certificate. There's nothing in your husband's medical history to lead one to expect a sudden death of this kind. He was a thoroughly healthy man. There'll have to be an inquest, and probably an autopsy will be necessary to find out the real cause of death.' He looked at her with the grave, considerate courtesy proper to the occasion, but she thought that he already knew the cause of death very well. If he did not, she could have told him; but perhaps he was not well informed about the wealth of risky material potters handle, and the volume of knowledge they possess about it.

'I expected that,' she said. 'I could see it wasn't a natural death.'

'That being so, it passes into the hands of the coroner now. I'm very sorry! If there's anything I can do—'

He looked a little embarrassed over his condolences, as if it were already in order to wonder whether she should really be condoled with or congratulated. It was, she thought, a fair warning of what was to come.

'Thank you, you're very kind. I quite understand the position.'

He went away with an almost imperceptible shrug, and left her to the sergeant. The police ambulance was in the yard by that time, and a thick-set little surgeon had bustled through the house to the studio, and after him the photographer, and an inspector, and an indeterminate young man in plain clothes, who might or might not be another policeman. The house was no longer either hers or Theo's, it belonged to the great British public and the administrators of its judicial system. That was something she fully understood.

'And now,' said the sergeant, 'if you feel up to it, I'd like you to tell me all you can about what's happened, Mrs. Freeland. Just in your own words, if you please! I may need to ask you some more questions afterwards, but we shall have a foundation to work on, then, shan't we?'

The sergeant was a middle-aged man, who had been in Great Leddington now for some years, and knew most of the inhabitants; a quiet, thoughtful, plaintive person with a level eye and a low voice. She had often seen him, occasionally talked to him; it surprised her a little now to reflect that she did not know his name. His constable was a bright little Londoner, alert and pale, prompt at his superior's elbow like an accomplished terrier.

'My husband worked all last night,' she said. 'It wasn't unusual for him to do that, if he felt in the mood, and was working on something that made it possible. He's done it a good many times. I never interfered with him. He was also . . . drinking fairly heavily, and had been for some days. That wasn't unusual, either, and it never stopped him working. I don't think I ever knew him really incapable.

'I had begun to load my kiln, late in the evening, but I was interrupted, and I didn't quite finish getting it ready to fire.'

'You were interrupted? By a visitor, or something?'

'Yes, a friend of ours called. Dennis Forbes – he was often here. So I didn't have time to finish what I was doing, and had to leave it until this morning. When Dennis went home I was tired, and I went to bed rather early.'

'Perhaps you could give me times,' suggested the sergeant, as she paused.

'He came about nine, and I think it must have been just turned half-past nine when he left, but I can't be positive to ten minutes or so. I suppose I was up for about half an hour after that. I must have gone to bed very soon after ten.'

'You didn't interrupt your husband in his studio – you and your friend?'

'It wouldn't have been much use, he was too drunk to care about people. No, we didn't go in there. We stayed talking in here for a while, and then Dennis went home, and I cleared things up a little, and went to bed.'

'You never heard any sound – any cry, for instance, from the studio – after you retired?'

'No, nothing.'

'And you weren't alarmed that Mr. Freeland didn't join you?'

'It wouldn't have alarmed me, no. But as I fell asleep quite soon, I didn't know whether he'd come to bed or not, until I got up this morning. We're not sharing a room,' she said, raising her eyes suddenly to his face.

'I see! May I ask – was that arrangement of old standing, or did it indicate a . . . a recent change in your relationship?'

'A very recent change,' she said, gazing thoughtfully into the plaintive eyes which studied her with so much solicitude and so pointed an intelligence. 'It's all right! I understand that you have to enquire into that part of our lives, too.'

She waited for him to probe farther, but he asked her, instead: 'What about this morning? Tell me about that.'

'I awoke about six – a few minutes before, I think – and remembered my kiln, and wanted to finish loading it, and fire it as early as possible. So I got up, and went out to the workshop. It wasn't until I saw the light on in the studio window, when I went out at the back door, that I knew Theo was still up. I loaded and covered the kiln, and fired it, and then I came in and began to get the breakfast ready. We often had it in the kitchen, and didn't light this fire until later. I made the coffee, and took it in to him. And found him – as you've seen him.'

'What time would that be?'

'About a quarter to seven, as far as I can make out. I didn't stop to look at the clock then, I called you as quickly as I could. I must have been on the line about seven or eight minutes after I found him.'

'You thought at once there was something wrong about his death? You had no doubt that he *was* dead?'

'I touched his hand,' she said, paling. 'I saw his eyes. You've seen him yourself. What doubt could I have that he was dead? And how could it be a natural death – or at least, how could I jump to the conclusion that it was – when he was never ill? He was a very fit and a very strong man, in spite of drinking rather a lot. Of course I thought there was something wrong with it!'

'You had no other reason for thinking so, apart from his appearance?'

'No. Wasn't that enough? I'd never had any reason to think of death at all in connection with Theo. He was always rather more alive than other men.'

'You never thought, for instance, that he might have taken his own life?' he suggested, almost meekly.

'No, never!' She said it almost blankly, as if the question seemed to her silly rather than shocking.

'What makes you so positive about that? The most unexpected people do commit suicide.'

'Theo was on the side of life,' she said vehemently. The temptation to hesitate, to avow a doubt she did not feel, had just touched her heart with the first true convulsion of guilt towards him, and in consequence her words had a ritual ring about them, like a phrase of exorcism.

'I don't understand quite what you mean by that,' he said humbly.

'I don't know how to make it any clearer. There *are* people who are on the side of life, who live with their doors wide open to experience and to relationships, who like to do, and feel, and make things, and don't know how to be bored or in despair. There are other people who spend their whole lives warding off other people and avoiding experience, who don't want to spend energy in feeling, or creating, or liking, or anything that isn't as safe as the grave. I can believe they might kill themselves rather easily. But Theo was the first kind. I don't say it couldn't happen, but I do say it's extremely unlikely.'

'The best of us,' he suggested, watching her steadily, 'may have short moods against our nature. It wouldn't take long then to do something fatal, and there'd be no taking it back afterwards.'

'I've said it could happen. I still think it very improbable.'

'But he had rather special reasons for being unusually depressed just now, if his relations with you were disturbed? You don't think that would be enough to turn him to a course even as far out of his line as suicide?'

'I don't know,' she said, intensely pale. 'I can only say what I feel. It never seemed to me even a possibility.'

'But he was unhappy about the situation with you?'

'Yes – yes, he was.'

'May I ask if you had made any plans? Did you intend to leave him?'

'I had no plans at all. I didn't look further ahead than tomorrow. You can surely understand that. We didn't want to hurt each other, and there wasn't anything you could call a quarrel. There was only a reality, something that had happened, and that we had to accept and get used to. How we were going to make the adjustments was something we hadn't solved.'

'It must have been very much on your mind,' said the sergeant sympathetically. 'On the minds of both of you.'

She said nothing; she had already said enough, and truth and lies between them were tearing at the cords of her mind. In a moment he went back placidly to the events of the morning. 'You found the room just as you left it for us? The light was on? You moved nothing? Touched nothing?'

'I put the cup down – it's there still. I touched his hand. That's all!'

'I see! Well, I think that's all for now, Mrs. Freeland. Thank you for being so frank. It helps us, you know, when people don't treat us as their natural enemies. In a few minutes I'll ask you to read your statement through, and sign it. Presently the inspector will want to have a word with you. He's a very easy man – very considerate. He won't worry you any more than he can help.'

She was sure of it. With tender and chivalrous solicitude they would all combine to put a rope round her neck if they could, and probably only the bright, avid eyes of the young constable would betray any satisfaction when the thing was accomplished.

She heard the studio door opened wide at last, and voices in the corridor. The ambulance men were taking Theo's body away.

4

It was the inspector who took the matter further, an hour later, when the ambulance was gone, and only the plain-clothes man remained at work in the studio. The inspector was a very different person from his subordinate, a smooth, square, dark man with the manner of a business executive. He had her statement before him, and she was well aware that the swerves the sergeant had made from too personal enquiries would serve only as signposts to this man. Perhaps indeed they had been left clearly pointing the way to her private life for precisely that purpose. It did not matter. It was her intention, no less than his, that this part of the truth should come to light early and convincingly, without too much reserve on her part, but still with the fastidious reluctance which might be expected from even the most candid of women upon such a subject. Since he had to hear about Dennis from one source or another, he should hear it from her, in circumstances which would fight on their side, instead of against them.

He asked her, looking up from the statement she had already signed: 'Mrs. Freeland, do you know of anything which might have caused your husband to take his own life? I gather you don't believe very much in that possibility, but you'll understand that we have to consider everything.'

'The idea seems to me so incongruous in connection with Theo,' she said, carefully and quietly, 'that I haven't been able to get my mind to entertain it at all. I'm trying to see it from your point of view, but I still can't believe in it. No, there was nothing that was likely to make him do a thing like that.'

'But you do know of at least one reason he had for being anxious and unhappy. Your statement makes that clear. His relations with you had undergone a change – a sudden change, after so many years together?' When she was silent, he went on, not ungently, but without any warmth: 'I know these are questions you would prefer not to have to answer. We would prefer, for that matter, not to have to ask them. But your husband is dead, and as you were very quick to perceive, his death was certainly not natural. It is absolutely necessary that we should not miss any clue to his state of mind.'

'I understand that. I am not trying to suppress anything – if it could shed any light—'

'You must let us be the judges of that. Had you quarrelled with your husband, for instance? Was there a complete estrangement?'

'No. It was not like that at all. You could, perhaps, call it an estrangement, but there was no quarrel. It was – just something that happened, and altered the relationship between us. Neither of us could have prevented it, even if we'd seen it coming. But it was no good pretending that everything was just the same as before.' She turned her head away from him, tormentedly. 'I'm not trying to suppress any of the facts – but you must understand that it isn't easy to find the right words. These are things one doesn't have to say every day, and accuracy is part of the truth, isn't it? I must get it right. Give me a little time to think!'

'You're afraid it may have something to do with your husband's death, after all?' suggested the inspector, watching her narrowly from under his broad, white and motionless eyelids.

'No!'

'Unhappy men shock their families daily by choosing a quick way out. Your husband was hardly likely to be any more immune from despair than the rest of mankind. You had really better tell me exactly what had come between you. There was, perhaps, some third person involved?'

'Yes,' she said in a very low voice, 'yes, there was.'

'A young man?'

'Yes,' she said again, in a deep and understanding sigh. He was not a native of Great Leddington for nothing; he knew already the body of the rumour, most probably he knew even the name.

'You had – fallen in love with him? If you care to go on in your own words—?'

She drew a long breath, considering him through her lashes with a look as cold as his own. 'Yes, I had fallen in love with him. Theo brought him home one evening – or rather, he brought Theo, who was gloriously drunk at the time. My husband was always picking up the most odd acquaintances, and making bosom friends of them, there was nothing at all unusual in it. I didn't see this man again for almost a month, then he came to the pottery exhibition I had in the town, and we met him again, and Theo invited him here. He became a regular visitor after that, we were both rather fond of him. And I – fell in love with him. And he with me. It was something none of us had bargained for.'

'I see!' he said, slowly and dryly. 'Your husband knew what had happened?'

'Not immediately, but lately he did.'

'How did that happen?'

'I told him. There was nothing secret about it.'

The first look of surprise, faint and under strict control, saluted this statement. She met it with a wide, dark stare, and went on with a hardening voice: 'If you have to know all the private parts of our lives, I prefer that you should have the facts correct. Rather more is involved than a bald confession of misconduct, you know. My husband and I have been married for ten years, and been the best of friends all that time. We had a lot in common, and we fondly believed – at least, I did – that we loved each other. You see, there are so many ways of loving people. This happened to be a way I'd never imagined before.'

'The young man has been your lover?' It was the kind of direct question she had invited, and she met it squarely, her eyes flaring green and bright.

'The young man *is* my lover.'

'You told your husband that, too?'

'Naturally! It was not a matter for less than the whole truth.'

'I see! And then you . . . felt unable to continue sharing a room with him any longer? Or was that his decision?'

'I have all the prejudices of the female brought up in a monandrous society,' she said, with a pale and savage smile, 'against being married to two men at a time.'

'And you considered yourself married to the man with whom you were in love?' The words sounded dry and practical in his mouth, like a formula, neither friendly nor inimical, but absolutely neutral.

'In every sense but the literal one, yes.'

'You had better tell me his name,' he suggested in the same tone.

'Is it really necessary? Oh, well, I suppose it is. His name is Dennis Forbes. He lives in Lancelot Road – I'm sorry I don't know the number, but I don't suppose that will give you any trouble. He works at Grover's Garage, on the London Road – that's how Theo got to know him in the first place. I mentioned him to the sergeant, too – he was here for half an hour last night.'

He made a note of it, without any change of expression. 'And what was the situation with regard to your husband? How did he take this?'

'He was very unhappy about it. I tried to discuss it with him. I hoped that between us we could find some decent arrangement that wouldn't hurt anyone more than was necessary. It had happened, there was no sense in pretending that we could go back and start again. But Theo preferred to avoid the issue. He would talk to me as usual about everything else, but not about that. I don't know whether he had any clear idea of what he was going to gain by it, but I think subconsciously he hoped that if he shut his eyes and took no notice of it, it would go away. And that's how it stood yesterday. He wouldn't meet us about it, but he wouldn't oppose us, either. He was waiting, and fending it off.'

'An intolerable situation for everyone,' said the inspector sympathetically.

'It was difficult – and painful.'

'You had no plans for ending it?'

'No. I didn't know what was to happen. We didn't want to hurt each other more than we had to, but I thought if we waited a little longer it might become easier to find a way out. No one can feel at the same intense pressure for ever, without any fuel at all. I was willing to wait. We had something worth waiting for, and I didn't want to dirty it.'

'But you don't think your husband may have taken his own way out?'

'I can't tell. But everything I know about him is against it. I don't believe he ever would.'

'It is possible,' said the inspector sombrely, 'that you might be the last person to realise how fatally you had wounded him? The mind makes all sorts of alibis for itself. It prefers, as a rule, not to acknowledge that one may have been responsible for another person's death.'

Suspiria's pale face whitened to the dead blanched texture of a waxen flower. Her lips said after him, soundlessly: 'It is possible.'

He left her then, to think about the final thing which he had not said, though she had felt it clearly formulated in his mind. 'Someone, at any rate, found a way out. If not your husband, perhaps you?' But all he said, as he buttoned his coat and pocketed his papers, was: 'The coroner has been informed, of course. I'm afraid you'll have a disturbed life for a few days, Mrs. Freeland, but we'll try to make it as easy for you as we can.'

'Motive and opportunity,' she thought, when he was gone, and she was alone in mid-morning with the sealed studio and the empty house, 'is about half of a case. And that's all you'll get. Beyond that, all you can hope for is to break me down into making admissions against myself – or him. And you won't get much that way. Motive and opportunity! For what they're worth, you'll have to be satisfied with those.'

5

Dennis read the note a second time at the back of the garage, while he was hanging up his coat. Then he put a match to the corner of the paper, and dropped the last remnant outside the door to burn out to a few fragments of black ash, which he ground to powder under his heel, and fanned away to the wind. He did not examine the reasons why he did this; the act was instinctive, and his mind, even had he questioned it, a turmoil of twisting threads of thought, to none of which could he find any end.

'Soon you will be questioned—' By whom, then, but the police? Who else erupts in people's lives at a moment's notice, and begins asking questions? 'You were never in the studio, you did not see him, there never was a biscuit beaker.' To these things she would be swearing, it seemed, long before anyone came near him. Whatever she said had to be buttressed into position, cemented, made safe at all costs. All right, be easy about that, at any rate, my love, my darling, my voice is yours, to say whatever you need said, and swear to it until I go dumb. I was not in the studio last night. I did not see Theo. I never saw any biscuit beaker there in my life. As for the rest, I shall come to you as soon as I can, and I love you, and always shall. And that's the whole truth.

But he worked through the morning with his heart every moment high in his throat, waiting for the expected figure and the interrogative voice, and nothing happened. George seemed to find nothing wrong with him, and his hands went about their business as competently as usual, though his mind was very far from Grover's Garage. The expected constriction of his senses did not come until he rode home for his dinner at one o'clock, and let himself into the house by the back door. He would have broken the ride at Little Worth, but for her injunction, sacred like everything she had enjoined upon him in this blind journey, that he must behave as usual. He had never called there at midday, nor even gone home by that way, so he did not do so now. To do what he regularly did every day was easy; to be as he was every day, with that flare of fear and uncertainty burning his mind into a dark void, was impossible, but he could do his best to seem so. He pushed open the kitchen door, and walked in on his family with:

'Hullo, whose is the bike outside? Have we got a visitor?'

Three wondering and wary faces, large and alert of eye, confronted him instantly with three wide, warning stares. His mother was sitting on the edge of her usual chair by the fire, while Winnie perched on the wooden arm with a hand reassuringly on her shoulder. Harold was at the table, but had not touched the contents of the plate before him. It was he who jerked a thumb meaningly over his shoulder towards the parlour door, and said in a low tone:

'There's a chap to see *you*. Been waiting twenty minutes.'

'Oh!' said Dennis, halting abruptly. 'Who is it?'

His mother said in a wailing whisper: 'It's a policeman!' The tone was the fatalistic lament of even the most law-abiding parent, confronted with a policeman anxious to interview her son. Her eyes looked as if they wanted to weep, but she was unused to tears and only a moist brightness rose to answer the deep, scandalised anxiety she felt for him. He stared at her with a puzzled frown, and the hint of an incredulous grin curling his lips.

'A policeman? After *me*? What on earth does he want with me?'

'Better go and see,' said Harold. 'He didn't tell us.'

'Oh – all right, I suppose I'd better.' It was not so hard to look mystified, and a little uneasy, and still a shade sceptical, too, as if the whole thing were no more than an elaborate leg-pull. He passed between them, still dubiously frowning, patted his mother's shoulder in passing, and said cheerfully: 'Well, don't look like that about it! He hasn't come to run me in, whatever it is!' But she did not laugh. She let him go by in foreboding silence, shaken by the contact of her deep disquiet.

He opened the parlour door upon the vision of the sad-eyed elderly sergeant, who was sitting with his back to the lace-curtained window, steadily watching the door.

'Mr. Dennis Forbes?'

'Yes. You wanted to see me?' He advanced into the room, and closed the door carefully behind him. Now that it was beginning, he was not so much afraid. Everything which has a form can be fought. He stood in the full light from the window, his face keeping its mask of slightly withdrawn and resentful bewilderment, and the slight, boyish uneasiness, too, as if he were searching his memory for minor sins.

'I shan't keep you very long, Mr. Forbes. My name's Grayne.'

'I know!' said Dennis. 'I've often seen you around the town, of course, Sergeant. But—'

'You're a friend of Mr. Theodore Freeland, of Little Worth, I believe?'

'Yes, I know him. Why, what—'

'An intimate friend? You often visited there, I'm told.'

'Quite often. Yes, I suppose you could say an intimate friend.' The mystified eyes, the minute, anxious frown pursued the enquiry, but he did not make a second attempt to put it into words.

'I'm enquiring into the sudden death of Mr. Freeland,' said Sergeant Grayne, striking the ground from under him without the quiver of a lash. 'Perhaps you'll be so good as to tell me when you last saw him?'

Dennis felt as if his knees had really given under him. He reached back for the edge of the table, and leaned back against it, feeling it groan as it took his weight. '*Dead?* Theo Freeland? But *how*? Why, there was nothing wrong with him last night – he was working in the studio when I was there.'

'Oh, you saw him alive and well last night?' said the sergeant, taking him up promptly and gently.

'Well, no, I didn't actually *see* him. But he was there, all right, I heard him moving about in the studio, and Mrs. Freeland said he'd been in there working most of the day.'

'You didn't actually go in, then, and talk to him yourself?'

'No. But she would have said if there'd been anything the matter. What on earth's happened to him? I don't understand how you come into it, anyhow, unless there's been an accident, or something. *Mrs.* Freeland's all right, isn't she?' His voice flew into a passion of consternation and concern, almost without any prompting, because for her his whole body and mind were already full of wild anxiety which was in desperate need of expression, and spilled easily and naturally into words. 'Do tell me, please! They're *friends* of mine!' Suddenly he understood that the twenty minutes the sergeant had spent there waiting for him had not been idle; he had already been at the other three for details of the connection with the Freelands, and especially for information about his movements on the previous evening.

'Mr. Freeland was found dead early this morning, by his wife. The cause of his death won't be known until after the post-mortem, but it seems likely it wasn't a natural one. That's how we come into it, Mr. Forbes.'

Dennis said: 'Oh, my God, poor Spiri! Is she all alone up there? There's nobody she can ask— Look, please, whatever you want from me, let's get on with it, quickly! I'd like to go and see her before I go back to work – the garage can wait, the hell with it if I'm a bit late! But I take it you want to know anything I can tell you at once, so please make it as short as you can!'

'Very proper concern in a friend, I'm sure,' said the sergeant, with a curious lack of all emphasis.

Dennis put up his head, almost after Suspiria's fashion, and gave him back a hot and arrogant stare, but said nothing.

'What exactly was your relationship with Mr. and Mrs. Freeland, if I may ask? A friend of his? Or hers? You didn't bother to disturb him last night, for instance.'

'He – didn't want to be disturbed, he was working. I was only there about half an hour, anyhow. I think it was just before nine when I got there. I went through to her workshop. She was loading the kiln, but she stopped work, and came through again into the house, and talked to me for a bit. The light was on in the studio, and he was hard at it in there, so we left him to it. We talked till just after half-past nine, and then I came away. She was tired, she said she was going to bed pretty early. As for whose friend I was – am – well, both of them. I knew him first, and he asked me there, and then I got to know her, too.'

'Quite intimately, I understand?'

Two small, hot flames of colour burned up in Dennis's cheeks, but he said nothing, deliberately and visibly shutting his lips hard upon an angry rejoinder.

'So you didn't actually see him, you only heard someone moving around in there? And when was the last occasion you really saw him?'

'I haven't seen him for eight days. Until yesterday I hadn't been to the house for a week.'

'Well, for the moment I don't think I need bother you any longer, sir, if you'll be so good as to come round to the police station as soon as you finish work this evening, and make a statement. Just the times, you know, to help to fill in all the details of yesterday evening. Nobody else was there to tell us anything about it, you see. A very lonely life, that, for a young woman.' His eyes dwelt speculatively upon the boy's face, and the burning spots of colour deepened into an angry flush, but still there was no answer. 'We'll expect you about six? Just what you've told me, you know. It isn't much, but every detail helps. If there's anything else you remember noticing— and as a matter of form, we shall need your fingerprints.'

He rose, gathering up his hat, and moved before Dennis out of the room, and with murmured leave-takings passed by the silent trio in the kitchen. Even when the door had closed on him they did not move for a moment, nor relax their strained poses. Then all their scared and outraged eyes turned and fixed upon Dennis.

Mrs. Forbes got up from her chair and threw herself into his arms, the grudging tears overflowing. 'Oh, Dennis, love, what is it? What did he want with you? You haven't done anything! All those questions he's been asking us – where were you last night, what time did you come in, how long have you known those Freeland people— Oh, what's happened? What have you been doing?'

He put his arms round her in a perfunctory fashion, and held her gently, but his eyes were straining past her towards the door, and his mind was already away, ahead of him, towards the lonely house under the hanging woods. 'I haven't been doing anything! It's all right, Mum, really it is! They have to ask everyone who might know something. Mr. Freeland's dead – suddenly. They don't know how, yet. I've got to go out again,' he said, drawing away from her.

'What, now, at once? Without your dinner?' she demanded indignantly, scrubbing at her eyes.

'It's all right, I don't want any dinner.'

'Nonsense, of course you must eat – such a cold day, and all! Oh, dear,' she wailed, breaking into fresh tears, 'why should he think *you'd* know anything about it, if the man's dead?'

'It's their job. They have to try everything. I was there last night. I was one of the last to see him, I suppose. Well, not *see* him, exactly, but I heard him knocking about in his studio. They'll be asking other people things, too, it isn't only me. Mum, really it's all right! Don't fret about it. Look, I've got to go—'

But she took him by the shoulders, and pushed him into a chair at the table, and to satisfy her he had to stay long enough to bolt a few choking mouthfuls. The other two, great-eyed still, watched him and stoned him with questions, while he turned his head restlessly this way and that to avoid them, as if they had indeed been missiles.

'They seemed to know all about your being so friendly with the Freelands. Did you know it was all over the neighbourhood, like that? What has it got to do with the police?'

'What's happened to him, anyhow? Are they going to say he didn't die a natural death?'

'It isn't going to turn out to be a scandal, is it? If he did himself in, why should you be supposed to know anything about it? And if – if somebody else killed him—' Winnie's voice faded out at the sudden and terrible thought.

'Oh, my God, Winnie, don't say such things!'

He flinched from his mother's cry, and shrank sideways from the arm she flung protectively round his shoulders. 'Oh, let me alone! I know no more than you do. What's the good of talking about it? I shall tell them what they ask me, I can't do any more.' He got up, and pulled himself roughly out of her hands, and plunged upon his coat.

'You're going to that woman!' said his mother, her voice shrilling upward in vindictive alarm.

'Yes, of course I am! For God's sake, why shouldn't I? She's by herself up there. Don't you stand by your friends when they're in trouble?'

'None of our friends ever got us into a murder case, that I can remember,' said Harold sharply.

'It wouldn't be any good their leaning on you, if they did, I know that.' He whipped up his helmet, and flung out, and in a minute more they heard the engine of the motor-bike stutter into life. He was away along Lancelot Road in a burst of frenzied speed, wild to overtake heart, and mind, and spirit in their indignant flight to Suspiria. He was free to go to her now. The police themselves had set him free. He had to behave normally, but normality for a man who had just heard of his rival's sudden death in threatening circumstances was precisely this headlong dash to sustain and protect the woman.

She knew the note of his machine, and was tearing open the door before he reached it. She walked into his arms, and he held her against his heart for an instant before she drew him into the house. Apart from an intense pallor and a look of strain she was much as usual, her eyes steady, her mouth a little drawn with tiredness, but remarkably composed and assured.

'It's all right, there's no one here. They'll be back again and again, but they're not here now.' She shut the door behind them, and caught him to her heart again in the warm obscurity just within it. He kissed her, a long insatiable kiss into which all their mutual disquiet seemed to flow and mingle, burning their lips with a bitter heat. 'You mustn't stay,' she said then, emerging. 'You must go back to work, everything has to be normal. They've been to you already?'

'They were waiting for me at home. They want a statement from me tonight. They're in no hurry with me, I think. It's *you* I'm frantic for.'

'It's no use being frantic. Listen, did you destroy my note?'

'It's burned – that's all right. I told them what time I came and left last night. I said I came to the workshop for you, and we came back in here and talked until after half-past nine. What did we talk about? Sooner or later they'll want to know.'

'About ourselves. About our hope of having a future together. We weren't likely to talk about anything else. Not about him – except to go on hoping he'd come to some compromise with us. Is there anything else?'

How little there was to be said, now that they were together! So little that their lips were as often locked silent in one motionless, intent knot as speaking. There were all manner of things which could have been said, but few which needed saying, and all that was not essential was swept aside out of their minds.

'Yes! Listen – if they ask you at what stage Theo found out, you don't know. You know I told him the truth, but not exactly when. Do you understand?'

'Yes, of course! A week isn't much – it's too apt. Yes, I understand! Spiri!' he said. 'We're conspiring – do you know that? Just as if we were guilty!'

'Yes, exactly as if we were guilty. We, or one of us. And listen – listen!' She took him by the shoulders fiercely, and shook him hard, so that in sheer surprise he froze into the stillness of a chidden and threatened child. 'The story I've told this morning is the story we've got to go on telling – without a single discrepancy, as often as we're asked, no matter what they drag out to try and shock us into changing it, that is our story. Do you understand? No matter what happens, if we begin to make changes they have us! The only way we can keep them in doubt for ever and ever is by being absolutely, patiently, perfectly consistent. It may be a thin story, it may be full of gaps, but if we tell it and tell and tell it until they give up hope of getting us to change it, *they cannot disprove it*! If ever there comes a time when you get nervous about it, and think you could make an improvement on it, don't do it! And, Dennis – if one of us is arrested—'

She heard the stab of his deep indrawn breath, almost as sharp as a cry. She put up a hand, and drew his head down to hers, cheek to cheek, her palm cupped softly about his temple, the fingers threading his hair. 'Hush, my dearest, my heart! You know it may happen. There is no one in this but the three of us. So remember, if it should be I – *you have got to hold your tongue*! It's the only thing to do. Any attempt to shift the suspicion would only bring both of us into it, and discredit everything we've already said. But if we stick it out to the end they won't get a conviction. There isn't any real evidence *unless we give it to them*. If you try to save me, you may well kill me. If I tried to save you, I might kill you. So be quiet, at all costs! Do you understand me? Then promise me, as I promise you?'

He whispered, deeply shaken: 'But they can't believe it's you!'

'They're wonderfully patient and consistent themselves. They don't believe it's anyone – yet. Not until they're sure of the cause of death. I'm only looking ahead. We have to be ready. Promise!'

'I promise – except that in an emergency I've got to be free to judge for myself. Something that hasn't been taken into account could easily happen. It might mean both our lives.'

'Promise, at least, not to change your story until you've asked me – for any reason. For my sake, Dennis!'

'All right, I can swear to that. Oh, Spiri, oh, my lovely!' he whispered. 'Was it very ugly?'

'It wasn't pretty. They've taken him away now. The studio is sealed up. Maybe they'll want some exhibits from there, when the inquest comes on. Did you tell them everything? About us?'

'No, but he knew. He said some things – pointed things –

trying to draw me. I said nothing. But some other way, I think I'd be glad to tell.'

'You can,' she said, 'I have. Everything. I was glad, too. And it's better told by us than by someone else, because by this time there are very few people in this town who don't know. But you understand it will be called a motive? The only motive!'

'All the more reason we should tell it our way,' he said fiercely.

'I thought so, too.'

'Spiri – what did you do with the beaker?'

'It's in the kiln,' she said. 'Nobody will ever identify it again. I was afraid they might tell me to switch it off, but nobody took much notice of it, and now it's too late, the glaze is already melted.'

'Then – it's a glost kiln you were loading when I came last night?'

'Yes – yes! For God's sake don't forget!'

'I shan't forget. Spiri, isn't there anything else I can do for you? Isn't there anything at all?'

'You can go on loving me,' she said.

'You know I shall always love you.' And after a while he sighed, almost too softly to be heard: 'Poor Theo!' and she understood that he was confronted for the first time, most piteously, with the thought of the impervious isolation of the dead, who are out of the turmoil of experience for good and all, past loving or suffering. He asked, after a moment's hesitation: 'They didn't tell me – perhaps they really don't know yet – how did he die? What *was* it that killed him?'

Suspiria held him off for a moment to look closely into his face, but she knew that the look would tell her nothing. There was so little time for considering anything but the mere fused urgency of their two lives. From now on they were one creature walking delicately among many dangers, directed by a single wild and frightened intelligence, and with no energy to spare for anything but the battle to remain alive. What point would there be in asking questions of which the answers would have no virtue? All creatures but those who have already renounced their lives will deny mortal guilt when they are challenged with it, and more than deny, act out the denial vehemently in every particular, even to challenging others with the same guilt. Ask if he loves you, ask if he would die for you, and you may get a pure truth in return, and know it certainly for what it is. But don't ask him if he doesn't already know what killed Theo, because there is only one answer to that, truth or lie, only one. And since you know what it is, why ask the question? And since you know what it is, you know how little enlightenment there can be in it. If you ask it, and he answers, you'll be no wiser than before.

So all she said was: 'It was poison – antimony oxide. The sediment was still lying in the beaker when I found him, that's why it had to disappear. They'll feel pretty sure I've tampered with the evidence, of course, but they won't be able to prove it. And feeling sure isn't enough.'

'Where would he get hold of antimony oxide? It isn't exactly – a household medicine, is it?'

'From my workshop,' she said. 'It's used for making a yellow pigment. You mixed a glaze for me once with it. Didn't you know?'

He was about to say: 'No!' when he realised that it would mean nothing if he did say it. And then, hard on the heels of this shock of knowledge, he recognised how little the question itself had meant, and turned back all the more wildly from making any answer. It was not as if it mattered now. There was virtually only one problem for either of them, and that was to preserve their two threatened lives. Nothing existed in the world but their love and their danger; there was no room anywhere for guilt or innocence.

CHAPTER SIX:

The Several Faces of Truth

1

'THERE ARE just five possibilities,' said Inspector Tarrant, hunched over his desk with the analyst's preliminary report before him. 'One, he took the stuff by accident; two, he took it deliberately, with the intention of killing himself, and putting an end to an intolerable situation; three, the wife and the boy fixed it up between them to get rid of him; four, the boy gave him the stuff without the wife knowing about it; and five, the wife did it by *her*self. There's nobody else in the affair at all. There never was a stage with fewer players on it.'

'Not a lot of cover,' admitted Sergeant Grayne, regarding him thoughtfully across the neat folder of papers. 'Take a bold person or a desperate one to plan a murder in those conditions.'

'Or a cool and able one, willing to make do with a near shave and the benefit of the doubt. Because, let's face it, if there's not much cover, there's hardly more material to hide. Never was a stage with fewer entrances, exits, or props, either.'

'You haven't got the surgeon's full report yet?'

'No, only the analysis of the vomited matter, but it doesn't leave much doubt. A high content of antimony oxide, more than enough to produce acute antimonial poisoning. The stuff acts rather like arsenic, with violent gastric symptoms. The attack may come on as early as ten minutes after taking, but more likely from an hour to two or three hours. Until we get a full report on this particular case we can't begin to consider the time element. What we can do is to have another look round for the stuff, and take a quick glance at our five possibilities – taking into consideration the nature of the death. Supposing you wanted to do away with yourself, Grayne, would *you* swallow something that was going to inflame your inside in an extremely painful way, and send you into convulsions?'

'No, sir,' said the sergeant, without any surprise. 'I've often thought, in a quite academic way, as you might say, that the only thing I could face would be a nice, quiet-flowing river. And then only in the warm weather. And then, you see, a man who wanted to get his wife back from another fellow, even if he had to be dead to do it, would take care to look a bit more romantic and dignified when found – if you see what I mean.'

'I doubt if they really think like that. To reach the point where you could consider getting out, I should think you'd have to pass the point where you cared how you looked. But I might be wrong, at that. And this was the artist. The proper presentation of form and proportion would mean more to him than it would to me. Maybe he wanted to make things worse for her by the offensive manner of his exit – she being an artist, too.'

'But she won't have it that he was a possible suicide. Very strong views on the matter she has. If genuine!' He looked very thoughtful for a moment, remembering the exact and scrupulous calm of the voice which had informed him that Theo was on the side of life. It had taken his fancy, because it was a means of classifying mankind which had never yet occurred to him, and he had caught himself trying to fit his superiors into these two simple categories, and achieving some curious results.

'That's a large question. But let's look at our five possibilities, and see what points can be made against them. One, the accident theory. Against that is the fact that so far we've found nothing in the studio which could possibly be the source of the antimony oxide. I gather it could be slipped in the sugar, or anything of that kind – but nothing he had consumable in the studio resembled it or would hide it. It is largely insoluble. The whisky and the soda are as innocent as they look. Not only is there no sign of the stuff itself, but there's no sign of any vessel in which he may have taken it. He'd nothing but drinks in there. And according to the map he left us in flake-white he must have spent several hours in the studio before he fell and died, without once going near the door. Traces of a murder may vanish, traces of a suicide, too, if a tidy or a vindictive mind planned it. But traces of an accident don't get cleared away by themselves, like that. His stove seems to have been burning until about three in the morning, but there's no sign of anything suspicious having been burned in it. Supposing he'd had some of this stuff there in a paper packet, and tossed it off in a toddy by mistake for sugar, he might conceivably have thrown the paper into the stove, and there wouldn't be any traces. But then there'd be the sediment of the stuff itself in his glass. And there wasn't.

'Two, the suicide theory. The same points are against it. He didn't leave the room to fetch the antimony. If he had it by him, and decided to use it, once again how did he take it? Empty it into his mouth, and swill it down with whisky, then burn the paper he had it in? It could happen, I'm not saying it couldn't. But there wasn't so much as the smear of anything odd on the lip of that broken glass, and I can't help feeling there would have been. Still, leave that in – it may not be probable, but it is possible.

'Third, the conspiracy theory.'

He hesitated, and sighed, watching his subordinate's face: 'What did you think of the young man?'

'My impression was that he was on the level. There was nothing that didn't ring right, nothing at all. Usually there's something, if it's only a word, that makes your hackles rise, and says: "Look out, you're being got at!" One thing I'm sure of, there's no lie about their being in love. Both of 'em! Poor devils!' he said. 'What can they expect to get out of it, even if they get over this business? Fourteen years, as near as need be, in between them, and as different as chalk and cheese. What sort of a set-up would that be in twenty years time? They'd better have poured poison into each other, if you ask me. It may come to that, in the finish!'

'Ordinarily one would say the most likely thing was they should both be in it. Look at all the cases that have worked out that way, two sides of a triangle getting rid of the third side so they could lie together. But there's a difference here. It gets in the way however you look at it. Do you know there's hardly a soul in Great Leddington, barring the ones who never follow the local gossip, who didn't know or guess that this boy was her lover? They went about fairly shining with it, so I'm told. They had it, and they meant keeping it. He knew – the husband knew. What had they got to gain by removing him? They weren't afraid of him, or of public opinion, as far as I can see. Marriage? Well, it might have been nice to have, but I can't see that either of them was much bothered about it. As she said, she felt pretty solidly married to the boy already. No, nobody was likely to remove Freeland so that they could get married – unless the boy had a lingering hankering after respectability. I'm pretty sure she had none.'

'Jointly,' agreed Sergeant Grayne diffidently, 'there wasn't much inducement. But I think, sir, that for her there might be something to gain – for her, personally. She was being torn in two between these two. A dead husband might be quite a relief, after one that was always there, and always a reproach to her. It wasn't that she wouldn't have done what she wanted, but she might not have been able to rest when she'd done it. With the other one gone it was a problem solved.'

'But did she really have any conscience towards her husband? Was she really being pulled two ways?'

'Oh, yes, sir – I think you needn't doubt that. They've lived here a long time, you see. There's never been a word before, and never a quarrel between them. It isn't a matter of a promiscuous woman, you can take my word for that. Apart from him she's been married only to her art, as you might say. They didn't live like most of the townspeople, of course, it was a loose sort of attachment. But up to now there's never been more than two people in it.'

'So you think she might have killed him, in the end, to be rid of the extreme problem of choosing between them?'

'To be rid of the reproach of having chosen the other one, more – because she had,' said Sergeant Grayne positively, and lowered his mournful gaze deprecatingly into the crown of his hat.

'So the motive would be a great deal stronger in her case than in the boy's?'

'Well, given a woman like that, that wouldn't be held by conventions, and knowing what young men are at about twenty-two or -three, I'd rather expect *him* to think it a pretty simple matter. Come away with me, and let him divorce you, and we'll start a beautiful new life together! It wouldn't be him that would see the complications. And there's another thing, sir, that points more to her, besides the fact that she was in the house alone with Freeland all night. The boy was home before ten, there's not much doubt of that. No, it's this – she being a potter by profession, I took the opportunity of borrowing a book or two on the subject. I'd need to refer to them again, but I believe this antimony oxide is mentioned among the colouring agents they use. She might have some in her workshop. I was thinking, if it meets with your ideas, I could go up there and have another look round this evening.'

'Do! And while you're there, go over the studio again, and see if we missed anything in the way of traces of the stuff. I don't think there'll be anything to find, but we can't afford not to look again. If there is antimony among her materials, you'll probably need to test all round the place for fingerprints, though I doubt if you'll find any but the residents'. Still, a negative answer is an answer of a sort. Take Martin with you.'

So Sergeant Grayne arrived once again at Little Worth, some thirty-seven hours after his first visit, just as Suspiria was opening her kiln. She did not hear his gentle tap at the front door; and when he tried the latch, and found the door unlocked, he let himself into the dark living-room and stood listening for a moment, and tracing the gleams of light which flowed under the curtain from the back premises. Then he walked through to the workshop, and through the soiled windows he saw her standing over the kiln. She was so intent that she did not hear him come into the room, and for the racks of pottery and hanging screens she could not see him until he chose to move forward from the doorway.

The kiln was still fairly hot, but sufficiently cooled for her to lift out the upper layers of pots with tongs, with only a slight risk of causing wounds on the glaze. All the glow of heat had already dulled from sight, though the workshop was warm with released air. She was standing the few intact pots round the rim of the kiln, and had reached the disordered mass in the centre, where even the bat shelves had been broken and welded into the lump of shattered ceramic. Colours emerged from the corners, clean and bright, shining across the wreckage. The young constable craned over Sergeant Grayne's shoulder to see Suspiria's face, and caught his breath with a shock of surprise, for she was crying.

She stood looking down into the pit, still palpitating with heat, with such a frenzy of sadness in her face that it was as if she were regarding another death. Hardly anything in the bottom of the kiln had survived. Only shining small curves of those beautiful things, the fruit of her mind and hands, rose here and there out of the raw, hot mass, the rapid strokes of her brushes leaping across them and into the fused clay monstrosity again, where they hid and were lost. She had killed them, and maimed herself. She wondered if she could ever forgive that to the innocent who had caused the crime, and whether indeed innocents who bring about murder and perjury ever should be forgiven. A few unregarded tears flowed down her cheeks, and hissed into dryness upon the dead body, but no miracle happened.

'Is anything the matter, Mrs. Freeland?' asked Sergeant Grayne, advancing round the racks suddenly to shatter her solitude.

She did not so much as start, only looked at him

incuriously over the hot grave, and said in the dullest of voices: 'I had a burst. One of the pieces has exploded in the firing, and smashed most of the others. It happens! It can't be helped.'

He felt that it was a tragedy, and had enough craftsman's blood in him to understand how the failing of the hand can excite the same passion of remorse and grief as a crime. It was not her mind that felt the guilt, it was her body, the coordinating muscles, the knowledgeable nerves, every particle of that intricate machinery by means of which she exerted her mastery over clay, and delighted in it. Only it seemed to him that her feeling of grief was extreme for one failure, rather the kind of desperation of loss which old men feel when the machinery has ceased to work smoothly or have validity any more. He was so sorry for her that he could not think of anything to say.

Suspiria lifted the tongs in both hands, and gripping the shapeless mass, hoisted it out of the kiln in a wave of heat, and let it drop heavily into the waste-bin, where all the fragments of bat and the rubbish of broken pots were thrown. His eyes followed it in helpless sympathy; and when she turned to him again her face was still sad, but the moment of artistic despair was over. He supposed that it was almost irrelevant now beside the giant anxiety of her personal predicament, and only for a moment had it been able to assert its identity and importance.

'There are a few survivors, at any rate,' she said, with a pale smile towards the row of pots on the edge of the kiln. 'I suppose it's only habit that makes me care about them. But when you've spent years of your life caring very much, you can't stop all at once. I'll leave these to cool off completely now. Do you want me? Or would you rather I just got out of your way for a while?'

Sergeant Grayne said simply: 'Well, you can help me, if you will. Do you happen to have any antimony oxide among your things here? It's used for a yellow colouring, isn't it?'

Her eyes opened wide, without the flicker of a glance away from his face. 'Yes, I've got some. Do you want to see it? It's here, in this cupboard.'

She was lifting a hand to open the little door, but he shut his fingers gently about her wrist.

'Don't touch it, if you don't mind. We'll do that, all in good time. Have you used any of it lately?'

She had to think back more than a month to recall the last occasion when she had wanted a yellow glaze. 'I think it's just over five weeks since I used it. But I keep these oxides in stock all the time, of course.'

'You don't lock them up? Some of them could be highly dangerous to people who didn't know much about them, couldn't they?'

'There was seldom anyone here who didn't know about them. One's friends hear so much about the whole business that some of mine know very nearly as much as I do myself. No, the doors were never locked – some of them haven't got any locks. But at night I usually locked up the whole workshop.'

'Would you be able to tell me how much of this stuff ought to be left, after the last time you used it?'

She shook her head at that, with a dubious smile. 'It's so long! The intervals often are. No, I couldn't even guess what weight should be there. Sometimes I use as much as eight per cent in a soft glaze or an enamel, as well as using it for pigments. I could find you the dealer's bill, that would give you the quantity and the date. I might be able to tell you how often I've used it since, but I'm not too confident of that, and in any case it wouldn't give us a record of how much was taken out at a time.'

'Thank you, it would help, all the same. You don't ask me any questions,' he said, looking at her steadily.

'You wouldn't answer them if I did. Besides, do you think I need to ask? It didn't take very much hard thinking,' she said with a tired smile, 'to connect for myself. Whatever you want from me, I'll supply it if I can.'

'Thank you, Mrs. Freeland. Now, if you wouldn't mind leaving us to do a little routine work here—'

When she was gone, Sergeant Grayne muffled his hand, and opened the cupboard. It was the smallest of half a dozen arrayed along the bare whitewashed wall, and had a well-fitting door with a knob greasy and polished from long years of handling, probably in a few other incarnations before this one. Inside there were two shallow shelves, each with a crumpled brown-paper parcel of powder. The larger packet was the bag of antimony oxide. He weighed it in his hand, wrapped in his handkerchief, and examined the dusty folds of the bag carefully. They had certainly been disturbed more recently than five weeks ago, for edges of cleaner brown showed, although the neck of the bag fell naturally into the lines it already bore from previous handling. He set it down on the bench, and gave his attention to the faintly smeared dust inside the locker.

'We'll need to take this bodily off the wall, and have it away with us. More effective than messing with it here, because it's going to be a delicate job getting much off it. At least,' he said with satisfaction, 'this is something her husband wouldn't normally be likely to touch very often. If we find his prints here it'll mean something. Not like the studio, littered with everybody's hands, and never telling us a thing.'

The young constable was still looking thoughtfully over his shoulder, after the vanished woman. He was not sure that he approved of these curious moments of intimacy with which Sergeant Grayne complicated his passage through a case. 'Why did you ask *her* about the stuff?' he wanted to know fretfully.

'Because I was sure she'd tell me, and it saved time. And to see how she took it. A remarkable woman, that!' said the sergeant, gingerly assembling the folds of his handkerchief about the parcel. The constable was still more shocked by the warmly appreciative note in his voice; he would never get used to the idea of admiring a woman while you were on your way to the consummation of hanging her.

2

The inquest on Theo Freeland opened on the following Monday, but after evidence of identification had been given the police asked for an adjournment of one week, the medical evidence being still incomplete. This was granted, together with the coroner's permission for the funeral to take place; and two days later Theo was buried, as quietly as was possible by then. The word had gone round. There were reporters in and out of the Great Leddington shops and pubs, and crowds of people gathered at the churchyard to stare, which they did with unwavering determination throughout the scene at the graveside, and as long as Suspiria, or Dennis, or one personal mourner remained in sight.

The widow was not even in black, said the scandalised witnesses afterwards, and whispered further that such disregard of the decencies proved she had murdered him. She had on the dark green corduroy suit she had often worn before, with a black lamb coat over it, and a small black hat, but that was not proper mourning. Even her stockings were only a soft sort of iris-grey. And what sort of woman would go to her husband's funeral with her lover beside her in the car?

Dennis suffered hideously on that ride, but would not be dissuaded from it. He knew that his family were in furious conclave behind his back, he knew that for once they were all united against him in the shocked recoil they had made towards their threatened respectability, about which they stood in a solid phalanx of protective rage. But he could not help it. There was no conflict, for he was aware of only one duty. His place was with Suspiria. The avid looks which followed her, the craning curiosity gaping at her across the churchyard wall, the flash of the cameras in her face as he helped her out of the car, these flooded his heart with such a passion of dedicated anger that he could not spare one thought for himself. And it had hardly begun yet. They both knew that.

The opening of the inquest had not attracted a great deal of notice, because the sensation was then so new, and its full possibilities hardly realised; but the resumed hearing was another matter. Everyone was well primed by then, a Sunday had passed, and the newspapers had their teeth well into the promising scandal, even though they had to confine themselves to carefully oblique suggestion of revelations to come. Dennis sat tense and sweating through Suspiria's evidence, his hand braced on the edge of her empty chair beside him, suffering vicariously everything she suffered, and perhaps some pangs of his own of which she knew nothing.

It was impossible that the coroner should let the obvious questions pass unasked, and hopeless for her to try to let them go only half answered. The affair was practically common property already, but this was the first time she had been forced to rehearse it before an audience so large, censorious, and greedy for sensation. There was an instant when her heart failed her, when she wanted to turn back from the ordeal, and put up a hand suddenly to cover her face. Dennis's heart heaved and struggled in his breast in a fury of helpless love, and his eyes fastened so intently upon her that she seemed to feel their compulsion, and suddenly lifted her head again, and returned their frantic look with a blazing green glance, eloquent and tender and fierce as fire. A quick flame of colour burned up in her pale face. She went on with her answer in a low voice, but very clearly:

'Not money worries, but there was – a domestic worry. He and I – our situation had changed, and he was unhappy about it. We both were.'

She hesitated for a moment, but this time it was not her resolution which had wavered, but only her intelligence which was busy selecting words. 'Our marriage had been disturbed because of my – feeling for someone else. I had told my husband about it, and told him that my feelings were not likely to change again. I had no plans to leave him, and no intention of causing him more pain than I had to, but I know he was very unhappy about it.'

The coroner was old, and had seen too much of sudden death to be quite as greedy or quite as censorious as the public in the body of his court. He pursued without warmth or curiosity: 'I understand you to say you had no plans, and it is quite easy to believe that you were unwilling to cause him pain, but you must have had some idea in your mind of what was to happen in the future. However vaguely, you must have known what was likely to follow your revelation.'

'I hoped,' she said in the same low voice, 'that we should be able to discuss it amicably, and come to some agreement.'

'I don't altogether see, if your mind was quite made up, and you saw no possibility of changing it again, what agreement could be reached, except that you and your husband should eventually separate. Would you agree to that as a fair statement of the position?'

She said, almost inaudibly: 'I didn't think of it as clearly as that.'

'So, however patient you were prepared to be, and however reasonable, your husband must have interpreted your declaration as meaning that his marriage and his life with you were virtually at an end?'

'Yes – I suppose so.'

He asked her – it was inevitable – if she did not think this blow might have affected her husband's state of mind in a way sufficient to cause him to contemplate his own death, at least in moments of depression precipitated by heavy drinking. She gave her rigid and proud answer, like a ceremonious bow in Theo's direction:

'I can't say it would be impossible. I can only say it would be against all the instincts of his nature, even under intense pressure.'

He said: 'Thank you, Mrs. Freeland!' and let her go. She came back to her chair beside Dennis with a fixed and motionless face, and sat like a stone woman for a few minutes, staring straight before her. In the shelter of his leaning body he laid his hand over her clenched hand; the rigid fingers opened passionately, and closed upon his, and they sat for a few minutes holding each other tightly beneath the folds of his coat, until the strained whiteness of her face relaxed, and a recovering flame of colour rose and warmed her cheeks.

As soon as the immediate pain subsided he was again aware of the greedy eyes clinging to them both, from the jury, from the public seats, from every corner of the room, creeping down the lines of their arms, feeling along the folds of the coat for the convulsive knot of their clasped hands. Worse than the conscious disapproval was the subconscious, gratified glee of these looks. There was a young woman in the jury who had a better view of them than the others; he thought he could hear her, clean across the clerk's table, purring like a fed cat.

What followed was what the public had come to hear, the medical evidence. First, the local doctor, who made a brief and mildly dull story of his being called to the house, his examination of the body, sufficient to inform him at once that this was no natural death, but a probable case of poisoning, and his notification of the case to the coroner. He gave it as his opinion that the man had died after swallowing some irritant poison.

Faint waves of excitement and horrified pleasure seemed to pass through the public seats at this. The police surgeon was even more satisfying, because he knew so much more. Yes, he had performed an autopsy on the dead man, and had come to the conclusion that the cause of death was the consumption of a large dose of antimony oxide, enough to bring on acute gastric symptoms in less than one hour. He went into minute particulars of the ascertainable amount swallowed.

'The onset of such symptoms in an acute case may take place in ten minutes or even less on an empty stomach, or as much as twelve hours afterwards if the stomach were full. More normally I should expect them in from half to one hour after the poison was taken. The symptoms are not unlike those of arsenical poisoning – heat and burning pain in throat and stomach, vomiting, great thirst, probable purging later, finally complete collapse. All the appearances in this case were consistent with this, there was both vomiting and purging, but there had also been a somewhat rarer but not unusual effect upon the nerve centres, with acute collapse, coma and death following fairly rapidly. The post-mortem appearances bore out this view of the case. There was considerable inflammation of the stomach and lungs, and some submucous haemorrhage. The vomited matter also yielded a large percentage of antimony oxide.'

'Were you able to form any opinion as to the actual time of death?' asked the coroner. He waved away the ready and unintelligible details, which the surgeon immediately began to proffer with the greatest placidity. 'Yes, yes, just the conclusion, please.'

'Everything points to a very rapid onset of coma and death in this case. I formed the opinion that the man died not later than about two o'clock in the morning. To be sure of the duration of the attack from the first symptoms to death is very much more difficult. There are certain complicating factors. He had been a heavy drinker, I should say for years, though his physical condition was remarkably good. However, on the whole I should say his attack began not earlier than ten o'clock, and probably not later than midnight.'

'I see. Which makes it probable that the poison was taken at some time between nine and eleven that evening?'

'Yes. Almost certainly not earlier than nine, but possibly rather later than eleven – I would say certainly between nine and eleven-thirty. In view of the condition of the stomach the attack may have taken rather less than an hour to develop, but is hardly likely to have taken longer.'

'Thank you. Can you tell us something about antimony oxide? The form it occurs in? What it would be doing in an ordinary household? How it might have been taken?'

'It occurs as a white powder, practically insoluble in water. There is no ordinary household use to which it can be put. But I understand that this was not exactly an ordinary household. Pottery was carried on on the premises. Antimony oxide has certain uses in colouring glazes, I believe. It would be quite usual to have it about the place in those conditions.'

'But it does not seem to you a very likely thing to be kept near food. You would not consider it an easy thing to take by mistake for something else?'

'It would be extremely unlikely to occur in the kitchen. If by any chance it did somehow get mixed up with sugar, or flour, or any other white solid, I would not preclude the possibility of accident.'

When he completed his evidence, the tide of invisible, inaudible but palpable excitement had risen until they felt themselves drowning in it.

Sergeant Grayne followed with the straightforward story of

what had happened after his arrival at Little Worth on the morning after the death. The picture of the cold studio, with its burned-out stove and its steadily shining lights, and the crumpled body discarded carelessly in the centre, emerged with a curious icy clarity from the official phrases. The sergeant was not a typical police witness; he went rather than proceeded. His mild and mournful eyes swept gently over the array of faces turned avidly upon him, and looked longest at Suspiria, who was not looking at him at all, but fixedly ahead of her through the wall.

'On the floor there was a tube of white oil paint, which had been dropped and trodden underfoot by the deceased. It had squashed out, and was all over the soles of both his shoes, and well trodden about the floor. The footprints were so numerous that it seemed likely the accident to the tube had happened several hours before death, and their grouping about the easel seemed to show that it happened while he was still fully capable of painting, and some time before he was taken ill. Considerably longer, I would say, than one hour. The photographs will show what I mean.'

The photographs were circulating while he spoke, the intricate patterns of Theo's oblique passage from world to world.

'It will be seen, sir, that none of these prints reach the door. He did not leave the room after he stepped on the tube. There is also in evidence, sir, an expert report to show that the state of tackiness of the oil paint on the shoes and on the floor can give a reasonable estimate of the time which had passed since it was exposed to the air. It tends to show that the tube got squashed and trampled probably as early as the middle of the evening, say, between seven and eight.'

'So the effect of the evidence is to show that the deceased did not leave the studio after about that time?'

'No, sir, unless on the assumption that he took off his shoes.'

'It would be difficult to show any reason why he should have done that. Go on, Sergeant!'

'On the following day, sir, Saturday, acting on the first received reports, I again went to Little Worth, to see if antimony oxide was kept in stock there in Mrs. Freeland's workshop. She at once showed me where it was kept, in a small cupboard on the wall, and gave me every assistance with regard to her bill for the purchase, and details of the last time of using it, which was some weeks previously. She was unable, however, to say positively what weight of the powder ought to be present, or to judge from its appearance whether anything had been taken out since she last used it. It did appear from the folds of the paper that the bag had been opened at some time recently. The cupboard and the bag were tested for fingerprints, and yielded only Mrs. Freeland's with any certainty, though there were some other, older traces, much overlaid, which could not be identified.'

'None could be positively identified as Mr. Freeland's?'

'No, sir. There were also some faint traces on the paper of the bag, which did not appear to be Mrs. Freeland's; but they were so fragmentary as to be of little use. It is a very rough-textured paper, and almost hopeless for our purposes. But no prints except Mrs. Freeland's were found on the cupboard. The door was tight-fitting. Quite a firm grip would be needed in opening it. Had any other person so opened it recently, I think the traces would certainly be present on that knob.'

'It is not, however, impossible that he might have helped himself at some time when the cupboard was already open? It cannot altogether be ruled out!'

'There would be nothing against it, sir. But it is fairly conclusive that he didn't do so after about seven or eight o'clock that evening, according to the footprints in the studio.'

'Is there anything to indicate how the poison was taken?'

'There was nothing eatable or drinkable in the studio, except an almost empty bottle of whisky and a siphon of soda. Both were entirely innocent, and so was the broken glass which lay beside the deceased. It showed traces of whisky and soda, but nothing else. Moreover, the oxide being insoluble, it could not have been taken by accident or unknown to the victim in a drink. No trace of antimony was found anywhere in the studio, though it was very thoroughly examined.'

'So he did not leave the studio to get it, and there is no evidence to show that he had any access to it within the studio?'

'No, sir.'

'It would appear, then, that unless he had it about him, and deliberately made use of it and disposed of the traces himself, the only alternative is that it was brought to him?'

'That seems to be the fact, sir.'

'The jury will keep in mind,' said the coroner, 'the times which have been quoted as possible for the swallowing of the poison. The period is from nine to half-past eleven. I should like to recall Mrs. Freeland for a moment.'

When she obeyed the clerk's summons, he asked her with a detached gentleness: 'During that period, Mrs. Freeland, from nine to eleven-thirty, did you take anything to your husband? Any tray of food? Or anything for which he himself asked?'

'No,' said Suspiria, 'I did not.'

'Did you go into the studio at all during that time, or until you entered it in the morning?'

'No.'

'And as to the dispositions of your workshop, was your husband familiar with them? Would he know where to find anything he wanted?'

'Yes, perfectly. He sometimes liked to work in clay himself. He was perfectly competent.'

'Were there others who would know where all your materials were kept?'

'Yes, several of our friends. There might be quite a list.'

'Local people, for instance? Were there any near neighbours who were in that relationship to you?'

'Most of the people we knew who were interested in that sort of thing lived in London, and came out only occasionally.'

'Most?' he prompted.

It had to come, sooner or later. 'Mr. Forbes, who visited me that evening, was frequently at the house, and knew something of the geography of the workshop, though not very much. There might be one or two others who were about equally informed.'

'Ah, yes, you mentioned you had a visitor for about half an hour that night. Is Mr. Forbes in the court, may I ask?'

'Yes, he is.'

The coroner conferred with his clerk for a moment in a quick undertone. Dennis had risen, excessively pale, but almost eager now to lift the burden of the eyes, the intolerable, pleased, titillated eyes, from Suspiria; eager, too, in a despairing way, to plunge into the cold flood which in any case was going to take him in the long run. He found himself flinching from it in a way which outraged his pride so grossly that the only reaction left to him was to plunge in headlong now, and give his agonised spirit no opportunity to escape.

'Yes, well— I think we had better call Mr. Forbes. Thank you, Mrs Freeland, that is all.'

Dennis answered to his name immediately it was called, and out of the desperate conflict of feeling within him, with almost too great alacrity, so that the faintest and most scarifying murmur of amusement, cold and a little hysterical, seemed to pass like a ripple through the watching rows of people. His face flamed, and then blanched to an even more painful whiteness.

He took the oath in a clear and rather stern voice, confronting himself terrifyingly with the syllables of his own undertaking. He knew he would soon be committing perjury; and in a few minutes he was pronouncing with just as much conviction:

'We didn't go into the studio. Mrs. Freeland said that he was working, and that . . . that he'd been drinking, and we . . . the sight of us might only have upset him.' He had brought himself quite deliberately, if not very coolly, to this declaration, wishing to make it himself, on his own terms, rather than to have it dragged out of him, at this or a later stage, by the questions of potentially inimical people. But still it was like putting his hand into the fire. 'It was through me,' he said through stiff lips, 'that their married life had broken up. Nobody had intended anything like that, but it had happened. And we didn't want to do any more damage than we could help.'

'I see!' The coroner looked him over with old and disillusioned eyes, but seemed to find him no more disagreeable a sight than any of the other people in the room. 'Well, well, we are not a court of morals. Our business is to determine how a man died. So you did not actually see or talk to the deceased that night?'

The assault of the eyes had achieved now its most pleased and greedy satisfaction, and he found himself able to sustain it. It would never again be quite so terrible as this first plunge, even if in the end he must go down far deeper. He lifted his head with a renewed pride, and said:

'No. But I saw the light was on in the studio, and heard him moving about in there. I stayed about half an hour with Mrs. Freeland, and then left, because she said she was tired. It must have been about twenty-five or twenty minutes to ten when I left the house. I was home just before ten.'

'You are acquainted with the house. Were you quite familiar with the materials in the workshop?'

'I wouldn't say familiar. I've helped sometimes with simple jobs there, and I know about the main processes, but I don't know anything about the various pigments, or about formulae, or any of the chemical side of it.'

'Would you know, for instance, where to lay your hand upon a particular ingredient? Let us say, the one in question, antimony oxide?'

'No. I could find it by going through the cupboards, because all the things had labels. But I shouldn't know where to look first.'

'You had never handled it?'

'Yes, I believe I had. Mrs. Freeland –' he caught himself back just in time from the admission that Suspiria had informed him of the cause of death more than a week previously, and sweating and burning with horror at his own carelessness, turned it aside as well as he could '– once asked me to mix a coloured glaze for her, and I remember this name on a label. But I didn't get it out of the cupboard myself. Still, anyone could find it who cared to give five minutes to looking for it. The materials were all more or less together. At least, these less bulky ones were.'

'Did the name mean anything to you then? Would you have known from seeing "antimony oxide" on a label that you were handling a poison?'

'No. I don't remember that I'd ever heard of it before.'

And that was all. He was dismissed, and went back to his seat torn between extreme relief and a queer, distinct feeling of being cheated. He had made his statement, a monstrous step towards his full identity, and nobody seemed to have recognised it. Perhaps in his heart he had wanted more to be made of it, had been prepared to welcome, even to enjoy, the questions which should parade his love defiantly before all those delighted and damning eyes. They should at least have known the breadth of the gesture, and made some large acknowledgment, whether angry or admiring he did not care. But all he had precipitated had been that dry, disillusioned glance, and that cold impartial remark: 'Well, well, we are not a court of morals.'

Because he felt young, and humiliated, and still very frightened, he sat with a rigidly erect back, and looked down the crowded room, seeking out eyes to meet, and hurting himself savagely against their oblique glances, which slid away from him even as they bruised. He had stared his way agressively almost to the back of the room when he looked full into the eyes of his sister Marjorie. Of course she would be there! The hint of an outrage which could in some degree be appropriated to herself would draw her clean across the county in midwinter, if need were. He stared bitterly into her eyes, already hearing within his mind the version of this scene with which she would fly hotly home before him.

The coroner was instructing the jury. What they had to decide was precisely this: how had Theodore Freeland met his death? No other judgment must be allowed to occupy their minds. They had to consider whether the cause of death was the consumption of a dose of antimony oxide, a point on which the medical evidence appeared to be decisive. If they decided that it was, they had then to consider how the dose was taken, and here the possibilities were three: that it had been swallowed by accident or mistake; that the deceased had taken it of his own will, with intent to end his life; or that it had been administered to him by some other person, in which case they must also consider whether it had been administered by mistake or of intent, in which latter case it would amount to murder. They should bear in mind the tendency of the evidence to show that the deceased did not leave the studio after at the latest eight o'clock, and had no access to antimony within the studio.

He told them exactly what inferences they were entitled to draw from the various testimonies they had heard, and pointed them meticulously away from conclusions not justified by the amount of the evidence. Straining his senses after the implications of that summary, Dennis found himself swinging feverishly between a hideous anxiety and a wild, laborious optimism. Were they being warned against crying murder, where there was almost nothing to support the charge except a situation, and a singular absence of evidence? Or were they being instructed that where sufficient details, even negative ones, tended all one way, they need not be afraid of acknowledging the full force of the evidence, and considering it solid enough to support a charge? From one moment to the next he could not be sure where the words were leading. He looked carefully at Suspiria, but her face told him nothing of what she was feeling. He was aware of her breathing, deep, even, and almost stealthy in its quietness, as if she held herself firmly braced against any shock.

The waiting seemed interminable, but the jury came back at last. They were a solid-looking lot, surely they wouldn't easily believe in the most melodramatic solution? He held his breath, waiting to take the first words from the foreman's lips, to turn them in his hands, and make them assume the shape he wanted. If only he even knew what he wanted! What could they say, that would round the obtrusive mystery away into the normal suave undulations of life in Great Leddington? Accidental death? But it so plainly wasn't! Easier by far to commit themselves to what it wasn't, rather than stake on what it was!

'We find, sir, that the deceased died as the result of swallowing antimony oxide, without sufficient evidence to show how the poison was taken.'

'That is a unanimous verdict?'

'Yes, sir.'

The sudden, quivering, aching passion of relief was almost more than he could bear. It was so careful, so inconclusive, that he fell into the natural error of supposing it to be a complete deliverance, until he looked eagerly at Suspiria's face, and saw that its wary stillness had not changed at all. She was looking at Sergeant Grayne, and her eyes, as they watched him, had a dark and informed expectancy. No illusion of safety had betrayed her into relief, even for an instant; she was waiting for the next move, and assembling her defences to encounter it worthily.

3

'You should have seen her,' said Marjorie, sweeping her long arm peremptorily about her assembled family to draw them into the net of her vision, 'sitting there like an image, never turning a hair, when it's as plain as your face she put him out of the way herself – *and* the police know it, too, only they're not ready to say so outright just yet. You'll see! It won't be long before we shall all be able to say in the streets what I'm saying now between you and me. She killed him, right enough! In her way, that's what he was! She'd done with him, she was after something a bit younger and greener. And our Dennis sitting there by her, holding her hand, as brazen as her! Well, he's done it now, the silly little fool! As good as told the court he's been carrying on with her for weeks, right under her husband's nose. If he'd got no shame about *doing* it,' she flamed indignantly, 'he might have had the decency not to get up and *say* it! There was no need. I will say she'd kept his name out of it up to then, not that that stopped anybody from knowing, mind you! Don't you imagine there's a soul in this town who hadn't got a good notion of what was going on, but now he's put it in their mouths himself. A nice thing! I have to get stopped by a whippersnapper of a newspaper man here in our own front garden! Would I care to make a statement? Could I give a few homely details about my brother? My God, he's right, I could, too! I could give the full facts about our Dennis!'

'I can't believe it!' said Mrs. Forbes, helplessly still in her chair, her hands knotted in her lap. 'Him and that woman, mixed up together in this terrible scandal! I just can't get it into my head. How are we ever going to look people in the face, after this? Such a disgrace!' She was trembling even at the word, oblivious of her husband's soothing hand upon her shoulder.

'Don't take on too much about it! Maybe the lad has been a bit of a fool, but nothing worse than that. He hasn't done anything *wrong*!'

'Nothing wrong? Carrying on with a married woman nearly old enough to be his mother, and you say he's done nothing wrong! And now it's worse than just that. Don't you make any mistake, he isn't out of this other wood yet, if he thinks he is. I can tell you, if I was in his shoes, after all that's been said in that court this afternoon, I'd be feeling pretty sick. He'll be lucky if he isn't in it with her, up to the neck.'

'Don't say such things!' said Mrs. Forbes almost violently, stirred out of her own hardly less bitter disapproval to defend her youngest son from the suggestion of a worse guilt than was already his. 'I don't say anything about *her*, but he wouldn't hurt a fly. It's been her fault all along. I wouldn't mind betting. He's only a boy. She must have got hold of him properly – if it's true, if he really has been— But to say he ever did her husband any other harm, that's a very different thing. You shouldn't go making charges like that against your own brother. You ought to have a bit of feeling for him, even if the rest of the world won't.'

'Feeling for him? Has he had much for us?'

'She's right, Mother,' said Albert, sitting prim and uneasy beside the fire. 'We've got to think of ourselves a bit, you know. This isn't going to do our name any good, whatever happens. I'm not saying he's been any worse than criminally foolish, but it isn't very nice for us, is it? Reporters in the road waiting for us to come out, and everybody pointing us out in the street if we dare to show our faces! It isn't just him, it's a matter for all of us. He ought to have had some thought for his family's good name, if he didn't have any for his own.'

'His family!' said Mrs. Forbes, unwontedly outspoken now that her blood was up. 'You should talk about having some thought for his family! The first time you've been near us for over six months, and now I expect it's only to tell us we shan't be seeing you again unless we put young Dennis somewhere out of sight until everything blows over. I can see your precious Nora's family sitting round chewing us over, and sending you down to tell us something'll have to be done to put things right, if it means kicking the kid out of the house – or you and the Loder tribe can't have anything to do with us for the future. I know their sort! We never were good enough for 'em, even when we were respectable. Well, all right, go on back to the fold. Go and tell 'em we shan't be expecting them or you around here again – not until you want something!'

'Mother, I never said it was anything to do with Nora's people! Not that you can expect them to be very pleased about it, I must say, when one of their in-laws gets himself mucked up in a murder case. All we want, any of us, is to see what can be done for the best, for all the lot of us. What's wrong with that?'

'I can't say it's going to do me any good at work,' said Harold, coming to his support. 'We've all got an interest, it's no good carrying on as if we were talking about throwing the miserable idiot out, the first time we say a word against him. You wait a day or two, Mum, and see how you like it when the news-hounds start on *you*. You needn't look for much peace from now on. You'll soon be spread across the headlines, unless I miss my guess.'

'In the papers? Me?' She could not grasp it. The expression of her face as she struggled to comprehend it was curiously dual, appalled, affronted, and yet lit up with a gleam of horrified pleasure. The flickering reflection of it shone in her children's faces, too. In a secret, ashamed way they would all find in it, loathe it as they might, an insidious enjoyment they could never, never acknowledge, even to themselves.

Winnie stood at the window, looking out between the curtains upon the arc of light spilt on the road. It was true, there were two men there now, questing back and forth uneasily yet eagerly, like scavenging dogs on a fresh scent. She had not said one word in the furious conference, though she was as shocked and morbidly excited as any one of them. Was she on their side, or his? She could find no answer. She had always stood up for him, because they were the two youngest, the victims of their own better fortune; and yet she wasn't going to find it very pleasant in the shop, after this, with the hot, inquisitive eyes of customers devouring her as they passed by her counter, and the occasional informative whisper sliding into her ears: 'See that girl? She's a sister of that boy – you know, the one in the murder case!'

And yet what she felt for him was not all pity or fear or resentment. There was a glow of envy, too, somewhere deep in her heart. How were people chosen to undergo these fatal passions of love? How did one become a name in a story, Iseult, Heathcliff, Lancelot? It might kill, but it made people immortal. And not only that, but the quality and kind of that love they had, briefly as they possessed and enjoyed it, must make everything else seem pale and flavourless by comparison. How strange it was to think of Dennis as touching, suddenly but unmistakably, that terrible pinnacle of feeling. Just an ordinary boy, like any other! Not bad-looking, of course, but nothing at all to write home about. And suddenly he was changed, he was tall as the most romantic of heroes, and tragic as Tristan. And she thought she would almost have been willing to have the terror and the shame, if she could have had the splendour, too.

She saw him come home, watched him thrust past the two reporters, and shake them from his elbows without looking behind. Already he seemed to her a different being. Because she could not warn him of what awaited him inside the house, she did not warn them of his coming, either. Let them both be without advantage.

Hearing his hand on the latch, they all turned their irate and frightened faces towards the door, rearing their heads abruptly as if to defend themselves from the opprobrium he brought in with him. He looked round them all in one quick glance, and said: 'What is this? A court-martial?'

His father said mildly, before Marjorie could say it for him and say it worse: 'Well, son, it looks as if you've got yourself into it properly this time.'

'Yes – myself. Not you. Not any of you.' He was too tired to bluster or shout, he just said it, as if nothing could be simpler. 'I'm sorry if you all feel you're contaminated, but there's no need for it. I'm not asking you for anything. This is my mess.'

'How can we stay out?' asked his mother, suddenly veering to the other side now that he opened the fight thus shamelessly. 'Do you suppose all those people in the court didn't know whose son you are? I'd like to know how you can expect us to feel anything but contaminated! I'd never have believed it,' she said fiercely, 'of a boy of mine! And now look at the fix you've got yourself into, going off the rails like you've done.'

Then they all began, all except Winnie, who stood clutching the curtains, and staring at her brother with intent and searching eyes, looking for the boy she had always known in this adult and stranger. Sometimes she saw him, in the spurts of temper and the querulous twists of his shoulders, sometimes heard him in a brief, stung retort, in the note of self-defence which leaped easily to his voice; but most of the time the newcomer, this harassed, desperate, calm young man, thrust him deep out of sight. They poured out on him all the alarm and shock, all the resentment and blame, they had been storing up for him. They demanded to know if he were not ashamed of himself, and he said quite arrogantly, and for a moment almost gladly: 'No!'

'It's no use going on like this,' said Albert hopelessly, 'wasting time squabbling about it, when the damage is done. Surely what we ought to be doing now is to find some way of making the best of it. There's nothing against you – not in a legal way, I mean. All we can do is keep as quiet as possible for a while, and make the best of it until it blows over.'

'It'll take some living down,' said Marjorie grimly, 'but

goodness knows he owes it to us to make the attempt, at least.'

'You'd find it better to get away from here for a bit,' said Harold knowingly. 'Jobs are easy enough to get in your line – *I* should get out, and strike out somewhere else for a year or so. You could use another name, couldn't you? There's nothing actually against you, as Albert says. And inside a year it'll be all over. Folks will soon forget about it, once—'

He stopped only because of the sudden flaming anger of Dennis's eyes, still at a loss what he had said to strike such a spark.

'Damn you, shut up! What do you think I am, to run away and leave her to face this by herself? My God, you make me sick!' he said in a fury of pain. 'And you ask me if I'm not ashamed! If I had your sort of mind I might well be!'

'You don't mean,' said Harold, groping incredulously after an attitude he could not grasp, 'that you're going on seeing her? After what she's dragged you into already? Christ, you must be mad!'

'You can't mean to carry on with her as if nothing had happened!' said Albert, paling. 'The sure way to get yourself and us in deeper than ever! You needn't expect *me* to have anything more to do with you, if you do anything so daft.'

'I don't! I don't expect anything from any of you, I keep telling you so. You don't owe me anything, it's my affair. If you all want to be safe, as much as all that, I'll clear out. It's all the same to me!' But this once, at least, he was lying. His lips shook with outrage as he said it.

'You'll do nothing of the kind!' cried his mother, bounding out of her chair. 'I'll box your ears if you talk to me like that, big as you are. This is your home, and here you'll stay, even if you are fool enough and ungrateful enough to get us all into trouble with you. But you won't,' she said, lifting her hands to take him by the coat and shake him into sense, 'you wouldn't be so silly and wicked. You won't go near her again, will you? Dennie, love, don't go making things worse!'

He stepped back out of her hands, though he looked at her as he recoiled with a shaky and distracted smile.

'I'm not making any promises. Or any bargains, either. I'm sorry, Mum, I don't expect you to understand. That's all right!'

'But it's you who don't understand! Can't you see that the only thing for you to do is to give up seeing her, and live as quietly and regularly as you can? The police will be watching every step you take. You've got your own life to think about.'

Winnie said from the window, in a queer, neutral voice: 'You're wasting your time. Can't you see he loves her?' She said it as if it were something from superhuman experience, out of the range of ordinary men; and perhaps it was the infection of her awareness that made them suddenly start back to stare at him with those inimical, alien eyes.

'Yes, I love her,' he said, with the simplicity of extreme weariness. He did not understand why they should stare at him like that; all he knew was a sort of grateful sweetness in his mouth, because he was saying it aloud at last in the only just words. 'I've been her lover for two months now,' he said. 'I shall go on being her lover as long as we're both free. And I shall go on loving her as long as we're both alive. You may as well get used to it,' he said, almost with compassion for their helplessness. 'There's nothing you can do about it.'

4

It took the police three weeks to comb out from the artistic recesses of London every intimate in whom Theo Freeland had ever confided, every drinking companion with whom he had shared the last joyless fling a week before he died; and a few days more to assess what they had got, and make up their minds to it that in all probability they would get nothing more. It was not a matter of time. There was just so much to be gleaned, just so many people to be taken into account; after that all that remained was to weigh the probabilities, and decide whether they had a case which could hope to stand.

Dennis had begun almost to disbelieve in danger by then.

Three weeks was an age to him, and every day of it increased the impetus of their withdrawal from the shadows. He wondered why she did not relax with him, and argued with her, wildly and tenderly, in an effort to erase the constant slight air she had of listening for a footstep, the careful smoothness of her face.

He was with her when they came at last, one evening in February, in the tearful, whispering softness of a thaw after a long frost, when the eaves were sighing and dripping into the puddles of the yard, and even the inner walls looked dewy and whitened with melting rime. He was at her feet on the rug, almost half asleep, his face hidden in the folds of her skirt, and his hands cupping her body above the waist, a body which seemed to him daily to dwindle in his arms. He was achingly full of physical content in her, and could not find room in his being for the instinctive disquiet with which she nevertheless tormented him. It went crying round the soft, sweet sleepiness of his satisfied mind, trying to get in. If only she would stretch out her body beside him, and lie heavily upon his arm, instead of sitting there like that, drawn neatly together into an active tension, ready to react to any touch without astonishment! That was what still frightened him, that she should keep herself ready night and day for something he wished to believe would never come.

He was just saying, his lips moving drowsily against the faint warmth of the silk which covered her side: 'It's nearly a month now – nearly a fortnight since they even came near you. It's all over, I tell you. They've given it up as a bad job. Nothing will happen now.'

It was then that she heard the car. There was only the faint watery purring of wheels along the ruts of the drive, moving slowly, but she knew it, and held him off from her by the shoulders so that she might rise and go to the window. He lifted his weight from her reluctantly, not yet afraid, only impatient that she should still be keyed to such instant responses. He turned his head and watched her as she parted the curtains and looked out. The flicker of one headlight fanned across the window.

She said, in the alert voice which of late had intruded even upon their intimacies: 'It's a police car.'

He plunged to his feet and came to her side, his arms reaching for her instinctively at the first threat of loss. 'Oh, no – impossible! You've got police on the brain. Why should they suddenly turn up now, after so long? I tell you they've given up.'

'They couldn't give up. I knew that from the beginning. There wasn't enough of a case to make a conviction certain, but there was too much to let pass without a charge. The only question was how soon they'd be ready to proceed. They're ready now,' she said, 'and they're here. It was only a matter of time.'

The sheen of the headlights as the car swung slowly round the curve of the drive passed glimmering across her face, and her eyes flashed green as a cat's for an instant, a hunting cat live and wary in the night. She turned her body in his fiercely clenched arms, and took him by the shoulders, forcing him off from her urgently.

'Listen! You remember what we agreed? You remember what I told you, if one of us was arrested? And what you promised me?'

'But I can't let you—' he said, panting. 'I never believed in it—'

'You promised it!' She shook him fiercely between her hands, for already the car was hissing to a leisurely stop in the puddles of the yard. 'I know what I'm doing. It's the only possible way for us both to get clear. If you try to do something crazy you'll only kill me. If you do as we agreed I'll come back to you, I swear it! If we keep our heads and stick to our story, they *can't* convict – there'll always be too much doubt. You want to help me, don't you? Then do as I tell you, damn you, or you'll be the death of us both!'

Over her voice they heard the knock at the door, discreet, decorous, almost prim. He tried to speak, but she shut her lips hard upon his as they parted, and held him trembling under her long, deliberate kiss, to silence his last doubts, for which there was no longer any time. Then she put him gently away from her, and went to open the door to Inspector Tarrant and Sergeant Grayne.

'Come in!' she said, stepping back from the moist swirling gleam of the night, suddenly illuminated behind their shoulders. She felt Dennis move to her side, and knew by the constraint of his steps that she had nothing to fear from him. A faint, curious smile touched her face as she closed the door behind her long-expected visitors, and looked up into their correct and expressionless eyes.

'Mrs. Freeland, I have a warrant for your arrest on a charge of the murder of your husband. I must caution you that anything you say will be taken down, and may be used in evidence.'

'Yes,' she said, 'yes, I quite understand. I suppose I'd better think about getting a solicitor.' She turned her head, and looked at Dennis, and her eyes seemed to grow and darken into a deep and vehement tenderness. 'Everything will be all right,' she said quietly, 'believe me. We've done nothing wrong. Everything will be perfectly all right.'

'Yes,' he said in his turn, and bending his head with the sudden austere delicacy of a schoolboy taking leave, gave her the strangest, briefest, most chaste and touching kiss she had ever received from him.

CHAPTER SEVEN:

The Illusion of Deliverance

1

HE DID not see her again until she was brought into the magistrates' court, a week later. The hearing lasted only two days, and provided no sensations, since she reserved her defence, and allowed herself to be sent for trial without displaying any interpretable degree of interest in the case the police made out against her. But the drama was not in the evidence. The Sunday papers had already begun, by then, the process of turning her into a myth.

There were hundreds of people outside the court, waiting to see her arrive, and at least a dozen photographers ran like excited terriers alongside the car as it drew up, elbowing for position and dancing backwards before her with their cameras at their eyes. She remembered, from somewhere at the back of her trivial experience of sensational reading, those pitiable pictures of men and women running head-down to avoid just such a barrage, their arms raised to cover their faces, crouched to half their stature in the effort to be invisible. She got out of the car with the composure and frigidity of a seventeen-year-old débutante arriving at a party, and walked through the ceremonial dance of cameramen as though they, and not she, lacked reality. Any effort to escape from her situation by short cuts and fantasies would in any case be wasted, and she could not afford waste.

What she had to do was conserve all her emotions, all her reserves of self-control, and patience, and intelligence. It was not that the eyes and the voices, and the half-sadistic and half-sentimental curiosity did not offend her, but rather that she could spare no feeling for them, so long as she had a life to play for.

Dennis was in court to see her come. He heard the attendant frenzy outside, and looking up quickly, caught the first glimpse of her as she was brought in. She looked a very long way off, curiously fresh and austere, and almost a stranger, in a severely pressed grey suit and a little blue snail-shell of a hat which hid all her hair except for one frail, curved black feather across her forehead. She looked as if she had dressed with exceptional care, not merely to make a good impression, as most people do when charged with a criminal offence for the first time, but also for more frustrating reasons, because for once in her life her active mind and hands had nothing real to do, and had been driven to expend themselves upon her appearance for want of any more urgent occupation. And in this careful and imaginative grooming she now looked a little lost and startled, as if so unfamiliar a preoccupation had upset her conception of her own personality, and left her in doubt when she had most need of confidence.

People in court craned, and goggled, and whispered, eating and drinking her. Behind Dennis's shoulder a girl said to her friend disparagingly: 'I thought she'd be better-looking than that!' And her friend replied knowingly: 'It isn't the looks that do it. It's sex-appeal, that's what she's got. You look at all the women who get fellows crazy about 'em – there's none of 'em all that much to look at.'

Every word aimed at Suspiria, however slight, however innocent of conscious offence, went into his heart now with a bitter and poisonous impetus, inflaming him with useless pain. He lifted his head and looked at her again hungrily, unable to understand why the very lines of her small, aristocratic bones did not move others as they moved him. She looked at him only once, but so straightly and deliberately that he knew she had been aware of him from the instant she entered, and conserved her glances in his direction only for fear of disturbing a composure she had not achieved without care and forethought. When her eyes did meet his they lingered for several seconds, regarding him steadily and without a smile or a change of expression. She sat through the outlining of the case against her, following the thread with an intelligent but motionless gravity, nothing left in her face but patience and resignation, two extraordinary characteristics to be displayed in her. She had never been known to possess more than a crumb of either; it was rather as if she had produced them suddenly at need, as little girls achieve breasts when growth forces them to become women.

Looking at her now, as she leaned slightly forward, turning her head alertly from her solicitor to the magistrate, from the bench back to her counsel, he could scarcely believe that he had ever touched or even spoken to this woman; and a kind of superstitious despair seized his heart and wrung it, contorting every remaining hope into a doubt. Even if this ordeal passed, and they came out of the din and glare and strangeness of publicity into a normal daylight again, they would be so changed that they would scarcely know what to say to each other. What they were trying to do was to make love stand still and keep its unity of spirit in the middle of a battlefield. They wanted a miracle, and nothing less.

'Why, she's going on forty,' said the younger girl, soft and indignant behind him, 'if she's a day! I don't see what makes boys go for old women like that.'

'It's just the green boys that fall for it. And once they're in love they go crazy. Well, you know how it is yourself, when you're just wild about somebody.'

'Oh, yes, but there's different ways of going crazy. I mean, they say he's young enough to be her son, nearly, and quite good-looking. What on earth did he see in her in the first place?'

He tried to shut his ears to the whispers, but they made corrosive patterns of acid upon his mind. Everything about Suspiria and himself belonged to the greedy senses of the public now, even their follies, even their magnificence. By the time both had been pawed over in the headlines, both would be unrecognisable for ever. They were losing their shape, they were being tailored to fit a gap in the news, a pause between the cosh boys and the divorce courts. For a moment he thought with astonished gratitude how safe Suspiria would be from this deforming pressure, once this hearing was over, and he wondered if she, too, felt as if she had ventured out of the only refuge now left to her.

There were no surprises; he knew already what was likely to happen. The case would go for trial, almost inevitably, so her solicitor had told him, so there was no point in expending themselves at this stage. Better to learn all they could about the police case, and give away nothing of their own.

Mr. Quinn, the solicitor, was a thin, cool, fastidious man of middle age, who had known the Freelands casually for some years; but in the course of his anxious interviews with him Dennis had been unable to discover how he felt about his client. Did he believe in her guilt? He looked as if he would find it easier to believe in the guilt of human beings than their innocence. Did he feel any of the exquisite fear and rage for her life which burned in her now, those violent sensitivities which hurt Dennis even across the crowded and voracious court, out of her silence and calm? He looked only like a little book on the law, grey unobtrusive, neatly bound, informative but without sympathy.

The Q.C. who was to defend her seemed to him to have scarcely more warmth. He was younger, bigger, a personable man of about fifty, with a name which might have meant something to a person who followed the proceedings of criminal law, but which Dennis in his preoccupation had heard and forgotten in a breath. Nothing mattered, except that he should be effective for Suspiria; but the very serenity with which he regarded her situation was unspeakable offence.

Following with painful intensity and some difficulty – for he could not concentrate as he wished – the curiously dull recital of the police case, he could not see that they had the means to prove anything more than that Suspiria had had motive and opportunity for killing Theo. He wished he knew more about the processes of law. He wished he could change places with Suspiria, but she had put it out of his power. All he could do was sit watching her and suffering for her, and keep silence, and wait. Wait without sight or touch of her, wait with his hunger for her daily renewed in him, and no secure promise that he would ever regain her, even if they both survived this ordeal.

Two days of this, and always more curious people milling about the pavement outside the court, craning and jumping to peer in at the windows of the car, always more dancing cameras, more avid-eyed girls gaping in the doorway and nudging one another as the victims came in sight, more greedily cheerful young men, pulling at his sleeve in the street, since they could not get at her. He thought she must have sighed with relief when it was over, and she was safely committed for trial at the Assizes, two months away, and could recoil into her walled solitude, and forget the weight of the eyes, all the shining, watching eyes, even his, which loved her.

2

He was not safe even at the garage. Even there cars came in for minor repairs, and their owners, penetrating insinuatingly into the particular rear corners where Dennis sought to hide himself, would suddenly have notebooks in their hands and aggressive professional charm in their mouths. If he said anything, anything at all, it was reproduced word for word, or with imaginative descriptive phrases, in the evening papers. If he simply turned his back and went on with his work, that, too, could somehow be made significant. He could not go into a pub for a drink, but some unknown young man would slide along the bar to his elbow, and begin again the persuasive whisper in his ear: 'Mr. Forbes? Look, I'd like to have a personal line on your story – nothing sensational at all, believe me, we don't use that kind of thing—' After a while he gave up saying that he had nothing to say, gave up being angry, gave up telling them to go to hell; he turned his shoulder on them at the first word, and went away himself. But they were everywhere, in his own front garden, on the very doorstep when he reached it, standing in the shadow of the lilac tree, waiting to step out and pluck at his arm before he could plunge inside and close the door.

The family lived in a state of siege. Each of them, before leaving the house, had to peer from behind the front curtains, and see if the coast was clear, or else leave by the back door and the gap in the garden hedge, which brought them on to the common field below. They never opened the door to any knock until it had been investigated from an upstairs window. And yet on Sunday morning, when the paper slipped through the letter-box, no less than three members of the family were waiting with ears strained for its coming, and hands itching to open it. They avoided his eyes when he came in and saw them scatter from it, but they converged again upon its headlines as soon as he was gone from the room. And in the afternoon Harold returned from a walk with two more newspapers in his pockets, and these, too, were circulated from hand to hand, and read greedily.

'Passionate Friends Case Electrifies Artists' Town'. 'Mechanic Lover of Accused Wife Shuns Publicity'. 'Star-Crossed Lovers in Great Leddington Tragedy'.

They read every word of every account, when he was not there. Fascinated, repelled, titillated, they turned back to read them again, and the phrases began to have a taste secretly almost pleasant. He could feel the half-horrified, half-sweet excitement in the house, fermenting, filling the air with a faint smell of fever.

On Monday Winnie came downstairs first in the morning, and had just put the kettle on for tea when the postman passed the window. She did not look to see if he turned in through the minute front garden, but a moment after his passing there was a brisk knock at the door, and she answered it automatically in the assurance that it must be he. A brogued foot inserted itself promptly in the door, and a young man in shaggy tweeds thrust his shoulder across the threshold, and angled his way in past her into the hall. She opened her mouth to begin the inevitable protests, and felt them falling a little dully into the abyss of his eager friendliness. She faltered, and he moved a step farther into the house, and very gently, very gradually, let the door close behind him.

'He doesn't want to see you or any other newspaper man,' she said protestingly. 'Why can't you leave him alone? You've no right forcing your way in here like this, you'd better go.'

'So I will if you insist. But, look, Miss Forbes, really, I don't want to do anything you wouldn't want. I only want to help you. Look, your brother's missing his tricks. I know what I'm talking about. There's a fund of sympathy for him among the public, it only wants tapping, and he's got a right to public support. There's no need to bother him about it, I know how he feels. But that's no reason why his side of the affair shouldn't be put across, is it? People only need to know the genuine facts to send out their sympathy to him. Real love isn't so common they run up against it every day! And in an ordeal like this, isn't it worth while putting his case fairly to as many people as possible? People in his position tend to look on us as their enemies, but that isn't so, Miss Forbes, believe me. We'd like your brother to get a fair hearing – and if you'll help us, you'll be surprised at the goodwill he'll find pouring in to his support. That's why I've taken the liberty of stepping in like this. I do hope you'll forgive me. If you throw me out, that's all right, I'll go.'

She was wavering; she looked at him with large dubious eyes, and said: 'I'd like him to get some support, certainly, but it's his affair. What can *I* do about it? He doesn't want to talk to you, *I* can't make him.'

'Well, for instance, there aren't any really good photographs of him, that I've been able to trace. I don't want to pester him with photographers, at a time like this, but you know, if you happened to have one in the house – a good one—? You see, it would put over half the story. An attractive personality, youth, good looks— People have a *right* to understand!'

She hesitated for a moment, and then suddenly turned and went into the parlour. There was a photograph of Dennis, her own favourite, in one of the table drawers. It was aggressively touched up and unnecessarily handsome, in the false studio manner; she thought it romantically pleasing, in keeping with a high and tragic love affair, and when she imagined it enlarged upon the front page of a Sunday paper her courage stiffened to the small, loving treason. She took it back with her into the hall, and gave it to the reporter.

'That's fine! Just what we needed! And if you could just tell me something, some little outline, about how he met Mrs. Freeland! It's a kind of fairy-tale, you know, because of her being an artist, and all that.'

Before she opened her lips she heard a foot upon the stairs, and looked up guiltily into Dennis's eyes. The intruder had recognised him, too, and backed rapidly towards the door, but as quickly recovered his balance, and even stepped forward with some assumption of confidence and honesty.

'Mr. Forbes? I was just asking your sister if you—'

Dennis reached the foot of the stairs, and stood looking at him with heavy dislike. He held out his hand for the photograph.

'If you'll give me just ten minues, Mr. Forbes, I can convince you—'

'You can give me that picture,' said Dennis, in a perfectly flat, disinterested voice, 'and get out.'

He gave up the photograph without any more words, startled into compliance by the very deadness of the voice. A moment he hesitated, shot an uncertain glance at Winnie, and then slid out through the half-open doorway, and made off thankfully down the road.

'I gave it to him,' said Winnie, staring at her brother with an anxiety far more intense than if he had broken into the hot rage she might have expected from him.

'I know.' He dropped the thing upon the table with a look of distaste, and went into the kitchen, and sat down to put on his shoes. She followed him closely, flushed but insistent.

'Why don't you make use of them? He wasn't a bad sort.

He wanted to put people in the picture for your sake, as well as just as a matter of business. He says you need to have your view put fairly, you need sympathy, you need as many of the public as you can get on your side. So you do! I wasn't trying to do you any harm. I wanted to do something *for* you!'

He tried to smile at her, because he knew it was true, and there was no point in quarrelling with her. But he felt sick, and full of a kind of inexplicable panic. She was the nearest to him of them all, and even she was now so far from him that sometimes he could scarcely see her, and the effort of speaking to her seemed hardly worth while, so improbable was it that his words would even reach her, or be in the right language if they did. So profound was this impression of separation that it was a serious effort to him to look up at her and say: 'It's all right, I know you didn't mean any harm. But it wouldn't have come to any good, you know. Don't give them anything! Keep them right off me – will you?'

This comunication at least had reached her, and been understood, for her face eased readily into a relieved smile. Perhaps the ears of people who have been fond of one another are always more ready to receive and interpret requests than any other formulae into which words can be fitted.

'All right,' she said, 'if that's what you want. But I wish—' She hesitated, in her turn despairing of making him hear and understand. No, there was nothing more she or anyone could do for him. She went away quickly, because her eyes were full of tears, and she did not want him to know.

3

He visited Suspiria as often as was permitted. Each time, when she was brought in to him, the sight of him touched her afresh with a painful and wondering tenderness, so that she felt the laborious erection of her tranquillity crumbling, and could not bear the too frequent repetition of so distressing a delight. She rebelled against the thought of being seen by him at all in this condition, confined, restricted, on guard, emaciated with her constant watchfulness; and yet she thought she could not have lived through it at all without the occasional dangerous joy of this confrontation.

Their meetings were always attended. The wardress would sit retired from them, making believe to see and hear nothing, seeing and hearing everything. She was a kind, hard, disillusioned woman, the one they usually had, so inured to her duty that she could dissolve into the background and be no more substantial to them than a shadow. It never occurred to her to wonder whether Suspiria was guilty or innocent; such words had almost no meaning for her. She did what she was paid to do, but it had ceased to be interesting.

When Suspiria entered Dennis would rise, staring at her with all the anxiety and hunger which had been burning in him since the last glimpse of her. Often he forgot to speak, so much of his being had flowed into the single look of his eyes. Throughout the brief interview those eyes would never leave her face. He stared at her as if he were defying change, precisely because he feared it so much, his eyes furiously denying that she was in any way diminished for him, or paler, or older, or less complete than when he had first loved her. And yet he knew that a terrible metamorphosis was taking place in both of them, that nothing would ever again be the same, that there was no going back. Sometimes, therefore, they sat through their short time together virtually without words, struggling towards each other through a panic of estrangement. Sometimes they were luckier, and a mere familiar word, a turn of the hand, a sudden flame of physical memory, would dissolve the distance, and leave them articulate at last in a passion of tenderness, their tongues hurrying to say everything while the gift remained to them; for then there was nothing, nothing in the world, they could not say.

'You're worrying too much about me. You know there's no need. It's harder for you. Try not to worry – in the end everything will be all right. It must! We've done nothing wrong, no one can prove that we have.'

'No,' he repeated obediently, the pale flame of her smile dazzling him. 'No one can prove what isn't true. If only there wasn't this awful waiting!'

'It hasn't done me any real harm,' she said. 'There'll be a lot of years after it, to make up for this. I'll soon put back the little weight I've lost.' And when she saw the uncontrollable convulsion of pain which wrung his face at the steadily nearing danger-point beyond which, in his darkest moments, there was no afterwards, she gave him a sudden beautiful, glimmering look of reproach and tenderness, and said, with the simplicity with which, in other circumstances, she would have enfolded and kissed him: 'My beloved darling, my heart's heart, you have got to believe in justice, as well as in me. I believe in it, and I promise you there will be an afterwards, and we shall spend it together, and all this will be forgotten. I love you,' she said, steadily shining upon him.

The words were like kisses, and the voice was like an embrace. The wardress knitted, and her face was indifferent as the wall, but she listened.

Dennis said, in the breathless murmur which belonged to the solitude and the dark; 'You're the only home I've got in the world, and if you even turn your head away from me I shall die.'

'I never shall, my darling. Don't be afraid of anything.'

After a moment he asked, drinking her face with wide, grey eyes: 'Are you never afraid?'

'No, never!' she said, lying with the most perfect and affectionate serenity. 'I've told you, everything is going to be all right. You mustn't even doubt it.'

'All right, I won't doubt it. But I wish I could have kept you from having to go through all this.'

'I think it's harder for you. No one can get at me here, but everyone can pester you. I'm sorry I had to bring you that gift, as well,' she said, with a soft and rueful smile.

'It doesn't matter. It happens to other people, too. They've made their own picture of us – we're being made to dance for them. But that's got nothing to do with the reality. It'll pass!'

In these moments of unhesitating communion they both believed these things. The sentimental shells in which the newspapers were trying to encase them fell off like a sloughed skin. And then suddenly, between the deliberate and defiant endearments, a tremor of fear and doubt would shake them both, and the pure image of their certainty would be torn shivering away, and they would be left struggling again in panic with all the arduous intricacies of language, and staring painfully upon each other to recover the lost conviction of their safety.

'Is there anything you'd like? Anything I could bring you?'

'I can't think of anything.'

'Do they give you enough books?'

'Oh, yes. I have plenty to read. I have everything I need.'

'I'll try to come again next week. If you'd like me to?'

They groped and touched clumsily, and could get no hold on each other. Even their voices had receded into a laborious unreality, and their bodies felt the weight of the grotesque headline images encasing them, making them heavy and slow, so that they could never again be molten together even by the fury of love.

'You'll talk to Mr. Quinn, and do everything he says?'

'Yes, of course!'

'We've only to stick it out now. Everything will be all right!'

But it was no longer possible to be sure of that. She saw him receding from her, and it was no longer a simple thing to believe that the separation was only for a short time. He would withdraw with many a look back over his shoulder, trying to recapture the certainty of victory, or at least to keep the full memory of the happiness which had already belonged to them once, and might help them to believe in its eventual recovery. But always, when the door had closed between them, she suffered a terrible moment of frenzy and loss, as if she had said good-bye to him for ever.

4

The trial came on at the Assizes at the county town, in the clear, melting weather of May, while the parks were full of tulips, stiff bright candles in their thick candlesticks of leaves. The judge's procession laid a devious course along the pavement between the flower-beds, weaving its way among the dimpled mirror-grey puddles almost with the eccentricity of Theo's labyrinth of flake-white; and in the skittish winds the little, shrivelled Judge looked unimaginably old and waxen and vindictive, huddled in his robes like a robin in its feathers, but without the bravado. He had not survived a lifetime of justice without injury; he was sick and saddened with humanity, and would not be able to adjust himself to deal fairly with his enemy for many more years, and even now the tension of his struggle had thinned him to a shred of skin, bone and nerves inside his clothes.

'You couldn't fall into better hands,' said Suspiria's Counsel, after reciting, with the candour almost of friendship, the curious qualities of this embittered old man. 'If there's one creature he hates more than a man, it's a woman. Because he's well aware of his own threatening disintegration, he'll fall over backwards to avoid being unfair to you. With a doubt the size of a walnut, you could draw a life's-worth of benefit out of him.'

At about the same time Sergeant Grayne was saying to Inspector Tarrant, with whom he had been over and over the meagre personal evidence they had collected on the Freeland marriage: 'It was worth trying. But we shan't get a conviction.'

'We can but try,' said Inspector Tarrant equably.

They tried their hardest. Not they only, for the Crown had the ambitious assistance of Vincent Perleman, Q.C., who had begun to collect spectacular cases as a means of advertising a talent already proven but not yet sufficiently inflated into legend. He estimated that the conviction of Suspiria Freeland might be precisely what his reputation needed at this stage. She was personable, she was an artist, she had rather more than a national name, and she was not of a dangerously sympathetic type, the public heart would not beat hotly for her, at least without an unconscionable amount of prompting. Too clearly she held herself apart from any appeal to them; too obviously, in her undemonstrative way, she despised them. She was a woman who might find a wave of facile emotion sweeping after her if she escaped, but would neither invite nor excite any partisan feelings if the verdict went against her. It needed success to make a success of Suspiria with the public. Moreover, she was a woman; he would lose nothing if he did not get her convicted, while gaining stature if he did. She was a double investment, and he extended himself to make the most of her.

His assistant in this laudable enterprise was a very young and very active man who had his name to make in the world, and would have followed a first-class principal to any kill. Between them they made a formidable team, capable of spreading a very little evidence a considerable way.

The court was crowded on the first day of the case, and in the shine and showers of the morning perhaps a hundred people waited outside throughout the hearing, avid for even secondhand news. Inside the court many Great Leddington people had managed to secure places, for this was something they could not afford to miss. They inspected a newly-sworn jury as motley and yet as respectable as most, a defendant who seemed to be every moment less of flesh and more of mind and spirit, burning bright in her fragility and her desperate attention. They kept their eyes fixed upon her as unshakably as she kept hers upon Perleman while he opened his case. It was a long exposition, because most of his material was in the circumstances, and he had no intention of letting the trivial answers he would get from his witnesses blur the clarity of the picture he himself knew so much better how to give, the picture of an established marriage suddenly shattered by the most illogical, the most hopeless, of love affairs.

He had a taste for form and symmetry, he wished to give

his attack an elegant and compact shape. He was a man of very moderate gestures, but Suspiria thought at times that his handsome hands centred and compelled truth as violently and determinedly as hers had been accustomed to compel the clay. He left it its nature, but imposed on it a shape of his own choosing. Was he within his artistic rights, she wondered? For without question he was an artist. She supposed that she, of all people, ought to acknowledge his claim to a craftsman's rights over his material.

'Such, then, is the picture of this household up to the dates with which we are concerned in this case. The marriage was ten years old, and might have been supposed to be about as nearly invulnerable as a marriage could well be. The couple were eminently suited to each other, had every interest in common, and had proved their compatibility and their affection by experience.

'Then, one evening early in October, something happens to this couple, something quite unforeseen, which is to alter both their lives. The husband has been in London, and is driving home early in the evening. He calls at a garage on the London road near Great Leddington, and the proprietor, who knows him well, sees that he is under the influence of drink, and in no fit state to drive. It was not a particularly unusual state of affairs with him, it appears. To avoid letting him run into trouble, the garage proprietor asks one of his hands, who is just going home, and lives only a quarter of an hour's walk from Freeland's house, to drive him home to Little Worth. The young man good-naturedly agrees, and on arrival is hailed into the house by Freeland, who made friends readily and indiscriminately even when sober, introduced to Mrs. Freeland, and detained for some time before he is allowed to go on home. This was the encounter which broke up the Freeland marriage. The parties met again by chance, and Freeland rashly adopted the young man Forbes into his household as a friend. There were frequent visits. The young man of twenty-two began to take an interest in Mrs. Freeland's work, and a still greater interest in the lady herself. Early in December he became her lover.

'That the infatuation was mutual and disastrous we have every reason to know, for its results are precisely what engages us at this moment. To look for reason in love is perhaps waste of time at best, but I ask you to consider the particular desperation of this case. On the one side a woman of culture, and of remarkable talent, a woman in her late thirties, admirably matched with a man of her own artistic calibre, of similar background, and of suitable age; on the other, a boy of twenty-two, a garage mechanic, cursorily educated, but without any intellectual resources which could bring him on to the same plane with her – incompatible in age, in temperament, in his whole scale of values. What could possibly be hoped from such a liaison? But remember this, it is precisely against such odds as these that infatuation acquires and asserts its most disastrous hold upon the human imagination. Where little is urged against an unwarranted affection, little will be attempted in order to retain it. Where nothing but the illogical fury of the heart promises any faint hope of successful fulfilment, monstrous feats may be performed to bolster up that hope. It is the Crown's case that the result here was the death of Theodore Freeland, and that he died as the result of poison administered by his wife.

'I will not cite precedents,' said Mr. Perleman, sweeping his magnetic gaze over the line of intent faces in the jury box. 'Your memories, like mine, will bring to mind the names of other such women, for this is a case which repeats itself with a curious persistency – the case of the ageing woman of parts, and the man who can match against her culture just two qualities made overwhelming by the time and the circumstances of their eruption into her life – his beauty and his youth.'

Suspiria's translucent face, which seemed to be only faintly shadowed by the bones within, gazed steadily upon him, and gave no sign of outrage or pain. She was thinking, with what energy she could draw off from her single devouring preoccupation with continuing to live: 'If I survive this, in less than a year I shall know how much of this is true.'

'By their own story,' went on Perleman, catching up the

skirts of the pause he had left them for digestion, 'they continued constant lovers from that day, so long as both of them were free. And before Thursday, January 29th, Theodore Freeland became fully aware of the liaison, for I shall call a friend of his, to whom he talked about his tragedy on that day, showing a full knowledge of the extent and the threatened permanence of his loss.

'On Friday, February 6th, at an early hour in the morning, Mrs. Freeland called the doctor and the police from the call-box at the crossroads near her home, and told them that she had just found her husband dead in his studio.'

He began to tell the story of that day detail by detail, the contorted corpse, the trodden paint, the innocent glass which should not have been innocent, the poison without a source.

'Precisely three people were in that house on the previous evening, and precisely three people appear in this case throughout. Apart from the husband, the wife and the lover, the stage is completely bare. That is the most notable thing about the entire set-up – it is a drama with only three characters.

'You will hear medical evidence which will show that the poison was swallowed by Theodore Freeland between the hours of nine and eleven-thirty on the night of February the 5th. The police evidence will tell you that there was a ready source of antimony oxide on the premises, in the accused woman's workshop. It is a material sometimes used by potters to obtain yellow colouring in glazes and pigments, and she had the greater part of a pound of it in one of the cupboards of her workshop. Access to it was easy enough during the day for anyone who was sufficiently familiar with the household to know that such an ingredient existed, and might be found there. But not one person appears in this case at all but the three angles of this most improbable triangle – the husband, the wife, and the lover. Is it not a reasonable supposition that if there existed one other person in the world with an interest in the death of this inconvenient husband, somewhere in the house, somewhere in the case, there would be a hint, a handprint, a mere whiff of that person? There is none. None whatever!

'Consider, then, the situation of these three people on the night of February 5th. The wife and her lover, as you will hear, have been temporarily disturbed in their relationship, for he has not been to the house for a week. Why? What has happened to upset their idyll? What new factor has appeared in the triangle? Only this – that the husband now knows what is going on. The first certain knowledge we have of his enlightenment is on Thursday, January 29th, remember. There is a week of abstention – something new between these infatuated people. At the end of it, the young man goes to visit his mistress again, but it is only a short visit – before ten o'clock he is home again. There is evidence to show that he must have left Little Worth only a few minutes after half-past nine. He spent, you will observe, about half an hour of the time in question within that house. He knew something of the lay-out of Mrs. Freeland's workshop, and had worked occasionally with her materials, but it seems fairly certain that he was not well acquainted with them, and knew very little about their chemical properties. It would not have been impossible for him to acquire the necessary knowledge for the act, nor does the time element rule him out completely, but on the face of it he is not a particularly likely poisoner. He has had what he wanted – the problem of the husband might, no doubt, be a painful one even for him, but how much more painful to the woman!

'And what of the remaining pair in the house? It was not a matter of a mere half hour together that night for them, but of the whole night, without interference, without witnesses. Take, then, the possibility which will certainly be presented to you at some point by the defence, the possibility of suicide.

'You may think that a man whose marriage has been shattered after ten years, and whose love for his wife is certainly as strong as ever it was, had a strong motive for putting an end to his life. But you may also think that there are several indications that he did no such thing. There was no farewell note, the door of the studio was not locked from within, as one might well have expected it to be if he intended to kill himself, the studio itself contained no traces whatever of the poison or of his means of swallowing it, and, most significant of all, the dead man himself left us a map of his movements for several hours before his death, in flake-white oil-paint – and it does not once approach the door of the room. However that antimony oxide got from the cupboard in the workshop into Theodore Freeland's body, he himself certainly did not go to the workshop that night in order to get it.

'Come, then, to the wife. She is alone with this suddenly troublesome husband all night. He is drunk, he has been drunk for some days and he has shut himself in his studio to try and satiate himself with work. She has the strongest possible motive for wishing him dead, since he threatens her not only with trouble and violence, but also, and more subtly, with the constant mirror of her own guilt, the reproach of his grief. A world without her husband would make everything smooth and simple for her. She alone is in a position to consider at once the full implications of her opportunity. She has an adequate supply of poison, to which it can fairly be claimed that her husband also has free access; she is perfectly aware of the properties of antimony oxide, she knows exactly where to put her hand on it at a moment's notice. She has all night to dispose of the immediate evidence – the food or drink in which it is administered. She cannot, perhaps, obliterate the traces of that obliteration. There will be, to say the least, a suspicious blankness about the scene. But she has the desperation, and the determination, to accept that risk.

'It is the Crown's case that this woman did precisely that. She took a bold risk to end an intolerable situation. She brought to her husband, at some time before half-past eleven that night, a drink, or possibly food, in which she had secreted a quantity of antimony oxide sufficient to bring on acute poisoning, and to kill before morning. Perhaps she had to use her persuasive powers as a woman in order to induce him to accept the attention from her. Perhaps she pretended a change of heart, a reconciliation. What is certain is that within those hours Theodore Freeland did indeed swallow the antimony, and did with complete finality die. It is the

Crown case that no one within the bounds of reasonable probability could have administered the poison to him, and removed the traces of the act, except his wife, Suspiria Freeland.'

He began to call his witnesses; first Inspector Tarrant with evidence of arrest, and the detailed picture of the studio, clear and cold in the frosty morning about Theo's body. He made the most of his man; and with the picture still uncorrected by cross-examination, the court rose for lunch.

Throughout the morning, Suspiria had not once looked at Dennis. He had sat through it all with his hands clenched and stiff with tension, his eyes unwavering upon her face, waiting for the instant of acknowledgment, and she had not granted it. Now turning in the dock to go down the stairs, the wardress's hand at her elbow, she suddenly lifted her head, and looked at him full, and it seemed to him that within the pallor of her cheeks there was burning a steady and fierce flame of anger and defiance, that every particle of fear and doubt had been fed into that flame and consumed. There was no tenderness in the look she gave him, only a white resolution and fury, intelligent, roused and implacable. It warned him that a like dedicated rage was demanded of him, if she was to live. It conveyed, too, that she had already taken the hint that the precise date of Theo's enlightenment was bound to come out, and that she meant it should come from her, and that he must bear her out. A lie less for you to tell, her eyes said to him, almost with pity, almost with disdain, as she turned and went alertly, angrily away out of his sight. He wondered that no one else had intercepted and understood the message, but they looked back at her curiously, and seemed to have learned nothing. Only he spoke the language.

5

The presentation of the case for the prosecution took two and a half days in all, and throughout that time the prisoner kept her intent eyes fixed upon the faces of her enemies, and her hand alert upon pencil and paper, and burned every hour more transparently away into a rage for life. The little Judge, shrunken and bitter as an ancient, shrivelled hazelnut, watched her without pity or aversion, but with an intelligence as fevered and tragic as her own interest in the police witnesses. It might have been his life, as well as hers, that rose and fell sickeningly upon the tide of feeling in the court, hesitant whether to sink or swim.

And what was there in all that torrent of words, when all was said and done? Not very much more than she had known from the first. Everything was in the medical evidence and the police evidence, and the few witnesses who had been dredged meagrely out of Theo's last visit to London served only to weaken and diffuse the hard, compact glitter of condemnation Sergeant Grayne had managed to focus upon the reported facts of the case. It was strange how much more damaging the sergeant was than his superior. His soft, sympathetic voice, his uncharacteristic preference for simple and direct words, gave him a terrible force of conviction, and his gentle and generous eagerness to concede every point in Suspiria's favour, and the discouraged sadness with which he described her willing co-operation, made cross-examination curiously feeble and ineffective. His manner of offering his admiration for her to full view made plain, at the same time, the measure of his regret that he nevertheless could not believe her anything but guilty. Trying to elicit points in Suspiria's favour from him was like pushing hard at an unfastened door, and falling flat on one's face over the threshold. They did better with Inspector Tarrant, in whose adamant professional manner it was easier to claw perceptible scars, and from whose stony assurance useful sparks could be struck.

The medical and expert witnesses, happy in having a relatively simple kind of truth to defend, maintained their opinions under attack, but granted without distress the possibility of a number of explanations fitting the same set of facts. No, Theo Freeland certainly had not left the studio to help himself to poison from the workshop that night. Yes, granted the idea of suicide had already entered his head, he could have helped himself, in readiness for just such a moment of despair, on almost innumerable previous occasions. He could have had the stuff in his pockets all the time. It was not their job to assess the relative probability of such a theory, but it was certainly possible. Granted it seemed unlikely that he should carry his death about with him, granted it strained belief a little further that he should thereupon dispose of every indication that he had done so, apart from his own contorted body, still the possibility remained obstinately possible. As often as it was obscured again by the circumstantial evidence, up sprang Sir Howard Fallon's tireless junior to unveil it again, to keep it for ever in mind. It was almost his only ewe lamb, and he did not mean to let it be side-tracked into the wilderness.

Nevertheless, the prosecution case stood squarely upon the solid ground of probability, and would not be shaken. Three weeks of arduous search for useful witnesses had hardly added anything to the structure. He had drunk himself as near as he could get to forgetfulness on that last visit to London with several people, some old friends, some strangers, but had opened his mind to only two. Both were produced in court. The first was a total stranger to Suspiria, a middle-aged clerk torn between fright and elation, who had merely shared a half-hour of sodden confidences with Theo just before closing-time, and testified that the fellow had said his marriage had broken up on him after ten years, and his wife had told him outright she was in love with somebody else, and never likely to change her mind about it.

From this witness there were no details of the time and place of the actual revelation, only a fairly shrewd observance concerning the state of mind of the victim. Did he seem to feel that his case was hopeless, and his life virtually ended? Well, he carried on as if he thought so, but all the time he really gave the impression that he didn't believe in it. He was cut up about it, all right, but in his heart he thought it would blow over, if he sat tight and held his breath. Like a kid with a nightmare, not too deep asleep, cleverly telling himself with the conscious bit of his mind: 'It can't really get you! You're only dreaming it!'

The second drinking-companion was an old friend, somewhat slipped out of their confidences since the war, but still a constant factor in their visits to London. He painted, desultorily but well, in an attic studio in Chelsea, and Theo had spent his single night in London, on this occasion, on his sofa, and poured out to him, with increasing coherence as the night wore on and the coffee grew blacker, the story of Suspiria's love affair. To this man it could be told, because he knew her, and was in a position to be just to them both. Only one detail seemed to have been omitted; there was no mention of the opening of the living-room door that night, and the two linked bodies starting apart as the latch relaxed softly into place. 'She came down in the night, and told me – she said they'd been lovers for two months—' Not: 'I found them—'

His host was a close friend, but only Theo's own skin, it seemed, had been close enough to be trusted with that one shattering moment. So now she knew exactly how much truth she had to tell, and the readjustment was not quite as terrible as it might have been.

Sir Howard Fallon, no doubt, expected her to avoid his eyes when he asked her about it that night. Instead, she gazed at him thoughtfully as she admitted the inaccuracy of this part of the story she had told him. There was even a slight, satirical smile on her lips, though no reflection of it touched his.

'Theo's report was perfectly accurate. The talk I had with him took place on the night of Wednesday, January 28th – or rather – let's be exact – in the small hours of the next morning. Malcolm seems to have got it the very next night, just as it happened. I suppose I'm lucky that it came out as it did, and not after we'd made some reference to the circumstances ourselves.'

He was watching her with a bleak and austere face, and for a moment he was silent. Then he said: 'I advise you to be very careful. Such a slip as that could make a very bad impression indeed – not only on the jury, either. Can you imagine that it makes things easier for me, to know that my client lies to me?'

'It can hardly make any impression on *your* faith in me,' said Suspiria, raising her hollow, exhausted eyes, 'for I know you have none. I'm perfectly well aware that you believe I killed Theo. I'm not so ingenuous as to suppose that it incommodes you at all, nor so disinterested as to feel obliged to fall out with you about it. I don't care what you believe, provided you're effective. Besides, it can hardly surprise or shock you to find a client lying to you. You're not that kind of hypocrite. You must know that very few people for whom you've acted have ever told you the whole truth.'

'It is commonly felt,' he said, not without the shadow of irony, though his face remained grave, 'that only the guilty lie in court.'

'That's hardly good enough for you, is it? Obviously the innocent lie just as desperately, and almost as often,' she said, pushing the disarranged plumes of her hair back from the broad, tired, boyish brow.

'Do they? Why do you think so?' It was a very soft and thoughtful question, as though he really wished to learn from her.

'Because, though your system of law may be the best in the world – I don't say it isn't – there are very few people with a sufficiently childlike trust in it to suppose that what it produces is invariably justice. Placing yourself upon your country is all very well on paper, but wait until you have to try it yourself. You'll find you have some reserves, too, and are trying to keep one of the strings of your life in your own hands. If there weren't some serious points against me, I shouldn't be here, and if I didn't look carefully round in every direction to see if I couldn't suppress some of them, I shouldn't be human. You are, no doubt, as good an advocate as I could have, but you're not the Archangel Gabriel yet – and I'm reasonably sure that little elderly monkey isn't quite as infallible as God, either.'

She waited for him to tell her, with a straight face, that nevertheless she must here and now dispose of any other lies she might have told him, and promise to tell him no more from this moment. She watched his face, and its gravity remained constant and severe; but he was not as obvious as she had suspected. All he said was: 'Well, we'll have to make the best we can of it. It won't look so good as if you'd told him about the affair some weeks earlier, of course. Why didn't you?'

'I don't know if you'll be able to believe me this time, but this time you can. It really didn't occur to me, until Dennis pointed it out, that it was any of Theo's business. That night he told me exactly how it was worrying him. He wanted us to have it out with Theo, and tell him the whole truth. It offended him that we weren't being honest about it.' A faint smile, blind and tender, made all the tired lines of her face tremulous for a moment. 'Until then I hadn't realised that we weren't, but I saw his point.'

'And why hadn't he spoken before? There'd been plenty of time.'

'That, again, is something that might easily not be believed. He thought at first that he'd merely been taken out of liking and pity. He thought it couldn't last, that in a very few weeks he'd be getting his dismissal, and I'd be going back to Theo. That being what he expected to happen, he thought it the opposite of honest to let any part of our little affair come to Theo's ears, to sour the future for him without any real cause. By the time he was convinced that the affair was not so little as he'd supposed, he'd kept it quiet so long that he didn't know quite how to bring it into the open. So he told me. And I talked to Theo. Much good it did any of us! Will the jury believe all that, do you think?'

'*I* believe it,' he said, without any change of tone, 'and *I know* you can lie.' And in a moment he added thoughtfully: 'By the time I've known you a little longer, it will be quite useless for you to tell me any lies at all.'

'By the time you've known me a little longer,' she said, with her angry smile, 'I shall either be free, or dead. In either case, no longer obliged to account for myself to you.'

'And you won't, I imagine, ever want to see me again?'

'I might have,' she said wearily, 'if we'd met in other circumstances. As it is – no, I shan't want to see you again. Even if I owe you my life,' she said, 'I'm never going to be able to be grateful to you or anyone for giving back to me a damaged version of something that was mine by right.'

He made no complaint of her. She thought afterwards that something in this conversation had reacted perversely against his disbelief in her, for from then on she could no longer be sure what he thought of her.

In the afternoon of the third day he opened the defence with a clear and unemotional speech, going over the points of the case briefly, and showing that the known facts were not in dispute upon either side.

'The prosecution has produced for you the story of Mrs. Freeland's liaison with Dennis Forbes in the manner of a conjurer producing a rabbit from a hat. But the curious thing about the whole proceeding, the thing which makes this line of attack seem quite frankly a dishonest one, is that this rabbit was perfectly tame, and well-known to every permanent resident of Great Leddington. The visits of Dennis Forbes to Little Worth were frequent, open, and a subject of scandal in a good part of the town for weeks before the tragedy of Theodore Freeland's death. It cannot be said that either of the pair took any steps to cover their tracks. They were lovers, and known to be lovers. What is now offered to you as a motive for murder – the desire to eliminate an obstacle to their love – becomes nonsense when you consider the fact that for nearly two months their love had known no obstacle at all, nor acknowledged the possibility of any. Admittedly Freeland himself was one of the last to learn the truth about what was going on, *but* when he did learn it, it was from his wife's lips. Why, then, should she want to kill him? Obviously she had no fear of him, obviously she had no intention whatever of letting him determine her future course of action. How, then, was he an obstacle? With lovers of a different kind you might be justified in supposing that they wished to eliminate him in order to be free to marry, and so regain – perhaps they might be ingenuous enough to say, rather, to retain – their respectability. But when you have heard the evidence of their proceedings, heard what the neighbours knew about them, and what the neighbours thought, and how much attention these singularly brave or singularly brazen lovers paid to public opinion – then I shall ask you with confidence to consider how much respectability meant to these two. Kill for it? You may find yourselves wondering whether they would so much as cross the road for it!

'Beware of accepting a conventional motive as credible in dealing with a woman to whom the conventions meant nothing! She had already thrown her good name, as we normally understand it, her reputation and his, and all the established course of her life, clean away for the love of a young man. But do not suppose that these things necessarily meant to her as much as they mean to you. What mattered to this woman was her art, and her single and responsible governance of her own life – and, after he appeared, her love for this young man. Her art she could carry with her any time she cared to walk out of her husband's house and her husband's life. It went wherever her body and her brain went, and she could not be asked to give it up. Her sense of her own integrity demanded that she should make her own decisions, by no standards but her own. This, also, was very portable luggage. Her love asserted its pre-eminence in her life, and dictated precisely one course – that she should accept it for what it was, and re-orientate her life to its acceptance. You will hear that she elected to do so, without any hesitation. What you have been asked, in fact, to regard as a lunatic infatuation, emerges on examination as one of the most deliberate, responsible and candid acts of free-will you are ever likely to meet, in a world where many of us allow all our actions to be dictated by the fixed patterns of society.'

Some of his phrases were headlined that night. He spent rather more time upon opening careful holes in all the prosecution's assumptions. Too much importance, for instance, had been attached to the emptiness of the stage. How dared they assume that because they had found no one else in the house, and no traces, therefore no one had been there, no one else existed in the case? He would bring witnesses to testify that the door of this most casual and most isolated house was almost never locked. Any casual tramp, any private enemy, could walk in as he pleased. How, then, could it be taken for granted that Mrs. Freeland was alone in the house with her husband throughout the night? Much had been made of the footprints which proved that Freeland had not left his studio for several hours before his death – or, at least, that his shoes had not. How could it be argued from this that he had not taken the antimony from the workshop himself, when it was known and admitted that he had been drunk, depressed, and pouring out the story of his loss a full week previously, and throughout that week had had every opportunity of helping himself to this particular means of ending his life? There were, said Sir Howard, many holes as large as these to be found, in the evidence on which they were being asked to convict a woman of murder. He mapped them all; but what the headlines wanted and took from his speech were the knife-edged phrases about 'singularly brave or singularly brazen lovers', 'lovers and known to be lovers'.

The legend was growing by then, and grew still more rapidly after Sir Howard had allowed his junior to guide his few casual witnesses through their paces, and had arrived at the point of putting Dennis into the witness-box. Suspiria was being saved for last, but here at least was the other partner in the scandalous romance. They crowded and craned to hear him, and ripples of excitement and gratification passed almost soundlessly through their ranks. He took the oath with the clear, fastidious attention of one about to break it the next moment. He looked once at Suspiria, and then fixed his grey eyes upon his mentor, and moistened his dry lips nervously, like a small boy facing an examination.

Suspiria saw that gesture, and a small tight spot of fear below her heart began to ache for him, because it was the only childish thing left about him. He looked taller than she had ever thought him, and older by the few decisive years which turn a grown-up boy into a man. He had lost flesh in the last weeks; how was it she had never noticed it before? His face had gained in clarity and form, and the young, vulnerable mouth, once firmly shut after that nervous caress of his tongue, had acquired a new length and stillness, and drawn out its soft lines to a tension of resolution. He would never look so defenceless again; but it needed only the one glimpse he had given her of his eyes to show her how he was suffering.

Counsel led him, coolly and practically and without any gentleness, through the story of his meeting with Theo and Suspiria, his association with them, his love affair, and the few days of grace for which Suspiria had asked in Theo's interests. What had she hoped to do? To manage to induce Theo to understand their situation, and help to resolve it without avoidable damage to anyone. They had hoped to keep his friendship, and thought it worth waiting for. Dennis answered the questions in rather a low voice, but one which carried easily to every ear; even from his voice, she thought, some slightly defensive, slightly truculent overtone had been exorcised by the reality of this danger, with which no imaginary grievances could live.

As soon as Perleman got to his feet, with that deliberate swirl of his gown about him, as insolently provocative as the shooting of a Georgian cuff, Suspiria knew that he had selected Dennis as the weaker vessel, and was about to set out on a long and calculating offensive to break him down. Perhaps he hoped to shatter her nerves, too, by tormenting her darling; she could well imagine him thinking in that way. The process, too, would be something he knew how to enjoy. He began modestly, almost tenderly, like a cat fondling a mouse, regarding Dennis across the court with a gentler face than Sir Howard had shown him, and an almost vague smile.

'I should like to be sure that I have understood you correctly, Mr. Forbes, in the matter of your attitude to this – romantic attachment. You wish us to infer that from the beginning there was no secrecy about it? That it was as open as the day?'

'There was no secrecy about it,' said Dennis. 'There was something that might have been mistaken for it, though. You don't have to be feeling guilty about a thing to want to keep it private and safe, if you value it very much.'

'But you had no desire to hide it from Mr. Freeland. That, I believe, is the gist of what you have said?'

'Not quite! I said *she* had no desire to hide it from him, and never thought it might look as if she was. At first *I* did want to hide it from him.'

Counsel's thick, straight eyebrows rose a little. 'I see! Why did you not make that plain in your answers to my learned friend?'

'I thought I had. If not, I'm glad to do so now. Certainly I wanted to keep it from him, at first. For maybe two or three weeks I felt like that.'

'So you did feel guilt in the matter, and did anticipate the kind of vulgar trouble which attends on affairs with other men's wives! The prospect of facing an outraged husband had some terrors for you, then, after all?'

Dennis looked back at him fixedly, and his cheeks were stained with two hot pinpoints of colour, but his composure survived the long, inimical stare without a tremor. There was no one left in his consciousness but the two of them, and there unseen, watching them, Suspiria, whose safety was at the moment the only thing on earth that mattered to him.

'There *was* something of that in it,' he said, 'naturally. Instinctively I was a bit scared of the kind of row there might be – that is, the kind husbands are supposed to make in the circumstances. But that had to come soon or later, if it was coming. What I was more afraid of was that we'd bring on the whole scene, and all for nothing. I didn't expect to be able to last long with her. I never thought she could feel about me as I did about her. And if I had to get out and let them alone in a very few weeks, what was the good of spoiling things for him? He might have had it on his mind all his life.'

'I see! It was pure consideration for the husband! Now we understand! You appear to be as modest as you are considerate, Mr. Forbes, since it seems you found it improbable that you possessed the necessary qualities to hold Mrs. Freeland's interest for long. May I ask how long it took to disabuse your mind of that idea?'

'I suppose after two or three weeks I began to believe that she – that it was going to last, after all.'

'So, of course, acting on the same heroic principles, you

made a clean breast of the whole thing to Mr. Freeland. It was no longer a point of decency to preserve your secrecy – I beg your pardon, reticence! – but rather a point of honour to tell him the full truth. You did that at once, of course? There appears to be a confusion in the dates here, Mr. Forbes. I understood from the evidence of Mr. Malcolm that it was not until January 29th that Mr. Freeland learned the facts.'

'I agree with that date. I have already agreed with it.'

'Then how do you account for the lapse of those additional weeks? You knew now that the case was serious, and that the only fair thing to do was to tell him. Why didn't you?'

Dennis said patiently: 'There were two reasons. Having begun by keeping silent about it, it seemed harder afterwards to change course. And then, it had to be agreed between the two of us, it couldn't be a gesture by one. And I found it very difficult to begin to talk about it to Suspiria.' He looked a little startled, even for a moment a little disconcerted, at having called her by that name, as if he had given away a piece of her which could be used in offensive magic. 'It was so obvious that she hadn't thought about it at all. I made several tries. That night – the Wednesday, January 28th, I managed it. As soon as she understood what was on my mind – as soon as she thought about his side of it – she agreed that we must have it straight with him. She told him the same night.'

'*She* told him? You were not present yourself?'

'No. She told him after I'd gone home.'

'Your own part in it doesn't seem to have been a very heroic one, does it?'

'We weren't concerned with what anyone else was going to think about either of us,' said Dennis. 'It was a simple matter of economy. It had to cost him the least we could make it, and she said that was the best way for him, and I knew she was right.' But he was affronted, his mind was rubbing the place that had been hit, and Perleman knew it. 'We agreed I should go back the next night, and we—'

'Thank you, yes, we quite understand. You agree, then, that whatever the reasons, the affair was suppressed – will you allow me that word? – for seven weeks from the beginning of your liaison? It seems that you shrank from the scene which would probably follow. Is that a fair statement?'

'*I* did. I wanted it out, but I won't pretend I looked forward to the process.'

'Mrs. Freeland, you wish me to infer – since you differentiate so carefully – Mrs. Freeland had no scruples?' asked Perleman pleasantly.

'Mrs. Freeland had no doubts or fears.' All his wincing indignation left him when he reverted to her. His voice was full, assured, assuaged, his tongue found the right words instinctively.

'Mr. Forbes, I would ask you to remember that you are on oath.' The volcanic eruption of Perleman's voice cast a startled cloud of ash over that good impression, knowing when to thunder. 'You have stated on oath that this – this humane and voluntary interview between husband and wife was the manner of Freeland's enlightenment, and that it took place at *your* will – yours and the prisoner's. After nearly two months of a liaison so careful, so furtive, that this man could live constantly in the same house with it, and have no suspicions, you ask us to believe that suddenly you and your partner in guilt decide to do the right thing, and tell him the truth! Out of your fundamental love of honesty, no doubt! Really, it won't do, you know! Let me help your memory! Wasn't what happened more like this: you were alone with Mrs. Freeland that night, while Freeland was painting, probably, in his studio. You were not, I suggest, wasting your time in talking. You had other ways of passing the evenings, had you not? And in the middle of your absorption in each other – *he came in*! It was that night he learned the truth, yes, but he learned it because he was so indiscreet as to walk in upon you in the act. And in a week he was dead! I put it to you that this – *this*, and not your gentle fiction – was the manner of Theodore Freeland's discovery of his wife's misconduct, and that you had everything to fear and *you knew it*. And one of you or both of you took steps accordingly! Answer me! He caught you in the act, did he not?'

'No,' said Dennis vigorously, grateful for the prompt weight of his own lie anchoring his mind to what was essential. 'He did not.' The shock of Perleman's inspired guess had passed by without even grazing him, because it was necessary for Suspiria's life that he should feel nothing, nothing at all, but what touched her. He wanted to look at her, but it was impossible, his eyes must hold Perleman fast, and give no sign of fear, or anger, or pain. The wide, patient, prolonged stare was certainly a victory.

Sir Howard was on his feet, ready to advance the obvious objection but it was not necessary. The old Judge leaned forward in his husk of clothes to observe with acidity: 'There appears to be support for this witness's version of the events in question, from one of your own witnesses. Precisely which witness are you trying to discredit, Mr. Perleman?'

'I am suggesting, my lord, that while Edward Malcolm's truthfulness is not in question for a moment, the account he had of that evening came from a deeply shocked man, who may very well have told him the truth, and nothing but the truth, but not the whole truth. I am suggesting that a discovery by the husband preceded and precipitated the wife's confession, and that, indeed, that confession would never have been made at all but for that discovery. I think it does not require much imagination, my lord, to understand why the husband did not feel like confiding the full extent of his injury, even in the state he was then in.'

'He does not appear to have been in the mood to keep very much back,' said the Judge dryly. 'However – very well, proceed!'

'You know the meaning of perjury, I trust, Mr. Forbes?'

'Yes, I know it.'

'And you insist on maintaining this most improbable version of the events of that evening? You don't wish to add anything?'

'It is what happened. I can't add anything, there was nothing else to add.'

'He can't know anything,' thought Suspiria, watching the smooth, recovered placidity of Perleman's face. 'If Theo didn't tell Malcolm he wouldn't tell anyone else.' But the recoiling pain of that moment of discovery, that moment that need never have happened, lay cold and quiet in her heart.

'Very well! Let us go on to the evening of the following Wednesday, the eve of Freeland's death. I would like to take you through the details of that evening once more—'

It went on and on, item by item through this and through that, dwelling suggestively on the week between, the renewed visits, the rapid death. All too apt, and too significant. He kept it up for over three hours, eliciting every smallest detail which might show Dennis up discreditably, and displaying an inspired gift for finding the most sensitive nerves of his victim's body; but there were no breakages. Her own examination and cross-examination, which occupied most of the following day, held no such terrors for Suspiria as she had felt for Dennis. She watched his eyes growing hollow and haggard in his head, and all the youth, all the colour, draining slowly out of him, and she was filled with an unbearable, a frenzied anger.

At the end of it, when Perleman relinquished him, Sir Howard Fallon rose, and said in his detached voice: 'Just one minute more, Mr. Forbes. Since your position has been somewhat obscured in an avalanche of detail, I would like to have it clearly restated for the jury's benefit. I'll be very brief. First, through no contrivance of yours or hers, you met and loved Mrs. Freeland, and she you?'

'Yes. Loved and love her! And she me.'

'Second, this love appeared to you both – appears to you both, I should say – as a sacred reality, which ought not to be either denied or relinquished?'

'Yes, that is how it appears to us.'

'Or defaced by any meanness? You can answer, perhaps, only for yourself, but I ask you to consider very gravely how you answer.'

'I can answer for both of us! We wanted it to be unmarked.'

'And have you – either of you – done anything to deface it? Have you, in particular, sought to make it permanent and safe by the final meanness of murder?'

'No. There was no need! It *is* permanent and safe. It always was.'

'Thank you, Mr. Forbes, that is all.'

6

The struggle between Suspiria and Perleman was longer and more deadly, but it came to the same thing in the end. He could not break her down on any detail of her story, or shake her steady denials; she could not close every avenue of doubt he opened. The impression she made in the witness-box, however, was good; her replies were all prompt, alert, forceful and angry, she fought him savagely, but with as much precision as if she had considered every answer beforehand. After that duel, the final speeches scarcely seemed to add anything.

Throughout the trial the little Judge had sat huddled in his robes, looking shrivelled and vindictive, and as if he could not get warm, for all the May sunshine that glittered between the showers. His rare interventions had all been phrased so briefly that it seemed impossible he could utter more than one short sentence at a time, but when he stirred irritably and emerged from his silence to sum up, there came out of his shrunken body a startlingly cold, lucid and musical voice, like a mountain river, that spoke in formed and fluent phrases, distastefully manipulating the exact measure of justice.

He knew that he would not last many more years. Perhaps this was the last woman who would ever sit with her eyes fixed insatiably on his face, trying to wrest the verdict out of his mind without reference to all those crippling intermediary stages through which it must pass before reaching her, his words, the mixed and imperfect understandings of the jury, their prejudices, their obstinacies. He did not look at her as he spoke, but he knew how she was looking at him. Every woman in the dock is only a variant, not a new species; even a woman like this one, who happens to be an artist and a lover as well.

He thought: 'I shall not destroy her, but I think the process of her destruction may already have begun, by another way.' And he looked at the boy, clinging to her clean across the court with the sick grey anxiety of his handsome eyes, and for a moment he almost pitied them. 'Ah, well, it's too late for anyone to save them from each other now,' he said to himself, relinquishing the instinct of regret with hardly a pang. 'It's gone too far – they'll never escape, now. Not even a strength like hers can drag them out of it after this.'

The summing-up was a model of its kind, comprehensive and just but without too much obscuring detail. He wondered that it had to be so long, when there was really only one thing to say, the thing they must surely have seen for themselves from the beginning:

'Remember that the onus is not on the defence to prove the prisoner's innocence, nor to suggest an alternative theory to account for the death. It is the business of the prosecution to prove the prisoner's guilt beyond any reasonable doubt. If you think that a doubt does remain in this case – and if you do not, you are not fit to serve on a jury, but you won't be the first jurors of whom that could be said! – you must give the accused the benefit of that doubt. You are not entitled to toss for it mentally, however much you would like to get out of it that way, and however much you dislike her, and would like to retain a chance of convicting her; you must find her not guilty.'

That was not what he said, though he would have taken pleasure in addressing them at last with that extreme and offensive simplicity. After all, guilty or innocent, why should they mind letting go? She was taken care of! She had made ber bed, and installed that wretched child in it, and there they would both find their particular circle of hell, like Paolo and Francesca locked for ever in an indissoluble and unremitting embrace, and blown about the windy spaces of their own emotions by uncontrollable winds of passion and despair. The headlines had married them, and no divorce would ever deliver them out of hell again. Two whom notoriety had joined might look in vain for a God or a man ingenious enough to prise them asunder.

They suffered, no doubt, a great deal during the eighty minutes of the jury's absence, and the woman's eyes when she came back into the dock to hear the verdict were sunken hollow and deep into her head, and the green flames within them cast a fierce despairing light upward out of the pit of her exhaustion. She wanted her life, that woman, she had stood over it like a wildcat for five days, daring them to try and take it; and now, if they gave it back to her, there was nothing on earth for her to do with it but put it into the arms of that terrified boy who had died with her so many times already. Much good it would do her there, but she had not looked beyond the verdict yet. She was standing in the dock, tearing at the foreman with the fury of her eyes, willing him to say the right words. And he, poor devil, looked as if he had been dragged through a few hedges and ditches during the retirement. Which of them had wanted to kill her, doubt or no doubt? The women?

'You are agreed upon your verdict?'

'We are, my lord?' He looked at the woman then, defending himself hurriedly from that fierce green stare.

'Do you find the prisoner at the bar guilty or not guilty of murder?'

'Not guilty, my lord!'

Her face of stone and flame softened and became flesh and blood before the old man's eyes, her hands relaxed upon the edge of the dock, and a surge of warm colour flooded her cheeks miraculously, like the sudden blooming of a rose. She turned her head, and looked full at the young man Forbes, and his eyes were like mirrors of her own, alive, eased, dazed with joy. They didn't understand properly yet; they thought they were free.

CHAPTER EIGHT:

The Chained Lovers

1

DENNIS BROUGHT her home to Little Worth next day, in a car lent by George Grover. The loan was offered with a warmth for which he felt a childish and unsuspecting gratitude, though even in the moment of acceptance it seemed to lay an unaccountable weight upon his spirit, slight but perceptible, like the touch of a reminding finger. It was something he did not understand, and was too tired to examine. He accepted it as pure kindness, like his mother's offer to go up to the house and put fires in, and air the bed for Suspiria's return, and Winnie's sudden whispered suggestion that it would be nice if they put some flowers in the living-room to welcome her. It was the soft compulsion of relief moving them all to demonstrative acts of kindness, and in his own still dazed state it made him tremble with gratitude, and weaken into an unreasoning affection. How good people were, after all, how generous!

Suspiria had elected to spend the night in a small hotel in the county town, to which Mr Quinn had brought her very quietly, under cover of the excitement. She had slept for about sixteen hours, an exhausted sleep, sunk far below the level of consciousness; and when she awoke and arose, it was into a world so new that it had little colour and almost no form. Presently, she supposed, there would be feeling again; but as yet she moved through a half-made void, trying to exercise her senses where there was nothing for them to taste, or hear, or touch. She had died, of course; one does not get over that in a single day. Even the pain and the rage take longer than that to leave the mind.

Their escape from the town was effected without hindrance or annoyance; and in the car, where pursuit and interference were no longer possible, she began to feel again. This was new, and of the new world, that she should sit shoulder to shoulder with Dennis, on her way home, and that there should be no shadow nor memory of another person between them. The warmth of his body came to her, first faintly, then with unbearably sweet reminders. They did not touch each other throughout the journey, nor speak more than a few words, until he helped her out of the car at her own door, in the cool, delicate sunlight of the May afternoon.

Suspiria stood in the yard, looking all round her with dilated eyes just stirring out of their drugged blankness. A blue coil of smoke was spiralling upward from the chimney, the curtains had been changed, and the windows cleaned. When she opened the door and let herself into the living-room, she was met by a subdued and disciplined gleam, for the room had been dusted and polished, an overcrowded vase of tulips stood on the piano, where she had been accustomed to see the gracious swelling lines of the green bowl, and all the pots on the shelves stood in prim rows, like unintelligent soldiers on parade. The books had been tidied so strictly into place that they looked only like paintings of books, created to fill vacant shelves and satisfy the eye. She stood looking round her blankly for a moment in the middle of this unfamiliar domesticity, and then a curious light came into her eyes. He could not be sure whether it was amusement or anger.

'I see someone's been busy!' She crossed to the hearth, where a compact fire burned, and stood with her back to him, warming her hands.

'My mother offered to come and put in a fire for you. You don't mind, do you?'

'It was very kind of her,' said Suspiria, in a voice he could not translate with any accuracy. 'And the flowers?'

'I expect that was Winnie. Give me your coat, Spiri! There, now sit down, and I'll go and make some tea.' But he hovered with his hands above her shoulders, wanting her to turn and fasten her arms round his neck, and draw him into her heart. It had always seemed to him that the homecoming could begin in no other way; there would be the closing of the door against the world, and then the instant, hungry meeting, everything they had missed through the weeks of waiting, but with a new and indescribable and desperate sweetness added. Now he hung over her sick with longing, and she did not move.

'I'm not an invalid,' she said, lightly and gently. 'So – your mother has cleaned the house for me, your sister brought me flowers – and George loaned the car to bring me home. It's touching, isn't it?'

He did not understand; he had been dwelling so much upon her that he had scarcely seen or thought of anything else.

'George has been very decent all round. He let me off the extra day from work without a murmur.'

'He expects to be well paid for it,' said Suspiria, 'one way or another. The first instalment will be payable tomorrow, I expect – you'll have to tell him all about it. Not just the trial, he can read that in the papers. No, the home-coming, and what we said to each other, and how I looked, and how we made love—'

Dennis took his hands away from her, and stood looking at her, not with the hurt patience she had expected, but in a dark, passive pain, as if she had merely held up a mirror to his eyes.

'They haven't taken out shares in us, if they think they have. We're not public property.'

'Oh, yes, we are! That's just what we are. We belong to the world, my poor little love. Everybody's rushing to buy into the company, and they all want value for their money. Those who can only get at us through the papers want fine, large gestures from us, that can satisfy their senses from a long way off. Those who're close round us will want the dialogue, too – appropriate, sentimental confidences, everything they've been led to expect. My God!' she said, 'what complaint have we got? We wrote our own parts to begin with, didn't we?'

'You don't regret it?' he asked, in a voice of such sudden suppressed terror that she put out her hand in protest, and laid it against his cheek, and the moment after was in his arms. This at least remained a vast and violent reality, the mutual tide of their passion, infallible above all their differences, making mere rack of the world that plagued them.

'Oh, no, no! Never, my own darling, my beloved little heart! Don't leave me – whatever I say or do, don't leave me!'

'Never, never— Oh, Spiri! Oh, my darling—'

She felt so fragile in his arms now, and her slight weight sank upon him so heavily, that even the hard-won delight of the moment faded from him into pure tenderness. He lifted her, and put her softly into the chair by the fire.

'I'm sorry! Not the time or the place! Listen, now, you rest there, as you're told, and I'll get some tea.'

He came in from the kitchen a few minutes later with a pile of letters, all nicely sorted into sizes; she thought she recognised again his mother's housewifely touch. 'They were on the table there. Look, mountains of it! Do you want to bother with them now?'

She took them from him with a frown, suddenly conscious of their ugly possibilities. The feel of his mother in the house had made her nudge herself wryly: 'A mother-in-law – that's something I never had before!' The sight of so many unopened envelopes, so many unknown hands, made her think more bitterly: 'Some of our millions of proprietors!' But she accepted them with authority, because they were a reality which had to be faced. By the time he came in again with the tea she had torn her way through most of them, and piled them round her upon the floor. The evening paper, fallen sprawling among them, opened to his wincing eyes headlines and photographs full across the page:

'TRAGIC LOVERS VINDICATED: Great Leddington Awaits Homecoming of Mrs. Freeland.
'Consistent and Fearless Throughout,' says Counsel.

And the large beginning of the text, splayed under a picture taken outside the court after the acquittal: 'Today young Dennis Forbes will bring home to her studio at Little Worth, under the hanging woods of Great Leddington, the woman whose love for him has triumphantly survived not only all the pressures of her society, but the ordeal of a murder trial. Acquitted yesterday of the slaying of her artist husband, Mrs Freeland returns unsubdued to her own art, and to the love which has successfully defended itself against conventional morality and the gravest of criminal charges.'

'Yes,' she said, seeing with what a passion of dislike he stood regarding it, 'they must have their satisfaction somehow. If they can't hang us, they must debauch us.' She reached down and turned the paper over, to hide the rest of it from him. 'It's nothing, it's almost dignified, only trying to be daring and broad-minded. Wait until the real scandal-sheets begin to compete.'

'They'll get tired of it,' he said, 'in time.'

'In time, we shall all be dead. Then nothing will matter.' She drew in her skirt fastidiously from the litter of paper she had strewn round her. 'Most of it's only fit for burning, but you should look through it before it goes. Yes, if you believe we've escaped, you should really add it all up, and see what the sum comes to. Some of them are just filth, the pathological kind people get when they've been through the headlines. Some are much more horrible, like the papers, but worse – oozing sentimentality about love, and pawing both of us all over. Even if they meant all they said, they'd be indecent; but they're dishonest, too.'

He put the tray on the table, and went to her and took hold of her hands, because she was shaking with silent laughter, and the very quietness of what he took for her hysteria terrified him. 'Don't look at them again! Don't think of them! I'll burn them all, you needn't see them any more. We *have* escaped, Spiri! We don't have to live the way they want us to, we belong to no one but ourselves.'

'And that's not all!' she said, as if he had never spoken. 'That's no more than the beginning, my poor little innocent. After all the suppressed romantics who want to congratulate us on losing the world for love, and the perverts who want us to go to bed together in public for them, the subtler insults begin. There are four offers here from newspapers, for my – or even better, our – exclusive story of martyrdom for love. Have you any idea how much money you could get, Dennis, my darling, for a five-hundred-word article in your own hand? I won't tell you, the temptation might be too much. I can understand now why people do exhibit themselves, people who've never had that much money in their lives. And then, think of the competition! You could force them to double their offers, easily, if you kept your nerve!'

'Don't!' he said, his voice rising into a cry. 'Stop it, Spiri, I can't bear it!'

'I'm sorry!' she said, light and quiet again, and freed one hand to touch his forehead, so softly that he could not doubt her calm. 'You mustn't be upset, I'm quite in control of myself. You shouldn't grudge my laughing – unless you want me to die of spite. Either it's funny or it's a horrible outrage, and I think I prefer to find it funny, but if you don't like it— And then, there are some more original angles, too. There are two dealers making me offers for London exhibitions, and a big shop wanting to put me on contract. They're specially interested in recent work – that means work I did while we made love to each other, and Theo painted away in happy ignorance in the next room. I'm a good business proposition now, Dennis, better than I've ever been before. It doesn't even matter very much whether the pots are any good, as long as they're my children by you.'

'You could have expected things like that,' he said, trembling nevertheless because he himself had never foreseen them. 'It'll all blow over in a few weeks. They'll let us alone.'

'And you think we shall still be intact? Intellectual and spiritual virgins? After wading through this? You haven't heard everything yet. The cream of the joke is still to come. There's a letter from a firm of caterers, offering to take care of all the wedding arrangements for us, discreetly and tastefully – in a style befitting the remarriage of a notorious widow, no doubt.'

This time he really did not understand. He sat there at her feet on the rug, still holding her hand between his own, his fingers tight upon hers as if he felt himself to be hanging on desperately to his own personality. She put her free hand over his eyes, because she did not want to see the beginning of understanding in them; and bending her head, kissed him very tenderly on the mouth.

'I shouldn't have told you. But even if I'd said nothing, some day you'd have realised all this. Close your eyes! Don't look at me yet! I love you!'

The long brown lashes lay obediently on his cheeks. After a moment he said, so quietly, with such strenuous serenity that she knew he had understood at last: 'What does it matter? We shall be doing what *we* decide to do. I want to marry you. I hope you want to marry me. I don't care about anyone else. They can go to hell, or queue up outside the gate to stare at us, it won't matter to me.'

Perhaps he even believed it, she thought; he had a furious faith in her, and in the person she had unwittingly made of him. He would ask God knew what miracles of them both!

'You didn't look forward to quite this kind of shotgun wedding, I suppose,' she said dryly.

The contortion of his face made her feel as if she had struck him. He opened his eyes upon her widely, then, and said in the same resolute tone, yet somehow with less conviction: 'I think you're making too much of it – too much of them all.'

'Do you? Haven't you realised yet that we've put ourselves in their power? We started a course of events, and we've no choice now but to go with it. If we love each other, as we've gone to a great deal of trouble to state as publicly and often as possible – if through no act of ours, as we've also sworn, the barrier between us has been removed – if we mean what we've said about both our love and our innocence, my poor child – then there's just one move open to us. If we make any other, can't you see all those eyes turning to look at us again, and all those minds beginning to wonder? We've even put it out of our power to delay for long, since conventions mean nothing to us! Oh, we've been wonderfully thorough, we've shut every escape route against ourselves! No, we've got to go on. There's just one end for us – to marry, and live together, and be perfectly, triumphantly happy, in full view of all our public. And if we don't make a good showing, can't you hear the whispers of murder going round again? As soon as we cease to provide value for money one way, they'll set out to get it another. We belong to them, now.'

'We belong to ourselves,' he said doggedly, 'and we can do what we please. If you want me to go away now, and leave you alone, I'll go. If you tell me not to come back—' But he could not end the challenge, it stuck in his throat and he could not get it out.

'I want you to continue to be the person you are. I want you to love me, and to let me love you, but oh, God, not their way!'

'It won't be their way, it will be ours. You needn't do anything you don't want to do. You shall only take me when you choose to take me. You shall work, and only sell your work where you choose to sell it – not at all, if you don't want to. We won't touch these damned dealers who want to cash in on the scandal. There must be others! We won't get married till we're ready – never, if you want to make a gesture. I don't care if they dig the case up again,' he said, rocking her hands against his burning cheek. 'They can't touch *you* again, I don't care if they try to get at me. I don't care if everyone turns against us! I won't have you bent out of shape!'

She felt the sudden heat and tremor of his tears upon her fingers, a slight and scalding dew, bursting out from his eyes to blur the image of her deformity and defeat. It was then that she knew he had understood; the violence of his recoil from the conviction of their helplessness shook him from head to foot in a convulsion of denial and despair. Ever-assertion of defiance was an acknowledgment of his hopelessness and disbelief, and a recognition of hers; and at the point where he knew his struggles for what they were, he suddenly ceased to make them, and the unwonted and ungovernable tears broke along his lashes, terrifying him and putting him to silence. She tore her hands free from his hold, and caught him to her breast with a soft, grieved cry.

'Don't listen to me! It's the reaction – it isn't really true! They can't change us! They can't make us change!'

But he did not look up. He shut his arms round her body and clung to her, while she strained him to her heart. They lay still in the chair, encircled and encircling, bound indissolubly together, like guilty lovers tied breast to breast and set adrift upon a fast-flowing river, to perpetuate to death and beyond one terrible embrace.

2

Afterwards, when the moment had passed and they had torn themselves apart, each blamed the other, pitifully and tenderly, for the remembered distress, and each refused to believe in it.

'It *was* just the reaction,' Dennis told himself, driving back alone to the garage. 'How could she be expected to come through that without a scratch? Of course the nervous strain is just coming out this way. In a few weeks she'll get over it, and be back to normal. I must be in a pretty low state myself – for a little while I really believed in it. We'll have to take things quietly for a bit, and wait for the whole thing to blow over. I must be very good to her.'

But the lingering uneasiness did not leave him. Of course they had made their stand throughout the case upon their love and their innocence – what else could they have done? But they hadn't given up one atom of their own personalities. They owed nothing to anyone, and nothing even to each other. If they wanted to get married, they could, now. But as for having to, that was ridiculous. There was no compulsion about it. They loved each other, but marriage was a practical step, something that had to be thought about. Suddenly he knew that he had never really thought about it at all. Even when he had talked about getting Theo to divorce her, he hadn't really begun to realise what the results would be. It had been just a kind of sweet, painful and remote dream, and its very remoteness had absolved them both from examining or regarding the possibility of its accomplishment. But now the impossible had become possible, and they would do well to step back and consider it from every angle, before they did something which could not be undone. For both their sakes!

Perhaps it was only this sudden realisation of the responsibility they had for the future that had caused her mind to recoil in rage and protest. She couldn't bear to take even what she wanted at the compulsion of the world. She needed an interlude of work to regain her passion of creative satisfaction, to feel her own vindicated stability again, to defy the world out of the rock of her own personality. Then she could give herself again, with the old candour and generosity, she who couldn't bear to have things snatched from her when all she wanted was to give them of her own free will. And he had to have something positive to give in return, an identity of his own to match with hers. Yes, she was right to resist the too hasty thrust of events. Only, he told himself vehemently, she would never have been afraid of the challenge at any other time; the despair had come from her nerves and her weariness, not from her spirit.

Left alone in the house, Suspiria sat gazing at the overcrowded tulips in their unsuitable vase, and sensing the strangeness of that neat, domesticated hand in her affronted possessions. It was late to wonder now what they had in common; perhaps it was too late. Perleman had put it all very plainly, and they had scarcely even heard him, so sure had they been of what they were and what they wanted – then, when it was still out of their reach, and therefore of passionate importance. '—the case of the ageing woman of parts, and the man who can match against her culture just two qualities, made overwhelming by the time and the circumstances of their eruption into her life – his beauty and his youth.' A very intelligent man, Perleman! But limited, too. He saw in obvious terms what was by no means obvious; until he spoke, they had neither of them had any age at all, and for each of them the beauty of the other had been so personal that it needed no standards of measurement or comparison. Now that there was no obstacle between them, they could see each other more plainly, armed already with all the advice and wisdom of the world.

'—a boy of twenty-two, a garage mechanic, cursorily educated, but without any intellectual resources which could bring him on to the same plane with her – incompatible in age, in temperament, in his whole scale of values.' She could not forget a word of it now, though at the time it had seemed to pass her by and leave no scar. She had denied it every word, in everything she said and every look of her eyes, and so had the boy, perhaps unconsciously copying her defiance, perhaps producing some magnificent obstinacy of his own out of the violent growth which was taking place in him every moment. 'It *is* permanent and safe. It always was.' And they had maintained their cause and won their case, and the world was convinced. What a curious victory, that in the process they should also have been infected by the arguments they had over-ridden. The world was convinced, and they had lost their conviction. The world was convinced, and had given them its inescapable blessing, from which they would never again find a hiding-place, and from the compulsion of which they would never, with all their late and convulsive struggles, be able to turn aside.

'I'm being a fool,' she thought, thrusting her shoulders back, and shutting her fingers against her breast, where his moist lashes had left the faintest and most piteous of stains. 'I'm Suspiria Freeland, I haven't changed at all, I still know my trade, I can still make things, and they'll still be good. I have an existence apart from him! And he exists, too, without my name to prop him up. When we marry, if we choose to marry, it will be on our own terms, not theirs – not as the two broken halves of a pot being cemented together.'

She had not yet been into the workshop, and suddenly her desire to recover her own course seemed to her to have no other starting-point. She rose and crossed the room, and in the doorway the long mirror brought her up short, face to face with her reflection. The wrought-iron frame had been carefully dusted; the attentive hand of Mrs Forbes, heavy and soft, was everywhere in the room. From within the frame her own face looked out, thinner, paler, more translucent than she had remembered it. Did she look, as now she felt, every one of her thirty-six years? She touched her cheeks, curiously; they were smooth but cold, and no colour mantled to the touch. 'An ageing woman of parts,' she thought. 'A woman in her late thirties!' It was perhaps rather ungallant to thirty-six and seven months, but it was broadly true. She supposed she had always been perfectly aware of her age; how was it that it had never seemed at all important? Apparently these things mattered, were almost a part of one's identity. She would be another woman, then, would she, when she turned thirty-seven?

She went into the workshop. The managing hand had not been there, perhaps Mrs Forbes had been afraid to interfere where there were poisons. The fine screens stirred along the wall when she opened the door, the draught rocking them upon their hooks. Going undusted and uncleaned for two months made no difference to this room, where no more cleaning was ever done than the minimum necessary to make work possible. Her spirit lifted a little as she stood looking about her, and moved between the wooden racks of shelves, touching the materials of her trade, the wheel, the rough bricks of the kiln, the heaped bats, the fantastic little improvised tools of hoop-iron half-embedded in the cracked white clay of the wheel-table. Only this pervasive dryness hurt her senses with an oppressive sadness. There were green pots standing on the shelves, hard and white now, past reclaiming, some of them cracked with their long waiting. Where there was usually a smooth, creamy pool of slurry there was now a miniature clay desert, a tiny Sinkiang, sterile and desolate.

The first small elation at touching her own again, at

re-entering her kingdom, melted away out of her heart, and left her sick with a desperate and senseless grief. She put her head down in her arms over the wheel, and broke into a passion of weeping, all the centre of her being molten into tears.

When the storm had passed, she lifted her head with a weary indifference, and saw the darker traces of her tears softening the desert beneath her hands. She pressed her fingers into the marks, and worked the dead clay into life again. It drank, it was recoverable, it creamed upward between her finger-tips, responsive and alert; but still she looked at it sorrowfully, and could not foresee that it would ever again blossom like the rose.

3

George Grover began to draw on the deposit of the borrowed car as soon as Dennis came back to work. It was not only his kind, inquisitive questions that bore out the very letter of Suspiria's prophecy, but even more than these the confident assurance of his eyes as he asked them. He took it as his right to know a little of their business now, even a little more than the ordinary man in the street, though he, too, had his rights in them to a lesser degree. Dennis fended him off with monosyllables, and made every excuse to withdraw into the inspection pit, or into the bowels of some repair job too intricate for conversation; but it was a losing battle. He was expected to pay his way. Why should he mind being paraded, being talked about, being sent out unwarily to serve petrol to people who had specially angled to have a close look at him? Naturally they were interested, who wouldn't be? But all he was asked to do was to serve them with petrol. Nobody was trying to make him dance and sing for them! George was astonished and injured when he flared up in protest.

'I'm a mechanic, not a vaudeville act. I haven't asked you to let me off anything, have I? If I'm unlucky enough to get that kind of customer myself, all right, it can't be helped, it isn't your fault any more than it's mine. But I'm damned if I'm going to be trotted out like a performing monkey every time some nosey parker misses his aim and gets you, instead!'

'I don't know what you're talking about,' said George, wiping his oily hands. 'You're feeling touchy about it, I can understand that well enough, but it's making you imagine things. *I* haven't been trying to trot you out for anybody's benefit. All I've asked you to do is take a bit of the serving off my hands when I'm busy with a job. I don't want to be hard on you, lad, but that's what you're here for, isn't it?'

'And you're paying me! Well, you're getting your money's worth out of me, aren't you? Without trying to turn me into a sideshow. If you think I don't earn what you pay me, say so, and I'll go somewhere else, it's all the same to me.'

'Now, now!' said George, soothingly, laying a large hand heavily upon his assistant's shoulder. 'You don't want to take it like that. Have I said you don't earn your money? You're in a proper state of nerves, that's what's the matter with you. Whatever any of us do just now won't be right for you. Anyhow, what if these folks do feel a bit of curiosity about you, and want to have a look at you? They're entitled to come here with their trade, aren't they? And what harm does it do you? They don't say nothing to you about it, do they? Well, then!'

'No,' agreed Dennis bitterly, 'they don't say anything to me about it. They've already been tipped off that they'd better not. The first time one of 'em says to me right out: "Good Lord, aren't you the Dennis Forbes that was in that murder case?" I'll know I've got an honest man – one you haven't been talking to beforehand.'

George said, heaving a large, tolerant, fatherly sigh: 'There you go! Nothing I do's right for you! If I try to spare your feelings, that's all the thanks I get!'

But if he went elsewhere, what was to be gained? Not everyone would be as adroit as George, perhaps, in turning his notoriety to account, but the shadow of his reputation would follow him to some extent wherever he went, and the newspaper men and the idly curious and the misguided romantics would find their way after it to his refuge. Even if he went away and used another name for a time, they would probably find him. And at that thought, in any case, his mind drew back, erect and adamant, refusing to approach the idea more closely. His name had never meant all that much to him while it was unblemished and unknown, but it meant the whole of himself as soon as he was driven to considering renouncing it. Nor could he bear to contemplate running away from his difficulty, even under his own name; whatever they chose to do, he could not leave Suspiria here to carry the load alone.

So he stayed, and swallowed his bitterness. In the end the sensation would die a natural death; the trouble was that from his position, harassed and humiliated and sick with frustration, like a bear prodded into an unwilling dance, he could not be sure that the end was even in sight.

He went to Little Worth only every third or fourth evening, not because he did not long for Suspiria day and night, but because he was afraid to go more often until he had recovered his confidence, and left her free to assert her own. Moreoever, he knew that she did not want him for ever on her doorstep. He knew it by the intense and wary tenderness with which she handled him, the care she took to avoid too outspoken, too hurtful a solemnity in their contacts. Delicately, with infinitely fastidious and selective care, they picked their way between the subjects on which their minds were really fixed, and would not notice the daily avalanches of letters with the ashes of which her fire was always choked, or the frequent ingratiating incursions of reporters which left her stiff with detestation and pain for hours afterwards, or the meagre and unsatisfactory results of all the time she put in at her wheel. He admired what she made, she expressed interest in what he did. They were resolute, practical and cheerful, and kept so intent a watch upon themselves that not even their bodies, embracing, made any desperate admissions or any appeals.

But when he did not go to her, when he went firmly home, and sat down to tea with the rest of the family, and wanted to feel the current which moved through them stirring as surely in his own veins, the pulse faltered in him, and the flow was halting and cold. It was then he began to panic. He fought hard to get back, driving his mind and his tongue savagely towards what he felt to be normality, but when he managed to touch it and wrap himself in it again, it did not fit him. He did not recognise the voice, nor the words, and withdrew in revulsion from something which, without any will of his, had become an affectation.

A curious change had come over their attitude to him. The dangerous part of his celebrity exorcised, the disreputable part stood upon its head and turned respectable, nothing remained but a queer, surreptitious pleasure and pride in him. They took a fond interest in his love affair, they preened themselves in his fame, silently but not discreetly. They were his millions of proprietors in a little compass. It was like living in the market-place. And yet what had he to complain of? They were almost exaggeratedly considerate of him, as though he had been an invalid, or a visitor.

In his heart he knew that he was a disappointment to them. They would have liked him to live continually on the plane of the witness-box. He had led them to expect it, and now he was letting them down badly. After all, they were his family, they wanted a larger share in the excitement and gratification of his headlined romance than the ordinary public could buy for the price of a newspaper, or the inquisitive achieve by patronising Grover's Garage. Through the first constrained and silent days they waited confidently, humouring him, no more impatient for their entertainment than theatre-goers before the rise of the curtain. But the days lengthened out one by one, and the curtain did not rise. And presently there began to be certain signs of restlessness, some shuffling of feet, not a little whispering. There would have been more and louder manifestations of dissatisfaction, but that they had become, in a curious sense, afraid of him. Only in suppressed whispers can you complain of the stranger in the house.

But when he was not there they discussed him roundly enough. They said that they couldn't make him out, that he wasn't carrying on as if he cared all that much about her, for all he'd said at the trial. They said that after the way they'd stood by him, you'd have thought he'd be a bit more appreciative, and make some response. They said that they'd made allowances for the strain he'd been under, but surely he ought to be getting over that by now, and anyhow, *they* weren't to blame for it, why take it out on *them*? Nobody wanted to pry into his affairs, but surely a normal brother would take his family a little way into his confidence. They might have been a bunch of lodgers in the house, for all the acknowledgments he made to their common blood. Marjorie, who had come back into conference as soon as the acquittal eased her of the fear of sharing in his disgrace, led the chorus. Winnie and his mother defended him stoutly; he was still sore, he mustn't be hurried, the reporters were still persecuting him, how could he be expected to get over an experience like that all in a week or two? They defended, but they did not justify him, for they were as hungry and unsatisfied as the rest.

It was his mother who ventured at last to try to step across the gulf which it seemed he could not bring himself to pass. She had never been wont to hesitate, she was no easily sloughed mother; and finding herself alone with him one night in the kitchen while his father was busy gardening, and the other two were out, was all the opportunity she needed to tempt her. She leaned across the table to him, where he was turning half-heartedly at the knobs of the wireless set, and said straight out:

'Dennis, when are you going to bring Suspiria to see us?'

He raised his head sharply, and looked at her with blank, astonished eyes. The name seemed so incongruous in her mouth that it was almost unrecognisable; and the attitude, however he tried to adjust his mind to it, would not be fitted upon Suspiria's person. He tried to think of her as a prospective daughter-in-law, to be brought to pass inspection by his parents. It ought to have been funny, but it was not; it was a distasteful familiarity, almost an indecency.

'I hadn't thought,' he said, 'of bringing her anywhere. It isn't quite that kind of case.' He had meant his voice to remain low and equable, but he could hear its stiffening arrogance for himself, and regret it as he might, he could not change it.

'Why not?' demanded his mother, bridling. 'It seems a queer thing to keep her in the background, as if she was a secret, or something – after all that's been said in public! Oh, I know! It's been a bad time for you both, and you want to get over it in peace – but it's no good letting it get over *you*! If she's going to be one of the family, surely it's only right that we should get to know her. I should think she'd be glad!'

He got up abruptly and turned his shoulder on her, so that she should not see the bitter face he made at the thought of trying to compress Suspiria into a mere member of the family. Over his shoulder he said, rather breathlessly: 'I don't know that she is, I don't know that she wants to. Hadn't we better leave that to her?'

'Oh, now, look, that isn't good enough! After all that's happened, you really can't try to tell me that she doesn't care enough about you to want to have things straight between you. I know you've kept all this to yourself, and you don't want to talk about it, but goodness gracious, child, I'm your mother! I'm not trying to get at you, you needn't be suspicious of me. What's the use being so secretive about things, after they've been dragged through the courts already?'

He said, with involuntary violence, but very quietly: 'What was said in court hasn't given me any proprietary rights in her – or her in me, either.'

'But, good heavens, boy, you must know what you intend to do! You're just being stupid, and obstinate, and determined to shut us out, that's all it is. What have we done to you, I'd like to know, to be treated the way you're treating us?'

'Don't be silly, Mum,' he said sharply, 'I haven't done anything to you. We haven't made any plans, how can I tell you about them? What are you complaining about?' He didn't want to quarrel with her, or to hurt her, but he spread himself angrily between her and Suspiria, because the thought of them together offended him bitterly, though he could not tell why. It was nothing to do with being proud of one or ashamed of the other; it was something infinitely more subtle and complex, but he could not understand it himself, much less explain it to her or anyone else. 'When there's anything to tell,' he said, with careful gentleness, 'you'll be told, of course. I can't say fairer than that, can I?'

She stood facing him for a moment in silence, with a suspicious and disapproving stare. Then she said in a tone of deep offence and concern: 'I suppose you know what's going to be said if you two don't make a move soon? They'll say there was something in it, after all. They'll say you're not so sure as you made out that she didn't do it, and you're not keen to go the same way he went.'

'My God!' he said, in a stricken whisper, 'you can't believe that!'

'It isn't what I believe that counts, it's what's going to be whispered around. What else are they to think, I'd like to know? You were mad to get her, you said it over and over. What *can* they think, when you don't make any move now the road's clear?'

She was frightened suddenly by the fixed and silent whiteness of his face, and the curiously distant look of his eyes, and she made a hasty step towards him, reaching out her hands to take him by the arms and shake some sense and feeling back into him; but somehow he moved back out of her hold, and left her clutching the air.

'Don't look at me that way, Dennie, love! *I* don't believe that, not for a minute I don't! But there's people who will, can't you see that? I don't know what's got into you both. There's only one decent thing for you to do, why don't you *do* it? I can't understand you – neither of you!'

'No,' he said, through stiff lips, 'no, I suppose not.'

'And you don't help me! You don't care about us now, any of us, we're not good enough for you. You tell us nothing! You don't consider us! Anybody'd think we were your enemies.'

'I'm sorry!' he said in the same tone. 'I don't mean to hurt you. I can't be any different.'

'You hate everything the papers say about you, but you won't give anything in your own words, to put it all in a better way. Nothing we say or do is right. The more we try to make it easy for you, the more you back away from us. What *are* we to do, to please you?'

'Just let me alone,' he said, rearing his head and turning his face away from her. 'That's all anyone can do, and it's the one thing you won't do.'

He saw the hands coming again, and longed to pull himself away from her and run out of the house, but what was the good of that? There was no sense in hurting anyone more than he need, and he was long past the stage where someone else's pain could ease his own. So he opened his arms to her, and let her cry on his shoulder, and hug him, and complain of him gratefully, while he made the little, laborious, comforting noises which alone were required of him. As soon as she was soothed and satisfied with touching him, and with the constrained caresses of his reluctant but resigned hands, she went back to her ironing, appeased, and he was free to do what he had to do.

She would think she had been effective, and sent him off to plan the future with Suspiria in order to achieve the compliant respectability which would stop tongues from wagging. Let her think it, then! What harm would it do? She would be happy about it, and that was something to the good. He could see her beginning to shine with secret gratification already, as he took his hat and slipped out of the house. 'I believe he's taken notice!' she was saying to herself. 'He's going to her, I do believe! After all, his mother's still got some influence with him!'

Yes, he was going to her, but not for so simple a reason. He was going to her because he had nowhere else to go, nowhere in the world where he belonged. Only now, when he had given up the struggle, and was running headlong for the only way of escape, did he realise the opaque dark wilderness of loneliness in which he had been trying to live. He had to get out of it, he had to find his way home. He was going to Suspiria, who was the only home he had.

4

At Little Worth the living-room was in darkness, but the door gave to his hand as in the old days, and from under the half-drawn curtain in the doorway opposite, the faint light from the workshop spread thin fingers across the floor. He went through the stony, echoing corridor, and let himself into the long, dusty, disreputable room.

Suspiria was standing by the open kiln, which filled the air above it with a gush of heat. A few small pots were ranged along the rim, breathing their heat into the air also, and her face as she stood staring down at the floor was flushed to a deep rose colour with their nearness. But it was not at them she was looking. The undistinguished survivors did not interest her, she was looking at the shards of a large blue and grey jar, still quaking with heat on the floor at her feet. She had looked at it living with the same baffled and desperate face which now contemplated its dead body. Its making had cost her untold effort, she had torn it upward to its prodigious proportions with straining arms and hands, and a mind tortured as savagely as the clay itself; and all the time her spirit had known what she had refused to acknowledge until this moment of its completion, that it was a monstrosity, grown out of nature, useless, unjustifiable, better killed and buried quickly. It was not the first thing she had destroyed since her return home, but it was the best and worst, the most terrible.

She heard Dennis come in, and looked up at him slowly, kicking the quivering shards out of her way. She put down the heavy tongs with which she had lifted the abortion from the kiln.

'I can't work, Dennis,' she said, in a high, hard voice, vibrating with tension. Her hands were shaking now that the weight was out of them, and they had nothing to which to cling. She fixed upon his face great blurred eyes, brimming with grief and terror. 'I can't work any more!' Her voice ran up into a lamentable, soft cry, accusing and appealing. She began to shake all over, as if she would disintegrate before his eyes. 'Dennis, help me!'

He put his arms round her with a wild, grateful gentleness, and lifted her into his heart. She lay tensed against him for a moment, then her body relaxed with a great sigh, and she fastened her arms about him fiercely and her mouth reached upward blindly against his cheek. He carried her back into the living-room, dim now with the deepening June dusk, and wonderfully quiet. Their muted murmurings hardly stirred the hush; the surrender, the whirlpool, the vortex of dark delight into which they drew each other down had almost no voice at all, its plunge was too abrupt, too still for sound. It dragged them down with so headlong an impetus that somewhere in the descent all the tatters of doubt and fear and failure, all the regrets and reservations and rages were stripped from them, and they reached the levels beneath light and consciousness as naked as flames, and lay there lulled and safe in the absolute, silent darkness, mindless, motionless, locked in each other's arms.

CHAPTER NINE:

A Marriage Made On Earth

1

THEY WERE married in the third week of July, in the register office on the first floor of the Georgian house which lay in a little court off the square. Once they were agreed upon it, there was no point in waiting. When it came to the planning of the future, suddenly it was she who laid every responsibility in his arms, and said yes, not listlessly, but pliantly and gratefully, to every suggestion he made.

'We won't make any secret of it. No one shall be able to say we hid. We'll keep it as quiet as it can be kept, but only as other couples do who don't like fuss. Just an ordinary register office wedding, without any guests except those who have business there.'

'Yes,' she said, faintly smiling, 'that's the best thing we can do.'

'And we won't budge from this town. Nobody's going to force us out of it. You'll go on working – don't worry about it any more, you *will* be able to work! – and I'll go on with the same job, at least for a year or so. We'll make a life for ourselves here, or for ever fail to have one anywhere. If we ran, it would be the end of us. We'll stay here! We'll live in this house! In a year most of the people will have forgotten all about it, and all about us.'

'There'll be plenty of people,' she said, 'waiting for the

whole thing to fall to pieces. You know that, don't you? We're not a good risk, Dennis.'

'They'll be disappointed. It won't fall to pieces. Why should it?' he said strenuously. 'I love you, you love me. Why should it fall to pieces?'

'Oh!' she said, brushing her hair back from her brow with a wild, regretful smile. 'Love— If that was all!' But she shut her fingers tightly over his hand the next moment, and folded it into her breast. 'Yes, yes, my darling! Everything will be all right. We shall make a good job of it, of course we shall!'

'You won't mind – I promised my mother I'd tell her what we planned to do. You won't mind if she comes to the wedding, and acts as one of our witnesses?'

'Of course not! Why should I mind?' But for a moment her eyes shone in the old, alert fashion, between alarm and amusement. 'I never had a family before, I shall be very bad at it. I never had any practice, except for an absentminded father who forgot I existed half the time, and fed me unsuitable literature the other half, and a placid mother who ignored me almost all the time. She read, too, anything she could get hold of. That was how she came to christen me Suspiria – did I ever tell you? She had a fancy for Oscar Wilde.' The gleam deepened for a moment, remembering. 'Yes, of course your family must come – if they can bear the spectacle!' She shut her lips quickly then upon the trend of her thoughts, because she was only too sure that he would understand it very well, and very readily. Once, his innocence and his youth, the very insignia of his wrongs, would have protected him from understanding that he was wronged.

'They want to know you,' he said, watching her steadily. 'I don't say it's only for the right reasons, though.'

'Why should it be?' she said, quite gently. 'That sort of thing does upset human relationship. We shall get used to one another in time.'

Anything, anything, she thought, the parents and the cousins, and the neighbours, and all, just to have him, and never to have to be alone again in the house with her own hands which had lost their knack, and her own mind which had lost its power of concentration, and her own spirit which had lost its peace. Anything to have that unfailing well of forgetfulness waiting for her need every night, his body, in which the long spiral hours of labour without achievement, the terrible fear of her own sterility, sank without trace, leaving not a ripple upon the dark perfection of her exhaustion and fulfilment.

So Dennis gave notice of their intention to marry, at the register office, and their names were duly inscribed in the notice book. It was very unlikely that any of the still persistent journalists would inspect the book, but if they did he could at least keep the actual date of the ceremony from everyone outside the family. But when he came to tell his mother what had been arranged, he found he could not bring himself to lay great emphasis on their desire for privacy. It was beneath his dignity and Suspiria's to beg off anything, and besides, his mother ought to understand without any prompting.

'I haven't told anyone but you. We don't want anyone there but our own people.'

'You don't want me to tell anyone else?' she asked, divided between pleasure and disappointment, her eyes triumphant upon his face. He had taken notice of her strictures, after all; he was still her little boy, for all the hold that woman had over him.

'I'd rather – we'd rather you didn't. They'll know soon enough.'

That was all he could bring himself to say. If he had pleaded with her for secrecy she would gladly have turned herself into the most furtive of conspirators for him, but when it came to the point he could not give her that satisfaction. So she was left with a request, but not a prohibition. She told every member of the family, and went out to telephone to Albert; she wanted the Loders to know, after the way they had drawn back from any contact with Dennis and his folks from the moment things began to look like trouble. She wanted them to know that everything was above-board, and to feel cheated that they had themselves made it impossible to attend the wedding. Shudder as they might at the idea of a connection of theirs being in the Sunday papers, she knew, none better, that they were eaten with secret envy, all the same.

She did not mean to drop so much as a hint in the way of the brash young man who came to the door one afternoon draped with an unmistakable press camera, and made himself agreeable to her upon the doorstep. She said she did not want to talk to him, and had nothing to say, but he seemed quite willing to do most of the talking himself. Finally, having tantalised and provoked her more than once to the point of confidences, he took his shoulder regretfully from the door-post, and said casually:

'Oh, well, it wasn't such a big story, really. Looks like there's no more chapters coming along. We spend a lot of our time running round after false alarms of one sort and another – we're used to it!'

'Maybe if you knew your job better,' she said, nettled, 'you'd find a lot more news than you do. If you were to look in the proper places, there's plenty to be picked up – instead of worrying hard-working women like me.'

He gave her a look which should have warned her to say no more, but as smoothly deflected it into innocence. 'Proper places, what proper places? We cover everything we can think of.'

'You do something you call the rounds, don't you? Courts, and hospitals, all those public places? You ought to extend the round a bit, and take in some other offices that's as open to you as to me. I'm not here to do your work for you,' she said, pleased with his helpless mystification, and withdrew into the house and left him still searching his mind for her meaning.

It took him the better part of a day to dredge up all the ideas he had concerning offices open to public investigation, but by the next morning he had arrived by a methodical process of elimination at the register office, and found the names in the notice book. It did not take very much detective work to determine, from the days their notice had still to run, the approximate date of the wedding. He went away very contentedly, and set himself to keep an eye upon their movements.

On Wednesday evening, the fifteenth of July, Dennis brought out Theo's old car from the garage at Little Worth, and cleaned and overhauled it. It was all the indication necessary that the day was imminent. The reporter went off happily to confide to one of his colleagues, with whom he had a reciprocal arrangement for sharing titbits, that the Freeland woman was probably getting married next day, and they spent the entire morning and half the afternoon in the back snug of a pub which had a window on the court. A few minutes before half-past three they saw Suspiria and Dennis arrive, with Mr and Mrs Forbes in the back of the car, and a taxi following unobtrusively with Winnie and Mr Quinn, who had been invited to be a witness because he was already so deeply involved in their affairs that his presence was no offence. They all went into the pillared doorway, and out went the hunters from ambush, to take station and await the departure.

'Look better, wouldn't it,' said the second reporter, critically surveying the deserted court, 'if we had a clamouring mob? I suppose that's why they avoided Saturday. Most Saturday afternoons in summer a few hopefuls hang around here, just in case somebody interesting turns up among the ruck. But weekdays nothing much goes on. Have it your own way,' he said detachedly, 'but me, I'd rather have some spectators. Won't *look* like a sensation otherwise.'

The first reporter went into the square, buttonholed a bright local delivery boy who looked suitable for the purpose, and told him what was going on in the register office.

'Run round, quick, and tell everybody you know who might want to have a look. Women! They'll come with their tongues hanging out. Run, quick, it doesn't take long to get hitched in that dump – none of your fully choral services there.'

The boy leaned hard on his pedals, and shot away, grinning gleefully; and presently the women came, his employer's wife first in the field at a scuttling trot. By the time the little registrar had got through his ten-minute ceremony, and the register had been signed, there were probably thirty people ringed round outside the door waiting for them, with a few children gaping between the elbows of the adults, and a stray dog or two playing among their feet.

'Pretty good!' said the second reporter approvingly, his camera at his eye. 'Get 'em when they come out on the steps, and see what's waiting for 'em. If they don't stand stock-still and give us a beautiful shot, I'm cheated. By the time they get through the ring there'll be time enough for a close-up or two, as well.'

Deep within the open doorway, beyond which a dim and dilapidated hall extended, Suspiria appeared. A child shrilled, a woman nudged her neighbour and cried all too clearly: 'That's her!'

The backward start she made from the sound, stiffening her shoulders, brought her into the hollow of Dennis's following arm, which took her fiercely about the waist and caught her close to his side, as if he expected an attack. It was a difficult shot, rather deep within the shadows of the doorway still, but the second reporter got it, and it duly appeared on the front page of his paper on the following Sunday. The next was easier, but less dramatically rewarding. She recovered herself, she put off her husband's shielding arm with a single touch of her fingers, and walked forward steadily into the light. Down the steps she came with the frozen assurance of a first-class mannequin ignoring a critical gallery of marchionesses. To the two reporters, however, who were used to penetrating such protective coverings, her eyes gave her away. The shock had got home, all right. Through the cool shell of her face the bitter heat of her loathing and revulsion burned with an incandescent brightness. There was a beautiful opportunity for a classic, symmetrical shot as she came down the steps, the boy pale and flaming with distress at her elbow, the relatives trailing after, divided between embarrassment and gratification, and ranged before them the meagre little group of onlookers which could be made to look so imposing in a well-cut print.

It had everything, in particular that oval, ice-cold face raised deliberately to the sunlight, with such clear lines, such sheer, polished bones, and those eyes in it a bitter bright green with distaste and disdain; that, and the boy's face following her with such agonised attention, his eyes not raised to the light, but fixed only upon her. A very good-looking lad, too, you could quite see her point of view! And a woman as experienced as this one knew how to get what she wanted.

'Evidently there wasn't a back door,' said the first reporter, scurrying down the steps from his doorway to intercept the procession across the court. 'I believe she'd have taken it if there had been.'

Suspiria moved quickly between the staring, gaping ranks which parted grudgingly to let her through. The ragged little gallery murmured excitedly as it followed at a loose distance to watch her get into the car. Two women passing the alley as she emerged gazed at her indifferently in passing, and the next moment nudged each other and turned to stare with the rest, remembering who she was, and realising from which door she had come.

Nevertheless, it was over. It had seemed an hour, and lasted only perhaps two minutes. Dennis was reaching past her to open the door of the car; the ancient cushions squeaked as he got in beside her. As soon as they were safely away, anonymous in the twirling thread of traffic spinning through the town, he heard her draw a great, violent breath, dragged down painfully to her heart. He did not dare to touch her; all he could do was to thrust the car to its most urgent speed, and withdraw her furiously from the lingering, corrosive memory of the witnesses to her wedding.

2

'She did drop the hint that brought them, of course,' said Dennis, when the door of the bedroom was shut, and the sighing summer quiet of the night had taken away, as it seemed, the house from under them, and left them swinging in a small, isolated world slung among the stars. The house by night had a way of seeming taller than it was, and the fields and the town more remote.

'It doesn't matter,' said Suspiria, brushing her hair at the open window. 'Don't talk about it.'

'But she probably doesn't even realise she did it. I don't think she meant anything like that to happen.'

'I've told you, it doesn't matter! After all, what did happen? Nothing new, for us!'

'But just today – I'd have given anything to keep them off us today!' he said, wrenching at the incurable distress.

She said nothing in reply to that, but only turned slowly from the luminous blue radiance of the clear sky, powdered with fine midsummer gold, and moved towards him with the inexpressible languor of the warm breeze in the leaves, or the soft drifting fall of her folds of blue nylon, settling and clinging again about her body as she stood beside him. Where the light fell upon her flesh through it, it warmed into a heliotrope glow, softening the sharp little hip-bones and the thin shoulders, slight as a girl's, into a suave delicacy of line. The fronds of her hair, cut short as a boy's now for the hot months, stood up from her head distrait with their own lightness and the stimulus of brushing, and quivered in the thread of breeze. The full, broad forehead looked as smooth as marble beneath them, and her eyes in their deep, arched settings shone upon him with a distant and sorrowful wonder. His wedding day, then, kept a sort of holiness for him, poor child, and he had not wanted it soiled. How he clung for safety still to the conventions of his already forsaken world, in the middle of the incalculable spiritual dangers she had brought upon him!

'It did hurt you!' he said insistently, as if she had denied it. 'It hurt you horribly.'

'Did I show it so badly?'

'Oh, no – no, you were kind!' He was so dizzy with gratitude for her forbearance with his mother that his tongue overstated it without any insincerity; and indeed, she wondered at it herself. 'But you won't hold it against her, will you? They don't think about things like that as you do. They can't understand.'

She noticed that he did not identify himself with either side. God alone knew where he felt himself to be! Somewhere in the gulf between them, perhaps, eternally falling.

'No,' she said, turning down the covers of the bed, 'no, I won't hold it against her.'

He slipped into the bed beside her, and reached up and put out the light. His hands folded her, and drew her into his heart. The cool of the night swung over them slowly, star by star withdrawing into infinite dark distance as they went down the long, plunging shaft of rapture to the abyss of peace. Like a deep, dreamless sleep, with conscious joy still awake and radiant at the heart of it; absolute stillness at last, absolute perfection of happiness, the whole being fulfilled, the whole life justified, wanting nothing, needing nothing. They lay dreaming in the profundity of ocean depths where no life survived, of enemy or friend, but their two matched and mated selves, fused now into one immaculate unity by the last convulsion of delight.

She lay for a long time motionless after thought began again; sleep drew back from her, but the exquisite conviction of safety and peace remained. Dennis's arm lay across her waist, so heavily that she thought he had fallen asleep; but when she turned to kiss his cheek, with delicate, still care for fear of disturbing him, his lifted mouth felt for her lips instead, and his hand cupped her breast, and lay there languid with content.

'Aren't you asleep? I thought you'd fallen asleep?'

'No, I was just thinking. I don't want to sleep.'

The ecstatic deliberation of their voices filled the night, though they made only soft shadows of sound within the bed. They had all time in which to think and speak, and no morning would ever come down into the profound deeps where they were.

'What were you thinking about?'

'About us. About our future.' He said it as though nothing else existed, and yet the world was full. 'You did have some doubts – didn't you? They won't last. You'll see! We can make it perfect, Spiri. In spite of everybody and everything –

perfect!' His lips, stirring between her breasts, prolonged the 'perfect' until they reached her heart.

Was it the shortening of her name that started another image out of the void? Suddenly her senses, springing upward out of the guarded deeps, recovered the touch of Theo's hand, half-asleep and triumphant after long hours of work, the weight of Theo's head low on her shoulder. More child than this child, when he was not intent on creation; more innocent than this touching innocence, when he was not sharpening his wits upon somebody's pretensions, like a street-urchin presented with a large and unblemished wall. She had never plunged into this ocean with him; he had never been able to make her realise that it existed, beyond all the levels of his light-hearted and exuberant love. What was the use of trying to allocate the fault now, if there had been a fault? Nevertheless, she felt the chill of his silenced mouth through the warm whispering lips which explored her breast.

'Perfect! Spiri, promise me – we'll share everything!'

'Everything!' she said, caressing him. 'Everything!'

'Spiri – we ought to have absolute truth between us two—'

'Absolute truth!' she said, bursting upward into full, cold consciousness. She felt the upward surge of his senses beside her, the night with its wary stillness was all about them once again, the alert and listening air leaned to their lips. 'There's something you want to say to me?'

He drew breath, and checked as silently before he spent it. The fingers which had strayed about her body as carelessly as a child trailing bare feet in the July grass, were still and gentle now upon her cheek, pleading with careful, wordless eloquence for her understanding. 'No – but you'd tell me anything I ought to know – wouldn't you? As I would you?'

Answering him beneath that touch was difficult and dangerous; so much might be conveyed even by the contraction of the muscles of her cheek, or the momentary arrest of her breath. But she said with the terrible stealth of one who must be convincing at all costs, this once if never again: 'Yes, of course! You know I would!'

She waited, but he only sighed: 'Yes—' and did not say any more. What was it he had just drawn back so stealthily into the closed places of his mind? A confidence? Or a question? The reasons for not asking questions were even stronger now. When neither the one who asks nor the one who answers can hope to prove the truth is in him, why ask? And why answer? For after all the trials and the acquittals, all the oaths and all the perjury, and all the torment and passion of truth among the perjury, the old, the inescapable fact remains. Theo is dead. Theo is dead, and his footprints did not reach the door. And there were only two other people in the case from first to last. The wife, and the lover!

When the silence had stretched to breaking-point, she said very quietly: 'Dennis!' There was no answer. 'Dennis, have you gone to sleep?'

His breathing, stealthily measured out slow breath by breath, sighed steadily into the pillow beside her. His fingers had slipped from her breast, his hand lay half-open and relaxed between them. She felt the tension and haste of his recoil making the air quiver faintly, and his mind trying to still the betraying tremors which he would take care never to provoke again. He did not move or speak; and after a moment she turned, very softly, and drew her hand away from touching him. It was more than an hour before either of them slept.

3

They had a week's holiday in Scotland, slipping with the car from village to village where they could pass unrecognised. Afterwards they remembered that belated honeymoon as a curious interlude of unreality islanded out of their lives, golden, rounded, idyllic, except that like all enchanted castles it had a door in it which they pretended not to see, and were forbidden to open. When the week ended, they came back to Little Worth, and settled doggedly to the resumption of their daily lives. He went back to his work, she to hers; they put on the routine with a brisk resolution in which neither of them fully believed.

It was early in September, one Saturday afternoon when they were shopping in the town, that Dennis edged himself backwards out of a narrow shop doorway in Crane Street, and backed into Iris Moffatt's arms. As he turned hastily to apologise they recognised each other, and exclaimed together.

'Iris!' He coloured richly at the too close and too sudden encounter, and she was blushing, too, but for all that she was not greatly embarrassed. It was rather as if he were no longer of sufficient importance to her to put her out of countenance. She looked prettier than he remembered her, less prim and defensive, less ready to find slights or evasions in other people's innocent phrases. She looked happy; that was what it was, happiness. His smile reflected her own, a gradual glow of pleasure. 'You're looking awfully well,' he said.

Propping the most precarious parcel back into the crook of his arm, she let her hand linger for a moment to steady it. Suspiria was sitting in the car at the edge of the pavement, and she saw the gloved fingers hover, touching his sleeve, saw the young face beaming into his. The light of its easy gaiety seemed to shine down into his eyes, and wake an understanding and answering brightness there. He looked purely twenty-two again, eager and astonished, a young man prompt at an assignation. Her heart was suddenly transfixed by a lightning-flash of incredible jealousy, suffocating her with rage and humiliation. She wound up the window of the car, so that she might not hear their conversation.

There must be dozens of them loose in Great Leddington, the girls, the contemporaries, the young things with whom he had grown up, who had known him years before he ever entered her emancipated life. Girls who had run around with him, sharing dances and cinemas, and the hectic youthful excitement of the motor-cycle and pillion, girls who had walked the lanes arm-in-arm with him, and kissed him lengthily at parting, long before he ever heard Suspiria Freeland's name. She tried to turn her face away, not to watch them, but the clear sound of their voices drew her head round again irresistibly, and her eyes fixed on them and clung with a hungry bitterness.

'Well, it's nice to see you again! It's been ages! How are you?' A little wary still, but well-disposed; too happy to hold anything against him now, he thought.

'Oh, not so bad, thanks! I don't have to ask you that – you look blooming.'

'I haven't had a chance to talk to you for months,' she said, and grew pink again, remembering, no doubt, how he had spent those months. But she was full of her own affairs, and for him could find only the impulse of pure kindness which comes from satisfied happiness. She wanted to give him a little piece of her well-being. 'I'm a bit late,' she said, 'but I'd like to congratulate you, just the same. I'm glad it came out right for you. I hope you'll be happy enough to make up for everything.'

'Thank you!' he said, warmed in spite of his constraint, because she had said it without a thought of curiosity or proprietorship, because she was making no claim on him, and wanted nothing from him. 'How have you been getting on? What's new with you? I don't seem to have heard any of the local news lately.'

'*I'm* getting married next month. I thought perhaps your mother would have told you.' So that was the reason for the glow she had; a comfortable, vindicated glow, all the brighter at the moment for the understandable satisfaction she had in flourishing her victory before these particular eyes. 'It's Bill Parkes – remember him? It's going to be a quiet little affair, if they'll let us get away with that. But he's got three younger sisters, and you know what they can be like! I can see me having a flock of bridesmaids, whether we want them or not.' But she would love it; she was radiant at the thought.

'I say, I am glad! That's grand news! I hope you'll be very happy.'

'As happy as you are?' she suggested archly, patting his arm. 'All right, I know that's impossible! But maybe we'll get somewhere near it.' She wanted to say something more personal, something intimate and magnanimous, something that would take the wind clean out of his sails, and make him remember her always with warm friendliness, perhaps even a faint recurring wonder if he had not been a fool to let her get away from him when he had her. 'I'm glad you stuck it out here, Dennis, really,' she said. 'You were right, and I'm sure you'll always be glad you did. It must be a bit difficult, sometimes, but don't take too much notice. You'll be all right in the end, I'm sure you will.'

Suspiria saw the warm flush mount Dennis's face, and his hand go out to take the girl's proffered hand. 'What do I know of his life up to a year ago?' she was thinking, her eyes upon the two glowing profiles. 'Nothing! He came out of an absolutely unknown past, and some day he'll go again, and disappear as completely. I shall have nothing left but this bit of his life to remember. Why should he give me anything else? I've been a kind of disease that drove him to bed for a time. When he gets over it he'll leave me. Why should I expect anything else? He's young, he belongs to his own generation. People like this girl! This girl – she knows him very well. Who is she? He never talked about any of them. What is there in her to talk about, anyhow? She's not good-looking, she wouldn't be noticed in a crowd, she doesn't look particularly clever—'

But she was young, young, young! The answer to everything!

The two on the pavement were separating now, their hands clinging for a moment as they drew apart, with that easy and confident flurry of last-minute words which marks old and intimate acquaintance. Dennis put a hand to the handle of the car door, and leaned inside to tip his purchases into the back seat. The girl had not realised until then that Suspiria was sitting there so close to them. She flashed a startled and conciliatory smile at them both, and made off up the street rather quickly. Dennis slid into the driving seat, and slammed the door, and the car moved away from the kerb jauntily, as if it had caught some of the encouraged lightness of his mood. The girl's touch had done him good. His eyes had a sparkle, his lips an eager half-smile, hopeful and boyish.

'Who was that?' asked Suspiria, drawn together extremely small and compact beside his shoulder.

'A girl I used to know,' he said cheerfully, noticing nothing amiss with her tone. 'Her name's Iris Moffatt. I haven't seen her for a long time.'

'No, it seemed to be a pleasant surprise, on both sides.'

This time he heard it clearly, the ice and acid bursting upward into the harmless words. He gave her a quick, astonished look along his shoulder, and said indignantly: 'It was on *my* side, at any rate. Why not? She's a nice girl, I've known her a long time.' The next moment he laughed aloud, it was so unexpected and so ridiculous that she could feel like that, just because he spoke to poor Iris.

'Don't be a fool!' he said. 'She's getting married next month, and she couldn't think of anything else. What do you suppose she wanted with me, except to tell me all about it? I haven't set eyes on her for – must be nearly ten months. Soon after I got to know you.'

'Really! I hope I didn't break anything up for you both? She looked as if she might have done rather well for you. Not very much imagination, perhaps, but you can have too much of that. And otherwise, yes, I'd say very suitable!' Her pure profile smiled, but not kindly. Her voice was as limpid as snow-water, and as cold.

'If you enjoy this,' he said, still not seriously disturbed, but vexed and chafing, all the same, 'I used to know several more girls. We could call round on a few of them, and you could have a really wonderful time.' He shook his shoulders, putting off the impulse of irritation.' 'Don't be so silly! How many men do you suppose I saw around you, those first weeks, without being mad with jealousy? Men who knew you intimately, and could talk to you as I didn't know how to talk. I could have killed the lot of them. But let Iris alone, poor girl, what harm's she ever done? If you want to know all about her, I can tell you. There isn't so much of it. We used to knock about together, before I knew you; and after I knew you, I broke it off. I haven't even seen her to speak to since, until today.'

'Do I detect a slight note of regret?' asked Suspiria, the

raging smile curling her lips more deeply. 'You may live to be sorry you were in such a hurry to make up your mind. One should never do these things too hastily.'

'I don't know why you want to quarrel with me,' he said, in incredulous exasperation, still only half in earnest, 'but it wouldn't take a lot of this to manage it. Do you have to behave like a jealous child because I speak to another woman in the street? What's got into you?'

There was no profit in it, but she could not let it alone. The very lightness of his voice, still unconvinced of danger, made her long to stab him with the pain she herself was experiencing, for it was new, and terrible, and she did not know how to deal with it. 'I'm simply interested,' she said. 'You never told me you'd had a regular girl in the days of your innocence. Do tell me more about it! Did you walk the monkey-run with her? And sit in the back row at the cinema? She didn't look the type to fill your days with unbearable excitement, I thought. I should imagine your mother was quite easy about you in those days. She must sigh over the memory of your Iris, sometimes.'

It was no use talking to her while she was in this utterly confounding mood, so he said nothing more, but his face had grown as hotly vindictive as hers. She went on wilfully goading him, out of her own fear and distress, out of the dread she felt of the young, smooth, girlish faces, and the unclouded eyes, and the light hearts of the generation to which he belonged, and she did not.

'A nice, healthy, straightforward girl, really rather like you temperamentally, I should say – and of course, the exact age for you.'

The moment she had said it, she knew it had recoiled into her own heart. What a fool she was, what a fool to fling it in his face with her own hands! He did not say a word, but only shut his lips hard, and tramped heavily on the accelerator, staring stonily ahead between the flashing hedges, the angry colour ebbing from his cheeks. She could feel in her flesh the turmoil of his distressed and resentful thoughts, could feel him counting the fourteen years which Perleman and all the voluble commentators in the Press had shaken in his face in vain. It had taken her bitter breath to quicken the seed of realisation into life. Well, he was not likely to forget again. Now he was hating her for saying it – soon he would be hating her because it was true, and she had known it all along, and had not seen fit to warn him. By acknowledging their ages she had forced him to acknowledge them; by feeling them as an offence against him, she had taught him that he was offended. What complaint would she have against him, when he threw them back in her face some day, and walked out?

She fell into a silence of despair, experiencing already in imagination the eventual and final terror of his loss.

4

In October Suspiria was offered an exhibition at a private gallery in London, on terms which did not offend her so grossly as to put her answer out of question immediately. It surprised her very much when Dennis urged her to take it. She had no daily contact now with the world which was most truly hers, and he was achingly troubled by the constant spectacle of her burning away in the ashes of her talent. Her mind could not focus, her hands had not regained the impetus of certainty, there was no joy in the clay. The pieces which satisfied her craftsman's conscience were few and meagre, the children of her delight would not come back at all. He wanted her to go back into her world, if only for a little while, by any door that opened. The spark might come to life again if she touched some other person's flame.

She evaded the idea for a little while, and then agreed to it, if he would go down with her for the week-end, and help her to arrange it. The show had a certain scandalous success, and amused her in a detached way. She kept Dennis close beside her on the afternoon of the opening, but he was not a great asset. Silent, handsome, not quite easy, not quite belonging anywhere, he moved among her friends and her works, only half assimilated. He was as deeply aware of it as she was, and as glad to get away from it, and go home again.

He travelled home to Great Leddington on the Sunday evening by train, leaving her the car for her return two or three days later. It was this accident of separation which caused him to pick up the crumpled and abandoned newspaper from a corner of his compartment, half-way through the short but tedious journey, and turn the pages listlessly in search of amusement.

From the middle page, wide-eyed, indifferently printed, his own face suddenly stared out at him. It was a popular paper of large circulation and execrable taste, which he did not normally see; no doubt Harold had thought it well worth the small risk that someone might make it his business to show it to him, for a paper like that could afford to pay handsomely for its dirt.

'MY BROTHER'S HEADLINE LOVE'
by
Harold Forbes

'The Intimate Story of the Love Affair Which Survived a Murder Charge, and Found its Happy Ending at Last.'

And inset into the larger photograph, one of the shots taken on their wedding day, startled, outraged, his arm about Suspiria in the doorway of the register office. No doubt the same persuasive young man had contrived this coup.

He sat with the paper spread before him, reading the thing from beginning to end with a slow, methodical care. Harold was a bright boy, Harold was saving up for his own wedding, and the prospect of such easy money must almost have torn the heart out of him long ago. His work was not more vulgar than most of its kind, it had a horrible, patronising kindness, it was corrupt and yet innocent. The most terrible thing about it was that it might have been written by any member of his family, except perhaps Marjorie, who would have written in vitriol instead of syrup. This was exactly how the rest of them thought of him now, a blurred figure of sentiment, a clothes-horse for their own sicklier day-dreams. All Harold had added was the offensive facility of the writing.

> '—our family resolved to stand by my brother come what might, through the long strain of the trial. At first we had had our qualms about the affection which we saw daily growing between Dennis and Mrs Freeland, but when the blow fell, and the terrible ordeal began, we soon realised that this was real love, which we must recognise with respect and admiration. The apparent barriers between them, the difference in their backgrounds, the discrepancy in their ages, all became as nothing beside that love. Poor Dennis's suffering during the time of waiting was terrible for us to watch, though we tried to share it with him as devotedly as we could. His faith in Suspiria was supreme—'

He read carefully, letting himself feel the fearful anger and hate which can only exist, perhaps, between brothers, because only brothers enjoy such intimate opportunities mortally to offend each other. 'I'll kill him!' he thought, half-choking with detestation. 'I'll kill him!' knowing very well he never would. If only it had been a little more loathsomely ridiculous, not still united by a slender, wavering thread to the truth! It had taken his family, in the end, to strip him naked and exhibit him for twopence-ha'penny a time. And there was worse, there was Suspiria, the affectionate, offensive use of her name, the coy uncovering of her proud and beloved flesh beside his own. He thought: 'Oh, God, if she ever sees it!' and again, with an almost childish descent of the heart: 'Somebody's sure to make it their business to show her!' And it was his people who had done this to her! He felt even his own love for her suddenly smeared with the inescapable Forbes vulgarity.

> '—Our hearts bled for Suspiria when she came home, shattered by her ordeal, which she had sustained so bravely while it endured. We tried to make the house

bright and welcoming for her return, to show her that we already loved her and recognised her as Dennis's wife. She was so pale and exhausted, so childishly small and fragile, that my mother and sister could not help crying over her. For a time she allowed no one access to her heart except Dennis, but we understood, and were content to wait patiently until she could bear to emerge from her mental convalescence, and become our sweet and touchingly grateful sister.'

And for the peroration, of course, all the most solemnly cloying phrases had been saved, a paragraph of pure cliché, saccharine on saccharine. 'Ideal happiness at last', 'true love has found its haven', 'in harbour after the storms of tragedy'. 'Her happy smile—' Her happy smile – that ravaged face, fixed in the pallor of disbelief, exhausted with unrewarded effort, stooped over the wheel, staring at her own disaster. 'It repays all our loyalty to see my young brother once again as radiantly happy as when we played together as children.' She, at least, was spared that! And he was radiantly happy, was he? It seemed to him that the adverb, at any rate, was a shocking joke at his expense, he who spent most of his life, now, fending and frowning people off from him for fear of new bruises. There had been happiness, yes, violent and destructive happiness, too intense to be borne, a kind of dissolution, a kind of nightly death; but he saw it as black rather than radiant.

When it was all read, he folded it together very carefully, and put it into his pocket; and when he left the train, though it was late for visiting, it was to Lancelot Road he went. He walked in upon them at the supper table, and knew by the abrupt flare of their startled eyes, and the quick, deflecting warmth of their welcoming voices, that they had been afraid of the next meeting with him, and suspected the worst from this sudden appearance. Still, they did their best. They hunted all together, he saw. All the others beamed at him with feverishly joyful surprise, and his mother rose to envelop him and kiss him. They were all in it, every one.

Stiff and unbending between his mother's hands, he held

back his head out of her reach, and shrugged her by as if her touch were wholly distasteful to him. He had not meant to be as convincing as that, but there was no room in his mind or heart for any complicating affection. He unfolded the paper, and dropped it among the dishes on the table, in the middle of the circle of their guilty eyes, which flew to it like pins to a magnet.

'Yes, I've seen it. I suppose you don't want to tell me it's a forgery?'

They were silent; even Harold, who was seldom at a loss for words, could find none at first gasp to defend his own too facile eloquence. His round, confident face grew pink, he licked his lips, and began: 'You don't want to take it too hard, Den. I never meant—'

'How much did you get for it?' His voice was low, and slightly hoarse with strain, but perfectly level. 'You sold me out pretty thoroughly,' he said, 'so I suppose the price was right. Are you splitting it among you, or does Harold keep the lot?'

They began to talk all together, in fits and starts, defending themselves, cajoling him, Harold already loudest and most voluble. 'What's the matter with it, anyhow? It's on your side. It's going to make friends for you, isn't it? I didn't think you'd mind all that much. Most fellows would be glad to think their families thought about 'em like that, and stuck to 'em like that. It wasn't the money! But if I hadn't accepted, they'd have paid some professional to write it all up a lot worse – without any of the true details and the – the good feeling—'

It was too much, he had to laugh. 'The good feeling! That's rich! The good feeling! You take the clothes off both of us, and stick us up under floodlighting, and you talk about good feeling!'

'Oh, now, Dennis, love, you're not fair! Harold wrote it beautifully! I'm sure you've no call to talk like that about it.'

'You're pathological about it,' said Harold strenuously, 'that's your trouble. They'll write these articles, whether you like it or not. You ought to have done it yourself, then you could have said what you like, and left out what you like. But you never would. I didn't see why it should be left to the newspaper men, when I could do it a lot better and more decently.'

'Decently!' said Dennis. 'You call that doing it decently. My God!'

'But really, you're not being fair! Harold never thought you'd feel so bad about it. He never meant any harm. He only thought—'

'That it was a lot of money, and he might as well have it as anybody else. I know. Well, make sure of your money, then – you've lost your goods.' He drew back from his mother's hands, which still sought ineffectively to envelop him, as boldly, as insolently, as if he had still been a small boy in a violent paddy, which would break in a storm of penitent tears if only she could once take his struggling form to her bosom. 'Don't! Don't touch me! You don't think you can do a thing like that to me, and then get round me with a little cheap cuddling! You knew perfectly well how I felt about it, how we both felt. Even if I didn't care for myself, I could never forgive you for doing this to her. I'm finished,' he said, his voice sinking to a parched finality of rejection.

His father, with dropping jaw, asked feebly: 'What do you mean by that?'

'What I say. I'm done with you, the lot of you. You've got your money, you can't expect to keep me as well.' He turned abruptly, and his hand clashed at the latch of the door. 'Good-bye!'

If only it had sounded petulant, or childish, or as if he were blackmailing them with his hurts, they might have sprung after him with humouring apologies, but the voice had a flatness and finality which paralysed. They let him go. Only Winnie suddenly pulled the door open after him, and ran down the path, and caught him by the arm, almost in tears.

'Dennis, don't go away like this – please! All right, we just hoped you wouldn't *see* it. It was such a lot of money— Oh, we oughtn't to have done it; I wish we hadn't, now!'

'It's a bit late, isn't it?' He pulled his sleeve out of her clutch, and went on; and when she pursued him still with a despairing babble of regret, he cried furiously: 'Let me alone!' and tore himself away from her at a pace only just short of a run. He wanted to be rid of them all, cleanly, with as little argument and as little distress as possible. What was the use of hanging about them, trying to make the best of a bad job, when it was clear that nothing could result but continued frustration and misunderstanding, for them and him? They had started as a family, but events had altered that, once for all. He no more belonged there now than Suspiria did.

She came home the next evening, two days before he was expecting her; and as soon as he heard the car in the yard, he knew that someone had called her attention to the article. She was in the doorway before he could go out to meet her. Her face looked small and pinched in the high collar of her coat, her cheekbones flecked with an angry, steady red. She looked at him without a smile, walked past him into the house, and dropped the folded paper upon the piano.

'I suppose you've seen it. Of course someone took good care to show it to me.' She dug her hands into her pockets, and wheeled on him suddenly with a protesting cry: 'Can't you keep your tribe off my throat?'

He had nothing to say. He searched for something helplessly, and could find nothing. He might have said that the worst of the humiliation this time had fallen upon him, but it seemed to him that they were so irrevocably one that such a defence meant nothing. He could have told her at once that he had broken with his family once for all as a result of this betrayal, but somehow the first raging note of her voice had made him fly to spread the arms of his spirit between her ferocity and their weakness. He thought he had done with them, but when she aimed at them she drew blood from him. He felt the vehement colour mount his cheeks, and tightened his hold upon his own sore feelings, to remind himself how delicately he must allow for hers. He said with strained quietness: 'Yes, I've seen it. I knew what you'd feel about it. I'm sorry!'

'Sorry!' She beat her hands together in a sudden, violent blow. 'Is that all you can say? My God, when I think of it!'

The thin, long fingers locked and clung, wrenching at one another. 'Wasn't it enough to have let them in on the wedding? Didn't they get enough fun out of us? What sort of appetites have your people got? But then, there was the money!' The flame of her tormented eyes lifted viciously to his face. 'Did you get a share, too? It would be only fair!'

'You don't mean what you're saying,' he said. 'You know I had nothing to do with it. I knew no more about it than you did until I picked up the paper in the train last night. I felt the same about it as you do. You don't need me to tell you that.'

'How do I know it? How do I know you might not find that sort of thing worthwhile, provided it pays a big enough fee? They don't see anything wrong with it, how can I be sure you do? You're one of the same tribe, aren't you?'

'It happened,' he said, his temples darkening into an angry crimson. 'I can't undo it now, I wish I could. What's the use of raving about it? If I'd had wind of it in time, I'd have stopped it, and you know it. I hate it as much as you do.'

'Then what have you done about it? Entered a mild protest and undertaken to smooth me down? What, and without even a share in the proceeds? Oh, my God!' she said, hoarse with loathing, 'what have I tied myself to? I knew it would be the devil for me to keep it up, but I didn't complain, did I, when that garrulous old woman turned our wedding into a sideshow? I never held it against her. But this – this—'

She turned her back on him, and fastened her hands upon the edge of the piano, swallowing the end of what she had tried to say. He approached her quietly, and taking her by the waist, made to turn her about to face him, but she sprang away from his touch furiously, wrenching her very sleeve out of his grasp.

'No, not like that! It isn't so simple! How often do you think I can be put up in your family's shop-window, and not bear any malice? If you've promised them to smooth me down again, you'll have a lot of explaining to do.'

'You talk as if I were on their side,' he said, aghast.

'Have you said anything to make me think you're not?'

'My God, what am I supposed to say? You want me to swear on the Bible or something? I tell you I had nothing to do with it, I hate it, I'd have stopped it if I could. If you expect me to bid for your trust by calling them a lot of filthy names, you'll be disappointed. I leave that to you – you're perfectly competent.'

It was the reproach of her impenetrable assurance that he couldn't stand. How could he bear to leave his family to her alien and aristocratic savagery, whatever their guilt? And yet to see her plying her fingers and writhing her body in the extremity of her humiliation and pain made him hate them as he had not known how to hate them on his own account.

'You want me to say it, then? They're third-rate people, with the sensitivities of blocks. They gloat over our celebrity. They terrify me! They're a little monument of vulgarity! And you belong to them! I should have known it,' she whispered, wringing her hands. 'I should have seen it! Oh, God, what a fool, to think you could be different!'

'You thought I could be changed,' he said, hitting back against his will. 'You were going to make a silk purse for yourself, weren't you? Who's to blame but you if it didn't come off?'

She shut her face between her hands, pressing her long eyebrows upward obliquely between her finger-tips, and staring from under them with distorted green eyes sick with frenzy. 'What have you done to me? I can't work since I knew you, I've lost myself, I've lost my self-respect, I've lost my peace. Oh, God, what am I to do? I wish I'd never seen you!'

'What have I done to you? What have *you* done to *me*? I was a whole person until you got hold of me. I had a decent life, and a place where I belonged. But you, with your passion for making something of things – what have you made of me? I don't belong anywhere. That's your doing! You made a monstrosity of me, just like those pots of yours – forced me out of my own nature without being able to give me another. I wish to God you'd let me alone! At least I should have been something, if it wasn't much – now I'm nothing at all!'

Such things ought not to be said, never to anyone, never even in the silence of the heart; he knew it, even while he was trying to rein in his tongue from finishing what it had begun. But every retort had gone a little deeper into the quick, and they were so locked by the claws that they could not struggle apart. The last reticences seemed to fall from them, there was nothing left but their wounds, and their frantic desire to wound. The violence of the quarrel rattled at their sanity, almost shattering them as glass is shattered by its own too intense key-tone mercilessly prolonged. They drove each other apart at last, shuddering and exhausted, until at night they had no words left, and no will, and lay side by side in the bed, motionless and silent, drained of life.

It was the most terrible, the most terrifying thing that had ever happened to them. It was like a death, like having the heart and the energy wrenched out of them. They lay without touching each other, too tired and broken to stir a hand across the crumpled sheet to reach for an answering hand. They fell into something which was less and more than sleep, a kind of grey semi-consciousness, with half-open eyes staring at the darkness over them, too listless to close completely and give them rest. The pain and fury of their disruption had become the long, dull ache of amputation; there was no cure for that.

Perhaps they fell asleep truly for a moment. She started into feeling again to find him suddenly trembling beside her, and in the instant of realisation she said: 'Dennis!' aloud, in a tone of such wild appeal and reproach that it startled him alive again. There were a hundred ways it could have begun, but only one in which it could end. He drew breath in a great recovering sob, and tore himself out of the drowning apathy of estrangement. The darkness shook and cried. His arms gathered her, and rigid for a moment, she melted into him as suddenly, moaning, winding her arms about his neck, groping with her blind, quivering mouth along his cheek and over the arched lids of his eyes, cool above the burning heat of his breaking tears.

They strained together wildly breast to breast, trying to lose themselves in each other, trying to break through the labouring ribs and gasping flesh into the centre of the heart, to be one and indissoluble for ever, to be safe. They hurt each other, the once-caressing hands now clinging like grapples of steel, the convulsively locked arms struggling to compress their two racked bodies into one. There were no articulate words between them at all, only the heaving gasps and lurching sighs of two tired animals driven to death. Even when the last paroxysm of desperate, agonised delight ebbed into stillness, and left them inextricably twined into exhaustion in the deeps of the private and illimitable sea, they lay without releasing each other, and slept so at last, afraid to relax their despairing hold, for fear their very bodies, pierced through and through by the violence of the storm, should disintegrate and be lost for ever.

They knew before they slept, they knew in awaking, that this was only the first of many such reconciliations, and the mildest of many such deaths. What they did not know, what they already wondered, was how many such violations body and spirit could bear before they shattered past reassembling.

CHAPTER TEN:

The Isolation of the Inseparable

1

BY THE time they were rid of that interminable autumn and winter, to reach the lost heaven was not more important to her than to escape from the ever-present hell. She had given up trying to make anything else of it. It was a hell of humiliating jealousy, of destroying quarrels and shattering reconciliations, in the recurring fires of which they burned incessantly. So when a respectable London gallery made the offer of a spring show of Theo's paintings, she accepted eagerly, and insisted on going down to help to arrange the exhibition. He was dead, and safe from the stings of publicity; and his work deserved all the honest notice she could get for it. It was a kind of propitiation to the sad ghost which would not leave them, nor let itself be forgotten.

She threw herself into the arrangements with all the demoniac energy which could find no outlet now through her own hands. She even bought new clothes, carefully chosen and unusually elaborate, for the opening, and went to meet the reviving publicity with a handsomely painted face and challenging eyes. It had become the lesser evil by then.

There was a certain amount of pure pleasure in the spectacle of Theo's pictures, well-hung to her own orders in a good light; and though a number of people came to the opening for the wrong reasons, still more were there out of a real artistic interest. Those who had known both Theo and Suspiria in the old days approached her with some constraint, but contacts limited to a few minutes of conversation in such an atmosphere confronted her with no difficulties. Nor, she thought, did they see much wrong with her. Perhaps she was even thinner than they had known her, but there was not time for them to find her greatly changed. She felt invulnerable; they could not help her, but equally they could not harm her.

She looked down the long room, on the second morning, and saw a tall, grey-haired man standing before her portrait, and studying it with a severe and thoughtful attention which was somehow familiar. She recognised the poise of the large head, the set of the heavy but straight shoulders. She had once told him she would not want to see him again, even if he gave her life back to her; but now she moved impulsively down the room, and touched his arm.

'Sir Howard! – I thought I couldn't be mistaken. I didn't know you cared about this kind of thing.'

'Psychological curiosity,' he said candidly, 'not artistic. How are you?' He looked at her, she thought, with every appearance of pleasure. For better or worse, they would always be more than acquaintances; there is no escaping from the facts of your past life. His presence was the acknowledgment of one such fact, and nothing more. Yet his eyes dwelt on her with a long and searching regard as he waited for the conventional reply.

'Very well, thank you! And you?'

'Thank you, I survive.' His eyes went back from her face to the uplifted face in the portrait. 'Your late husband was a very considerable painter.'

'I think so. I'm glad you agree.' She looked up at the singing colours, the vibration of the reds and greens, the cool, limpid greys. The touch of Theo's lively hand was everywhere in it, clearer than any signature. Poor Theo, who had never had justice yet!

'Are you happy?' Sir Howard asked her abruptly.

'Happy? What is that? I'm alive. I said I should never thank you for it, but I do. I wanted to remain alive. Perhaps it was an instinctive desire rather than a responsible one, but I wanted it.'

'If I'm not too grim a reminder,' he said, encouraged by the patience with which she had followed him so far, 'will you come and have lunch with me?'

She went with him almost gladly. His interest in her had a weight and thoughtfulness in strong contrast to the emotional inquisitiveness to which she had become accustomed. To be regarded with respect, even a disapproving and detached respect, was almost a novelty; and at least he was a peaceful companion in this, that he knew far more about her than most people knew. The things she might say to him would need no explaining; he had the language.

Over a secluded table in the most discreetly hidden of restaurants he looked up at her suddenly, and said: 'I heard that you married him.'

'Yes,' she said, 'I married him.'

He did not comment, but she knew that he had seen, as clearly as she saw them herself, the little insidious threads of necessity by which they had been drawn to the register office. 'We did what was expected of us,' she said, and was disturbingly aware of the bitterness in her own voice. It needed so little to steer this man's intuition into the secret channels where no one should ever be allowed to penetrate. And yet she was tempted, for the first time in her life, to the violent confidences of the confessional.

'There was nothing else for you to do,' he said simply. 'That was easily seen from the beginning.'

'I suppose so, at least from where you were sitting. But you see, I've not been used to going a step out of my way either to do what was expected of me, or to avoid doing it. It did something to my equilibrium. All the qualities I had have gone out of gear.' She added with a wry smile: 'It didn't do Dennis any good, either. For me it was a dangerous step away from my own individuality. For him it was something worse, a step *towards* his. Oh, it was what was expected of him, in the circumstances, too. But the only way he could have got back on an even keel was by running away like mad from the whole issue. He did try. We both tried, but what other way was there for us to go? If we'd run off together, somewhere abroad, where nobody knew us, that would have been a violation of the truth, too.'

'And if you'd broken loose from each other, once for all?'

She raised her fierce eyes, and looked through him into a terrifying emptiness. 'Did you ever try to break loose from your own blood and bones?'

He tilted the wickered bottle of Orvieto, and filled her glass, and for a moment sat gazing into the pale amber light of the wine. 'I often wondered!' he said, more to himself than to her.

'What did you wonder? How far Perleman was right in calling it an infatuation?'

'No,' he said unexpectedly, 'I was never in any doubt about the passion being genuine enough, on both sides. No, what I always wondered was who did give Freeland the poison. And what it was going to be like for you both, when you had time to wonder about it, too.'

The upward flare of her lashes, swift as it was, was so smooth and steady that he knew she felt no surprise, the flash of her eyes blazed recognition and response. 'You seem to have given up the idea,' she said, 'that I might be the one person who knows the answer to that.'

'I gave that up during the trial. To be exact, when Forbes was in the witness-box. It became so plain then that you were afraid *he* was the one who knew the answer. At that stage,' he said carefully, 'it didn't matter much to you, I realise that. All that mattered was keeping him and yourself alive. It was his possible danger, not his possible guilt, you were seeing, but I couldn't help wondering how you would get on when the danger was gone, and you were left with the guilt.'

'You are really a very subtle person,' she said softly. 'Have you also considered the possibility that, after all, Dennis didn't do it, either?'

'I had an open mind about it. But you were so insistent that he wouldn't have done it himself, you see. At first I thought that was a curious piece of chivalry, a gesture of honour towards a man you had pushed out of your way, but whom you wouldn't have traduced, even in so sympathetic a fashion. It was one of the chief reasons why I felt you probably had killed him – having the opinion of you which I had formed by then, it matched. But when I became sure that you hadn't done it yourself, it lost that quality of atonement. It left me no option but to think that it was a simple statement of truth. You knew him – and he was not a likely suicide.'

'I see! So it was I myself who reduced the three to one.'

'Not quite that, there were still two. One of them, according to you, is an unlikely starter, but the possibility remains a possibility. You ought to be the first person,' he said seriously, 'to be able to assess the full force of your loss on a man. But you're probably the last.'

She was silent, looking down at her hands, in which she turned the stem of her glass steadily. 'I don't know. I just don't know. No amount of thinking will bring me any nearer knowing. Of course it could have happened! Any time during that last week, except that final evening, he could have helped himself to it, if he'd wanted it. All I know is that for him to want it would be against everything I knew of him. But then, what do you ever know of another person? How reliable is what you learn in ten years of living together? When it comes to the point, every one of us is alone.' She looked up, fixing her tormented eyes on him insistently. 'If what you say is true, and you've been in no doubt now for a long time that *I* was not the murderer, then you must also know very well that I went to a lot of trouble to suppress half the evidence. I expect you took that to mean that I knew the answer, and the answer was Dennis. But I didn't! I don't know now! All I knew was that there were just the three of us involved, and my part of the responsibility, whatever it might be, had nothing to do with antimony oxide. Which left just two people, both, in a way, my victims, though heaven knows I never intended any harm to either of them. The only way to be fair to them both was to protect them both. And as for what I myself thought, I made my guess like all the rest, and knew no more than they did whether I was right or wrong.' And supposing, only supposing, that I was wrong, and you were right, and Theo killed himself. Supposing that Dennis doesn't know the answer, either?'

'Then he will still be looking for it, like you. And like you, he'll have only one place to look.'

'Yes,' she said in a very low voice, 'exactly! He knows he did it, or he believes I did it. Which is it? Can you tell me of a way of finding out the answer to that? Do you know any kind of test for it? I don't. I've listened to him, and watched him, and weighed everything he said and did since I began to have time to care about the answer. The variety of interpretations that can be put upon even the least word a man utters is something to marvel at. Asking and answering is no good, you see. The question was asked and answered so often and so definitely by both of us in court; 'did you' and 'no, I swear I didn't,' don't mean anything at all. And yet there's only one other person it could have been, and neither of us really believes in that solution. Once, he began to try me out, he said something about having absolute truth between us – and then he drew back, and left it standing there as a pious generality. He took fright, and couldn't go on. Why? Was he going to ask me? Or tell me? I've wondered ever since, but there's never been anything to tell me the answer, there never will be anything. If you are a murderer, and love someone better than your own life, you don't tell the beloved what you are. If you love someone better than your own life, and feel reasonably sure she's a murderer, you don't ask her. Partly because you don't want to be sure past all hope, partly because even silence between the two of you is a kind of protection for her. So he didn't ask me, and he didn't tell me. And a silence like that is something you don't break from the other side, either. I doubt if there's any way over it, or through it.'

'Then what do you propose to do? Live with it?'

'And bear it. What else?'

'You can't do it!' he said, almost angrily. 'No one could! You're asking too much of yourself, and of him.'

'What do you suggest, then? Forget it? Show me a way,

and we'll be happy to try it. Break up the marriage as a hopeless proposition, and leave him? I should be leaving my life. Besides, even if we were ever driven to consider breaking up that marriage, has it occurred to you how completely unbreakable it is? The forces that made it inevitable have taken good care to make it permanent, too. Oh, no,' she said, watching him fixedly across the table with her beautiful and haggard eyes. 'We shall never get away from each other in this life. We shall never even be able to long for it with an undivided mind. We still love each other, you see. Of all the married and damned living in this world, my dear man, we're the farthest beyond help. There isn't any escape – except, of course, the way Theo escaped.'

He drew back then from further discussion, as suddenly as if he had found himself walking over the edge of a cliff, to which he had come unnoticing. The conversation was wrenched into safer channels, and she followed indifferently, willingly entering into consideration of Theo's paintings. There was nothing wrong with her critical faculties, and her mind still glittered; only it had no stability, and no peace. Some disintegration of despair had begun within her, and was eating her substance away; the disorganisation of her hands had begun in her heart. And what was there to be said to her? What could be said, that would not be an impertinence? She was a woman capable of seeking her own solutions, and taking them at whatever cost. She wanted neither advice nor sympathy. She had, perhaps, made use of him this once to help the definition of her diagnosis, as men maddened by silence may talk sensibly to their mirrors to break the spell; but he knew, when she gave him her long, cold hand at parting, that she would never let him approach her so closely again. Never, unless the problem somehow solved itself, and set her free. He had served his purpose. Like the mirror he would be silent; but she would never again care to be with him, or to read back the confidences she had printed into his memory.

She released her hand, withdrawing strongly, and walked away from him towards Bond Street, the draped folds of her fashionable coat swirling back richly from her shoulders. He thought he had never seen nor imagined a figure so erect, and so lonely.

2

The spring came early and radiant; the last frosts wept away into a quick, bright thaw, the hanging woods behind the house budded into delicate green, softer and vaguer than the down of young birds, and all the carefully tended gardens of Great Leddington burst into a passion of flowers yellow as sunlight; but still they watched each other silently and compassionately through the dark mist of their memories of Theo, waiting for a word which was never said, a movement which was never made.

On the eve of May Day she fired her kiln early. She had been experimenting with a new glaze, of which she said restlessly that she had great hopes; but she knew that it was a lie, even as she said it. She had no great hopes at all, of anything she did. The gift was gone out of her fingers. How they had suddenly torn that one great, delicate bowl out of the clay, after so many months without reward, she could not understand. Now it stood invisible, rose-red in the cooling kiln, waiting for the evening again, with all that was left of her spirit burning within it.

Her mind had made this a final test; it had the full organic beauty of form which had eluded her for a year, and if she had brought the glaze to as high a perfection, then she was still alive, and an artist. If she had failed with it, after the wild encouragement of a first success, she was finished, and the spark had flowed out of her fingers only to mark the final death of the fire within. All day long she prowled in and out of the workshop, unable to work or rest, making excuses to remain beside the kiln, and yet the more deeply disquieted while she remained there.

'You're making too much of it,' said Dennis. 'If it came out a failure it would still be only a failure like any other – you're trying to make an oracle out of it. If you go on making crisis after crisis of every piece you throw, how can you expect to get back into form? You're ill, you ought to throw up the whole idea of work for a bit, and let it come back naturally.'

She looked up at him across the kiln, her thin shoulders arched cat-like to fend him off, as if he had threatened her last stake. He saw again, with a slow contraction of his heart into pain, how her eyes had burned up half her face, and her cheeks had sunk into gaunt hollows under the gleaming bones. He should have known better than to argue with her, everything he did was suspect now; he could not warn her against anything, even her own frenzy, without warning her against him.

'I know you don't believe in it,' she said, 'you don't have to tell me that. You'd like to be the breadwinner, wouldn't you? It would give you your bearings again.'

He made no answer. Unless she found some way of goading him off his balance against his will, he seldom quarrelled with her now. He would stand there staring steadily at her with his blank, compassionate eyes, while her blows bruised him and recoiled unacknowledged. For whole days she would be aware of those eyes upon her, smoothed clear of any betraying light or feeling, offering her no fuel for her angers or her despairs, and no unwary tenderness, but only a distant and detached pity, against which no weapon of hers could produce a wound.

'In any case you can't do anything until it's cooled off,' he said patiently. 'Why don't you come out into the garden, while the sun's out? It's nice if you keep out of the wind. It won't cool any the quicker for you standing and watching it.'

She felt how carefully, how arduously, he nursed her aside from her obsession, how even his voice had assumed the same opaque quality as his eyes. It was necessary to tread thus gently, because they had learned from scarifying experience that the slightest incautious step might hurl them into the screaming dark. Sometimes she could not bear the labouring calm, she wanted to end it at all costs, and longed for the very violence they went so wincingly to avoid. Sometimes she cast about her for a means of drawing blood from him, and forcing him to strike back at her, but it was not so easy as it had been. He kept his veiled quiet, his eyes continued their watch upon her without rest. Then, recoiling, she would think wildly: 'Poor Dennis! What hell for him! If he were free of me he could still be happy – he's only young, he has time!'

She went out with him into the garden; he had been busy all the Saturday afternoon breaking up the neglected butts of ground within the rear fence, under the shade of the woods, which were foaming into a bright and tender green of full leaf. He was flushed from digging, and his forehead smudged with earth from his hands, and sun and exercise had moved him to strip off his collar and tie, and unbutton his shirt. 'He looks,' she thought, 'like my son.' And her body ached with her love and hate for him.

She stayed with him a little while as he worked, and he was comforted, and bent his back to his digging again with all his attention; but when he relaxed for a moment, and turned to reassure himself that she was still there, he had already lost her. She had gone back silently to her vigil by the kiln. It was no use pursuing her and bringing her back again. Her mind was there, she could not help going back to it. And was it possible that he felt easier when she was gone? The lift of his heart, the deep sigh, could not be mistaken for anything but relief. Did he wish himself rid of her? Not often had he gone so far as to contemplate that question; the mere uneasy foreboding that he was approaching it set him baulking like a driven horse, and swerving from the line of thought which must bring him hard against it at last if he persisted.

He loved her as terribly as ever, more terribly, he could no more give her up than he could give up his own heart from his body. As long as they both lived, they could not live without each other, and yet they could not live with each other, either. It was not all their fault, events had made their task impossible from the start. In the end they would destroy each other. He knew in his heart that he was afraid, that the despairing patience and gentleness with which he watched her acquired its calm from the very force of the fear he felt within. If a way of escape from her offered, would he take it? Could he? He did not know, he dared not wonder.

He put away his tools and went and made the tea himself; she would have no awareness of time or hunger now, except as they touched her obsession. When he was drying his hands, he found that he had broken a nail in his wrestlings with some of the overgrown bushes in the garden. Suspiria's handbag was lying in one of the chairs in the living-room, and somewhere in its habitual chaos she carried a nail-file, so he opened the bag gingerly, and began to search through the accumulation of letters, cosmetics and keys for what he wanted. He did not find it, but he found something else.

There was a little phial of tablets with a chemist's label, and Suspiria's name upon it; small white tablets, with a very slightly translucent texture, and a mica-like gleam about them. He sat staring at the little bottle as it lay in the palm of his hand; and at first he thought he would simply put it back where he had found it, and ask nothing, as she had volunteered nothing. That ready, watchful fear in him stirred quickly, burning up newly-coloured, like salty flames. Yes, he knew he was afraid. He liked his life, he wanted it; it could be hell upon earth, but still he wanted it. Then he thought: 'No! I *will* tell her I've seen them.' There were too many things hidden and unsaid, he was not sure that the silent places of their minds could hold any more, or how much more his self-respect could bear.

When she came in reluctantly in answer to his call that tea was ready, he opened his hand beneath her eyes, and showed her the phial. She looked from it to his face, and her eyes were sombre and ready to be angry, though the emaciated lines of her face remained severe and still. 'Well?'

'You never told me you'd been to a doctor. I asked you to – remember? Several times!'

'I had to sleep,' she said. 'When it got too bad, I went to him, that's all. There's nothing else the matter with me.'

'I should have thought he could have done something better for you than just give you dope. What are they?' he asked, steadily watching her.

'I don't know. Chloral hydrate, most likely. Something

better than a bromide, anyhow.' She reached out her hand for them, and the authority of the gesture could not be denied. 'What were you doing in my bag?'

He told her; her lips curved upward into a cold and famished smile, but she believed him. She shrugged it off indifferently, and sat down to pour out tea, slipping the phial into the deep pocket in the skirt of her dress. He watched it out of sight, noticing how her fingers folded it tightly and thrust it down to the bottom, and how she instantly lifted her hollow, intent eyes to encounter his again, as if she waited for him to challenge her further.

'Why didn't you tell me you'd been to him?'

'What difference does it make? Either they're effective or they're not, your blessing isn't going to make them work any better. Besides, I'm not proud of needing a doctor. You're more interested than I expected,' she said in a curiously flat voice.

'I don't much like such things as sleeping drugs, that's all. They're only a way of patching at it, instead of finding out what's really wrong. You'll be careful with them, won't you?'

'I'm not likely to make any mistakes,' she said.

Across the table they watched each other steadily, wearily, aware of every movement. For a long time their life together had been like that, a contest of watchfulness, a match of eyes. He had not often ventured to question what he expected to see, nor why his life should seem to hang so heavily upon his senses; but he knew they were killing each other, and which of them was to die of it first, and by how rapid or how slow a pain, was something he found himself wondering now without disguise. What was the use of pretending that such things did not happen? Theo was dead. Such things had happened.

In a little while Suspiria got up and left him, and he heard the back door shut after her. She was going back to the kiln, because she could not keep away. He went into the garden again, and kept watch upon her movements unobtrusively through the windows, as often as he could make an excuse to pass that way. Inside the workshop, she was as assiduously inventing occupations for her hands, which flew from tool to tool with distrait fury, beginning and abandoning. He would have liked to avoid the moment of crisis when it came with the sunset, but he dared not leave her to face it alone, she had hung too much upon the issue. So when the full light began to fail, he put his tools away, and went to wash his hands at her sink, making that his excuse for entering the workshop. She had the first bricks off already, and went on lifting and stacking them, without paying any attention to him. Through the widening gap a column of hot air quivered fiercely, and the feathers of her disordered hair shook in it, and erected themselves, groping uncertainly upward like living things. Her face flushed vividly in the heat as she leaned over to stare into the interior. Beads of perspiration broke upon her forehead, and the softest tendrils of hair darkened and lay limply against her damp temples. He held his breath because she stared so long and so intently, shielding her eyes with the fingers of one hand.

He approached quietly, looking where she looked. The contents of the kiln stood intact, the bowl in the centre, large, eager and shapely, surely as fine as she could wish. It shaded upward from cream into a soft, dull gold, and at the rim into a deep chocolate-brown as furry in texture as the face of a Siamese cat. What more could she want? She prowled round it, circling, angling for every conceivable view of the thing. When she dared, she began to lift out some of the smaller pieces from round it, to have a clearer view; one of the small pots cracked as she closed the tongs on it. She drew back quickly, and waited again, never sparing another glance for the nondescript little thing she had broken, but taking to heart the warning for the single piece which mattered to her.

'It's all right, you see,' said Dennis, carefully unemphatic in her ear. Her movements, the way she quested about distractedly and longed and feared to touch, hurt him abominably. But she only gave him a dark look, almost of derision, and turned her eyes fiercely back to the kiln.

She had made too much of it; if a miracle came out, after this anguish of waiting, it could not satisfy her. He saw that clearly now. She had lost sight of truth and balance, everything went into the distorting mirror of her despair, and flashed back into her eyes grotesquely changed, a caricature of itself. He felt a terrible adoring pity gather hotly about his heart, filling him with pain. He remembered her as he had first seen her in this house, sweeping aside the curtain from between them with a gesture of her arm, and holding her grey and glistening hands before her while she stared at him imperiously from under her arched brows, angrily repulsing the invaders of her dedicated peace. A slut, he had called her, with shocking clothes and a dirty face; but all the time he had recognised and feared the magnificence of her absorption into something larger than anything he possessed in his limited life, and envied her the superb conviction with which she strode through the complexities of her daunting world, creating with assurance and joy things which were their own justification. The flowers of clay that came out of her hands rose and stood erect, knowing themselves to be works of art; they reared themselves up like man coming to his full height in the intoxication of knowing that he could go on two feet; they thrust with their ardent curves against the sustaining air, making a place for themselves as of right. Now she threshed uneasily about the still quivering heat of her kiln, waiting for one bowl, only one, to come forth uncrippled, and encourage her to go on believing that she was still an artist.

The disintegration terrified him, because he knew that it was his work. He had not meant it, but that did not absolve him. For a long time he had tried to comfort himself with the belief that this was only the aftermath of emotional disturbance, and would pass in time, and she would regain that unifying peace of the mind which makes creation possible. So she might have done, if the causes of her disruption could pass. But there was always, at the heart of everything they did or said or thought, the question without an answer, the question which would never be anwered. There was Theo, there would always be Theo. 'How she must long to get rid of him,' thought Dennis, watching her insatiably, 'even at the cost of getting rid of me! If she could break loose from us both she might amount to something yet.'

The heat subsided slowly. She pushed back her hair from her damp forehead, and stripped away more of the smaller pots which obscured the great one, until finally she could lift it out. She set it down without damage on the edge of the kiln, and stood back to consider it more critically.

A fine, full, vegetable shape, thrusting roundly outward, energetically making room for itself, as positive and confident as a great flower, and with something of a flower's texture. It was fluted with the marks of her fingers, it stood poised as accurately and proudly on its narrow base as a tulip on its stem. She had seen a world of hope in the form, what was she seeing now in the finished bowl? What did she make of the glaze, that she stared at it still with unmoving face and fixed eyes?

She had taught him, perhaps too well. He found himself examining his own reactions rather than hers. He liked the glowing yellow at first sight, with its furry chocolate lip and its creamy-white base. The gold was rich and soft as she had meant it to be. But had it, perhaps, a slight heaviness, a thought too much positive colour for the beautiful waxen shape, smoothed like flesh beneath her palms? It was not the singing gold of tulips, but a less live, less vernal yellow; it turned the vivid, responsive flesh back to clay. And the slight metallic tint in the brown of the rim gathered to a bluish-grey bloom where the light rested, defacing the furry, warm softness which was the unique quality of the glaze as she had intended it to be. The clay, where it showed like light beneath a curtain at the base, no more than a hair-thin line, had fired to a reddish russet; he was more aware of it than he liked, and it did not please him. And yet the thing came so near to being wonderful! But he knew it was a failure. The yellow was a surface yellow, no internal light came up through it, it was laid on from without, adroit, accomplished, unsatisfying.

Was it possible that she had so lost her orientation that she did not know? She went all round it, looked at it from every side, and then at him across it, her hungry eyes still dark with anxiety. 'Well? What do you think of it?'

'I like it!' The lie came out almost without his knowledge.

Anything, anything, to see that look of intolerable tension soften and ebb from her face; and if she did not know, what harm could it do? It was hardly a lie for any other creature but their two selves. The thing would pass with half the critics for a minor masterpiece, so subtle were the things that were wrong with it. 'Can't you see for yourself that it's a success? What more do you want?'

'You really think it succeeds?' she asked, the green glitter waking in the depths of her eyes; and she looked down again at the bowl, and the first spasmodic tremor of a smile began to shake the corners of her lips. 'The glaze, too? Do you think the glaze came out right? Could you fault it at all?' Her voice was quiet, and yet breathless. She watched his face, hanging upon his answer.

He looked back at her gently, and said: 'No, I couldn't. I can't see anything I'd want altered. It's perfect!'

She stood looking at him for a moment with her lower lip caught between her teeth, and then she began to laugh. There was nothing hysterical about it, it came up out of the deep recesses of her throat with an aching bitterness of amusement; and in the middle of it she suddenly put out her hand, and flattened it against the hot golden side of the bowl, and thrust it into the kiln. It fell with a shattering noise, and burst into a shower of fluted petals, breaking a dozen things besides in its fall. He had opened his mouth to cry out, and then made no more than a faint, guilty gasp like a sob, and was speechless before her.

'Liar!' she said, dragging herself back out of her laughter into a blaze of anger. 'Damned liar! You know as well as I do the thing's bad. If you don't know it, what use are you to me?' She stood there looking down into the kiln at the fragments of her last hope. 'It's no good! I'm finished! And all for you,' she said, incredulous between grief and laughter, 'all for you!'

CHAPTER ELEVEN:

On the Other Side of the Night

1

THE QUARREL flared up and burned out, leaving them languid in the deep twilight, silent and exhausted, motionless because from that battlefield they knew no place to which they might go. There was no energy left in either of them for the violence of regret which commonly followed their frenzies. Even the struggle, while it lasted, was not the familiar disrupting paroxysm of frustrated love; it was all hers, a threnody of grief and rage, ebbing away into despair; while he did no more than defend himself stoically, holding her off, suffering her, crying out a little when she hurt him beyond what he could bear, but not this time – oh, never again! – striking back at her wound for wound. He could not fight with her any more. It was not as if there remained anything profitable to be said, or any ease to be had for his own pain in striking at her. All he could do was endure it, and wait for it to pass.

The living-room was still in twilight, the soft, bluish May dusk clung at the window, diaphanous and cool. Now that they were silent they could sense how large was the silence outside the house, no wind stirring in the woods, no traffic in the lane, only the faint sounds from the town coming in tentatively upon the very edge of hearing, as if from an infinite distance, another world.

Suspiria lay so still in the depths of the big chair that he could scarcely detect her presence except by the one lax hand lying open and empty over the arm, and the almost imperceptible stirring of light which marked the rise and fall of her breast. She breathed long and deeply, but without ease, and lay half-dead, as sometimes in the exhaustion of love, incapable of any effort but the soft, limp effort of breathing, and continuing to live, and following him with her eyes if he moved a step away from her.

The tide of passion, which had been wont to go out devastatingly as the recoiling sea, wringing their hearts, rolling them about and about in its breaking waves like so much drift on the Atlantic ebb, sighed away now into a terrible quietness. Dennis sat in the corner of the window-sill, half-hidden by the curtain, his cheek against the cold glass, his half-closed eyes on the vast, clear, impersonal cobweb-greyness of the night. He was spent, there was nothing in him but the ache of her remembered outcry against him, and the hollow silence he had opposed to it. Everything, all that tumult and defiance and splendour, had come down to this flat and quiet end.

'We can't go on like this,' he heard himself say; but he said it without resolution or protest, only pointing out what was obvious. 'You see that!'

But what was the use of saying it, when for all their writhings and turnings they could do nothing but go on like this? They knew only too well that their course was fixed.

She said nothing; she had so sunk into the shadows of the chair that she seemed rather to have dissolved away, leaving only that discarded hand, open and empty, outstretched towards him but making no appeal and offering no promise, meaning nothing.

'What are we to do?' he said in a whisper, to the silence, not to her.

The twilight scent of foliage was coming in through the open window in faint, recurring drifts, the perfumed breath of the May night. Somewhere there were young poplar saplings, late in coming to full leaf, for they still had the sweet and drunken scent of their buds about them.

'I never meant to hurt you,' he said. 'I love you! But I've only done you harm.'

She still said nothing, but he saw a stirring of the dim outlines in the chair, as she gathered herself slowly together, dragging herself upright by the crooked fingers of the one visible hand. There was a small, pure pallor which was her face. He supposed she would not speak because she hated him for what he had done to her by blundering into her proud, inviolate life and breaking it to pieces. Or perhaps she had not yet the heart or the will to speak, for speech, too, can be an intolerable burden. She had pulled herself to her feet, and with a lame movement was shaking her skirts into order, a hand buried in the big pocket on her right thigh, so that the thin arm ended at the wrist. When she turned her back on him, and began to cross the room, she went like a cripple, groping her way.

'Where are you going?' he asked.

'Nowhere.' The slight, grey voices, dwindling into the greyness of the dusk, hardly troubled the silence. She was at the whisky cabinet, he heard the glasses clink; he wondered listlessly why she did not switch on the light, and almost got up to do it for her, but it did not seem worth the effort, nor did he yet want to see or be seen too clearly. She went fumbling patiently in the dark, and was about it a long time.

'If only there were something we could do!'

She was coming towards him across the room, moving between the piano and the lamp with a drifting lightness, as if she had no weight. She had a glass in either hand. Untroubled by alternations of light, their eyes could find the way very well as yet in the deepening dusk. She stood in front of him, holding out one of the glasses. He saw her face as a floating oval of sourceless light, and half of the light again translated into a great twin darkness and brightness of eyes.

He put out his hand to take the drink she was offering him, and then, abruptly, horribly, he was afraid. It made no sense, it came out of nowhere, a stabbing reminder, full of humiliation, because fear between them was an offence, and he felt it as such without understanding it. He got up quickly, and went past her, and switched on the light.

The first thing he saw, in the sudden dazzle, was the small glass phial lying at the rim of the circle of light cast by the lamp upon the open cabinet. It was pushed in there beside the whisky bottle, the screw cap lying beside it; and it was empty.

So now he understood everything. He turned and looked again at Suspiria; she was standing where he had brushed past her, gazing at him with eyes slightly narrowed against the suddenness of the light, and still holding the two glasses before her carefully, one in either hand. The eyes which watched him had a glitter he had never seen in them before. Tears were so alien to her that for a long moment he did not recognise the source of that shining along her lashes; then he saw that she was weeping for him, silently, with a motionless face. He understood everything. Yes, by this method, then, if there was no other, he could be free and set her free. He had been waiting for it with fear for a long time, but now it was quite different. He found himself thinking, strangely, almost gratefully: 'The great thing is not to be afraid – never to be afraid of anything. Fear is the only real violation.'

He reached back quietly with one hand, in the shelter of his body, and picked up the little bottle, and slipped it into his pocket; then he went towards her. He felt that he was smiling, but could not understand what there could be in his face to hold her eyes so imperiously. She drew back the one glass towards her breast, and held the other a little towards him. Her eyes had dilated again, there was little left of her but that great, shining stare, and the sheen of tears which would not gather and fall. She was filled with grief, drowning in the flood of her pity. He wished he could think of something comforting to say to her, but he knew that she would understand his silence afterwards.

He took the glass from her, the one she offered to him so carefully. She put the other one to her lips and then she seemed to lose the impulse to drink, and stood gazing at him over the rim, every other sense drained into the intensity with which she watched him.

He drained the glass, shivering at the slight bitterness that wrung his mouth. When it was all gone, he smiled at her with the most tender reassurance. There was nothing he need say, no advice he need give her. She would be all right when he was gone; and surely she would understand that he acquiesced, that he knew there could be no other way out for them. She was suffering now, but she had done only what she had to do.

He put down the glass, and going to her quietly where she stood, took her by the shoulders and kissed her on the lips, very gently and restrainedly, as he might have kissed a shy child who must not be startled. All the time she held the untouched drink before her in both cupped hands; and as his lips touched hers she drew breath sharply, and he felt her tremble between his palms. The tears spilled, and ran silently down her cheeks. Her eyes, as he turned from her, had a stunned and uncomprehending look that hurt him, and caused him to keep his chin on his shoulder, still smiling back at her, as he moved towards the door.

He did not want her to torment herself. Into the last look he gave her he poured all the love, all the tenderness he could find in his liberated spirit. That was what she did not yet understand, of course; that was why she continued to stare after him as he withdrew himself from her; but afterwards she would understand. She would know that he had consented of his own will, that at the last moment he had lifted the burden from her; and in her recovered liberty she would be able to remember him without guilt or bitterness.

She was just opening her lips as he closed the door between them. He almost expected her to cry out after him, but she did not, and the last picture he had of her was of the frozen oval face blanched with wonder, and the tragic eyes following him to the last glimpse in a valedictory passion of love and regret.

2

He walked round the house, climbed through the fence at the end of the garden, and went up the steep rise of the hanging wood, because she would not look for him there, and he did not want her to follow him and find him, now that it was done. He did not want her to see him again, it was better that he should be found somewhere else, by some other person, some independent witness. At best her position would not be easy this time, but he thought he could make it secure.

He wondered how long he had before the tablets began to take effect; the very thought made him quicken his pace, scrambling upward through the clinging bushes and the tufted grass. He had lost the anchorage of time, because he would never again have any need of it; but before sleep came over him he must put a decent distance between himself and Suspiria, so that she might truthfully disclaim all knowledge of where he was, and be in some obscure and merciful way absolved from all responsibility for him.

The night was still, without a breath of wind, and yet full of sounds. He felt the stirring of silent and furtive life all about him, among the bushes and the trees, and he was not aware of any loneliness. The interlacing of branches above his head made a pattern of black filigree upon a luminous blue sky, and away through the tangles of the wood behind him he could see the glow of the town's lights, and the long unrolling chain of stars which was the high road. They seemed an infinite distance away, and the quiet air brought to him only a very faint murmur of traffic, a mere hum in the remotest edges of hearing. He might have been many miles from any evidences of humanity. The house was lost already, its single light cut off from him by the rising curve of the hill; and she had not followed him.

There was no moon yet, and the sky had too much innate light for the stars to be able to show themselves. He went up steadily to the crest of the ridge, and over it to the edge of the fields which belonged to the upper farm, rough chalk pasture gently undulating along the top of the hill for some distance, before the richer fields declined towards the valley and the village beyond. There was a stone wall along the rim of the wood, and just within the gate the remaining half of a straw stack, sheeted against the weather. He sat down there on the crackling litter of straw, and settled his back against the stack. It was as good a place as any other. What point was there in withdrawing himself to a still greater distance, when here was a solitude into which no one was likely to intrude before morning? Remote enough to preserve him from the indignity of being rescued, and harried, and walked up and down all night, and filled up with coffee, by interfering people who had no right in his affairs or Suspiria's; but not so remote that he could lie undiscovered for so much as one full day after his death.

He had to think of so many things. He did not want to be too ugly when they found him; she might have to identify him, and if his looks had ever given her pleasure, he wanted her to keep the last sight of him as a not unpleasant memory. After all, it was the easiest, the most serene of deaths, his tranquillity would leave no burden of horror upon her such as Theo had left.

No weight of sleep hung upon his eyelids as yet. He supposed narcotics had to have time for their work. He could think of only one thing more he must do. Suspiria's prints would be on the bottle, but that was right, that was needed, because it was her prescription, and he had stolen it; his own prints would be found overlying hers. But suicides, especially considerate ones who take care to remove the act from sight and hearing of their wives, almost invariably leave notes behind them. It was a poor light here for writing, even now that his eyes were accustomed to it, and found so much radiance within the dark; but if the results were readable, that was all that mattered.

He had a small diary in his pocket, and a propelling pencil, a cheap one his mother had given him while he was still at school, and which had outlived many subsequent and more expensive ones. He wished there had been time to make things up with his family, they would feel badly about it, and he did not want any untidy ends of grief left behind to strangle other people; but it was late for wishing now, and it could not be helped. He poised the pencil, and found himself momentarily without words. It had to be brief, it had to look sufficiently like his hand, and the matter of it had to convince the authorities; but more than that, it had to say something to Suspiria, too. What would be the good of accepting this way out at her hands, if he left another ghost to trouble her? No, he had not only to go cleanly away from her of his own indestructible will, but to take Theo's shadow away with him. Who had a better right?

He wrote: 'I didn't want my wife to be the one to find me. Give her my love, and ask her to forgive me.'

That was all. Suicides do not explain, or justify themselves, they leave the world with some tired utterance which means far more to them than to those who will puzzle over their death when they are gone. He thought it was enough; he was sure she would understand it. He put the book back into his inside pocket, and stretched out his legs before him, leaning back warmly into the straw. Now he was ready, he almost wished that sleep would hurry to take him. And yet the world opened about him in the soft and lambent night with an invincible beauty.

Fear is the only real violation. He was not afraid to love life, now that he was leaving it. He was not afraid to feel its enchantment tightening upon him, and to open his heart to a passion of conflicting gratitude and regret. What he had done he had done with his eyes open, not out of temper, or despair, or arrogant self-sacrifice, but because it was the only way he could see of cutting them both loose from an untenable situation. He had never ceased to want life, he wanted it now, but if they could not remain together without mutual destruction, nor separate without as inevitable an end, it was true economy that one of them should make an exit by this single infallible door, and he could not bear that the issue should be complicated by arguing who should go and who should stay. She had more to give the world than he had; and she had taken the decision for both of them, and he endorsed her judgment. They would both abide by it.

He would have liked a cigarette, but was not sure that he might not fall asleep too soon, and let it fall still burning into the straw, so he did not light one. It was growing cold; he shivered a little, and arched his shoulders strongly back into the shelter of the stack, drawing up his knees and locking his arms round them. It was not important, he would not feel the cold for very long. Already he seemed to feel a weight upon his eyes, a soft, muffling weight that confused his vision, and made the undulations of the meadow rock gently before him like the waves of a calm sea.

You have to know what you are, and abide by what you are – every one of you, Theo and Suspiria no less than Dennis Forbes. He found himself believing in a judgment, a sort of supernatural justice which corrected all faulty balances, all untrue proportions, for whose who had the courage and the honesty to know what they were, and answer for it. He was not paying for Theo's life with his, he was adjusting an exquisite equilibrium which had been thrown out of gear. If there was no other way, this way would do. He had no complaint to make.

He sat and watched the night, and his mind drifted into a kind of spacious peace, through which the memory of Suspiria moved poignantly, a restored Suspiria, intact and full of the virtue of her gift, creative, erect, a work of art like the best of what she made. A soft and indefinable sorrow, mute and without regrets, came over him out of the darkness, out of the May night and the spring; and the heaviness of his eyelids burdened him like the weight of the world. There was a dryness in his mouth and throat, a minor discomfort which somehow displeased him acutely. He was slipping low out of the world, sinking down into a drowsy confusion of mind where everything had grown shadowy. He knew that he was dying, but the tired calm in which he lay was not shaken by the knowledge. He let his eyes close unable to sustain the weight any longer; and instead of the cool and impervious night he saw only Suspiria's face, and her body inclining to him out of the darkness of his senses, until all that remained of his consciousness was an aching sweetness of recollection, an ebbing anguish of longing.

His hands relaxed from about his knees, and lay open in the straw. A breath of wind came stirring across the field, rousing in the cold of the deepening night, and went shuddering through the trees over his head, over the sheltered roof of Little Worth; but it came too late for him to hear it, for sleep had already come with a remarkable stealth and gentleness, and taken him.

3

He awoke to an instant discomfort of cold and cramp, staring round him wildly at a dove-grey world of pre-dawn, and a thinly clouded sky, and the lurching downward run of the field before his face. For a moment he was filled with blind panic, recognising nothing, remembering nothing, and the tingling stiffness of his body, the pain of his coldness, seemed to him the attack of a hostile and alarming world never yet known to him.

He started up in the straw, huddling his feet under him, shivering violently, not yet fully awake. The desolate early morning was shockingly unfamiliar without walls and a bed, and he had leaped so suddenly out of sleep, stung by the cold biting into his flesh, that his head swam again, and he had to shut his eyes tightly, and shake his head fiercely, to clear his vision. But the second time he looked at the field before him, and the distant grouping of the farm buildings in their circle of trees, he knew the scene, and as abruptly remembered the occasion.

He was alive! The weight of his body, its complicated aches from being misused thus in the cold May night, assured him that he was truly alive. He felt at his shivering flesh, he stared at the desolate indifferent monotone of the daylight, reluctantly beginning to tint the darkness with a suggestion of dawn. Sounds came out of the wood behind him, a fluttering flight, small among the bushes, a tentative, sleepy call. All these overwhelming things fell upon his senses as if there had never before been sight or hearing or touch. Even so faint a light dazzled him with its implications of radiance, even such stiff and painful movements delighted and astonished him with the marvel of his own intricate and exquisite body, and the faint first call of the bird in the wood filled his ears with the whole possibility of music. He was not dead. He breathed, he felt, he exulted, he was alive! It had all been a folly, a dream!

Then his mind cleared, and he knew that it had been no

dream. He was surely alive, but the empty phial was in his pocket, the two glasses had been realities, the imminence of death no illusion. Only it had not come for him.

The terrible thought lifted him out of the straw, and drove him fumbling and clawing at the heavy latch of the gate in the stone wall. Two glasses, and one of them she had held so carefully, so scrupulously against her breast, for fear he should mistake which was meant for him! While she watched him with the strange tears on her lashes, and that look of withdrawal and farewell upon her face! She, who had never intended violence against his or any other life, except her own! Except her own! Yes, they had come to a nadir out of which only one of them could hope to climb. Only her answer had been different. Now he knew! Now he knew everything!

He did not wonder, or question his knowledge. Why should it be so clear to him that because she had not poisoned him, she had not poisoned Theo, either? He did not know, but he knew that it was clear, that nothing could ever call it in doubt again. He had the answer to everything, the insecurity which had lived within them and eaten them from within was gone, like a cloud torn down out of the sky to uncover the sun. Only he was afraid in his heart, he cried out with fear at every step of the scrambling, gasping way home, that the sun had come out too late.

He plunged through the level rim of the trees, and began to drop down through the wood by its steepest slope, direct to the corner of the garden. It seemed an infinitely long and wearisome distance, the spur of trees devilishly prolonged, draped with a deceptive twilight to hamper his journey, beset with trailers of bramble and low-growing thorn trees to fend him off. He went down through it in a series of leaps, crashing through the clawing undergrowth, tearing his hands and cheeks on the hawthorns, tripping and wrenching his ankles among the broken, pitted surfaces and the tussocky grass. Recklessly, spreading his hands blindly in front of him where the light did not penetrate, to thrust himself off from crashing into trees, he plunged downhill, out of breath and gasping with the urgency of his fear.

She was everything she had ever been to him, she was the heart in his body, the centre and reason of his life. It needed only the suggestion of loss to quicken his mind to the realisation of the value he set on her. It no longer mattered that they had cost each other a world of pain, and brought each other to the final lost levels of despair. That was over and done, and if it were not, what did he care? Nothing must or should induce him to turn away his eyes again from the greatest experience he was ever likely to know. Let her bring the world down over his head, if only she would be there alive when he reached the house, and remain beside him until the sky toppled upon them both. Now he knew everything. Now there was no Theo standing sadly between them; the guilt they shared towards him was no more than they could face and bear. They had not killed him. Some instinct in Theo himself had taken the material of their love, and translated it into a death, and if they must answer for that, some day, somewhere, they would answer. But they had not killed him! Now he was answering the question which had never been asked, which never need be asked. They had broken through the silence, they could meet again, a true meeting. If only she had not drunk it! If only the doctor had given her something harmless, the sort of suggestive nothing you give to neurotics who induce their own insomnia! 'Oh, let her be alive!' he thought, stumbling down the last rough course of grass, and leaping over the ditch full of brambles at the foot. 'Oh, Spiri, don't die, just when I'm alive again!'

Grey in the grey garden, touched here and there only faintly with the first positive, visible greens of daylight, the house crouched under its hanger, unlighted, no thread of smoke rising from its chimneys. He climbed into the roughly broken ground he had turned only yesterday, and ran to the door of the workshop, but it was empty and cold, the uncovered kiln still cradling indifferently the wreckage of shards, and the undamaged pots about which Suspiria had felt so little curiosity.

He circled the house, his feet slowing now, his knees failing under him. He wanted to cry out to her, but he was mortally afraid of the following silence, and his throat was so dry with dread that he doubted his own voice. He skirted the corner of the yard, and came to the front of the house.

She was sitting in the open window of the living-room, coiled up in the corner of the sill through the darkness and into the twilight of the dawn, her elbows on her knees, her chin in her hands. She was staring steadily, intently down the rutted lane of the drive, towards the gate through which she expected him. Her eyes looked as if they had not once closed, so single and fierce was that stare. The drink she had poured for herself last night stood on the window-sill, close beside her, and he saw that it had not been touched.

He stood still, leaning against the wall, indistinguishable as yet in the vague half-light which had shown her already a dozen illusions of him. He felt so weak, so limp with relief that for a moment he could not trust himself to leave the support of the wall, and walk into her sight. He could not look away from her, she seemed to his new and eager eyes so beautiful; but as if she had been a prism of coloured crystal, he saw the house and the field and the world through her. The sky which had seemed all a monochrome of grey was just beginning to quiver with suggestions of rose and gold, and the green of the grass, putting on colour valiantly, shone with its own vernal light. It was May, the fury of growth throbbed through the soil under his feet, and an excitement as piercing as music was on the little dawn wind. It was going to be a lovely day. He saw everything as if for the first time, and Suspiria as if for the first time after a long journey and a longer absence. After all, he had been dead, and he was alive again; there was every reason for things to look new.

He went towards her at last, almost shyly, and suddenly she heard his step, and turned her head with a passionate lightening of her eyes, and saw him. A blaze like the aurora sprang into her face, though he could not see that it was changed by anything so ordinary as a smile. She sat gazing at him without moving for several seconds, and then she picked up the glass, and emptied its contents suddenly out of the window. As though the action had somehow released them from a constraint which enjoined stillness and silence, he sprang towards the door, and she slid down from the window, and rushed to meet him.

He shut the door behind him, and she was in his arms, pressed to him breast and hip and thigh, and he could do nothing but hug her, and press his cheek against her uplifted cheek, and feel with every nerve and sense, in every contact of their linked bodies, that she lived as newly, as exultantly as he. She felt at him anxiously with her adoring, praying hands, and could not have enough of him. There was nothing he could find to say that made any sense, only the coaxing, apologetic little endearments men use to disarm their wives when they have done something silly. But how exquisite, how adult, how far from any apology was the joy it gave him to have her fast in his arms again, against his heart.

'You're wet!' she cried, feeling at his coat, which indeed was damp with dew. She had even a new note of exasperation in her voice, a delighted impatience with his follies. 'Silly child, staying out all night in the cold – without even a coat! You're sure to catch cold. I can feel you – you're frozen! Dennis! Haven't you got even the sense you were born with?'

'I know!' he said, shaking and laughing, his arms tight about her body. 'I've been such a fool!' And suddenly, convulsed by the memory of his terror, he hid his scratched face against her hair, and clung to her trembling. 'Oh, my dearest – my lovely—'

'You weren't the only fool,' she said, stroking the cheek that was smeared with little beads of blood from the brambles. 'Never mind it! Oh, don't, my darling! It's all over now! Everything's all right now!'

'Oh, Spiri, I was so afraid—'

'I only kept it in case you didn't come back,' she said, 'that was all I was afraid of.'

'Spiri, I thought – I thought—' But there was no need to explain anything, no need at all; they were long past the necessity for words, all that was left behind with the silence.

'I know! You thought I'd given you poison, just as I did to Theo. Never mind it! I didn't, I didn't, but never mind it any more. That was how I knew at last that *you* hadn't, either. I was so slow!' she said, her lips against his cheek. 'I couldn't understand why you looked at me like that, without a word – why you went out as you did— It was only after you'd gone it dawned on me. The bottle was gone, too, you see, and I knew you must have taken it, and then I understood why. So I had every reason to stay alive, hadn't I? And all I was afraid of then was that you'd never come back. I didn't know where you'd gone, all I could do was wait. It seemed a long time, waiting,' she said.

As long, he thought, as it had seemed to him, that age-long journey down the shoulder of the wood. To have all the crooked places suddenly made straight, and then to fear the loss of your only true companion by the way!

'It was because of the kiss you gave me,' she said, 'that I didn't drink it. Suddenly you were so strange and sweet, and I couldn't understand – and then, when you were gone, and I looked for the bottle – then I realised.'

'And I realised, too, when I woke up.' He put his head back suddenly, and laughed aloud, to think what a fool he'd made of himself, to think that he had been dead, and was alive, that it was May, and Sunday, and there was a whole world of rediscovered miracles inside the house and out, only waiting for him to have time for them.

'I'll light the fire,' she said, feeling reproachfully at the coldness of his hands. 'You're frozen! You're sure to have a cold. Go and get a hot bath while I make some coffee – the geyser won't take long.'

He began to go, obediently, but turned back in the doorway to look at her again, to reassure himself of her reality, and his miraculously regained unity with her. 'I love you!' he said. He could not help it, the words welled up in his lips, and would be said.

'And I love you, you crazy kid!' I can, she thought, now; there isn't any curse on it. I love you as I did at the beginning of it, and as I shall at the end. I'll stand by it and answer for it at whatever judgment there is, but I'll never give it up, any more than I'll give up my life. My life! She remembered what years of atonement she owed to herself, what prodigies of achievement.

He went out, satisfied, and she heard his footsteps recede down the stone corridor with a joyful alacrity, heading for the bathroom. The boy's smile had come back to his man's face, she had the dazzling memory of it in her eyes all the time she was laying and lighting the fire. You cannot turn back, but the road may circle, perhaps, and bring you again a prospect you had lost, and this time a nearer and clearer view of it. Nor could she ever have wished to turn back, it was not in her nature. There was only one honourable way to go, and that was forward.

When the fire was drawing nicely, she made for the kitchen, to prepare breakfast. Her own eyes shone upon her from the long mirror. On its austere round table in the corner the royal purple jar drew to itself the golden red of the morning light, and flushed into the deep crimson of a dark rose. She rang it with her finger-nail as she passed, and it gave out an astonishing, high, full note, purer and less complex than a bell's tone, a confident natural harmony, serene as its beautiful body. She thought: 'I must clear away all that rubbish in the kiln. But I'll work on that glaze, I believe it's worth it. I believe I can get it right next time!'